D0839339

KING ARTHUR'S KNIGHTS

KING ARTHUR'S KNIGHTS

HENRY GILBERT

CLUNY

Providence, Rhode Island

Cluny Media edition, 2021

This Cluny edition is a republication of *King Arthur's Knights*,
originally published by Thomas Nelson and Sons in 1911.

For more information regarding this title
or any other Cluny Media publication,
please write to info@clunymedia.com, or to
Cluny Media, P.O. Box 1664, Providence, RI 02901

VISIT US ONLINE AT WWW.CLUNYMEDIA.COM

ISBN: 978-1685950026

Cover design by Clarke & Clarke
Cover image: Dante Gabriel Rossetti, *Sir Galahad at the Ruined Chapel*,
Watercolour, bodycolour, gum arabic on paper, 1857/1859
Courtesy of Wikimedia Commons

Contents

In tholdé dayès of the King Arthour,
Of which that Britons speken great honour,
All was this land fulfilled of faery.

The Canterbury Tales

✤

Preface

THIS BOOK IS AN ATTEMPT TO TELL SOME OF THE STORIES OF King Arthur and his Knights in a way which will be interesting to every boy and girl who loves adventures.

Although tales of these old British heroes have been published before in a form intended for young people, it is believed that they have never been related quite in the same spirit nor from the same point of view; and it is hoped that the book will fill a place hitherto vacant in the hearts of all boys and girls.

No doubt many of you, my young readers, have at some time or another taken down the *Morte D'Arthur* from your father's bookshelves and read a few pages of it here and there. But I doubt if any of you have ever gone very far in the volume. You found generally, I think, that it was written in a puzzling, old-fashioned language, that though it spoke of many interesting things, and seemed that it ought to be well worth reading, yet somehow it was tedious and dry.

In the tales as I have retold them for you, I hope you will not find any of these faults. Besides writing them in simple language, I have chosen only those episodes which I know would appeal to you. I have added or altered here and there, for in places it struck me that there was just wanting a word or two to make you feel the magic that was every-where abroad in those days. It seemed to me that some mysterious adventure might easily be waiting in the ruined and deserted Roman town on the desolate moor, or even just round the mossy trunk of the next oak in the forest drive, through which the knight was riding; or that any fair lady or questing dog which he might meet could turn out to be a wizard seeking to work woe upon him. Nevertheless, I was always sure that in those bright days when the world was young, whatever evil power might get the mastery for a little while, the knight's courage, humility, and faith would win through every peril at the end.

In this book, besides reading of wonderful adventures and brave fighting, you will learn just what sort of man a perfect knight was required to be in the chivalrous times when men wore armour and rode on errantry. The duties of a "good and faithful knight" were quite simple, but they were often very hard to perform. They were to protect the distressed, to speak the truth, to keep his word to all, to be courteous and gentle to women, to defend right against might, and to do or say nothing that should sully the fair name of Christian knighthood.

Although, therefore, these stories of King Arthur and his men treat of knights and their ladies, of magical trolls and wonder-working wizards, and it might seem for that reason that they can have little or nothing in common with life of the present day, it will be seen that the spirit in which they are told conveys something which every boy and girl can learn. Indeed, the great and simple lesson of chivalry which the tales of King Arthur teach is, in a few words, to merit "the fine old name of gentleman."

The history of King Arthur and his Knights is contained in two books, one being the *Morte D'Arthur*, written by Sir Thomas Malory, the other being the *Mabinogion*, a collection of old Welsh stories, first translated by Lady Charlotte Guest in 1838. I have selected thirteen tales from the number which these two books contain; but there are many more, equally as interesting, which remain.

Little is known about Sir Thomas Malory, who lived in the fifteenth century. We only learn that he was a Welshman, a man of heroic mind who, as an old writer relates, "from his youth, greatly shone in the gifts of mind and body." Though much busied with cares of state, his favourite recreation was said to be the reading of history, and in this pursuit "he made selections from various authors concerning the valour and the victories of the most renowned King Arthur of the Britons." We know, further, that these selections or tales were translated mostly from poems about Arthur written by old French poets in the eleventh and twelfth centuries, and that Sir Thomas Malory finished his translation in the ninth year of King Edward the Fourth (1469). This, of course, was before printing was introduced into England, but no doubt many written copies were made of the book, so as to enable the stories to be read to the lords and ladies and other rich people who would desire to hear about the flower of kings and chivalry, the great King Arthur. When, in 1477, Caxton set up his printing press at Westminster, the *Morte D'Arthur* was one of the books which then saw the light of day.

The *Mabinogian*, which contains other tales about King Arthur, is a collection of old Welsh romances. Though our earliest collection of them is to be found in a manuscript written in the thirteenth or fourteenth century, some of them are probably as old as the time when Welshmen clothed themselves in the skins of the beaver and the bear, and used stone for their tools and weapons.

It may be that, when you get older, you will go back to the two books I have mentioned, and you will find them so fascinating that you will be impatient of any other book which pretends to tell you the same tales. But until that time arrives, I hope you will find the stories as I have told them quite interesting and exciting.

Henry Gilbert
June 1911

I

How Arthur Was Made King and Won His Kingdom

IN THE HALL OF HIS ROMAN PALACE AT LONDON, KING UTHER, Pendragon of the Island of Britain, lay dying. He had been long sick with a wasting disease, and forced to lie in his bed, gnawing his beard with wrath at his weakness, while the pagan Saxons ravened up and down the fair broad lands, leaving in their tracks the smoking ruin of broken towns and desolated villages, where mothers lay dead beside their children on the hearths, fair churches stood pillaged and desecrated, and priests and nuns wandered in the wilds.

At length, when the pagans, bold and insolent, had ventured near London, the king had been able to bear his shame and anguish no longer. He had put himself, in a litter, at the head of his army, and meeting the fierce, brave pagans at Verulam (now called St. Albans) he had, in a battle day-long and stubborn, forced them at length to fly with heavy slaughter.

That was three days ago, and since then he had lain in his bed as still as if he were dead; and beside him sat the wise wizard Merlin, white with great age, and in his eyes the calmness of deep learning.

It was the third night when the king suddenly awoke from his stupor and clutched the hand of Merlin.

"I have dreamed!" he said in a low shaken voice. "I have seen two dragons fighting—one white, the other red. First the white dragon got the mastery, and clawed with iron talons the red one's crest, and drove him hither and thither into holes and crannies of the rocks. And then the red one took heart, and with a fury that was marvellous to see, he drove and tore the white dragon full terribly, and anon the white one crawled away sore wounded. And the red dragon walked up and down in the place of his triumph, and grew proud, and fought smaller red dragons and conquered. Thus for a long time he stayed, and was secure and boastful. Then I saw the white dragon return with a rage that was very terrible, and the red dragon fought with him; but his pride had softened him, so he drew off. Then other red dragons came upon him in his wounds and beat him sore, which seeing, the white dragon dashed upon them all—and I awoke. Merlin, tell me what this may mean, for my mind is sore distraught with the vision."

Then Merlin looked at the trembling king, wasted with disease, and in his wise heart was great pity.

"It means, lord," he said in slow grave tones, "that thy people shall conquer—that a red dragon shall rise from thy kin, who shall drive out the loathsome pagan and shall conquer far and wide, and his fame shall go into all lands and for all time."

"I thank thee, Merlin, for thy comfort," sighed the wearied king. "I have feared me these last years that the pagan will at the last drive my people into the western sea, and that the name of Christ shall die out of this fair land, and the foul pagan possess it. But thy words give me great heart."

"Nay, sir," said Merlin, "take comfort. Great power will come to this people in a near time, and they shall conquer all their enemies."

Anon the king slept, and lay thus for three further days, neither speaking nor moving. Many great lords and barons came craving to speak with Merlin, asking if the king were not better. But, looking into their crafty eyes, and seeing there the pride and ambitions of their hearts, Merlin knew that they wished the king were already dead; for all thought that King Uther had no son to take the kingdom after him, and each great baron, strong in men, plotted to win the overlordship when the king should be gone.

"If he dieth and sayeth not which he shall name to succeed him," some asked, "say, Merlin, what's to be done?"

"I shall tell you," said Merlin. "Come ye all into this chamber tomorrow's morn, and, if God so wills, I will make the king speak."

Next morn, therefore, came all the great barons and lords into the high hall of the palace, and many were the proud and haughty glances passing among them. There was King Lot of Orkney, small and slim, with his dark narrow face and crafty eyes under pent eyebrows; King Uriens of Reged, tall and well-seeming, with grim eyes war-wise, fresh from the long harrying of the fleeing pagans; King Mark of Tintagel, hurly of form, crafty and mean of look; King Nentres of Garlot, ruddy of face, blusterous of manner, who tried to hide cunning under a guise of honesty; and many others, as Duke Cambenet of Loidis, King Brandegoris of Stranggore, King Morkant of Strathclyde, King Clariance of Northumberland, King Kador of Cornwall, and King Idres of Silura.

Now, when all these were assembled about the bed of Uther, Merlin went to the side of the sleeping king, and looked long and earnestly upon his closed eyes. Anon he passed his hands above the face of the king, and Uther instantly awoke, and looked about him as if startled.

"Lord," said Merlin, "God's hand is drawing you to Him, and these your lords desire you to name your successor ere you pass from life. Is it not your desire that your son Arthur shall take the kingdom after you, with your blessing?"

Those who craned towards the bed started and looked darkly at Merlin and then at each other; for none had heard of the son whom the wizard named Arthur. Then in the deep silence the dying king raised his hand in the sign of blessing, and in a hollow whisper said:

"Such is my desire. With God's blessing I wish my son Arthur to take this kingdom after me, and all that love me must follow him."

His eyes closed, a shiver passed down the tall frame as it lay beneath the clothes, and with a sigh the soul of Uther sped.

In a few days the king was buried in all solemnity with the dead of his kindred in the Roman temple that had been made a church, where now stands St. Paul's. Thereafter men waited and wondered, for the land was without a king, and none knew who was rightfully heir to the throne.

As the days went by, men gathered in groups in the marketplace of London, whispering the rumours that mysteriously began to fly from mouth to mouth—how King Lot of Orkney and Lothian was gathering his knights and men-at-arms; and King Uriens and Duke Cambenet of Loidis had got together a great host, although the remnant of the pagans had fled the country. The faces of the citizens went gloomy as they thought of the griefs of civil war, of the terrors of the sack of cities, the ruin of homes, the death of dear ones, and the loss of riches. Nevertheless, some were already wagering which of the great lords would conquer the others, and take to himself the crown of Britain and the title of Pendragon.

As it neared the feast of Christmas, men heard that the Archbishop of London, who was then chief ruler of the Church, had sent his letters to each and all the great nobles, bidding them come to a great council to be holden at the church of St. Paul at Christmas.

When men heard that this was done by the advice of Merlin, faces lightened and looked more joyful.

"Now shall things go right," said they, "for the old, old Merlin hath the deepest wisdom of all the earth."

On Christmas Eve the city throbbed with the clank of arms and the tramp of the great retinues of princes, kings, and powerful lords who had come at the archbishop's summons, and by day and night the narrow ways were crowded with armed men. Long ere the dawn of Christmas Day, the lords and the common people betook themselves along the wide road which led across to the church, which then stood in a wide space amid fields, and all knelt therein to mass.

While it was yet dark a great strange cry rang out in the churchyard. Some ran forth, and there by the wall behind the high altar they saw a vast stone, foursquare, that had not been there before, and in the middle thereof was stuck a great wedge of steel, and sticking therefrom by the point was a rich sword. On the blade were written words in Latin, which a clerk read forth, which said, "Whoso pulleth this sword out of this stone and wedge of steel is rightwise born King of all Britain."

The clerk ran into the church and told the archbishop, and men were all amazed and would have gone instantly to see this marvel, but the archbishop bade them stay.

"Finish your prayers to God," he said, "for no man may touch this strange thing till high mass be done."

When mass was finished, all poured forth from the church and thronged about the stone, and marvelled at the words on the sword. First King Lot, with a light laugh, took hold of the handle and essayed to pull out the point of the sword, but he could not, and his face went hot and angry. Then King Nentres of Garlot took his place with a jest, but though he heaved at the sword with all his burly strength, till it seemed like to snap, he could not move it, and so let go at last with an angry oath. All the others essayed in like manner, but by none was it moved a jot, and all stood about discomfited, looking with black looks at one another and the stone.

"He that is rightwise born ruler of Britain is not here," said the archbishop at length, "but doubt not he shall come in God's good time. Meanwhile, let a tent be raised over the stone, and do ye lords appoint ten of your number to watch over it, and we will essay the sword again after New Year's Day."

So that the kings and lords should be kept together, the archbishop appointed a great tournament to be held on New Year's Day on the wasteland north of the city, which men now call Smithfield.

Now when the day was come, a certain lord, Sir Ector de Morven, who had great lands about the isle of Thorney, rode towards the jousts with his son, Sir Kay, and young Arthur, who was Sir Kay's foster-brother. When they had got nearly to the place, suddenly Sir Kay bethought him that he had left his sword at home.

"Do you ride back, young Arthur," he said, "and fetch me my sword, for if I do not have it I may not fight."

Willingly Arthur turned his horse and rode back swiftly. But when he had arrived at the house, he found it shut up and none was within, for all had gone to the jousts. Then was he a little wroth, and rode back wondering how he should obtain a sword for his foster-brother.

Suddenly, as he saw the tower of St. Paul's church through the trees, he bethought him of the sword in the stone, about which many men had spoken in his hearing.

"I will ride thither," said he, "and see if I may get that sword for my brother, for he shall not be without a sword this day."

When he came to the churchyard, he tied his horse to the stile, and went through the grave-mounds to the tent wherein was the sword. He found the place unwatched, and the flashing sword was sticking by the point in the stone.

Lightly he grasped the handle of the sword with one hand, and it came forth straightway!

Then, glad that his brother should not be without a sword, he swiftly gat upon his horse and rode on, and delivered the sword to Sir Kay, and thought no more of aught but the splendid knights and richly garbed lords that were at the jousts.

But Sir Kay looked at the sword, and the writing, and knew it was the sword of the stone, and marvelled how young Arthur had possessed himself thereof; and being of a covetous and sour mind he thought how he might make advantage for himself. He went to his father, Sir Ector, and said:

"Lo, father, this is the sword of the stone, and surely am I rightful king."

Sir Ector knew the sword and marvelled, but his look was stern as he gazed into the crafty eyes of his son.

"Come ye with me," he said, and all three rode to the church, and alit from their horses and went in.

Sir Ector strode up the aisle to the altar, and turning to his son, said sternly:

"Now, swear on God's book and the holy relics how thou didst get this sword."

Sir Kay's heart went weak, and he stammered out the truth.

"How gat you this sword?" asked Sir Ector of Arthur.

"Sir, I will tell you," said Arthur, and so told him all as it had happened.

Sir Ector marvelled what this should mean; for Arthur had been given to him to nourish and rear as a week-old child by Merlin, but the wizard had only told him that the babe was a son of a dead lady, whose lord had been slain by the pagans.

Then Sir Ector went to the stone and bade Arthur put back the sword into the wedge of steel, which the young man did easily.

Thereupon Sir Ector strove with all his strength to draw the sword forth again, but though he pulled till he sweated, he could not stir the sword.

"Now you essay it," he said to his son. But naught that Sir Kay could do availed.

"Now do you try," he bade Arthur.

Arthur lightly grasped the handle with one hand, and the sword came out without hindrance.

Therewith Sir Ector sank to his knees, and Sir Kay also. And they bared their heads.

"Alas," said Arthur, "my own dear father and brother, why kneel ye so to me?"

"Nay, nay, my lord Arthur, it is not so," said Sir Ector, "for I was never your father. I wot well ye are of higher blood than I weened. For Merlin delivered you to me while yet ye were a babe."

The tears came into Arthur's eyes when he knew that Sir Ector was not his father, for the young man had loved him as if he were of his own blood.

"Sir," said Ector unto Arthur, "will ye be my good and kind lord when ye are king?"

"Ah, if this be true as ye say," cried Arthur, "ye shall desire of me whatsoever ye may, and I shall give it you. For both you and my good lady and dear mother your wife have kept and loved me as your own."

"Sir," said Sir Ector, "I crave a boon of you, that while you live, your foster-brother, Sir Kay, shall be high seneschal of all your lands."

"That shall be done, and never man shall have that office but him, while he and I live," replied Arthur.

Then hastily Sir Ector rode to the archbishop, and told him how and by whom the sword had been achieved from the stone. Thereupon the archbishop let call a great meeting on Twelfth Day of all the kings and barons.

So on the day appointed, all men gathered in the churchyard of St. Paul's, and the tent was removed from about the stone. From day dawn to the evening the kings and princes and lords strove each in his turn to draw the sword from the stone. But none of them availed to move it.

While they stood about, dark of look, gnawing their lips with rage and disappointment, the archbishop turned privily to Sir Ector and bade him bring Arthur.

The young man came, quietly clad in a tunic of brown samite, of medium height, with curly hair above a fair face of noble, though mild mien. As he came among the richly clad nobles, they looked haughtily at him, and wondered who he was and why he came, for as yet none had been told that the sword had been drawn by him.

The archbishop, tall, white-haired and reverend, called Arthur to him and said in grave tones:

"My son, I have heard a strange tale of thee, and whether it be true or false, God shall decide. Now, therefore, do ye take hold upon this sword and essay to draw it from the stone."

The proud barons, some with looks amazed and others with sneering laughter, pressed about the young man as he stepped towards the stone. Arthur took the handle of the sword with his right hand, and the sword seemed to fall into his grasp.

Thereat arose great cries of rage, and angry looks flashed forth, and many a hand went to dagger haft.

"Ho, archbishop!" cried King Lot, fiercely striding towards the tall ecclesiastic. "What wizard's brat are you foisting upon us here to draw the sword by magic?"

"'Tis a trick!" cried Nentres of Garlot, his bluff manner falling from him, and all the savage anger gleaming from his eyes. "A trick that shall not blind men such as we!"

"Who is this beggar's boy that is put forth to shame us kings and nobles?" said King Mark, and his hand sought his dagger as he disappeared among the crowd and wormed his way towards where stood young Arthur. But Sir Ector and Sir Kay, seeing the threatening looks of all, had quickly ranged themselves beside young Arthur, and with them went Sir Bedevere, Sir Baudwin, and Sir Ulfius, three noble lords who had loved King Uther well.

"Peace, lords!" said the old archbishop, calmly meeting the raging looks about him. "Ye know what words are about the sword, and this youth hath drawn the sword. I know naught of tricks or wizardry, but I think high Heaven hath chosen this way of showing who shall be lord of this land, and I think this young man is rightful King of us all."

"'Tis some base-born churl's son that the wizard Merlin would foist upon us!" cried the barons. "We will have none of him!"

"A shame and dishonour it is, so to try to overrule us, kings and lords of high lineage, with an unknown youth," cried others.

"We will have the sword put back and set a watch over it," cried King Uriens, "and we will meet here again at Candlemas, and essay the sword. And at that time, my lord archbishop, thou shalt do the proper rites to exorcise all evil powers, and then we will try the sword once more."

So was it agreed by all, and ten knights watched day and night about the stone and the sword.

But it befell at Candlemas as it had befallen at Twelfth Day, that for all their strength and might, none of the kings or barons could draw forth the sword; but into the hand of the unknown Arthur the weapon seemed to fall.

Whereat they were all sore aggrieved and rageful, and resolved that they would have yet another trial at Easter. It befell at the feast of Easter as it had befallen before, and this time the kings and lords for angry spite would have fallen upon Arthur and slain him, but the archbishop threatened them with the most dreadful ban of Holy Church.

They forbore, therefore, and went aside, and declared that it was their will to essay the sword again at the high feast of Pentecost.

By Merlin's advice the young Arthur went never about, unless the five friends of Uther were with him, that is to say, Sir Ector and his son Sir Kay, Sir Bedevere, Sir Baudwin, and Sir Ulfius. And though at divers times men were found skulking or hiding in the horse stall, the dark wood by the hall, or the bend in the lane, in places where Arthur might pass, no harm came to him by reason of the loving watch of those noble knights.

Again at the feast of Pentecost men gathered in the churchyard of St. Paul's, and the press of people was such that no man had ever seen the like. Once more the kings and princes and great barons, to the number of forty-nine, came forward, and each in turn pulled and drew at the sword in the stone until the sweat stood on their brows. Nevertheless, though the sword point was but the width of a palm in the stone, not the mightiest of them could move it by the breadth of a hair.

King Mark of Tintagel was the last of them who had to stand back at length, baffled and raging inwardly. Many were the evil looks that would have slain Arthur as he stood among his friends.

Then a cry came from among the common people, and so strong was it that the nobles looked as if they hated to hear it.

"Let Arthur draw the sword!" was the call from a thousand throats.

The venerable archbishop came and took Arthur by the hand, and led him towards the sword. Again the young man held the rich pommel with his single hand, and that which none of the forty-nine great men could do, he did as easily as if he but plucked a flower.

A fierce cry leaped from among the thousands of the common people.

"Arthur shall be our King!" they cried. "Arthur is our King! We will no longer deny him!"

Many of the princes and barons cried out with the commons that this was their will also; but eleven of the most powerful and ambitious showed by their arrogant and angry gestures that they refused to own Arthur as their lord.

For a long time the uproar raged, the cries of the common folk becoming fiercer and more menacing against the counter-cries of the eleven kings and their adherents.

At length from among the people there came the governor of London, who, in his rich robes of office, leaped upon the stone where but lately the sword had been.

"My lords, I speak the will of the commons," he cried, and at his voice all were silent. "We have taken counsel together, and we will have Arthur for our King. We will put him no more in delay, for we all see that it is God's will that he shall be our King, and who that holdeth against him, we will slay."

With that he got down from the stone, kneeled before Arthur, put the keys of the city in his hands, and rendered homage unto him. The great multitude kneeled likewise, bowing their bare heads, and cried him mercy because they had denied him so long.

Because they feared the great multitude, the eleven kings kneeled with them, but in their hearts was rage and rebellion.

Then Arthur took the sword between his hands and, going into the church, he laid it on the high altar, and the archbishop blessed him. Then, since Arthur was as yet unknighted, King Kador of Cornwall, who was brother of King Uther, made him a knight.

Standing up in the sight of all the people, lords and commons, Arthur laid his left hand upon the holy relics; then, lifting up his right hand, he swore that he would be a true king, to stand forth as their ruler in justice and mercy, to keep them from oppression, to redress their wrongs, and to establish right throughout the length and breadth of his dominions.

Men went forth from the church in great joy, for now they had a king they loved, and they felt that the land was safe from civil strife and the griefs of war.

When Arthur in his palace at London had received the homage of all the lords and princes from the lands south of Humber, he appointed his officers. Sir Kay he made seneschal or steward, and Sir Baudwin was made constable, and Sir Ulfius he named chamberlain of

his court. By the counsel of Merlin he made Sir Bedevere Warden of
the Northern Marches, for the lands of the eleven kings lay mostly in
the country north of Trent, and though those princes had yielded lip
service to Arthur, Merlin knew that in their hearts they nurtured the
seeds of conspiracy.

King Arthur made a progress through all his territories, staying at
the halls of those who did service for the lands they held of him, and
he commanded all those who had suffered evil or wrong to come to
him, and many came. The king's wrath when he heard a tale of women
and orphans wronged or robbed or evilly treated by proud or powerful lords and knights, was terrible to see. Many were the pale captives he released from their deep dungeons, many were the tears he
wiped away, and hard and heavy was his punishment of evil lords who
thought their power would forever shield them from penalty for their
cruelties and oppression.

When this was done, he caused a proclamation to be uttered, that
he would hold his coronation at the city of Caerleon-upon-Usk, at the
feast of Hallowmass then following; and he commanded all his loyal
subjects to attend. When the time came, all the countryside on the
marches of Wales was filled with the trains of noblemen and their
knights and servants gathering towards the city.

As Arthur looked from the window of the palace which the
Romans had builded, and which looked far and wide over the crowded
roads, word was brought to him that six of the kings who had resented
his kingship had come to the city. At this Arthur was glad, for he was
full gentle and kindly, and would liefer be friendly with a man than his
enemy.

Thinking that these kings and knights had come for love of him,
and to do him worship at his feast, King Arthur sent them many and
rich presents. But his messengers returned, saying that the kings and
knights had received them with insults, and had refused to take the
gifts of a beardless boy who had come, they said, of low blood.

Whereat the king's eyes flashed grimly, but at that time he said no
word.

In the joustings and knightly games that were part of the festival of the coronation, the six kings ever ranged themselves against King Arthur and his knights, and did him all the despite they could achieve. At that time they deemed themselves not strong enough to hurt the king, and therefore did no open act of revolt.

Now it happened, when the feasting was over and many of the kings and lords had departed home again, that Arthur stood in the door of his hall that looked into the street, and with his three best nobles, Sir Kay, Sir Bedevere and Sir Baudwin, he watched the rich cavalcades of his lords pass out of the town. Suddenly, as he stood there, a little page boy, fair of face but for the pitiful sorrow and gauntness upon it, dashed from the throng of a lord's retinue which was passing and threw himself along the ground, his hands clutching the feet of the king.

"O King Arthur, save me!" the lad cried, spent of breath. "Or this evil lord will slay me as he hath slain my mother and my brothers."

From the throng a tall black knight, leaping from his horse, strode towards the boy, and would have torn his hands from their hold upon the king's feet.

"Back, sir knight!" said the king. "I will hear more of this. Who are you?"

The knight laughed insolently.

"I? Oh, I am one that the last king knew well to his sorrow. I am Turquine, brother to Sir Caradoc of the Dolorous Tower."

"What is this boy to you?"

"He is Owen, the caitiff son of a brave father, who gave him to my care to train in knightly ways. But 'tis a puling fool, more fitting for the bowers of ladies."

"Nay, king, he lies!" said the lad who kneeled before the king. "I am his nephew. His hand slew my dear father treacherously, and he hath starved my mother to her death. For our lands are rich while his are poor, and my father warned me of him ere he died. This man hath kept me prisoner, used me evilly, starving me and wealing me with cruel blows daily. I think he hath my death in his heart."

"I can speak of this thing," said a knight who came forth from the throng. "I am Sir Miles of Bandon. I know this lad speaks truth, for his father was mine own dear cousin. This Sir Turquine is a felon knight."

The brow of the king went dark. He looked from the cruel insolent face of the black knight to the wan beseeching face of the lad.

"Hark ye!" said Arthur to Turquine, and his voice was terrible, for all that it was very quiet. "Ye shall answer to me and my justice for any evil you have done this young boy or his people. When I send for thee, come at once, or it will be worse for thee. The boy stays with me. Now begone!"

The big knight looked with hatred and surprise in his eyes, and for a while said naught. Then, with an insolent laugh, he turned and vaulted on his horse.

"I may come when thou dost not expect me, sir king!" he said, mocking, and shot an evil look at the young page.

Thenceforward the young page Owen stayed in the court, doing his services deftly and quietly, with an eye ever on the king to do his bidding. One night, when a storm raged and the town lay dark and quiet, King Arthur sat in his hall. Sir Kay and Sir Bedevere told tales, or the king's bard sang songs to amuse him, while about them moved young Owen, noiseless of step, quick of eye, and as restless as an unquiet spirit.

Anon the lad would pass through the arras, creep to the great outer door, and look at the porter in his room beside it. Then he would stand at the wicket and listen to the rare footsteps pass down the road, and when the rising wind keened and shrilled through the crannies, he would glance about him with quick looks as if in fear of an enemy.

Once he went to Falk, the king's porter, and said:

"'Tis a stormy night, Sir Falk. I doubt few are about the streets of Caerleon on such a night."

"Few indeed," said Falk.

"Yet methought but now I heard the rattle of a bridle in the distance, as if a steed stood in armour."

"I heard naught," said Falk. "'Twould be but the grinding of a chain beside a horseblock."

Young Owen went away, and sat where the king and his knights listened to the marvellous tales of the wise Gildas, who told of most terrible witches and warlocks in the wizard woods of Brittany.

Again the lad approached the door and listened; then going to the porter he said:

"This drenching storm will tear the last poor leaves from the forest trees, I ween, Sir Falk."

"Of a truth," said the porter, "'tis overlate for leaves. They be stuck in the mire of the rides long ere this."

"They could not be blown so far in this gushing storm," said the page, "and therefore I have deceived myself. But I thought I heard the rustle of leaves on the stones before the door but now."

"It could not be," said the porter; "it was doubtless the gouts of water from the roof of the hall thou didst hear."

Owen went away, but in a little while returned, and softly opened the wicket panel in the door a little way, and looked forth into the roaring darkness of rain and wind.

"Think you, Sir Falk," he said, going to the porter, "that the witches from the woods of Denn do send their baleful fires on such a night as this to lead poor houseless wretches into the marsh below the wall?"

The porter laughed.

"Thou'rt over-full of fancies tonight, young sir," he said. "Have no fear of witches. We're all safe and sound here till the blessed daylight comes, and none need stir out till then."

"Methought I saw a flash in the dark but now," said Owen, "as if 'twas the gleam of a sword or a wandering marsh fire."

"Not a doubt 'twas but a lightning flash," returned the porter. "Now go ye, for I hear the king moving towards bed. Sleep soundly, lad; no need to fear this night."

In a little while the palace was sunk in darkness, and in silence save for the smothered cries of sleepers in their dreams. Outside, the rain still sobbed at the eaves, and the wind beat at the narrow casements. Time passed, and for all his weariness young Owen could not sleep.

His spirit had been heavy all the day, and vague and dreadful fears had haunted him. Something told him that the life of the beloved king, who had taken him from the foul and cruel power of Sir Turquine, was threatened. He rose in the dark from his pallet of straw in the hall where lay the other pages, and stole softly out. He would make his way to the king's door, and, wrapped in his cloak, would be before it.

He felt his way softly along the corridor in the deep darkness. Suddenly he stopped. Something alive was near him in the dark. Even as he turned, a hand seized him by the throat, and a hateful voice which he knew growled in his ear:

"Lead us to the king's room, or this shall sink in thy heart!"

He knew at once that all his fears of the day and the night had been true. He had indeed heard the stealthy footsteps before the door of the hall, and had seen the dull gleam of a sword in the hand of one of those who lay in wait to murder the king.

"Speak!" said the voice again. "Is the king's room backward or forward?"

"I will not tell thee!" he gasped, and heard a low mocking laugh.

"'Tis thee, my caitiff boy!" sneered Sir Turquine, for he it was. "Then this for thee!"

With the words he thrust his dagger into the body of the struggling boy, who swooned and dropped to the floor.

In a few moments Owen stirred, for his struggles had caused his enemy's dagger to swerve, and though weak from loss of blood, the young page knew that he must act at once to save his hero from the murderous knives.

He heard the stealthy footsteps of the murderers going backwards to the hall, and, filled with joy, he pressed forward. His head was dizzy, he felt as if every moment he must sink in a swoon; but at length he reached the door, turned the handle and fell in.

"The king!" he cried. "Save the king! Turquine has broken in and seeks his life."

At his shrill cry there was the rush of men and torches along the corridors and into the room. Sir Bedevere was at the head of them, and in a moment he, with twenty half-dressed knights behind him, was scattering through the palace seeking the murderers, while the king ordered his leech or doctor to attend instantly to Owen's wound.

This was soon found not to be severe, and the lad was laid at the foot of the king's bed, glad and proud to hear the king's words of praise.

Then Sir Bedevere entered, saying that the murderers had fled as soon as they found they were discovered.

"But, my lord king," he said, "this is no murderous attempt by one insolent lord. It means, my king, that thou wilt have to fight for thy kingdom. It is civil war!"

"What mean you, Sir Bedevere?"

"Sir Turquine is but one of them, my king," replied Bedevere. "He is but the tool of the six kings who have put such great despite upon you. For with them also in this midnight murder-raid I saw King Nentres of Garlot and Duke Cambenet."

Suddenly, as he spoke, the tall grey form of Merlin took shape before them, for so great and marvellous was the power of this wizard, that he could come and go unseen, except when he willed that men should see him.

"Sir," said Merlin, "ye owe your life to this brave lad here, and he shall be a passing good man when he shall have attained his full strength, and he doth deserve your high and gracious favour."

"That shall he have," said the king, and smiled at young Owen, and the smile made the lad forget all the burning of his wound for very pride and gladness.

"And now," said Merlin, "if ye will gather your men I will lead you to the hold of those murderous kings by a secret way, and ye should give them such a sudden blow as will discomfit them."

In a little while all was ready, and then, silently, with muffled arms, the men of Arthur were marching forth down the narrow dark lanes of the town to where the place was ruinous with old houses left forsaken by their Roman masters when they had gone from Britain fifty years before.

Merlin led them to a great squat tower which stood beside the wall, wherein a single light gleamed at a high window. Causing some to surround this place, Merlin led others to a broken door, and there they entered in. Then was there a sudden uproar and fierce fighting in the rooms and up the narrow stairs.

In the darkness King Lot, with a hundred knights, burst out through a rear door, and thought to escape; but King Arthur with his knights waylaid them, and slew on the right and on the left, doing such deeds that all took pride in his bravery and might of arms. Fiercely did King Lot press forward, and to his aid came Sir Caradoc, who set upon King Arthur in the rear.

Arthur drew from his side the sword he had so marvellously taken from the stone, and in the darkness it flashed as if it were thirty torches, and it dazzled his enemies' eyes, so that they gave way.

By this time the common people of Caerleon had heard the great outcry and the clang of swords on armour. Learning of the jeopardy of their beloved king from midnight murderers, they ran to the tower, and with clubs and staves and bills they slew many of the men of the evil kings, putting the rest to flight. But the six kings were still unharmed, and with the remnant of their knights fled and departed in the darkness.

A few days later King Arthur journeyed back to London, and on an evening when, in the twilight, he stood upon the roof of the palace overlooking the broad Thames, he was aware of a shadow beside him where no shadow had been before. Before he could cross himself against the evil powers of wizardry and glamour, the steel-blue eyes of Merlin looked out from the cloud, and the magician's voice spoke to him as if from a great distance.

"I stand beneath the shaggy brows of the Hill of Tanyshane," said the voice, "and I look down into the courtyard of the castle of King Lot. There I see the gathering of men, the flash of torches on their hauberks, the glitter of helms, and the blue gleams of swords. I have passed through these northern lands, from the windswept ways of Alclwyd to the quaking marshes of the Humber. Eleven castles have I seen, and each is filled with the clang of beating iron, the glow of smiths' fires and the hissing of new-tempered steel. Call thy council, and abide my return, for now you must fight for your kingdom, O king, and for your very life."

The voice ceased, and the shadow and the vivid eyes it half concealed died away with it.

Into the council chamber three days later, while men waited for they knew not what, Merlin entered.

"What news do you bring, Merlin?" they cried.

"Of civil war!" he said. "I warn you all that the six kings ye gave a check to at Caerleon have taken to themselves four others and a mighty duke. They will to thrust Arthur, whom they call base-born, out of his life. Mark you, they are passing strong and as good fighting men as any alive—pity it is that great Uriens is with them, the wisest and noblest fighter of them all!—and unless Arthur have more men of arms and chivalry with him than he can get within this realm, he will be overcome!"

"Oh, but we be big enough!" cried some.

"That ye are not!" said Merlin. "Which of ye have single-handed beaten back the pagan hordes from your lands? Which of ye can match King Lot for subtlety and craft, or the great Uriens of Reged for wisdom in war?"

"What is to do, then? Tell us your counsel," said they all.

"This is my advice," replied the wizard. "Ye must send an embassy to King Ban of Brittany and King Bors of Gaul, promising to aid them when King Claudas, their common enemy, shall fight them again, if they will come and aid our king in this his fight for life and kingdom."

In a few weeks this was done. King Ban of Brittany and his brother, King Bors, crossed into Britain with five thousand good knights, sworn to aid Arthur in this great conflict.

With King Ban came his son, young Lancelot, who was later to make more fame and more dole than any knight of Arthur's court.

On a day in early spring, the hosts of Arthur and his two allies were encamped in Sherwood Forest, and the fore-riders or scouts, which Merlin had sent out, came hastening in to say that the host of the eleven kings was but a few miles to the north of Trentwater. By secret ways, throughout that night, Merlin led the army of Arthur until they came near where the enemy lay. Then did he order an ambush to be made by some part of their men, with King Ban and King Bors, by hiding in a hollow filled with trees.

In the morning, when either host saw the other, the northern host was well comforted, for they thought King Arthur's force was but small.

With the pealing of trumpets and the shouts of the knights, King Arthur ordered his men to advance, and in their midst was the great silken banner with the fierce red dragon ramping in its folds. This had been blessed by the Archbishop of London at a solemn service held before the host left London.

All day the battle raged. Knight hurled and hurtled against knight, bowmen shot their short Welsh arrows, and men-at-arms thrust and maimed and slashed with the great billhooks and spears.

King Arthur, with his bodyguard of four—Sir Kay, Sir Baudwin, Sir Ulfius, and Sir Bedevere—did feats of arms that it was marvellous to see. Often the eleven kings did essay to give deadly strokes upon the king, but the press of fighting kept some of them from him, and others withdrew sore wounded from the attack upon him and his faithful four.

Once the five held strong medley against six of the rebel kings, and these were King Lot, King Nentres, King Brandegoris, King Idres, King Uriens, and King Agwisance; and so fiercely did they attack them that three drew off sore wounded, whilst King Lot, King Uriens, and King Nentres were unhorsed, and all but slain by the men-at-arms.

At length it appeared to Arthur that his host was yielding before the weight of numbers of the enemy, and then he bethought him of a strategy. He took counsel of his nobles, and they approved; he sent a trusty messenger to the Kings Ban and Bors, who still lay in ambush; and then, commanding his trumpets to sound, he ordered a retreat.

As had been agreed on, the knights on Arthur's side made their retreat in a confusion that seemed full of fear; and the enemy, joyfully shouting their cries of triumph, pursued them headlong.

King Lot's host, led onward thus unthinking, were sure of victory.

But their cries of triumph were short and quickly turned to woe; for when they had passed the place of ambush, they heard cries of terror in their rear, and turning, they found a great host pouring forth from the hollow combe, thick as angry bees from a hive.

Then, indeed, taken in the rear and in the front, there was little hope of victory, and King Lot's men fought for dear life.

Seeing King Bors, where he hewed terribly in the press of battle, King Lot, who knew him well, cried out:

"Ah, Mary, now defend us from death and from horrible maims, for I see well we be in fear of quick death! Yonder is King Bors, one of the most worshipful and best knights in the world; and there is his twin brother, King Ban, as terrible as he. How came they and their host into Britain, and we not know it, alas?"

"By the arts of that wizard Merlin, I doubt not," said King Uriens. "And I doubt not we shall all be sped. Look you, Lot," he went on, "whoever that Arthur may be, I'll swear by my head he is not of low-born breeding, but a very man and a marvellous fighter."

"If you lose heart now, why, go and swear fealty to him!" sneered King Lot.

"Keep your sneers," said Uriens sternly. "I'll pay the price of rebellion to my last breath, as I have vowed."

By now the great mass of King Lot's host was either slain or run away, and the evening drew on; but the eleven kings, wounded, spent, and full of anguish at defeat, drew together with a few hundred of their knights, and vowed to die fighting. When they looked to see where they stood, they found that Arthur had penned them upon a little bluff of land that ended steeply over a deep river, and that no way was open for them to escape from the death of swords, unless they chose to leap on the rocks below the cliff.

"See!" said Uriens, with a laugh. "While we fought like wild boars, and thought of nothing but the killing, this base-born king kept his wits and moved us like pawns on a chessboard, we all unwitting. First, he drew us into ambush, and now he thrusts us into a chasm. We war-wise fighters, grown grey in battle, checkmated by a boy!"

Nevertheless, though wearied, full of dread and shame, and looking death in the eyes, the little band of men withdrew backwards, waiting until Arthur should command his lines of glittering knights to dash upon the remnant of the rebel kings.

"The proud evil men!" said Arthur in anger, looking upon them. "Though they know death is upon them, they will not crave mercy of me, a base-born king, as they name me!"

"Ah, sir king," said King Ban, "blame them not, for they do as brave men ought to do, and they are the best fighting men and the knights of most prowess that ever I saw. And if they were belonging unto you, there would be no king under heaven to compare with you for power and fame and majesty."

"I cannot love them," said Arthur sadly, "for they would destroy me."

"Now, this is my counsel," said King Lot to his ten fellows, as he looked over the field strewn with the dead, "that we stand together in a circle and swear to die together—we and our few knights. We have aimed at a kingdom and a crown, and we have failed. But we will die like kings and warriors. When they press upon us at the last, let no one of us break away. If any see another dress him to flee or to yield, let him slay him. How say ye?"

"It is good!" said they all.

Then, for all their aching wounds, they mended their broken harness hurriedly, and righted their shields, took new spears from the hands of their squires, and set them upright on their thighs, and thus, with the low red light of the westering sun behind them, they stood still and grim, like a clump of tall leafless trees.

Arthur gave the order to advance, and his knights leaped forward over the heap of the slain. But just then Sir Kay came to the king, bringing a knight from the north who had just been captured, bearing messages to the eleven kings, and Arthur asked him who he was and why he came.

"Sir king," said the man, "I am Sir Eliot of the March Tower, and I have ill tidings for my master, King Uriens, and his friends, but it seems my news is no worse than their fate. If my great lord is to die, I would lief die with him. Therefore, lord, despatch me now, or let me go stand beside my lord in the last rally."

"What is thy news?" asked King Arthur.

"It is that the pagans, the savage Saxons, have landed in three places beyond Humber, and all the lands of my lord and his ten fellows shall suffer fire and sword again."

"But if I slay your master and his fellow rebels, whose lands are those the pagans overrun?"

"Yours, lord, of a truth, if you can dash the pagans from them."

"If I and my host have swept these rebel kings from before me, think you I cannot sweep the Saxons from the land?"

"I trow you could, sir king, for on my way hither I have heard of the marvellous deeds this day of yourself and your knights. But, lord, I see the press of knights about my dear lord. Ah, that I might strike a blow for him before I die!"

"Thou shalt strike a-many yet," said Arthur, and Sir Eliot marvelled.

Arthur commanded his trumpets to blow the retreat, and the knights, wondering and half-unbelieving, withdrew them from about the eleven kings.

Then, surrounded by his chief lords, Arthur rode to the group of wearied kings, who, with dented and broken harness, from which the blood oozed in many places, still kept their seats with undaunted mien.

At King Arthur's command Sir Eliot told his news to King Uriens.

"Now this I have to say to ye," said Arthur, lifting his vizor and showing a stern countenance. "Ye are in my hands, to slay or spare as I choose. But ye have fought like brave men, and I would that, for your prowess, ye were my friends rather than mine enemies. Now this I have to offer ye. Swear here and now to be my lieges, as ye were to King Uther before me, and I will aid thee to thrust the pagans from your land, and thenceforth we will aid and cherish each other as true subjects and true lords should do. But if ye refuse, then your folly be on your own heads, for then I take your lives and your lands both."

With that King Uriens threw down his sword and put up his vizor, and turning to the others, said:

"Fellow rebels, we should be mad to refuse gifts so kingly and kindly offered. We have tried a throw with this young king, and we have been worsted. Better now to own ourselves lesser men than this wise lad here, and try to live in peace with him henceforth."

The other kings agreed, but King Lot, mean and revengeful, and the Kings Nentres and Brandegoris, suspicious that, as had been too often with themselves, fair words had covered foul intent, held back a little, until the others swore to leave them to the penalty of their folly. Whereupon they all knelt down upon the stricken field, and each put his hands between the hands of King Arthur, and swore upon the honour of their knighthood to be his true and faithful men while they lived.

As they rose from rendering their homage, Merlin came riding on a great black horse.

"Ye have done wisely well, my king," he said. "For by this kingly deed you shall rivet the hearts of the good men among these former rebels closer to your own than with rivets of steel. Thus well and wisely have ye won your kingdom and the fealty of these brave men."

"Now," he went on to the eleven kings, "ye doubted whether Arthur was of noble birth, and rightful king. Know ye that he is the son of the noble King Uther, who by my counsel hid him away on his birth. Ye will remember how Gorlois, Duke of Cornwall, hated Uther for taking Igraine for wife, whom Gorlois had captured and sworn to wed for her beauty and her wealth. And how all the turbulent lords did cling to Gorlois, and how for years King Uther had much ado to keep those rebels from dismembering the kingdom. Gorlois had vowed to slay by poison or treachery any son of Uther's, and so I took young Arthur into safe keeping. None knew of him until King Uther named him as his rightful heir upon his deathbed in the presence of you all. So, therefore, ye do well to give your homage to this your king, for Arthur is the son right worshipful of the great Pendragon, and the lovely lady, Igraine of Lyonesse."

All that stood by marvelled, and most of the eleven kings were glad that they had a king so noble in birth and doing as Arthur, the son of Uther Pendragon.

II

Sir Balin and the Stroke Dolorous

IT HAPPENED THAT ON A DAY KING ARTHUR, WANDERING FROM his court, had fought and vanquished a valiant knight, but he himself had been sore wounded. Merlin, coming to his aid, had taken him to a hermit's cave, and there with many marvellous salves had searched his wounds, so that in three days the king was whole again.

Riding forth together, Merlin led the king deeper and deeper into a wild and desolate country where he had never been before, and where there were no pathways. Arthur looked to and fro over the waste, but saw no sign of man or beast, and no bird flitted or piped. Great gaunt stones stood upright on the hillsides, solitary or in long lines as if they marched, or else they leaned together as if conspiring; while great heaps or cairns of stone rose here and there from the lichen-covered and rocky soil, in which the grass grew weakly in small crevices.

The mists now rose and drifted before them as they rode, the light was low and sallow, and the wind began to whisper shrilly among the great stones, and in the crannies of the cairns.

The king crossed himself, and looked at the white, old, and wrinkled face of Merlin; but the wizard seemed sunk in thought. Then Arthur bethought him that, in case some fiend-shape or wizard knight should assail him in that desolate waste, he could not defend himself, inasmuch as his sword—the sword he had drawn from the stone—had snapped when he fought the knight, and he had no other weapon with him.

"Merlin," he said, "this is a place of ancient death and terror, and if aught should assail us of evil, I have no sword."

"For that reason I bring thee here," replied Merlin, and would not utter another word.

Then, through the mists, which writhed and twisted as if they were fell shapes that would tear down the passing riders, Arthur became aware that their way was leading downwards, and soon the smell of water rose up to him.

He heard the beat and suck of waves upon a shore, and in a little while the mists cleared as if at a word, and there before him Arthur saw a lonely lake or sea, hedged round with salt-rimed reeds and sedges, and stretching out its waters, dull and leaden-hued, to so great a distance that his eye could see no end.

"What is this place?" he asked of Merlin.

"It is the Lake of the Endless Waters," said the wizard.

"Why bring ye me to this desolate lake in the wilderness?"

"You shall visit it once more—ere you die!" replied Merlin. "But look you there in the midmost of the lake."

Looking to where the wizard pointed, Arthur saw a great hand, clothed in white samite, stretched above the lapsing waves, and in its grasp was a long two-handed sword in a rich scabbard.

With that they saw a barge riding over the water, and it came without oars or any sail, and in the prow sat a woman, tall and comely, with a face lovely but sad. A frontlet of gold and pearls was bound about her rich red hair, and her robes, of green samite, fell about her as if they were reeds of the shore.

"What lady is that?" said the king.

"It is the Lady of the Lake," said Merlin, "and she comes to you. Now, therefore, speak fair to her, and ask that she will give you that sword."

Then the barge rasped among the reeds where Arthur sat on his horse, and the lady said:

"Greeting to you, O king!"

"Greeting, fair damsel!" replied Arthur. "What sword is that which the arm holdeth above the water? I would it were mine, for I have none."

"Sir king," said the lady, "that sword is mine; but if ye will give me a gift when I ask it of you, and will swear an oath to give me back the sword when ye shall be dying, then shall ye have it."

"By my faith, I will give ye the gift when ye shall desire, and when I am dying I will truly give back the sword."

"Then do you step into this barge and row yourself unto the hand and take from it the sword. And know ye that the name of that sword is Excalibur, and while you keep the scabbard by your side, ye shall lose no blood, be ye never so sore wounded."

So King Arthur and Merlin alighted, tied their horses to two stunted trees, and went into the barge. The king turned to look to where the tall green lady had stood but a moment before, and marvelled to see that she had vanished.

When they came to the sword which the hand held, King Arthur saw that the water where the hand rose forth was all troubled, and he could see naught. He took the sword by the handle, and the great fingers of the hand opened and then sank. So they came afterwards to the land, and rode on their way to Camelot, and reached it after many days.

When King Arthur entered his hall, and had been welcomed by his knights, the seneschal brought forth a messenger, who had come from King Rience of North Wales, and the man with insolent looks uttered this message:

"My lord, King Rience, hath but now discomfited and overwhelmed seven kings, and each hath done him homage, and given him for a sign of their subjection their beard clean cut from their chins. And my lord hath caused a rich mantle to be hemmed with these kings' beards, and there yet lacketh one place. Wherefore my lord hath sent me to demand that ye give him homage and send him thy beard also. Or else he will enter thy lands, and burn and slay and lay waste, and will not cease until he hath thy head as well as thy beard."

"Now this is the most shameful message that any man sent to a king!" said Arthur, "and thy king shall rue his villainous words." Then he laughed a little grimly. "Thou seest, fellow, that my beard is full young yet to make a hem. So take this message back to thy master. If he will have it, he must wait until I grow older; but yet he shall not wait long before he sees me, and then shall he lose his head, by the faith of my body, unless he do homage to me."

So the messenger departed, and King Arthur set about the ordering of his army to invade the land of Rience.

Later, on a day when the king sat in council with his barons and knights, there came a damsel into the hall, richly beseen and of a fair countenance. She knelt at the feet of the king, and said humbly:

"O king, I crave a boon of ye, and by your promise ye shall grant it me."

"Who are ye, damsel?" asked the king.

"My lord, my lady mother hath sent me, and she is the Lady of the Lake."

"I remember me," said Arthur, "and thou shalt have thy boon."

Whereat the damsel rose and let her mantle fall, that was richly furred, and then they saw that she was girded about the waist with a great sword.

Marvelling, the king asked, "Damsel, for what cause are ye girded with that sword?"

"My lord," said the damsel, in distress and sadness, "this sword that I am girded withal, doth me great sorrow and remembrance. For it was the sword of him I loved most tenderly in all the world, and he hath been slain by falsest treachery by a foul knight, Sir Garlon, and nevermore shall I be joyful. But I would that my dear love be avenged by his own good sword, which my lady mother hath endowed with great enchantment. And the knight of thine that shall draw this sword shall be he who shall avenge my dead love. But he must be a clean knight, a good man of his hands and of his deeds, and without guile or treachery. If I may find such a knight, he shall deliver me of this sword, out of the scabbard, and with it do vengeance for me."

"This is a great marvel," said King Arthur, "and while I presume not to be such a knight as thou sayest, yet for ensample to my knights will I essay to draw the sword."

Therewith the king took the scabbard and drew at the sword with all his strength, but in no wise could he make it come forth.

"Sir," said the damsel, "ye need not draw half so hard, for lightly shall it come into the hands of him who shall draw it."

Then the king bade all his knights to attempt this feat, and all tried their best, but it was of no avail.

"Alas!" said the damsel in great sadness. "And shall my dear love go unavenged, because there is no knight here who shall achieve this sword?"

She turned away through the crowd of knights who stood abashed about her, and went towards the door.

It happened that there was a poor knight in the court of King Arthur, who had been a prisoner for a year and a day, by reason of his having slain a kinsman of the king's. His name was Sir Balin the Hardy, and he was a good man of his hands, though needy. He had been but lately released from durance, and was standing privily in the hall and saw the adventure of the damsel with the sword. Whereat his heart rose, both to do the deed for the sorrowing maid and because of her beauty and sadness. Yet, being poor and meanly arrayed, he pushed not forward in the press.

But as the damsel went towards the door, she passed him, and he said:

"Damsel, I pray you of your courtesy to suffer me as well to essay as these knights, for though I be poorly clothed, my heart seemeth fully assured that I may draw the sword, and thy sorrow moveth me."

The damsel lifted her large sad eyes to him, and she saw he was goodly of form and noble of look, and her heart was stirred.

"Though ye be poor, worthiness and manhood are not in a man's rich raiment, and therefore," she said with a sorrowful smile, "do you essay the sword also, good knight, and God speed you."

Balin took the sword by the scabbard, and drew it out easily, and when he looked upon the sword it pleased him well.

Then had the king and barons great marvel, but some of the knights had great spite against Balin.

"Truly," said the damsel, "this is a passing good knight, and the best man of ye all, and many marvels shall he achieve. But now, gentle and courteous knight," she said, "give me the sword again."

"Nay, this sword will I keep," said Balin.

"Ye are not wise," said the maiden sorrowfully. "My lady mother sent the sword to find which was the knight the most worthy to rid the world of an evil knight that doeth his foul treacheries and murders by wizardry, but if ye keep the sword it shall work great bane on you and on one you love most in this world."

"I shall take the adventure God shall ordain for me," said Balin, "be it good or ill."

The damsel looked sadly into his eyes and wept.

"I am passing heavy for your sake," she said. "I repent that I have brought this to you, for I see you lying wounded unto death, and I shall not be near to comfort you."

With that the damsel departed in great sorrow.

Anon Balin sent for his horse and armour, and took his leave of King Arthur, who was almost wroth that he should depart upon a quest that promised but misfortune. He would have him stay with him in his court, but Balin would not, and so departed.

For many days, by lonely ways and through forest drives, Sir Balin fared, seeking for the felon knight Sir Garlon, but nowhere could he get word of him. At length one night, as he made his way to a hermitage by the edge of a thick wood, he saw the arms of his younger brother, Sir Balan, hung upon a thorn before the holy man's door. Just then Sir Balan came out and saw him, and when he looked on Balin's shield, which had two crossed swords, he recognised his brother's device, and ran to him, and they met and kissed each other, and that night they were happy together, for it had been long since that they had parted, and each told the other his adventures.

"It seemeth, then, that this King Arthur is a right worshipful lord," said Balan, when his brother had told him the adventure of the damsel and the sword, "but I doubt me he will not withstand King Rience and his host. Already that king hath come into this land and is harrying and burning."

"That were great pity," said Balin, "and I would that I could do some deed to stay the power of Rience, who is evil-minded and of an arrogant nature. I would put my life in any danger to win the love of the great Arthur, and to punish King Rience for his shameful message."

"Let us go then tomorrow," said Balan, "and try our prowess. King Rience lieth at the siege of the castle Terabil, within ten leagues of this place."

"I will well," said Balin, "and if we slay King Rience, his people will go astray and King Arthur shall easily make them yield."

Next morning early they rode away through the gay woods, drenched with dew, which sparkled where the sunlight lit upon it. Long and lonely was the way, until towards the evening they met with a poor old man on foot, ragged, lame, and dirty, and bearing a great burden. It was in a narrow ride of the forest, and there was but room for one person to pass, and though the brothers were making great speed, since they doubted they had lost their way, they would not ride down the poor man, as many knights would do.

But Balin, with a cheery call, said, "Old man, give me thy pack, and do thou climb up and sit behind me. For it is late and lonely that such poor old bones as thine should be abroad."

The old man, either from fear of the two great knights in their black armour, or from suspicion, mumbled out a few words and refused the offer, while yet he would not budge from the narrow path.

"Well, then, tell us thy name, old man," said Balin, laughing at his obstinacy.

"At this time I will not tell you," croaked the old fellow, stumbling under his pack.

"I doubt that great pack hath many rich things that never owned thee master," said Balan with a laugh.

"It is full evil seen," said Balin, "that thou art a true honest man, when thou wilt not tell thy name."

"Be that as it may," snarled the old man, "but I know your name, my lordlings, and why you ride this way."

"By the faith of my body, but ye are some wizard if ye know that," said Balan mockingly.

"And who may we be?" asked Balin. "And whither do we ride?"

"Ye are brothers, my Lords Balin and Balan," answered the old man. "And ye ride to pull King Rience's beard. But that ye shall not do, unless ye take my counsel."

"Ah!" cried Balin, "I know thee, Merlin! We would fain be ruled by thy counsel, old magician."

So it came about, with Merlin's aid, that Balin and Balan came upon King Rience that night with but a small band of his knights, and with a sudden attack out of the dark wood the two brothers seized the king and slew many of his men that tried to save him. And when they had ridden some way towards Camelot with the king, wounded and bound, between them, Merlin vanished from beside them.

Then they rode to Camelot at the dawning, and delivered Rience to the porter at the gate, to be led to King Arthur when he should sit in hall, and the two knights rode away. So, by the capture of King Rience, his host was put to naught, and the king paid his homage to King Arthur, and swore on the sacred relics of the Abbey of Camelot to be his true man while he should live.

At that time Balin could not meet with the felon knight, Sir Garlon, who wrought evil by wizardry, and he and his brother went their different ways seeking adventure. Sir Balin returned to King Arthur and became one of his most valiant knights.

It happened on a day that King Arthur journeyed with his knights from Camelot to London, and he lay in his pavilion in the heat of the day. As he rested he heard the noise of a horse, and looking out of the flap of his tent, he saw a strange knight passing, making great complaint and sorrowing, and with him was a damsel.

"Abide, fair sir," said Arthur, "and tell me wherefore you are troubled."

"Ye may little amend it," answered the knight, and passed on.

Later came Sir Balin and saluted the king, who told him of the strange knight sorrowing as he rode, and the king bade him follow and bring back the knight to him, "for," said he, "the sorrows of that knight were so piercing that I would fain know his grief."

Sir Balin took horse and lance and rode many miles through the forest, and by evening he came upon the knight and the lady.

"Sir knight," said Balin, "ye must come with me unto my lord, King Arthur, for to tell him the cause of your sorrow."

"That will I not," answered the knight, "for it would do me none avail."

"Sir, make ready," replied Balin, "for ye must needs go with me, or else I will fight with you and take you by force."

"No heart have I to fight, for all joy of life is dead with me," said the knight, "but I am on a fierce quest, and ye must be my warrant if I go with you that I be not kept from my quest."

"I will gladly warrant you," said Balin, and together with the lady they turned back.

"I fear not to tell you my sorrow," said the knight as they rode. "I but lately returned from fighting the pagans in the north, and when I came to my father's hall, men told me that the lady that I loved most tenderly had been robbed away by a villain knight. And as I sorrowed and went forth to seek the knight to slay him, lo, there I saw my lady, who had escaped unscathed from his evil hold. And much joy we made of each other, for we loved each other tenderly. But even as we kissed, there came an arrow through the air and pierced my dear lady to the heart, so that she fell dead in my arms. And there was none to see who shot the arrow, but men said it was the felon knight who had taken my lady, and he had killed her by black magic. So now with this damsel, my dear sister, who was her friend, do I go through the world seeking the invisible knight. And when I find him, with God's help I will surely slay him."

The good knight Balin was much moved by the sad story.

"Ah," said he, "it is the same fell knight whose death I seek by this good sword! And we will fare together, you and I, and take his evil life when God leads us to him."

Even as Sir Balin spoke, out of a dark glade by their side came a lance hurtling, as if held in rest by an invisible rider, and while they turned their heads at the sound of its hissing through the air, it pierced the side of the sorrowing knight and stood deep in the wound.

"Alas!" cried the knight, falling from his horse, "I am slain by the traitorous and wizard knight. His punishment is not for me, sir knight, but I charge you, seek him out and slay him for my sake, and for the sake of my dead lady."

"That will I do," said Balin, sorrowing, "and thereof I make a vow to you and this damsel by my knighthood."

When Balin had told all to his lord, King Arthur, the king made the knight to be buried in a rich tomb, and on it engraved his sad story, together with his name, Sir Herlew, and that of his lady love, Gwenellen.

Balin and the damsel rode forward the next day and for many days, and ever the lady bore the truncheon of the spear with her by which Sir Herlew had been slain.

Then on a day they lodged at the house of a rich knight named Sir Gwydion, an old grey gentleman, of a sad aspect. When night came, Sir Balin lay sleeping in the hall beside the fire, and suddenly he awoke at the sound of one sorrowing quietly near him. He rose up and went to the pallet and saw it was his host, and he asked him why he mourned in the dark.

"I will tell you," said the old sad knight, "and the telling will comfort me. I was but late at a jousting, and there I jousted with a knight that is brother to good King Pellam. And a full evil kinsman is this knight of so good a king. I smote the evil man from his horse twice, and he was full of rage that I, an old man, should overcome him. Therefore by treachery he assailed my son, a young and untried knight, and slew him. And I cannot avenge my dear son, for the evil man goeth invisible. But I pray that I may meet him in a little while."

"Is not his name Garlon?" asked Balin.

"Ye say right," said Sir Gwydion.

"Ah, I know him," replied Balin, "and I had rather meet with him than have all the gold of this realm."

"That shall we both do," said his host. "For King Pellam, his brother, king of the land of Holy Hallows, hath made a cry in all this country, of a great feast that shall be in twenty days, and that evil knight, your enemy and mine, shall we see there."

On the morrow they rode all three towards the town of King Pellam, and when they came within the country of Holy Hallows, Sir Balin saw how fair and happy was the land and its joyful people. Their meadows were rich with grass, the cattle were thriving and sleek, the trees were loaded with fruit and the cornfields full with rich ripe corn.

"Why doth it seem," asked Balin, "that this country is the fairest and happiest that ever I saw?"

"It is for this," said Sir Gwydion, "that in the Castle of Holy Hallows, whither we wend, King Pellam hath some holy relics of a passing marvellous power, and while he keepeth these his land is rich and happy, and plagues cannot enter it nor murrain, nor can pestilence waste the people."

When they reached the castle they found a great throng of lords and ladies, and because Sir Gwydion had no lady with him he could not sit at the feast. But Balin was well received and brought to a chamber, and they unarmed him. The squires brought him a festal robe to his pleasure, but he would not suffer them to take his sword.

"Nay," said he, "it is my vow that never shall I and my sword be parted, and that vow will I keep or depart as I came."

So they suffered him to wear it under his robe, and he was set in the hall with his lady beside him. Anon, when the meal was ended and the mead horns were set, Sir Balin asked his neighbour whether there was a knight at that court named Garlon.

"Yonder he goeth," said the knight; "he with that dark face and piercing eye. He is the most marvellous knight that is now living, and though King Pellam loveth him dearly, because he is his brother, yet he suffers bitterly the evil magic of Sir Garlon. For that knight rideth invisible, and slays so that none may know how they get their death."

Sir Balin's heart rose at these words, and he trembled with his great anger.

"Ah, well," said the good knight. "And that is he?" He considered long within himself what he should do.

"If I slay him here in this crowded hall," he said, "I shall surely not escape, and if I leave him now, peradventure I shall never meet with him again, and much evil will he do if he be let to live."

He could not remove his eyes from Sir Garlon where he walked between the tables, proudly talking and laughing with those he knew, and making soft speeches to ladies, though many showed fear of him, and crossed their fingers while he spoke to them, to fend off the evil of his eyes. Very soon Sir Garlon noticed the fixed, stern look of Sir Balin, and came across to him and flicked his gauntlet across his face.

"This shall make thee remember me when next thou seest me, knight," he said. "But thou hadst better do what thou earnest for, and fill thyself with mead."

"Thou sayest sooth," said Balin, and clutched the sword under his robe. "Too long hast thou done evil and despite, and now will I do that for which I came."

Rising, he drew his sword fiercely and swiftly, and cleaved the head of Garlon to the shoulders.

"Give me the truncheon wherewith he slew thy brother!" said Balin to the damsel beside him.

From beneath her robe the lady brought forth the broken truncheon, and striding to the slain man, Sir Balin thrust it fiercely into his body.

"Now," cried he aloud, "with this lance thou didst treacherously slay a good knight, and for that and all thy other cruel murders have I slain thee."

With that arose a great outcry, and men ran from the tables towards Sir Balin to slay him, and the foremost of them was King Pellam, who rushed towards him, crying:

"Thou hast slain my brother when he bore no sword, and thou shalt surely die."

"Well," said Balin, "come and do it thyself."

"I shall do it," said Pellam, "and no man shall touch thee but me, for the love of my brother."

Pellam snatched an axe from the hands of one standing by, and smote eagerly at Balin; but Balin put his sword between his head and the stroke, and the sword was struck from his hand.

Then, weaponless, Balin dashed through the circle of guests towards a door, looking for a weapon while he ran, but none could he find. King Pellam followed closely behind him, and so they ran from chamber to chamber, and up the narrow stair within the wall, until at the last Balin found that he was near the top of the tower, and thought that now he must surely be slain, for no weapon had he found.

Suddenly he came upon a door, and bursting it open he found himself in a large room marvellously bright and richly dight, and with a bed arrayed with cloth of gold, and one old and white and reverend lying therein. And by the side of the bed was a table of virgin gold on pillars of pure silver, and on it stood a spear, strangely wrought.

Balin seized the spear, and turned upon King Pellam, who stood still in the doorway with terror in his eyes. But, marking naught of this, Balin thrust at him with the spear, and struck it in his side, and King Pellam with a great cry fell to the ground.

With that stroke the walls of the castle drove together and fell in ruins to the ground, and a great cry of lamentation beat to and fro from far and near, and Balin lay under the stones as one dead.

After three days Merlin came and drew out Balin from the ruins, and nourished and healed him. He also recovered his sword and got him a good horse, for his own was slain. Then he bade him ride out of that country without delay.

"And never more shall you have ease," said Merlin. "For by the stroke of that spear with intent to slay King Pellam thou hast done such a dolorous deed that not for many years shall its evil cease to work."

"What have I done?" said Balin.

"Thou wouldst have slain a man with the very spear that Longius the Roman thrust into the side of our Lord Jesus when He suffered on the Rood; and by that thou hast defiled it, and caused such ill that never shall its tale be ended until a stainless knight shall come, one of those who shall achieve the Holy Grail."

"It repents me," said Balin heavily, "but the adventure was forced upon me."

As he rode through the land, he saw how it seemed that a dire pestilence had swept over it; for where he had seen the golden corn waving in miles of smiling fields, he saw it now blackened along the ground; the trees were stripped of their leaves and fruit, the cattle lay dead in the meads, and the fish rotted in the streams, while in the villages lay the people dead or dying in shattered or roofless cottages.

As he passed, those that were alive cursed him, and called down upon him the wrath of Heaven.

"See, see," they cried, "thou murderous knight, how the evil stroke thou gavest to King Pellam by that hallowed spear hath destroyed this happy land! Go, thou foul knight, and may the vengeance strike thee soon!"

Balin went on, heavy of mind, for he knew not why he had been caused to do this evil.

For many days he passed through the saddened land, and he felt that in a little while death would meet him.

Then suddenly one day he came upon a castle in a wood, and he heard a horn blow, as it had been at the death of a beast.

"Here," said Balin, "shall I meet my death-wound, for that blast was blown for me."

As he came on the green before the castle, many ladies and knights met him and welcomed him with fair semblance, and gave him good cheer.

"Now," said the lady of the castle, when he had eaten, "ye must do a joust for me with a knight hereby who hath won from me a fair island in a stream, and he hath overcome every knight that hath essayed to win it back for me."

"Well, as you claim it for your good cheer," said Balin, "I will e'en joust, though both I and my horse are spent with travelling, and my heart is heavy. Nevertheless, show me the place."

"But, sir," said a knight, "thou shouldst change thy shield for a bigger. For the strange knight is a strong one and a hardy."

Balin cared not, and so took the shield with a device upon it that was not his own. Then he and his horse were led to a great barge, and so they were poled across the wide stream to an island.

When Balin had landed and mounted his horse, he rode a little way towards a stout tower, and from it a knight issued, his armour all in red, and the trappings of his horse of the same colour. They couched their lances and came marvellously fast together, and smote each other in the midmost of their shields; and the shock of their spears was so great that it bore down both horses and men, and for a little while the knights were dazed.

The stranger rose up first, for Balin was much bruised and wearied; and the red knight drew his sword and came towards Balin, who thereupon got upon his feet, and they fought most fiercely together. So they fought till their breaths failed.

Many were the bouts they fought, and they rested oftentimes, and then to battle again, so that in a little while the grass of the sward where they struggled was red with the blood of their wounds.

But the more wearied they were the fiercer they fought to vanquish each the other, so that their hauberks were in tatters, their helms were broken, and their shields were rived and cracked. At the last the red knight could not lift his shield for weakness, and then he went back a little and fell down.

Balin also sank to the ground, faint with his wounds, and as he lay he cried out:

"What knight art thou? For ere now I never found a knight that matched me."

The other answered him faintly:

"My name is Balan, brother to the good knight Balin!"

"Alas," said Balin, "that ever I should see the day!" And therewith he fell back in a swoon.

Then Balan crawled on all fours, feet and hands, and put off the helm of his brother, and might hardly know him by his face, so hewn and stained it was. Balan wept and kissed his face, and with that Balin awoke.

"O Balan, my brother, thou hast slain me and I thee!"

"Alas!" said Balan, "but I knew thee not, my brother. Hadst thou had thine own shield, I would have known thy device of the two swords."

"Ah, 'twas part of the evil hap that hath followed me," cried Balin. "I know not why."

Then they both swooned, and the lady of the castle came and would have had them taken to a chamber. But Balan awoke and said:

"Let be! Let be! No leech can mend us. And I would not live more, for I have slain my dear brother and he me!"

Balin woke up therewith, and put his hand forth, and his brother clasped it in his, very eagerly.

"Little brother," said Balin, "I cannot come to thee—kiss me!" When they had kissed, they swooned again, and in a little while Balin died, but Balan did not pass until midnight.

"Alas!" cried the lady, weeping for very pity. "Alas that ever this should be! Two brothers that have played together about their mother's knees to slay each other unwittingly!"

On the morrow came Merlin, and made them be buried richly in the green place where they had fought, and on their tomb he caused to be written in letters of gold, deep and thick, these words: "Here lie Sir Balin and his brother Sir Balan, who, unwittingly, did most pitifully slay each other: and this Sir Balin was, moreover, he that smote the dolorous stroke. Whereof the end is not yet."

IV

How Lancelot Was Made a Knight, the Four Witch Queens, and the Adventures at the Chapel Perilous

WHEN KING ARTHUR WAS ARRIVED AT THE AGE OF TWENTY-FIVE, his knights and barons counselled that he should take a queen, and his choice fell upon Gwenevere, the daughter of King Leodegrance, of the land of Cameliard. This damsel was the most beautiful and the most gracious in all the realm of Britain.

When the marriage was arranged between her father and Merlin, King Leodegrance said that, for her dowry, instead of broad lands, of which King Arthur had many, he would give to Arthur the Table Round, which Uther Pendragon had in friendship given to him many years before. For, as King Arthur was already famous for his prowess and nobleness and his love of knightly men and brave deeds, Leodegrance knew that this would be a gift beloved of Arthur.

With the table were to go the knights who were its company. It seated one hundred and fifty when it was complete, but many had been slain, and now they numbered but a hundred.

When King Arthur heard from Merlin of the coming of Gwenevere, with the hundred knights bearing the Round Table with them, he was very glad, "for," said he, "their noble company pleaseth me more than great riches." He charged Merlin to go and espy through all the land of Britain for another fifty knights, so that the tale of the noble company of the Round Table should be complete.

Now, it chanced that while Arthur sat in the hall of his palace at London, waiting for Gwenevere to come to him, and for Merlin to return from his quest, King Ban, who had aided him in his fierce battle against the eleven kings, sent his young son Lancelot to Arthur's court, to learn knightly deeds and noble prowess.

None knew who he was but Arthur, who kept the matter secret. Many had smiled at the huge limbs of Lancelot, until his great strength had caused them to respect him; and being but a young man he had not yet got all the courtly bearing and noble manners for which in later time he was famous throughout all Christendom. So that many knights and ladies smiled sourly upon him, but others saw that he would shortly prove a fine man of his hands, full courteous and gentle, and of a noble nature and great presence.

At the court was also young Gawaine, son of King Lot, and nephew of the king. Both Lancelot and Gawaine were as yet not knighted, but together they tilted at each other in the lists beyond the walls, and spent their days in sword-play and all knightly exercises. Lancelot was the stronger and the better fighter; and though Gawaine never overcame him, yet did they twain love each other passing well.

Now Gawaine went to the king one day, and asked of him a gift, and King Arthur said he would grant it.

"Sir," said Gawaine, while Lancelot stood a little way off, fondling the hounds that licked at his hand, "I ask that ye will make me knight the same day that ye shall wed fair Gwenevere."

"I will do it with a good will," said the king. "And Lancelot," he said, calling to the young man, "have ye no boon to ask of me?"

"Not at this time, sir," replied Lancelot, "but in a little while I may."

Into the hall next day, as the king sat at dinner, came an old woman, bent and feeble, but with reverend white hair and gentle face, and she kneeled at the king's feet.

"What is it, dame?" said Arthur. "What is't you crave?"

"Justice, lord king," she said in a weak voice, while the tears gushed from her eyes. "Or else I die beside the gate where you do give the justice that all men praise."

"Who hath done evil to you?" said the king.

"Sir Caradoc of the Dolorous Tower in the Marsh," replied the old woman. "I and my son, lord, did build a little hut of wattle on a little plot which we banked from the marsh, near the great wall of the rich baron, deeming it safe to rest within the shadow of the strong lord, and though his hard rule was hateful to those whom he oppressed, we were so humble that we thought he would not notice us. And meagrely we reared our living from the ground, and sold our poor herbs to Sir Caradoc, his steward, or to the people in the villages in the marsh about us. But soon the Lord Caradoc desired the land on which our little hut was standing, to make his lands the broader. He tore our poor home down, and scattered all, and thrust us out to wander in the marshes; and when my poor son pleaded with the lord, he had him whipped, and he was brought and cast half dead at my feet as I waited outside the hall. Now if thou givest us not justice, we shall surely die."

"Doth any know Sir Caradoc?" asked the king of his knights.

"Yea, sir," said one, "and he is a great man of his hands, fierce and bold, of strong family, and his brother is Sir Turquine of Camber, who tried to slay thee at Caerleon, and was with the eleven kings in battle. Sir Caradoc liveth in a strong tower beyond the marshes to the south of the river, and he slayeth all that desire to pass them, unless they pay him all he demands."

"What!" said the king with fierce anger. "Within a few miles of this my justice-seat doth such tyranny rule unchecked, and ye tell me naught of it? Are ye then more fearful of this marsh robber than of me your king?"

The knights hung their heads abashed, and were silent.

Then Lancelot came and stood before the king.

"Let me, sir king, go and summon this tyrant to your presence," he said, "so that this poor dame may have justice, and that ye may punish him for his oppression."

"I fear me, Lancelot, thou art over young for so fierce a knight," said Arthur.

"I shall but bear thy words, sir," said Lancelot, "and he will not harm thy messenger."

"Take two stout men-at-arms with you, then," said Arthur, "and say to this Sir Caradoc that if he come not back with thee to answer unto me, I will come and take his life and burn his evil tower to the ground."

Many of the younger men that had despite against Lancelot for his greater prowess at the sword and the lance thought that now, indeed, they would be ridded of him, for they deemed Sir Caradoc would slay him.

Two days later came young Lancelot back with his two men-at-arms, and with them, bound upon a great horse, was a full fierce and raging knight, red of face, large of body, his clothes all tossed and torn, and his mouth full of dire threatenings against Lancelot. Men made way for them marvelling, and together Lancelot and his captive rode up the hall to the king.

"Here, lord, is Sir Caradoc of the Dolorous Tower in the Marsh," said Lancelot. "He would not come when I gave him your message, so I bided my time until he was sunk in wine, and was sleeping alone, and I have brought him secretly from his hold. Now, lord king, I think Sir Caradoc would joust with me, if you will give me knighthood."

"Joust with thee, thou smooth-faced boy!" cried Sir Caradoc, straining at his bonds. "I will spit thee on my lance if I may get at thee, and when thou art slain I will fight with this little king of thine—and his death shall wipe out this insult thou hast put upon me!"

At his rage and fierce bearing men marvelled and many were afeared, seeing that Sir Caradoc was great in lands and kinsmen, and big of his body.

"Thou art full young, Lancelot," said Arthur, "to joust with so strong a knight. Let an older man have ado with him."

"Sir king," cried Lancelot eagerly, "I claim the first battle with this strong tyrant. He is my captive, and I claim it."

"Have it as ye will," said Arthur, "and God speed you. But I misdoubt me much 'twill end in your sorrow."

"Ay, and thine too, thou gentle lady's knight!" sneered Sir Caradoc.

"Peace, man, peace," said the king sternly. "I think God will fight in this battle, for I have inquired far, and the tale of thy evil deeds is over-full."

Therewith King Arthur made young Lancelot knight, and men eagerly rushed away to the tilting-ground to see the battle between the virgin knight, Sir Lancelot, and the old robber knight, Sir Caradoc. And when Sir Caradoc was released and armed, he laughed and shook his lance, so sure was he of revenge right speedily.

Then they hurtled together most fiercely, and young Sir Lancelot was thrust from his horse by Sir Caradoc. Quickly he rose from the ground, and dressed his shield and drew his sword, and cried, "Alight, Sir Caradoc, for I will fight thee on foot." But Sir Caradoc, being traitorous, rode at Sir Lancelot with his spear, as if he would pin him to the earth, and the young knight had much ado to avoid him. All the knights cried out upon Sir Caradoc for a foul knight, and for shame he threw down his lance and alighted, and rushed at Sir Lancelot full fiercely, in order to slay him instantly.

But that was not easily to be done, for however wise Sir Caradoc was in sword-play, he was mad with wrath, and therefore thought of naught but to slay his enemy instantly. He raged like a wild boar, and gave Sir Lancelot many evil strokes, yet never did he beat down the young knight's guard. Soon men perceived that Sir Caradoc's great fierceness was causing him to make blind strokes, and then Sir Lancelot seemed the more wary. Suddenly they saw the young knight leap forward, and beat so heavily upon the other's helm that it cracked. Sir Caradoc strove to guard himself but Sir Lancelot was so wroth, and so mighty of his blows, that he could not. At last Sir Lancelot beat him to his knees, and then thrust him grovelling to the ground. Sir Lancelot bade him yield, but he would not, and still sought to thrust at the other. Then the young knight struck at him between the neck and the head and slew him.

Both the knights and the common people shouted with joy, and acclaimed Sir Lancelot as a noble and mighty knight. But the young man was full modest, and withdrew from the press. King Arthur gave unto him the Dolorous Tower and the lands which had belonged to Sir Caradoc, and Lancelot caused the old dame and her son to be given a fair piece of land and a hut, and many other wrongs and evil customs that had been done by Sir Caradoc, Sir Lancelot caused to be righted.

The kinsmen of Sir Caradoc went apart and conspired to have Sir Lancelot slain, but for a long time they could not come at him.

Then, when the queen came unto King Arthur, there was great feasting and joustings and merry games, and Sir Lancelot, for his knightly prowess in the lists, and for his gentle courtesy and noble manners to all, both poor and rich, high and low, was sought by many, and for some time rested himself in knightly games and play.

Then, on a day in June, when a sudden wind from a lattice blew upon his face as he laughed and jested with ladies and knights in silks and rich garments, he bethought him of the fair green woods and the wide lands through which lonely roads were winding. And departing from the hall forthwith, he bade his horse and arms be brought to him, and rode into a deep forest, and thought to prove himself in strange adventures.

Thus faring, he rode for two days and met with naught. On the third day the weather was hot about noon, and Sir Lancelot had great list to sleep. He espied a great apple tree full of white blossoms, and a fair shadow was beneath it, and he alighted and tied his horse unto a thorn, and laid his helmet under his head and slept.

While he thus lay, there rode by him on white mules four ladies of great estate, with four knights about them, who bore a canopy of green silk on four spears, so that the high sun should not touch the faces of the ladies. Then, as they rode by, they heard a warhorse grimly neigh, and looking aside, they were aware of Sir Lancelot all armed, and asleep under the apple tree.

The ladies came nigh him, and of them there was Queen Morgan le Fay, who was wife of King Lot, and an evil witch; the Queen of Northgales, a haughty lady; the Lady of the Out-Isles; and the Lady of the Marshes. And when the Lady of the Marshes saw the knight she cried:

"Now this is as good hap as ever could be, for this is he that slew my brother, Sir Caradoc of the Dolorous Tower; and for revenge of that, I would have this knight taken to my tower and torture him before I slay him."

"That is well said," said Morgan le Fay, "for he bids fair to be one of the most strong knights of Arthur, whom I hate. This man, Sir Lancelot du Lake, is the favourite of all the ladies at that court, who hate me. So will I lay an enchantment on him, so that he shall sleep."

Then the evil queen laid her hands over the face of Sir Lancelot, and said strange words that none could understand, and then he was laid across the crupper of one of the knights' horses, and he did not wake.

When in the twilight Sir Lancelot awoke, he found himself on a straw pallet in a strange room, and he leaped up and went to a narrow arrow-slit in the wall and looked out. Before him for a great distance was a black watery land, with the sun sinking far away on the very edge, and the pools of the marsh were as if they were of blood.

Then he beat at the door and called, but none responded, and for wrath he could have dashed the door down, but it was too stout, and he had no weapon, for his arms had been taken from him.

When it was dark, suddenly it seemed to Sir Lancelot that the room smelled foul, as if he had been carried into the midst of the quaking marsh, and was sunk deep in the slime and weeds of a pool. Then, through the arrow-slit, he saw many strange lights come, dim and blue like the wild lights that dance and flit over the lonely marshes by night; but that which made him marvel was that these lights were two together, as if they were the eyes of evil things. And they came up to him with a breath that was cold and dank, and they seemed to peer into his face, but he could see naught of their bodies. The hair upon his head rose, and his skin went cold. They pressed all about him, and to defend himself he struck at the eyes, but his blows beat only the air. Then suddenly Sir Lancelot felt sharp pains, as if small keen knives had been thrust into his flesh at many places. The stabs increased in number and in pain, and Sir Lancelot beat about himself and ran to and fro in the narrow chamber to escape the evil eyes and the stabs, but it was in vain, and thus all night in much misery he suffered. When for sheer weariness he lay down and tried to close his eyes, the evil things would not let him, but ever they tore at him and stabbed him. He was in anguish of mind more than he could bear, and for all his thought he could not think of any way to fight against the evil powers which followed and tortured him wherever he ran.

But at dawn they fled, and then the door of the room opened, and a damsel appeared, and in her hands was a manchet of sour bread, and a beaker of water from the ditch of the moat. The damsel was evilly clad in rags, and seemed like a scullion maid.

"These," she said, "my mistresses bid me say shall be your food until you die."

"Damsel," said Lancelot, "tell me who hath brought me here and used me so evilly."

"It is Queen Morgan le Fay," said the damsel, "and the three witch queens, the Queen of Northgales, the Queen of the Out-Isles, and the Lady of the Marshes."

"I doubt not, then, that they would slay me?" said Lancelot. "But why hate they me?"

"It is for this," went on the damsel, "that you did slay Sir Caradoc, the brother of the Lady of the Marshes."

"Alas, then," said Sir Lancelot, "there is no pity for me, and none of my dear friends shall learn of my shameful death."

"And so that you should suffer much ere you are slain," went on the damsel, "they sent in the night the Coranians, the marsh fiends, to torture you. Thus will they do until you die, unless, sir knight, you are a knight with a stout heart, and a good fighter, and will do me justice. If you will be ruled by me, and will give me a promise, I will aid you."

"Damsel, that will I grant you," said Lancelot, "for this would be an evil death for a knight. And full of terror hath been this night, from the foul things which have beset me."

"I may not stay further now," said the maid, "lest they think I tarry over-long. But by evening I will come again."

The day passed and twilight came, and Sir Lancelot was adread for fear of the night. But anon the damsel came secretly to him and said:

"Now must you promise me this, that you will release my father, whom Sir Turquine, Sir Caradoc's brother, hath kept in his foul dungeons since I was but a little child. And all his lands did Sir Turquine rob from him, and me he gave as a kitchen wench to Morgan le Fay, and evilly have I been treated who am a good knight's daughter. Now, will ye promise to free my father?"

"That will I, my poor damsel," said Lancelot, "and I will, God aiding me, slay this Sir Turquine as I slew Sir Caradoc his brother."

So at the dead of night the damsel opened his door, and with the keys that she had stolen, she opened twelve other locks that stood between them and the postern door. Then she brought him to his armour, which she had hidden in a bush, and she led forth his horse, and he mounted with much joy, and took the maid with him, and she showed him the way to a convent of white nuns, and there they had good cheer.

Then, on the morrow, she led him to a thick forest with many hills therein, and anon they came to a fair ford, and over the ford there grew a tree, and on it there hung many good shields, each with the device of some knight thereon, and Sir Lancelot was astounded to see the shields of many of King Arthur's knights hung there. And on a bole of the tree there was a bason of copper.

"Now," said the damsel, "I have brought you here where is Sir Turquine, the mightiest knight that ever was found, as men say, and was never overmatched by any. And in his dungeons are many poor knights, and my dear father, Sir Darrel. Now strike the bason with the butt of your spear."

Sir Lancelot beat such strokes that the bason burst asunder, and then he was aware of a great knight riding on a black horse. "This is he," said the damsel, "and now God aid you!"

"What needst thou, sir knight?" cried the other.

"To try my strength on thee," cried Lancelot, "for thou hast done great despite and shame unto many good knights of the Round Table."

"Art thou of that caitiff crew of ladies' knights?" sneered Sir Turquine. "Then I defy thee."

"Thou hast said enough," replied Lancelot.

They put their spears in their rests, and came like the wind against each other, and either smote other in the middle of their shields, so that both their horses' girths broke. Then, lightly avoiding their beasts, they came at each other with great fierceness, and so fared for two hours, feinting and striking, and so heavy were their blows that each bled from many wounds as they stood. At last, for sheer breathlessness, each leaned upon his sword.

"Now, fellow," said Sir Turquine haughtily, "answer me these questions I shall put to thee."

"Say on," said Sir Lancelot.

"Thou art," went on Sir Turquine, "the biggest man that ever I met with, and like one knight that I hate above all others, and I would liefer be thy friend than thy foe. Now, therefore, I will give up to thee my captive knights if thou wilt tell me thy name, and if thou art not the knight I hate most."

"Willingly," said Sir Lancelot. "But what knight hatest thou above all other? And why?"

"It is Sir Lancelot du Lake," cried the knight, "for he slew my brother Sir Caradoc of the Dolorous Tower in the Marsh, who was one of the best knights living. And ever I have sought this Lancelot, and slain and maimed many good knights and imprisoned others in the quest. To slay that fellow I have made a vow, and him I would meet above all others."

"Ha!" laughed Sir Lancelot. "And I am the first thou hast met whose love thou wouldst liefer have than my hatred? Well, I will have thee to wit that I am he ye seek, Sir Lancelot du Lake, and thy brother was an evil knight and an oppressor."

"What sayest thou?" cried Sir Turquine. "Thou art he I seek? Then, Lancelot, thou art unto me most welcome as ever was any knight, for we shall never part till the one of us be dead."

Then they ran at each other like two wild boars, lashing and dashing with their swords and shields, so that sometimes in their fury they slipped together on the grass, which was wetted with blood, and fell striking at each other. But at last Sir Turquine waxed faint and tried to avoid Sir Lancelot's blows, and his shield sank low, for his arm was very weary. Seeing this, Sir Lancelot leaped upon him fiercely, and got him by the banner of his helmet, and thrust him on his knees, and slew him at a stroke.

When he had rested a while, he went to the castle of Sir Turquine and released all his prisoners, and was rejoiced to see the damsel find her father alive. He caused the old knight to have his lands again, and bade the others that they should betake themselves to the court of King Arthur to be cheered and comforted, while their possessions, which Sir Turquine had robbed of them, should be given back to them.

Then fared Sir Lancelot further afield, glad exceedingly that he had escaped the foul plots of the four witch queens, and also that he had vanquished the evil Sir Turquine.

Then he rode a great while in a deep and dark forest, and as he followed the winding ways, suddenly he saw a black hound before him, with its nose to the ground as if seeking a scent. He followed the beast, and ever she looked behind her. Soon she left the forest, and picked her way through a great marsh, and Sir Lancelot followed, until in the wide distance he saw a little hill with trees upon it, and in the midst a ruined manor.

The hound went towards the ruin and Sir Lancelot followed. The wall was broken down in many places, and the path all overgrown and weedy, and as he came to the courtyard before the house, he saw the fishponds choked with weeds and the horseblock green with moss, and in the great doorway grew charnel and hellebore, and the spiked hemlock waved and spilt its seed in the wind. The windows hung by their hinges, and the green moss crept down the wide wet cracks in the walls.

But the dog ran over the drawbridge into the house, and Sir Lancelot gat from his horse and tethered it to the post beside the horseblock, and so went across the bridge, which was full sodden and worm-eaten, and bent beneath his weight.

Coming into a great hall, foul with many rotting leaves, he saw a table in the midst thereof, and on it was a knight that was a seemly man, and he lay as if he were dead, and the black hound licked his wound. And by his side there was a lovely lady, who started up, weeping and wringing her hands, and she said:

"O knight, too much evil have you brought to me!"

"Why say ye so?" said Sir Lancelot; "I never did harm to this knight, for hither did this hound lead me, and therefore, fair lady, be not displeased with me, for grief is upon me for your sorrow and your sadness."

"Truly, sir," said the lady, and she laid her face in her hands and sobbed full sorely, so that Sir Lancelot was much stirred thereat. "I trow, as ye say it, that you are not the knight that hath near slain my love and my husband. And never may he be healed of his deadly wound except some good knight aid me. But he must be so bold and valiant a man, that never, I think, may I find such a one in the little time I have before my dear lord shall die!"

"Now on the honour of my knighthood," replied Sir Lancelot, "I do not presume that I am such a one as you desire; but if I may aid you and ease your sorrow, that would I do most willingly. What is it I should do?"

"Oh, sir knight!" cried the lady, and her lovely eyes looked full thankfully at Sir Lancelot. "If ye would, it were the greatest deed you have ever done, however bold a knight ye may be. For this my lord is sore wounded by a knight whom he met in the forest this day, and by one thing only may he be made whole. For there is a lady, a sorceress, that dwelleth in a castle here beside, and she hath told me that my husband's wounds may never be whole till I may find a knight that would go at midnight into the Chapel Perilous beside the Mere, and that therein he should find before the high altar a sword, and the shroud in which the dead wizard knight is lapped, and with that sword my husband's wounds should be searched, and a piece of the shroud should bind them."

"This is a marvellous thing," said Sir Lancelot, "and I will essay it. But what is your husband's name?"

"Sir," she said, "his name is Sir Meliot de Logres."

"That me repenteth," said Sir Lancelot, "for he is a fellow of the Round Table, and for him will I do all in my power."

Going to the table, he looked upon the ashen face of the wounded man, and it was Sir Meliot, even as the lady said.

"Now, sir," said the lady, when Sir Lancelot had mounted his horse, "do ye follow that hard way across the marsh, and it will lead ye by midnight to the Chapel Perilous, and may ye speed well."

Right so, Sir Lancelot departed, and the sun was near its setting.

For some hours Sir Lancelot fared across the marsh, until it was deep night, save for the stars; then he came upon a broad road, grass-grown and banked high, where the night wind piped in the long grass. This he knew was a road which the great Roman necromancers had wrought, and he thought he had missed his way, for there was no other path.

As he stood marvelling, the figure of a man, tall and gaunt and but half-clad, came down the broad road towards him, and cried in a hollow voice:

"For the love of charity, sir knight, give to a poor man who is outcast."

Sir Lancelot pitied the sunken eyes of the poor man, and gave him alms.

"God give thee comfort, poor soul," said the knight, "and get thee a roof, for the night wind blows chill."

"God bless thee, sir knight," said the man, in awful tones, "for courtesy and pity such as thine are rare. Whither goest thou this night?"

"I seek the Chapel Perilous," said Sir Lancelot.

At which the shape threw back its head and cried out as if with great sorrow.

"God fend thee, sir knight," he said, "and bring thee safe alive. What thou gettest there, keep thou in thy hands until the dawn, or thy soul shall suffer death."

Then he vanished, and Sir Lancelot knew it had been a phantom.

Then as he crossed himself, he looked up, and through some thin and withered trees a little way off upon a slope he saw the shimmer of light, as if a chapel was lit up. He went towards it, and he saw a high wall that was broken down in many places, and an old grey chapel beyond, and the windows were shimmering with a ghostly light. As he came through the trees he saw they were all dead, with neither leaf nor twig upon them, their roots were crooked out of the ground as if they would throw his horse, and their limbs were stretched as if they strained to clutch him.

Coming to the gate in the wall, his horse trembled and plunged, and would go no further; whereat Sir Lancelot alighted, and tied it to a thorn tree, and went through the gate. By the ghostly light that came from the windows of the ruined chapel he saw that under the eaves were hung fair shields, with rich devices, and all were turned upside down. Many of them were those of knights he had known or heard of, long since dead or lost. When he had made a few steps on the grass-grown pathway towards the door, of a sudden he saw, coming from the church, thirty tall knights, each a foot higher than he, each in black armour, and each with sword uplifted, as they rushed towards him.

Their feet and their armour made no sound as they pressed forwards, and a thin blue flame licked about each naked sword.

They came upon him, but Sir Lancelot, with a prayer to God, dressed his shield and sword and stood firm, though his flesh quaked and his tongue clave to the roof of his mouth. They mowed and gnashed at him, and heaved their swords about him; then suddenly their vizors went up and he looked into their faces. And at that he was sore adread, for he knew they were dead men.

But he would not be overcome, and said in a loud voice:

"In the name of God, avaunt ye!"

He made a step forward, and they scattered before him, but followed closely behind. Then he went into the chapel, where he saw no light but a dim lamp burning upon the altar. It was an old, old chapel, with dust upon its floor like a thick carpet, the walls and windows were holed and broken, and the timber of the seats was rotten.

He went up to the high altar, and saw before it a trestle, and upon it was a dead man, all covered with a cloth of silk. Sir Lancelot stooped down, and with his sword cut a piece of that cloth away.

With that his blood seemed turned to water, and his feet seemed eager to run towards the door, for with a mighty roar the earth shook beneath him, and the walls of the chapel rocked. But he looked for the sword which he must take, and saw it under the trestle, and picked it up and went out of the chapel.

The ghosts of the knights pressed about him as he walked, and strove to tear the sword from his grasp. But he would not suffer them to take it, and when he reached the gate they could no further go, and so left him.

At the gate there came running up to him a fair damsel, crying to him:

"O brave knight, give me the sword and the cloth, that I may take them at once to my mistress, the lady of Sir Meliot, for he is at the point of death, and she is waiting in sorrow and tears beside him."

But Sir Lancelot remembered the words of the phantom beggar, and made reply:

"Fair damsel, I shall take them myself to the lady of Sir Meliot, for these things I may not give to any until the dawning."

The damsel would have torn the sword and the cloth full hastily from his hands, but he was aware of her intent, and hindered her, and bade her in the name of God to withdraw.

Whereat, with a great shriek, she vanished.

"Now," said Sir Lancelot, "may God, who has brought me through these evil adventures, shield me from any further subtle crafts of these foul things."

Straightway he mounted his horse, and took his way towards the marsh, so that he should give the sword and the cloth into the hands of the lady of Sir Meliot, for the healing of her lord.

But at the dawn Merlin met him.

"Sir Lancelot," said the old white wizard, "ye have no need to go to the ruined manor, except ye would have the proof of what I tell you."

"And what is that?" asked Sir Lancelot.

"That all that hath befallen thee hath been done by evil magic," replied Merlin. "The black dog that led thee to the manor was a fiend, the fair lady that entreated ye was an evil witch, and she and the damsel at the chapel were the same, and all was caused by the witch queens who had you in their tower; and the likeness of the wounded knight to Sir Meliot was formed by wizardry. They that craved your death did hope that ye would fail at the terrors of the Chapel Perilous, and that your soul would be lost as have the souls of those evil or weak knights whose ghosts assailed ye. But by your courage and great heart ye won through all."

"This is a great marvel," said Sir Lancelot, "and I thank God that He hath shielded me of His mercy."

When Sir Lancelot was returned to Camelot, and Merlin had told King Arthur of the knight's adventures, the king made him one of the knights of the Round Table.

"Ye do well," said Merlin privily unto the king, "for he shall prove the most man of worship that is in the world, and all your court and all your Round Table shall be by him made more famous than by any knight now living. Yet shall he not be one of those three that shall achieve the Holy Grail."

IV

The Knight of the Kitchen

It was the feast of Pentecost, and King Arthur was holding his court of the Round Table at the city of Kin-Kenadon, hard by the sea in Wales. In the high hall the tables were set for dinner, and the floor was freshly strewn with rushes, flowers, and fennel, so that the place smelled as sweet as a field. The cook and his scullions came to and fro through the door of the kitchen with anxious faces, for they feared lest the meats should be overdone, but as yet King Arthur would not sit to dinner. For it was his custom never to go to meat on that day until he had heard or seen some great marvel or adventure.

Sir Gawaine stood looking from a window in the bower where the king sat with the queen, and suddenly he turned with a laugh, and said:

"Sir, go to your meat, for here, I think, cometh a strange adventure."

And even as the king took his seat on the high dais in the hall, and his knights sat at the Round Table, through the great door of the hall came two men, well beseen and richly dressed, and, leaning on their shoulders, was a tall, fair, young man, as goodly in strength and breadth as ever was seen, with hands large and fair. But he was either lazy or ill-conditioned, for he leaned upon his fellows as if he were unable to stand upright. And the three of them marched through the hall, speaking no word, and they came to the foot of the dais, while men sat silent and marvelling. Then the young man raised himself upright, and it was seen that he was a foot and a half taller than those beside him.

"God bless you, O king!" said the young man, "and all your fair fellowship, and in especial the fellowship of the Round Table. I come to crave of your kindness three gifts, and they are such as ye may worshipfully and honourably grant unto me. And the first I will ask now, and the others will I ask at the same day twelvemonths, wheresoever ye hold your feast of Pentecost."

"Ask," said the king, "and ye shall be granted your petition."

"The first is this," said he, "that ye give me meat and drink and lodging here for a year."

"Willingly," said the king, "but what is your name and whence come you? Ye have the bearing of good lineage."

"That is as may be," was the reply, "but I may tell you naught, if it please you, lord."

Then King Arthur called Sir Kay, his steward, and bade him tend the young man for a year as if he were a lord's son.

"There is no need that he should have such care," sneered Sir Kay, who was a man of a sour mind. "I dare swear that he is but a villein born. If he were of good blood he would have craved a horse and harness. And since he hath no name I will dub him Beaumains or Fair Hands, for see how soft are his hands! And he shall live in the kitchen, and become as fat as any pig!"

But Sir Lancelot and Sir Gawaine reproached Sir Kay for his mocking of the young man, "for," said Sir Lancelot, "I dare lay my head he hath the making of a man of great worship."

"That cannot be," said Sir Kay; "he has asked as his nature prompted him. He will make naught but fat, for he desires only meat and drink. On my life I would swear he is only some lazy fellow from an abbey, where food hath failed, and so he has come hither for sustenance."

So Kay sat down to his meat laughing, and Beaumains went to the door of the hall, where the varlets and boys ate the leavings from the table; but he fared badly there, for they jeered at him as Sir Kay had done.

Afterwards Sir Lancelot, of his great gentleness and courtesy, bade him come to his chamber, to be better fed and clothed; and Sir Gawaine, because of a liking he felt in his heart for the young man, proffered him good meat and drink and a soft bed. But then, and at all other times, Beaumains refused, and would do nothing but what Sir Kay commanded.

Thus he lived in the kitchen, eating broken scraps, and lying at night where the scullions lay, except that he was given the chilliest spot furthest from the fire. But he did what he was bidden to do with a cheerful air and was ever willing to work. And if there was any jousting of knights or any other sights of prowess, these would he see with the greatest delight. In any sports or trials of strength or skill among the serving-men, he was ever foremost, and none could overcome him in wrestling or at quarterstaff, nor could any throw the bar or cast the stone so far as he could, no, not by two yards.

Whenever Sir Kay met him about the hall or the kitchen he would laugh mockingly, and to those about him he would say, "Well, how like you my huge boy of the kitchen?"

But to such sneers, and to all the scorns and insults of the varlets of the kitchen, Beaumains would answer naught, and was ever quiet and mild whatever he endured. And to all was he ever gentle, both man and child, and he never put forth his great strength in anger.

Thus a year passed, until again it was the feast of Pentecost, and at that time the king held it at his chief city in Wales, Caerleon-upon-Usk. And again the feast was royally prepared in the great hall of the court, but the king would not give the signal to sit to meat until he should have heard or seen some strange adventure.

But about noon a squire came to where the king waited, and said, "Lord, I am bidden to say ye may go to your meat, for there cometh a damsel with some strange adventure."

Quickly the king sat on the high seat, and the cooks brought in the smoking collops of meat and the dishes of savoury stews. And as they began to eat, there came a maiden of a plain sharp visage, who made her way to the step of the dais, and there kneeling, cried:

"Succour and help I crave of you, O king!"

"For whom?" said the king. "And for what reason?"

"Sir," said the maiden, "my lady sister is of great beauty and renown, and is besieged in her castle by a tyrant-knight, who will not let her go forth from her castle; and because it is said that here in your court are the noblest knights in all the world, I come to you praying for aid."

"What is your lady sister's name?" asked the king, "and where doth she dwell, and tell me who is he that doth besiege her?"

"Sir king," said the lady, "I may not tell you my sister's name, but she is of great beauty and of wide lands. And the tyrant-knight who besieges her is the Red Knight of Reedlands."

"I know him not," replied the king.

"Sir," cried Sir Gawaine from his seat, "I know him well. He is one of the perilous knights of the world, for he hath the strength of seven men, and from him I once escaped barely with my life."

"Fair lady," said the king, "I would help you willingly, but as ye will not tell me your lady's name, none of my knights here shall go with you with my consent."

The damsel looked about the hall with a quick angry glance, and the knights that sat there liked not her sour looks. Then from the crowd of scullions and kitchen lads that hung about the serving-tables at the side of the hall came Beaumains, his dress smirched, but his handsome face lit up and his eyes burning with eagerness.

"Sir king!" he cried, holding up his hand. "A boon I crave!"

As he came to the step of the dais the damsel shrank from him as if he had been something foul.

"Say on," replied the king to the young man.

"God thank you, my king," went on Beaumains. "I have been these twelve months in your kitchen, and have had my full living, as ye did graciously order, and now I ask for the two further gifts ye promised."

"Ye have but to ask," replied the king.

"Sir, they are these," said Beaumains. "First, that you will grant me this adventure of the damsel."

"I grant it you," said King Arthur.

"Then, sir, this is the other, that ye shall bid Sir Lancelot du Lake to follow me, and to make me a knight when I shall desire him."

"All this shall be done if Sir Lancelot think it well," said the king.

But the lady was exceedingly wroth, and her eyes flashed with scorn as she turned to the king:

"Shame on thee!" she cried. "Will you give me a kitchen scullion to aid me?"

With that she hastened from the hall, mounted her horse and rode away. Even as she went forth, a dwarf in the dress of a page entered the hall leading a great horse richly caparisoned, and on the saddle was piled a splendid suit of armour. And the dwarf went up to Beaumains and began to arm him, while men asked each other whence came all this fine gear.

When he was dressed in armour, all the knights marvelled to see how goodly a man he looked. Then Beaumains took leave of King Arthur and of Sir Gawaine, and asked Sir Lancelot to follow him.

Many people went to the door of the hall to see Beaumains mount his horse and ride after the damsel, and the way he sat his steed, with its trappings of gold and purple, excited their admiration. But all wondered to see that Beaumains had neither shield nor spear, and some laughed and said, "The ignorant churl! Doth he think the mere sight of him on horseback will affright his enemies, that he carries neither shield nor lance."

Sir Kay sneered with them, and suddenly getting up from his seat he cried:

"By my faith! I will go after my kitchen boy and see whether he will still know me for his better!"

"Ye had better bide at home," said Sir Lancelot, and Sir Gawaine agreed.

But Sir Kay laughed them aside, and having swiftly put on his armour, he took his spear and shield and rode after Beaumains. He caught up with the youth just as the latter reached the side of the damsel, and Sir Kay cried out, with a scornful laugh:

"What! Beaumains, do ye not know me?"

"Ay," replied Beaumains, "I know ye for the most ungentle knight in all King Arthur's court, and therefore keep you off from me."

"Ah, churl!" cried Sir Kay. "Thou needst a lesson from me. A beggar, though he be on horseback, is still a beggar."

With that he put his lance in rest and dashed towards Beaumains, expecting an easy victory. But the young man, putting the lance aside with his sword just as it was about to strike him, rushed upon Sir Kay, and with a deft thrust struck him through a joint of his armour, so that Sir Kay fell backwards off his horse to the ground. Swiftly leaping down, Beaumains took possession of his opponent's spear and shield, and commanded his dwarf to mount upon Sir Kay's horse.

Then, after remounting, Beaumains rejoined the damsel, who had seen all that had taken place, but said nothing.

At that moment they saw Sir Lancelot coming towards him. He had seen Sir Kay's discomfiture, and wondered at the mastery which Beaumains had shown.

"Fair sir," cried Beaumains, turning and drawing rein as Sir Lance-lot approached, "I would joust with you, if ye will."

"Have at you, then!" replied Sir Lancelot with a laugh, and with spears in rest they set their horses at a great gallop. They came together so fiercely that they were both thrust backwards from their saddles and fell to the earth, half-stunned and greatly bruised.

Sir Lancelot recovered first and ran to help Beaumains to his feet, and then, with their shields before them, they continued the combat with swords. For an hour they strove fiercely, thrusting, striking and parrying like two great boars in a forest clearing. Sir Lancelot was astonished to feel how great was the young man's strength, how swift were his thrusts, and how powerful were his blows. He recognised that Beaumains was a dangerous fighter, and that he himself would have much to do to overcome him.

"Beaumains," he cried at length, "fight not so hard, lad. Our quarrel, if we have aught, is surely not so great that we cannot leave off."

"That is truth!" said Beaumains, laughing, as he dropped the point of his weapon. "But, Sir Lancelot, it doth me good to feel your wondrous skill and the strength of your arm. Yet, my lord, I have not shown the uttermost of mine."

"By my faith, I believe ye," cried Sir Lancelot, "for I should have much ado to keep myself from shameful defeat if you should really push me to the utmost. Therefore I say that you need not fear any earthly knight."

"I thank you for your good words," replied Beaumains. "And do you think I may hope at any time to become a proved knight?"

"Fight as you have fought with me, and I have no doubt of you."

"Then, I pray you, my lord," said Beaumains, "give me the order of knighthood."

"Ere I do that, you must tell me your name and of what kin you were born," replied Sir Lancelot.

"If you will promise to tell no one, I will reveal it."

Sir Lancelot gave his promise, and Beaumains, going closer, whispered some words into Sir Lancelot's ear.

"Ah, sir," said Sir Lancelot, taking the young man's hand in his, "I am glad I was not deceived. I knew you must come of great kin, and that you had not come to King Arthur for meat or drink. Kneel now, and I will make you knight."

So Beaumains knelt before Sir Lancelot, who lightly touched him on the shoulder with his sword, naming him knight.

Thereupon they parted with many kind words, and Beaumains made haste to overtake the damsel, who had long since disappeared.

As for Sir Kay, he was lifted upon Sir Lancelot's shield and taken back to the court, and there slowly he recovered of his wound. Men laughed him to scorn for the beating he had received from his own "kitchen boy."

"Lo," said some, "the proud knight went forth to cuff his own scullion, and the scullion beat him sore and took his weapons for spoil."

When Beaumains reached the side of the damsel, she pulled up her horse and turned upon him with flashing eyes and angry looks.

"What doest thou here?" she cried. "Away from me—thou smellest of the kitchen, knave! Pah! Thy clothes are foul with grease and tallow! Dost thou think to ride with me?"

"Lady," said Beaumains, and he spoke full gently, "my clothes may be smirched, but my arm, I trust, is as strong to defend you as any that is wrapped in silk."

"Out upon thee, saucy churl!" she cried. "Thinkest thou I should allow for that knight whom you thrust from his horse but now? Nay, not a whit do I, for thou didst strike him foully and like a coward! I know thee well, for Sir Kay named you. Beaumains you are, dainty of hands and of eating, like a spoilt page. Get thee gone, thou turner of spits and washer of greasy dishes!"

But for all that she raved, Beaumains would not reply in angry words, though his heart burned within him.

"Damsel," said he courteously, "ye may say what ye will to me, but I will not go from you whatever you say. I have given my promise to King Arthur that I will achieve this adventure for you, and that will I do or die in the trial of it."

The girl laughed mockingly.

"*You* will finish my adventure—*you* will come to our aid!" she cried in scorn. "Fie on thee, thou upstart kitchen page! But if you will not go from me, then come, fool, and I shall see thee quickly shamed. Thou art proud with the too good living thou hadst in Arthur's kitchen, but one I know whose face thou wilt not dare to look into, my knight of the kitchen!"

So saying, she pushed on her horse, and thus in silence they went on together.

In a little while they came to a dark wood, and suddenly as they rode, a man with white scared face started from behind a bush and ran to the side of Beaumains.

"Go not that way, sir knight," he said, "for there be six knaves who have taken my lord and bound him, and now they will surely take you and your lady unless you go back. I barely escaped with my life, and hid when I heard you, thinking you were of their thievish company."

"Take me to them!" cried Beaumains, and the poor squire, holding the knight's stirrup-leather, ran with him. And surely, in a little while, three knaves rushed forth before them in the green drive and bade Beaumains stand. But grimly he dashed at them, before ever they could recover. Two he cut down with his good sword as they stood, and the third, trying to escape, was run between the shoulders.

Then turning, Beaumains saw in a glade near the drive where three other knaves stood beside a knight bound to a tree. They dashed towards Beaumains with spiked clubs uplifted. But the squire rushed at one, tripped him up and despatched him; and the others suddenly decided to turn and flee. Their resolution came too late, however, for Beaumains cut them down as they ran.

The knight was quickly released by his squire, and came up to his rescuer, and thanked him heartily for his speedy help.

"Come with me," he said, "you and your lady, to my castle, which is but a little way hence, and I will fittingly requite thee for the saving of my life."

"Nay," said Beaumains, "I will have no reward. All I do henceforth is but my duty, and I will take naught in payment. Moreover, I must follow this lady."

The knight went to the lady, and begged that she would accept his hospitality, for the twilight was deepening and they were yet far from a town. The damsel consented, but, on reaching the castle of the knight, she would not permit Beaumains to sit at the same table with her.

"Take the knave hence!" she cried haughtily. "He is but a scullion from King Arthur's kitchen, and is not fit to sit with a lady of rank. He is more suited, sir knight, to dine with your turnspits."

"Lady, I do not understand your words," said the knight, "for this gentleman hath proved himself a man of knightly courage and courtesy this day."

"As for that," said the lady, "I count it naught. He took the rascals unawares, and they had no heart. They were but sorrier knaves than he is."

"Well," said the knight, "since you mislike him so, he shall sit with me, and you shall sit alone."

So it was done, and while the lady sat eating her meal in chilly silence at one table, Beaumains and the knight, his host, laughed and talked merrily over their dinner at another.

Next morning, early, Beaumains and the lady were up and away while yet the dew shone on the leaves. Soon they passed through a great forest and approached a wide river. In a little while they rode down to where a roughly paved way ran into the water, and, looking to the other bank, Beaumains was aware of two knights on horseback, stationed as if to hinder his passing the ford.

"Now, sir kitchen knight," laughed the lady mockingly, "what sayest thou? Art thou a match for these two knights, or wilt thou not turn back?"

"I would not turn if they were six," replied Beaumains quietly.

With that he rushed, with spear at rest, into the ford, and one of the waiting knights came swiftly against him. They met in the midst with so great a shock that their spears were splintered. They then closed fiercely with their swords, and hurtled about in the foaming, dashing water, beating at each other. Suddenly Beaumains struck the other so hard a stroke on his helm that he was stunned, and fell from his horse into the stream, which whirled him away into the deeps, and there drowned him.

Then Beaumains rode swiftly towards the other knight, who with his lance dashed against him. But Beaumains parried the spear stroke, and with one great heave of his sword, clove the other's helm in twain, so that the knight fell like a stone.

"Alas," cried the lady, as she came across the ford, "that ever kitchen knave should have the mishap to slay two such noble knights! Doubtless thou thinkest thou hast done mightily, sir knight of the turnspit, but I saw well how it all happened. The first knight's horse stumbled on the stones of the ford, and the other thou didst stab from behind. 'Twas a shameful deed!"

"Damsel," said Beaumains, quiet in words though hot of mind at her words, "ye may say what ye will. I only know that I fight fairly, as God gives me strength. I reck not what ye say, so I win your lady sister from her oppressor."

"Thou knave of impudence!" cried the lady. "Thee to speak of winning my lady sister, high of rank and rich in wide lands as she is! But thou shalt soon see knights that shall abate thy pride."

"Whatever knights they be, I care not, so that I win good words from you at last," said Beaumains.

"Those thou shalt never have, thou churl," replied the lady scornfully. "For all that thou hast done has been by chance and misadventure, and not by the prowess of thy hands. But if thou wilt follow me, why, then, come, and I shall the more quickly be rid of thee, for of a surety thou wilt soon be slain."

Beaumains answered naught, and so they went on their way.

Thus they fared until evensong, and then they came to a wasteland, where their way led through a narrow darkling valley. And at the head thereof they entered upon a wide land, black and drear to the very skies, and beside the way was a black hawthorn, and thereon hung a black banner and a black shield, and by it, stuck upright, was a long black spear, and beside it was a great black horse covered with silk, and a black stone fast by it.

And upon the stone sat a knight in black armour, at sight of whom the damsel cried:

"Now, my kitchen knight, 'tis not too late. Fly back through the valley, or this knight will surely slay thee."

"Nay, I will not," said Beaumains, "for I fear him not."

The black knight came to the damsel and asked if she had brought this knight from King Arthur's court to be her champion.

"Fie!" she said angrily. "He is no knight. He is but a knave that was fed for alms in the king's kitchen, and would follow me in spite of all I say. And I would that you would rid me of him. Today he slew two noble knights at the passage of the water, and all by evil chance."

"A strong knave, in truth," answered the knight, "and a saucy one. Then this will I do. He shall leave me his horse and armour, for since he is but a knave, my knightly hands may not harm him."

"You speak lightly of my horse and armour," said Beaumains, "but I will have you know that you get naught from me, and moreover I will pass these lands with this lady in spite of you."

"Thou knave!" cried the knight angrily. "Yield me this lady and thyself without ado!"

"Let me see what thou canst do to take us," replied Beaumains, and laughed gaily.

At this the knight in a rage leaped upon his horse and they thundered together. The black knight's spear broke, but Beaumains' lance pierced him through the side and broke off short. Nevertheless, though badly wounded, the black knight drew his sword and fought manfully, striking Beaumains many mighty blows and bruising him sorely.

But suddenly his lifted sword fell from his hand, and turning in his saddle, he dropped to the ground in a swoon, and shortly died.

And Beaumains, seeing that the black armour was better than his own, armed himself in it with the aid of his dwarf squire, and rode after the damsel.

But ever as before she railed at him, telling him he had conquered the black knight by a cowardly blow; but Beaumains would answer her nothing in anger.

Anon they came to the edge of a vast and dark forest, and from its shadows came a knight in green armour, who cried to the damsel:

"Lady, is that my brother the Black Knight whom ye bring riding behind ye?"

"Nay, sir knight, it is not your brother," she replied. "It is but a kitchen knave who by treachery hath slain your noble brother, the Knight of the Black Lands."

"Thou traitor!" cried the green knight. "Now shalt thou surely die, for my brother, Sir Percard, was a most noble knight and a valiant. And to think that he fell by the dirty hand of a knave is great shame."

"I am no knave," said Beaumains, "but of lineage as high as thine, maybe! And I slew your brother in knightly fashion."

But the green knight stayed not to answer, and they hurtled together, and clashed midway as if it were thunder. And Beaumains' stroke was so mighty that both the green knight and his horse fell to the ground.

Swiftly the green knight rose to his feet, and then, Beaumains having alighted, they rushed together with their swords, and stood a long time hacking, thrusting, and parrying. And each hurt the other sorely.

"Oh, my lord, the green knight," cried the damsel, "why do ye stand so long fighting with that kitchen knave? A shame it is to see a proved knight matched by a dirty scullion! Slay him for me and be done!"

Shamed by her words the green knight gave a fierce stroke and clove Beaumains' shield in twain. Then Beaumains, smarting with this blow, and in anger at the words of the lady, suddenly gave the green knight so great a stroke that he fell upon his knees, and then was thrust grovelling upon the earth.

Swiftly Beaumains cut the fastenings of his helm, and, tearing it off, lifted his sword to strike off the other's head.

But the green knight prayed his mercy and pleaded hard for his life.

"Thou shalt plead in vain," said Beaumains, "unless this lady shall beg thy life of me."

"Shame on thee, thou kitchen knave!" cried the lady, biting her lip with anger. "Thinkest thou I shall crave aught of thee, and be so beholden to thee?"

"Then he shall die!" cried Beaumains.

"O lady, suffer me not to die!" cried the prostrate knight, "A fair word from you will save my life! And you, sir knight, give me my life, and I will yield myself and thirty knights to be your men and do your commands while they live."

"Now that is a grievous shame!" cried the lady. "What, Sir Green Knight, art such a coward as to crave thy life of a scullion knave, and promise him thirty knights' service!"

"You and your thirty knights shall avail you naught," said Beaumains grimly, "and since this lady will not beg thy life of me, why, now I shall slay thee."

With that he raised the sword, but the lady cried out:

"Put down, thou rascally knave, and slay him not, or thou shalt repent it!"

"Lady," said Beaumains, and bowed full gently, "your command is to me a pleasure, and at your desire I give him his life."

Then the green knight did homage to Beaumains and gave up his sword. Afterwards he took them to his castle near by, where they passed the night.

Next morning the green knight, whose name was Sir Pertolope, accompanied them some distance on their way, and at parting he told Beaumains that he and his thirty knights would do service when and where he might desire. Thereupon Beaumains told him that he must go and yield himself and his knights to King Arthur, and this Sir Pertolope promised faithfully to do.

And again, when they had gone some way and had reached a little town, a knight challenged Beaumains, who, having fought with the stranger and overpowered him, threatened to slay him unless the lady begged for his life. This she did, after she had said many bitter and evil things, and Beaumains commanded the knight to go, with threescore knights which were in his service, and yield himself up to King Arthur.

Then Beaumains and the lady went on again, and the lady was full of rage in that she had been compelled a second time to plead with him for the life of a knight.

"Thou shalt get thy full wages today, sir kitchen knight," said she, "for in a little while there will meet us the most valiant knight in the world, after King Arthur. Methinks thou wouldst do the better part to flee, for the evil luck which thou hast had with the three knights you have overcome will not avail thee upon this one."

"Madam," said Beaumains, "ye know that ye are uncourteous so to reproach me. I have done you great service these three days, but ever ye call me coward and kitchen knave. Yet those who have come against me, whom you said would beat me, are now either slain or have yielded homage to me."

"The greater shame," said the lady, "that so lowborn a churl as thou art should have knights yield to thee who should have slain thee."

Beaumains answered nothing more, but his heart was very heavy at the thought that, do what he might, he could not win this lady to speak fairly of him.

Towards noon, as they rode, they saw the white towers of a fair city, and before its gates was a field newly mown, with many tents therein of divers rich colours.

"Lo, there is the town of the man that shall cut thy comb, thou proud varlet!" said the lady. "A brave and proved knight is he, by name Sir Persaunt of Mynnid. And he hath a following of five hundred knights and men-at-arms."

"A goodly lord, indeed," replied Beaumains, "and one I fain would see."

The lady laughed mockingly.

"Thou shalt see him too soon to please thee, I doubt not," she replied, "for he is the lordliest knight that ever whipped a knave."

"That may well be," said Beaumains, "and the more desire I have to see him."

"Thou fool!" cried the lady angrily. "Thou hadst better turn and flee while there is time."

"Not a step will I," replied he with a laugh. "For, look you, if he be so lordly a knight as you say, he will not set his five hundred knights on me at once. But if he will send but one against me at a time, I will do my best till my strength goes from me. No man, be he knave or knight, can do more."

At his quiet brave words the lady's heart smote her. She repented of her evil tongue, when she thought how valiant and true this unknown man had been on her behalf.

"Sir," she said in a gentler voice, "ye make me marvel. Thou hast spoken boldly, and, by my faith, thou hast done boldly, and that makes me wonder of what kin thou art. But as ye are so brave, and have done, you and your horse, great travail these three days, I misdoubt that ye will get hurt if ye go further. Therefore I bid you turn, or ever it be too late."

"Nay, I will not," said Beaumains. "It would be a great shame that now, when we are but a few miles from your lady sister's oppressor, I should turn back."

"But, sir, I counsel ye to do so," said the lady. "For the strength of Sir Persaunt, even if ye conquer him, is but little compared with the great strength of the Red Knight who doth oppress my sister. And I am sure you have little hope of overcoming him."

"Nevertheless, lady, I will essay to conquer him," said Beaumains, "for it is but my duty and my desire to rescue your lady sister as I have resolved."

"I marvel what manner of man ye be," said the lady. "It must be that ye come of noble blood, for no woman could have spoken or treated you more evilly than I have done. Yet ever you have courteously suffered all I said."

"Lady, it is but a man's duty to suffer a woman's wayward words," said Beaumains, "and they have not been without service to me. For the more ye angered me the more strength of wrath I put into my blows, and so was enabled to overcome your enemies. And as to what I am and whence I came, I could have had meat in other places than in King Arthur's kitchen, but all that I have done was to try my friends. And whether I be knave or gentleman, I have done you gentleman's service."

"That is truth, Sir Beaumains," said the lady, all soft and penitent now, "and I beg of you forgiveness for all my evil words."

"I forgive ye with all my heart," said Sir Beaumains, "and I tell you, lady, that now that you speak kindly to me, it gladdens me greatly, and I feel that there is no knight living whom I could not strike down for the sake of yourself and your lady sister."

By this time Sir Persaunt had seen them, and had sent a squire to ask Beaumains whether he came in peace or war.

"If he will not let us pass," replied Beaumains, "it shall be war."

At that they saw Sir Persaunt array himself in his armour and mount his horse, and now he came rushing across the field at utmost speed, his lance in rest. Beaumains also made his horse leap forward swiftly, and the two knights met with so great a force that both their lances splintered in many pieces, and their horses fell dead upon the field.

But the two knights instantly disentangled themselves, and fought on foot with shield and sword. So furiously did they hurl themselves at each other that often they fell to the ground. For two hours the duel raged, till their hauberks were tattered and their shields were hacked, while both were sorely bruised and wounded.

At length Beaumains thrust Sir Persaunt in the side, and the latter's attack became less eager. Finally Beaumains hit the other so great a stroke that he fell headlong, and instantly Beaumains leaped astride of him and unlashed his helm, as if about to slay him.

Then Sir Persaunt yielded him and pleaded for his life, and the lady, who had stood watching the combat, ran forward, placed her hand on Sir Beaumains' sword arm, and cried:

"Of your mercy, Sir Beaumains, yield him his life for my sake."

"I do it willingly," cried he, helping the knight to rise, "for he hath nobly fought and so deserves not to die."

"Gramercy," said Sir Persaunt, "and now I know thou art the strong knight who slew my brothers the Black Knight of the Thorn and the Green Knight of the Wood. And now I will be your man, and five hundred knights of mine shall do your service as and when you will."

And that night they supped bounteously in Sir Persaunt's castle, and the lady besought Beaumains to sit by her at the same table, and all three made merry company.

In the morning, after they had heard mass and broken their fast, Beaumains and the lady set out again, and Sir Persaunt went with them to the drawbridge.

"Fair lady," said he, "where dost thou lead this valiant knight?"

"Sir," said the lady, "he is going to raise the siege which hath been set by the tyrant knight of the Reed Lands."

"Ah, then he goes to Castle Dangerous, and on the most perilous adventure that any man could take. For they say the Red Knight hath the strength of seven men. And he doth oppress one of the fairest and sweetest ladies in the world. I think you are her sister, Dame Linet?"

"That is my name," replied the lady, "and my sister is Dame Lyones."

"This Red Knight is the most dangerous knight in the world," said Sir Persaunt to Beaumains, "and hath besieged that fair lady these two years. Many times he might have forced her for terror to have married him, but he keeps the siege in hopes that Sir Lancelot or even King

Arthur would come to rescue the lady. For he hateth all true knights, but those two with most bitterness."

So they parted from Sir Persaunt and rode onwards, and the lady spoke now full friendly to Beaumains.

In a little while, when they had passed through a fair forest, they came upon a plain, and in the distance was a high castle with many tents about it, and men passing to and fro between them. And as they rode under some withered trees by the edge of the forest, they saw, hanging by their necks from the bare boughs, many goodly knights in armour, with their shields and swords hung before them.

At this shameful sight Beaumains checked his horse and asked: "What means this?"

"Fair sir," said Linet, "abate not your cheer at this dreadful sight, for ye have need now of all your courage, or else are we all shamed and destroyed. These dead knights are those who have come against the Red Knight trying to rescue my sister from his power. But the tyrant knight hath overcome them, and slain them thus shamefully by hanging."

"Now Heaven aid me," said Beaumains, "for this is a most shameful and unknightly custom, and well doth that evil knight deserve death."

"Nevertheless he is a knight of great prowess and force, though of evil custom," replied the lady, "and no one hath ever borne him down in battle."

With that they came to a sycamore tree which stood alone in the plain, and on it was hung a great horn of elephant bone, with gold work curiously wrought.

"Fair sir, ye must blow that horn if ye wish to do battle with the Red Knight. But, sir," went on the lady quickly, and caught at Beaumains' arm that already had lifted the horn, "be ye not overbold. It is now the hour of prime, and it is said that the Red Knight's force increaseth to the strength of seven men until it is noon. Wait, therefore, until noon shall be past, and his strength shall diminish."

"Nay, nay," said Beaumains, "speak not thus to me. I will assail him however mighty he be, and either I will beat him or die with honour in the field."

Therewith he lifted the horn and blew so great a blast that instantly knights came in a great press from the tents, and people looked out from the walls and windows of the castle. Then Beaumains saw a tall man come running from a tent, arming himself as he came. Two barons set his spurs upon his heels and an earl buckled his helm upon his head. He was all in red armour, from the plume which waved upon his crest to the cloth which was upon his horse. And his shield was all of red, with but a black heart in the centre thereof.

Then he waited for Beaumains in a little hollow before the castle, so that all that were therein might see the combat.

"Now, fair sir," said Linet, "it behoves you to have great courage and heart, for yonder is your deadliest enemy, and at yonder window is my lady sister, Dame Lyones."

Beaumains looked to where Linet was pointing, and saw at a window the loveliest lady he had ever seen. And as he looked she smiled and bowed to him, and he felt his heart burn with love for her.

"Truly," he said, "she is the fairest lady I have ever looked upon, and she shall be my lady."

"Cease thy looking at that lady," called the Red Knight in a harsh and angry voice. "She is my lady, and soon shall she see thy foolish body swinging from the tree for the ravens to pluck, as others hang there afore thee."

"'Tis for that shameful sight and for the love of this lady that hates you and your evil custom, that I am resolved to slay you, if God so wills," was the stern reply of Beaumains.

"A boastful rogue thou art," cried the Red Knight, and laughed scornfully. "What is thy name, and whence come ye, Sir Black Knight? For surely from your talk you must be one of those prating and soft fools of the Round Table?"

"I will not tell thee my name," said Beaumains. "And as yet I am not of the worshipful company of King Arthur's Round Table. But when I have slain thee and rid the world of so shameful a knight, then shall I crave the king to receive me into that high fellowship of noble and courteous knights."

"Make thee ready!" shouted the Red Knight in a furious voice. "I will talk no more with thee."

With that they withdrew a little from each other, and then, spurring their horses, and with lances in rest, they hurled themselves towards each other. With so great a crash did they come together that both their spears were broken into a hundred pieces, and their breastplates, girths, and cruppers burst, and the two knights fell to the ground half-stunned with the shock.

But in a little while they avoided their struggling horses, and leaping towards each other with their swords, they cut and hacked each the other so fiercely that great pieces of their shields and armour flew off.

Thus they fought till it was past noon, and would not stop, till at last they both lacked wind, and thus they stood swaying, staggering, panting, yet feinting and striking with what strength they had. The Red Knight was a cunning fighter, and Beaumains learned much from him, though it was at the cost of many a gaping wound.

When it was evensong they rested by mutual accord, and seated on two molehills near the fighting place, they had their helms taken off by their pages and their worse wounds bound up. Then Beaumains lifted up his eyes to the lady at the window, and saw how her looks were tender with pity for him.

So heartened was he at the sight that he started up swiftly, and bade the Red Knight make him ready to do battle once more to the uttermost. Then they rushed fiercely at each other, and the fight raged more hotly than ever. At length, by cunning, the Red Knight suddenly struck Beaumains' sword from his hand, and before he could recover it, the Red Kmght had with a great buffet thrown him to the ground, and had fallen upon him to keep him down.

Then cried the Lady Linet piteously:

"O Sir Beaumains! Sir Beaumains! Where is your great heart? My lady sister beholds you, and she sobs and weeps, for surely she feels the evil Red Knight hath her almost in his power!"

At that, so great a rage possessed Beaumains, that with one great effort he thrust the Red Knight from him, and, leaping up, he seized his sword again, and so fiercely did he beat upon his enemy that the Red Knight sank to his knees, and then was thrust grovelling to the ground.

Beaumains leaped astride him, and cut the fastenings of his helm. Then the Red Knight shrieked for mercy.

"Thou recreant and coward!" said Beaumains. "Did not any of those knights that thou hast hung cry to thee for mercy? What pity and what mercy didst thou give them? And thou deservest none from me, nor from any man!"

With that he slew him at a stroke, and the people in the castle cried out with joy.

Their leader being dead, his following of earls, barons, and knights came and did homage to Beaumains, and he commanded that instantly they should betake themselves to the court of King Arthur and yield them into his hands.

Then for ten days the Lady Linet made Beaumains rest him in the Red Knight's tent, while she tended his many sore wounds. But ever Beaumains desired to go into the castle to see the lady he loved, but his hurts forbade him.

On the eleventh day he would no longer be denied, but having armed himself, all except his helm, which his page carried, he rode up to the castle gate. But as he came thither he saw many armed men, who pulled up the drawbridge before him, so that he should not enter.

Therewith he saw a knight at a window, who called to him.

"Fair sir, I am Sir Gringamor, brother to the Lady Lyones," said the knight. "I will that ye enter not yet. We know that you have proved yourself a bold and brave fighter, but we know not who you are. Therefore, unless you tell me your name and kindred, I may not suffer my sister to see you."

"I know naught of thee, sir knight," cried Beaumains sternly. "My business is with the lady, from whom I think I deserve a little kindness, for I have bought her deliverance and her love with some of the best blood in my body. Must I go away then, thinking she cares more for a name and noble lineage than for brave deeds and devotion? Tell me, Sir Gringamor, is this the will of the Lady Lyones?"

"Ye have but to tell us thy name and of thy lineage, brave man!" said Sir Gringamor.

"Nay, that I will not!" said Beaumains, for his heart was hot with shame and anger. "If I were but a churl, I should reckon myself a nobler man than the recreant knight from whom I have rescued you and your sister. But since he was a knight, it seems ye would reckon him as of greater honour than the brave churl that slew him for his evil deeds?

"Nay, nay, it is not so!" came a sweet voice crying in tears, and Sir Beaumains saw the tender face of the Lady Lyones at the window where Sir Gringamor had been. "My brave knight, think not ill of me, for this is none of my will, for I am mocked and my pleasure denied in my own castle by this my over-careful brother. I love thee, sir knight, whatsoever thou art, for I feel that thou art gentle and brave, and as good a man as any lady might love. And I beg you go not far from me, for I will have my will erelong, and I tell you now that I trust you, and I shall be true to you, and unto my death I shall love you and no other. And whenever I may come to you I will, in spite of this my brother."

Saying these words, the lady sobbed as if her heart would break, and hiding her face in her hands she was led away by her women.

With that Beaumains' heart smote him, and he was resolved to reveal his name and lineage for the sake of the dear lady who loved him. But even as he thought this, he was aware of a party of knights coming towards him from the plain, and soon he recognised that they were of the company of King Arthur's Round Table.

And the foremost knight, who bore his helm in his hand, rode forward to him, crying:

"O Gareth, Gareth, my brother, how hast thou deceived us all!"

Then did Sir Beaumains clasp the other's hand right warmly, for this was his own brother, Sir Gaheris, sent from King Arthur to bring him home.

When Sir Gringamor knew of the coming of these knights, quickly he bade the drawbridge to be lowered, and in a little while the knights were being welcomed in the hall.

"Sir Gringamor," said Sir Gaheris, "I find that I come at a lucky chance for the happiness of my brother. Already the fame of his brave deeds has reached King Arthur, for the knights he hath overcome have put themselves in the mercy of the king."

"Sir Knight of the Round Table," said Sir Gringamor, "tell me who is this brave knight that will not say his name?"

"He is Sir Gareth, my brother, the youngest son of the King of Orkney," replied Sir Gaheris, "and fit for the highest lady in the land. He hath played this trick upon us all, to test us. We did not know him, for he hath grown up to manhood while we have been long away from home. But ever he hath had an adventurous and witty mind."

"Sir, I thank you," said Sir Gringamor, and taking Sir Gareth by the hand he led him into the bower where sat the Lady Lyones, who sprang to meet Sir Gareth. To her Sir Gringamor told all that he had heard, and then left Sir Gareth to tell her more of himself.

And in a little while, at the court of King Arthur, they were married with great feastings and joustings and with all things to make merry. And Linet was wedded at the same time to Sir Gaheris. For though the Lady Linet was sharp of tongue, she was of great and good heart, and well beloved of all who knew her well.

V

How Sir Tristram Kept His Word

In the days when King Arthur had established his kingdom, he was called Emperor of Britain and its three islands. Nevertheless, there were kings who were rulers in their own lands, but they held their sovereignty of Arthur and had done homage to him and sworn fealty. In Wales there were two kings, in the north were eleven kings, and these he had conquered in a great battle by Sherwood Forest; in Cornwall were two kings, and in Ireland three kings, but all gave service to the great King Arthur. That part of Cornwall which was called the lands of Tintagel formed the kingdom of a prince named Mark, and he owed certain yearly tribute or truage to King Anguish of South Ireland. It befell one day that King Anguish sent a messenger, who came to King Mark as he sat in hall, and said:

"Sir king, my master bids me say that the truage which you owe unto him is unpaid for seven years past, and if it be not paid he will demand of you double the sum."

Now King Mark was a man of a mean and covetous mind, and he loved not to give money. Therefore, to put off the payment for a little while, he made answer thus:

"Tell your master that we will pay him no truage; and if your lord says he will have it, let him send a trusty knight of his land that will fight for his right, and we will find another to do battle with him."

When King Anguish heard the message he was wondrous wroth, and called into him the brother of his queen, Sir Marhaus, a good knight of prowess nobly proved, and, besides, a knight of the Round Table. The king craved of him to go and do battle for the truage due from Mark of Cornwall.

"Sir," said Sir Marhaus, "I will gladly go and do battle for you on this saucy king or his knight. I ween ye shall have your truage to the last groat, for I fear not the best knight of the Round Table, unless it be Sir Lancelot, and I doubt not King Mark hath no knight of such worth and prowess as I."

So in all haste Sir Marhaus set forth in a ship, and in a little while cast anchor fast by the shore where, on two high cliffs, the castle of Tintagel frowned upon the sea. When King Mark understood that so noble a knight as Sir Marhaus had come to do battle for the truage, he was full of sorrow, and wept as he looked upon the bags of gold in his treasure-chest. He knew of no knight of his court that dared face Sir Marhaus, and he feared much that he would have to part with his gold.

Daily Sir Marhaus sent a message up to the castle gate, demanding payment of the truage, or that a knight should come forth to do battle against him.

Then King Mark let make a proclamation through all the lands, that if a knight would fight to save the truage of Cornwall he should fare the better as long as he lived. But the days and weeks went by and no knight came forward. Then Sir Marhaus sent at the last a message which said that if within a day and a night a champion for King Mark came not forward, he should depart.

All that day King Mark was sore and ill of mind and haggard of face, and could never stay still, but was forever faring with his barons to where he could look down upon the ship of Sir Marhaus, and see the knight waiting in his armour.

Late in the afternoon, as the king stood thus, gnawing his nails for rage, and so hot and wrathful that none of his barons dare speak to him, there came two horsemen riding swiftly into the courtyard of the castle, and at the sound of their horses' feet King Mark turned eagerly.

A young squire was the foremost rider, and he was a youth full handsome and tall, with brown curly hair and blue eyes. He was dressed in a surcoat of red satin and a mantle of crimson, trimmed with gold; and on his head was a cap of rich purple, and his feet and legs were clad in fine leather, with gold bosses on his shoes. Alighting easily, he doffed his hat and came towards the king:

"Sir," said he, "if ye will give me the order of knighthood, I shall do battle to the uttermost with Sir Marhaus of Ireland."

King Mark looked the young man up and down, and saw that though he was young of age, yet he was passing well made of body, with broad shoulders and of big limbs. The heart of King Mark became light.

"Fair son," he said, and his barons marvelled at his soft words, "what are ye and whence come ye?"

"Sir," said the youth, "I come from King Tailoch, Prince of Lyones, and I am a gentleman's son."

"And your name and birthplace—what are they?"

"My name is Tristram, sir, and I was born in Lyones."

"Young sir," said the king, "I like your manner, and I think ye should be a good man of your hands. Therefore will I make you knight if ye will fight with Sir Marhaus."

"That is why I have come," said Tristram.

Eagerly the king bade a baron give him his sword, and commanded Tristram to kneel, and then and there he tapped his shoulder with the flat of the sword and bade him rise, "Sir Tristram of Lyones."

The king commanded his scrivener to come to him, and on the low wall overlooking the sea the man of inkhorn and goosequill laid his parchment, and wrote a letter to Sir Marhaus at the king's dictation, saying that a knight would battle with him in the morning. A messenger was sent therewith without delay, and the king went into supper, snapping his fingers and joking with his barons in great glee.

But in the midst of supper a parchment was brought to the king and his face fell, and he commanded the new-made knight to come from his seat and stand before him.

"Hark ye," he said, his face dark, "this prideful Sir Marhaus, waiting so long, hath made his terms the harder. I fear, good fellow, your knighthood hath been earned of me too easily, even if ye are not in league with this pesky Irish knight," he went on, his narrow eyes gleaming with suspicion. "He sayeth now that he will not fight with any knight unless he be of blood royal on his mother's side or father's. Say, are ye some starveling knight's brat, or what are ye?"

Sir Tristram's face went hard and his eyes flashed.

"No starveling's brat am I, king," he said, "unless ye are that thyself."

"What mean you? Have a care of your saucy tongue."

"I fear thee not," laughed Sir Tristram, "but this I would have you know. I am thy nephew, son of thy sister Elizabeth, who died in the forest, and of King Tailoch of Lyones."

At these words the king rose from his seat and embraced Sir Tristram, crying:

"Now, in the name of Heaven, thou art right heartily welcome unto me, dear nephew."

That evening he made great cheer of Sir Tristram, and had his bed made next to his own in his own royal chamber. On the morrow the king had Sir Tristram horsed and armed in the best manner. Then he sent a trumpeter down to the seashore, and let Sir Marhaus know that a better born man than he was himself would fight with him, and that his name was Sir Tristram of Lyones, son of the King of Lyones and his queen Elizabeth, King Mark's sister. Sir Marhaus was right blithe that he should have to do with such a gentleman.

Then it was ordained that the two knights should battle on a little island near the ship of Sir Marhaus, and so young Sir Tristram and his squire were rowed thereunto, and when he departed, King Mark and his barons and all the common people were rejoiced to see the young knight's noble and high bearing, and wished him Godspeed.

When Sir Tristram landed he saw Sir Marhaus waiting armed in the shadow of his ship. Sir Tristram's squire brought his master's horse to land, and clad his master in his armour as was right, and then the young knight mounted upon his horse and rode towards Sir Marhaus.

While he was as yet six spear-lengths from him the knight of the Round Table cried unto him:

"Young knight, Sir Tristram, what doest thou here? I grieve me of thy courage, for ye are untried, while I have been well essayed in jousts and tournaments with some of the best men of their hands as are now living. I counsel thee to go back."

"Fair and well-proved knight," said Sir Tristram, "I am for thy sake made knight, and I have promised to fight thee, and I will do so, as much for mine uncle's sake as for what worship I may win from doing battle with ye, who are one of the best renowned knights of the world."

"Then I would have ye know, fair sir," said Sir Marhaus, "that no worship shalt thou lose if thou canst only stand against three strokes of mine, for, by reason of my noble deeds, seen and proved, King Arthur made me knight of the Round Table."

Sir Tristram answered him naught, and then they dressed their spears and spurred their horses, and ran so fiercely each against the other that both were smitten to the ground, both horses and men. But Sir Marhaus had struck a great wound in the side of Sir Tristram, yet so eager was the young knight that he knew not of it. They leaped up and avoided their horses, and drew out their swords, and with shield on arm they lashed at each other like fierce wild boars. Yet for all Sir Marhaus' strong and bitter strokes he could not beat down the young knight's guard, and in despite he began to aim at his vizor and his neck. At this Sir Tristram was wroth, and struck him more furiously. Thus for two hours the battle waged, and both were sore wounded. But Sir Tristram was the fresher and better winded and bigger of limb and reach; and suddenly he heaved his sword up high, and closing upon Sir Marhaus he smote him with so mighty a buffet upon his helm that the blade shore through the steel even into the brain-pan.

So fierce had been the stroke that the sword stuck fast in the bone and the helmet, and Sir Tristram pulled thrice at his sword before it would loosen. Sir Marhaus sank to his knees with a deathly groan; then he threw away his sword and shield, and rising, staggered away towards his ship. Sir Tristram swooned and fell; and his squire came running to

him, just as the men of Sir Marhaus' ship came and drew their master
on board. Then they swiftly set their sail and flew over the sea.

Great was the mourning of the barons and the people of Cornwall
when it was known how deep and wide was the wound which Tristram
had received from the lance of Sir Marhaus. Many famous leeches
came and searched the wound and strove to close it, but none availed.
When two months had passed, came an old, old woman, a witch wise
in leechcraft beyond all others, who was called the Mother of the
Mists, and who lived in the Great Shuddering Moor, where only trolls
dwelled, and no man ever dared to go. She also came and searched his
wound at the king's desire.

When she had made her search, with many mumblings and
strange words, she turned and looked keenly at the king. Her eyes
gleamed like beads, her skin was wrinkled and dark, and she laughed
a little soft laugh.

"Lord king," she said, "this fine man's wound is poisoned, and
naught can heal it this side of the great water. But if he goeth whither the
spear came from which poisoned it, he shall get whole of that wound."

"'Tis well," said the king, "he shall be sent to Ireland."

"Ay, ay, ay," said the old woman, and laughed in Sir Tristram's face.
"Thou shalt be healed, fair chief, but the hand that shall heal thee shall
give thee a deeper wound—a wound that shall never be healed this
side o' thy grave."

Forthwith King Mark let a fair ship be purveyed and well stored
with necessary victuals, and Sir Tristram was carried thereto and laid
on his couch on the deck, and Governale, his faithful squire, went with
him. In the sunshine and the brisk wind Sir Tristram felt joyful, and
the merry waves slapped the sides of the ship full prettily as it cleaved
through the blue seas towards the west.

In the evening they saw the white cliffs and the brown rocks of
Ireland, and Sir Tristram took his harp and played thereon, for he had
learned to harp most featly in France, where he had lived seven years,
to learn all manner of courtly and noble pastimes. Soon the shipmen
cast anchor in a wide sheltered cove beneath a castle which stood on a

high rock beside a fair town.

Sir Tristram asked the master of the ship the name of that town.

"Cro-na-Shee, if it please you, my lord," said the master.

"It pleases me well," said Tristram; "it should mean that there dwell therein brave and noble knights, and damsels like unto fairies."

Out of the merriness of his heart he thrummed his harp with so blithe and strange a time that in a little while the very folk upon the shore came listening, and some began to dance, while others looked sad. For though the tune was very merry, there was sadness also peeping from it.

It happened that King Anguish and his court were in that castle by the sea, and a handmaiden of the queen came to where they sat and told them of the knight that sat in his ship and harped so strange a lay that it made one glad and sorry at the same time.

Then King Anguish sent a knight and begged the harper to take cheer with him, and Sir Tristram was brought in a litter, and all the damsels were sad at his sickness, and the knights sorrowed that a knight so noble-looking should be so wounded. King Anguish asked him who he was and how he came by his wound. And Sir Tristram, having learned that this was the King of Ireland, whose champion he had worsted in the battle, and thinking that his own name would be known, replied:

"I am of the country of Lyones, and my name is Sir Tramor, and my wound was got in battle, as I fought for a lady's right."

"I pity thee, sir knight," said the king, who was a right noble king and lovable, "and by Heaven's aid, ye shall have all the help in this country that ye may need."

The king told him of the battle which Sir Marhaus had had on his behalf with a knight named Sir Tristram, and how Sir Marhaus had come home wounded unto death, and was dead this two months. On which Sir Tristram feigned to be sorry, but said not much thereon.

Then did the king order his daughter to come before him. She was called La Belle Isoude, for that she was the most lovely damsel in all Ireland and the Out-Isles, and withal gentle and kind; and her father bade her tend and minister to this stranger knight, who had come to Ireland to heal him of his wound.

In a few weeks, so soft was she of her hands and so learned in leechcraft, she had cleaned Tristram's wound of all poison and he was hale and strong again. As some reward he taught her to harp, and gave her many good and costly presents. These she took, but valued them not so much as his kind words and smiles. More and more she loved to hear his voice, and when he was gone out hawking or looking at jousts she was sad and thoughtful, sitting with her fair hands in her lap and her eyes looking far away, and when she heard his step or his voice in the hall, then would her sad eyes light up, and a merry tune would hum upon her lips, and she would gaily talk with her handmaidens, who, whispering and glancing and nodding to each other as they sat about her at their spinning frames, knew of her love for Sir Tristram before she was aware of it herself.

Sir Tristram cared not overmuch to be with ladies, but was more joyful to be in hall, talking of hunting, jousting and hawking. All men regarded him highly for his great knowledge of these things, but as yet, for fear of hurting his wound which was but freshly healed, La Belle Isoude forbade him gently to take violent exercise. Sir Tristram was impatient to be in the saddle again, with lance in rest and his great charger leaping beneath him.

Now, to the court of King Anguish there had lately come a knight named Sir Palomides, famed for his knightly deeds, though still a pagan, and he was well favoured both of King Anguish and his queen. Sir Palomides came and made great court to La Belle Isoude, and proffered her many gifts, for he loved her passing well. Indeed, for her sake he declared he would be christened and become a Christian knight; but La Belle Isoude had no care for him, and avoided him as well as she might.

On a certain day King Anguish made a great cry that a joust and tournament would be held, wherein only unmarried knights should join, and the prize would be a fair lady called the Lady of the Laundes, near cousin to the king. The heralds further said that he who should win her should marry her three days after, and have all her lands with her. This cry was made in all Ireland and Wales, and in Logres and Alban, which are now called England and Scotland.

It befell the same day that La Belle Isoude came to Sir Tristram, and she seemed distressed of mind and as if she had wept secretly.

"Sir Tramor," she said, "this tournament shall exalt Sir Palomides beyond all other knights, unless a better do come forward and overcome him."

"Fair lady," said Sir Tristram, "Sir Palomides may well win the prize against any knight, except it be Sir Lancelot. But if ye think I am fit to joust I will e'en essay it. Yet he is a proved knight, and I but a young one and but lately ill; and my first battle that I fought, it mishapped me to be sore wounded. Yet I will essay it, for I love not this Sir Palomides."

"Ah, but I know thou wilt do well in the battle, and thou shalt have all my prayers for thy safety and success," said La Belle Isoude.

On the first day of the jousts Sir Palomides came with a black shield, and he was a knight big of his body and on a great horse. He overthrew many knights and put them to the worst, among them being many of the knights of the Round Table, as Sir Gawaine and his brother Sir Gaheris, Sir Agravaine, Sir Kay, Sir Sagramore le Desirous, Sir Owen, who had been the little page boy who had saved King Arthur's life in his hall at Caerleon, and three other knights. All these he struck down, and the others were adread of him. The people had great marvel, and acclaimed him with much worship as the victor of the first day.

The next day he came and smote down King Morgant, the pagan King of Scotland, as also the Duke of Cambenet. Then, as he rode up and down the lists proudly flourishing his lance, dressing his shield and waiting for the other knights to offer themselves to him, he was aware of a knight all in white armour, with vizor closed, riding quickly through the gate as if he came from the seashore.

The stranger knight came with swiftness, lifting his lance in token of challenge. Whereat Sir Palomides rode to the other end of the lists, dressed his lance, and together they put their horses in motion. Like two bulls the knights thundered against each other in the centre of the lists. The white knight's lance hit the shield of Sir Palomides full in the centre, and with the shock the pagan knight was lifted from his saddle, carried beyond his horse, and fell with a great thud to the ground, while his horse careered onward riderless.

Sir Gawaine and his fellows marvelled who this stranger knight might be. Then Sir Palomides, rising from the ground, caught his horse, and full of shame, would have slunk from the field. But the white knight rode after him and bade him turn, "for," said the stranger, "he would better prove him with the sword."

Then, alighting, they lashed at each other with their swords. Now Sir Palomides was a powerful man, and his strokes were passing heavy, but Sir Tristram, for the stranger knight was he, felt so full of strength and joy after his long leisure, that he played with Sir Palomides, and men wondered at the might of his blows, and his swiftness was a marvel to see. In a while, with a great buffet on the head of the pagan knight, Sir Tristram felled him to the earth.

"Now yield thee," said the white knight sternly, "and do my command, or I will slay thee of a surety."

Sir Palomides was sore adread, and promised.

"Swear me this," said the stranger, "that upon pain of thy life thou leave my lady La Belle Isoude, and come not unto her ever again, and for a year and a day thou shalt bear no armour. Promise me this, or here shalt thou die!"

"I swear it," said Sir Palomides, "but I am forever shamed."

In his rage Sir Palomides cut off his armour and threw it from him and fled away on his horse.

Then the white knight also went away, and none knew who he was. The king sent after him, to tell him he was the winner of the lady, whom he should wed, but the messengers could not find him. Men marvelled much at this, that the victor knight should not come to claim the rich lady for his wife with the wide lands that went with her.

When Sir Tristram returned to the private postern where La Belle Isoude had led him forth secretly, he found her standing breathless, and she was pale and red by turns, and could not speak at first.

"Thou—thou hast not failed?" she said, and clasped her hands.

"Nay," said Sir Tristram, laughing. "He will never trouble you again. And, by Our Lady, I wished there had been six of him, for I never felt more full of fight and strength than I do this day."

"But—but have ye not claimed the prize?" said La Belle Isoude, and hid her face that was so deathly white.

"Nay, nor will I," said Sir Tristram, "for I crave not to be married. I would be free and go forth into strange lands to seek adventures."

He went from her, with the tune of a hunting song upon his lips, and saw not how La Belle Isoude trembled against the wall and was near to swoon.

For La Belle Isoude herself was the Lady of the Laundes who should be given to the victor, though this was known to none but herself and the king and queen.

The king and queen and all the court marvelled who should be the stranger knight, and why he had departed, and some suspected Sir Tristram, but none knew of this except La Belle Isoude and Governale his squire, and none dared charge him therewith. La Belle Isoude kept her counsel, and strove to seem lighthearted.

It fell upon a day that Sir Tristram was disporting himself with other knights at a game of ball upon the green before the castle, and had left his sword hung upon the post beside his seat in hall. The queen, with La Belle Isoude, passed through the hall to go to see the men at their sport, and on her way she espied Sir Tristram's sword, and the strange device of a serpent which was upon the handle. She said it was a marvellous piece of work, and never had she seen the like of it. Then, by ill hap, she drew the sword from the scabbard, and they both admired it a long time, looking at its keenness and brightness and the words of mystery engraved on it.

Suddenly the queen gave a little cry as of terror, and she pointed to where, within a foot and a half of the point, there was a piece broken out of the edge. Then, very hastily, the queen ran with the sword into her bower, and from her treasure-chest she drew a casket, and from the casket she drew a tiny piece of doeskin, and from that she took a fragment of steel.

While her daughter marvelled what it all might mean, the queen took the piece of steel and placed it in the broken part of Sir Tristram's sword, and it fitted so that the break could hardly be seen.

"Alas!" said the queen, "this is the piece of sword that the leech took from the brain of my brother, Sir Marhaus, and this Sir Tramor is the traitorous knight that slew him!"

The heart of La Belle Isoude stood still for fear of the ill that would befall Sir Tristram, for she knew her mother's rage.

The queen caught up the sword fiercely in her hand and rushed from the room. Midway through the hall there met her Sir Tristram himself with his squire Governale, and the queen sped to him and would have run him through, but for Governale, who snatched the sword from her, though she wounded him in her wrath.

Finding her rage thus put to naught, she ran to King Anguish, and threw herself on her knees before him, crying out:

"Oh, my lord and husband, here have ye in your house that traitor knight that slew my brother and your champion, that noble knight, Sir Marhaus. It is Sir Tramor, as he falsely calleth himself, but the piece of steel that was taken from my brother's brain fits a notch in his sword."

"Alas," cried King Anguish, "then am I right heavy, for he is as full noble a knight as ever I knew; and I charge ye, have not to do with him, but let me deal in this matter."

The king went to Sir Tristram and found him fully armed, as if ready to fight for his life, for he knew that now the truth had been discovered.

"Nay, Sir Tramor," said the king gravely, "it will not avail thee to fight me. But this will I do for the love and honour I bear thee. Inasmuch as ye are within my court it would be no worship for me to have thee taken and slain, and therefore will I let thee freely depart if thou wilt tell me this: Who is thy father and what is thy name? And didst thou truly and rightly slay Sir Marhaus?"

"Tristram is my name," replied the young knight, "and I am son of King Talloch of Lyones. For the truage of Cornwall I fought for the sake of my uncle King Mark, and the battle with Sir Marhaus was the first I had, for I was made knight for that alone. Sir Marhaus went from me alive into his ship, though he left his sword and shield behind him."

"I may not say that ye have done aught but what a good knight should do," replied the king, "but I may not maintain you in this country unless I would displease my wife and her kin."

"Sir," said Sir Tristram, "I thank you for your goodness and for the kind cheer which I have had here of yourself and your queen and La Belle Isoude. I will depart straightway when I have bidden your daughter farewell, for I owe my life to her gentle hands; and I promise this, that I will be your daughter's servant and knight in right or wrong, to shield her and fight for her, and do all that a knight may do in her behalf, as long as I live."

Then took he his leave of La Belle Isoude, and he told her all how he had come to that land. He thanked her heartily for all her gentleness to him and for her healing of his wound. At first she stood silent, changing red and white of face, and with downcast eyes, her fingers straining about each other. When he swore that he would be her knight, to fight for her whenever she should send for him, and bade her good-bye, she took the hand which he held forth, but would not look at him.

Tristram wondered why her fair hand was so cold. "Good-bye and God be with ye always," La Belle Isoude replied in a faint voice, and then turned and went from him. Tristram thought she was angered with him for the slaying of her uncle.

So in a little while he rode forth with Governale down to the seashore and looked back not once. There he entered by a ship, and with good wind he arrived at Tintagel in Cornwall, and King Mark and all his barons were glad that Tristram was whole again.

Then Sir Tristram went to his father King Tailoch, and there was made great cheer for him, and wide lands were given him. Nevertheless, he could not rest long in one place, but went into Logres and Alban and Wales, seeking adventures, and his fame for prowess was almost as great as the fame of Sir Lancelot. Wherever he went he took his harp, and in hall and bower his favourite songs were those that praised the beauty of La Belle Isoude, her gentle ways and her soft white hands.

After a year and a day he returned to the court of King Mark and lived there, and all the knights and ladies admired him, and the praise of his courtesy was in the mouths of all, noble and simple, high and low. Then King Mark his uncle began to hate him for the love that all bore him, and since he had never married and had no son to whom his kingdom should go after his death, he saw that Sir Tristram would have it, for he was his next kin, and then, with Lyones and Tintagel, the fame and power of Tristram would increase abundantly.

So the king began to cast about in his mind for a way whereby he might do some hurt to Sir Tristram, or even destroy him.

He called the young knight to him one day and said:

"Dear nephew, I have been thinking a long while of taking unto myself a wife, and I hear much of the beauty and goodness of the king's daughter of Ireland, whom men call La Belle Isoude. Now I would that you go to the king and bear my message to him."

Sir Tristram was troubled in mind at these words. Since he had left La Belle Isoude he had had no ease of spirit, for now he knew that he loved her. Though she had been angered with him for his slaying her uncle, and he knew that the queen and other kinsfolk of Sir Marhaus would surely slay him if they could, yet had he hoped in a while to have gone to King Anguish and found some way to win Isoude for his wife.

"Ye are feared to go, then?" sneered King Mark, noting the silence of Sir Tristram. "Then I will e'en send some other knight that is bolder."

At that Sir Tristram flushed hotly and said:

"I fear not to go there or anywhere, and I will bear thy message, sir."

"It is well," said the king. "I will send thee with a fine ship, and a rich company of knights, and I will get my scrivener to write my message."

Now King Mark said all this by reason of his craft and treachery. He had heard how Sir Tristram had been full of the praises of La Belle Isoude, while yet, as he had learned, Sir Tristram had not promised himself in love to her. By his crafty speech King Mark had hoped to make Sir Tristram promise to go to Ireland to obtain her, not for himself, but for King Mark. So, therefore, if the king married La Belle Isoude, this would cause some grief and hurt to Sir Tristram.

But King Mark cared not overmuch whether he wedded La Belle Isoude or not. He believed that Sir Tristram would of a surety be slain by the kin of Sir Marhaus in Ireland, and, if so, King Mark's plot would succeed to the full.

Sir Tristram, sad and troubled, went apart, and rode into a forest, for now he knew that he had done himself an ill turn. The lady he loved and whom he wanted to wife for himself he had now promised to woo for another.

As he rode moodily through the forest drive, a knight came swiftly riding on a great horse, its flanks flecked with the foam of its speed.

"Fair knight," said the stranger, "will ye of your courtesy tell me where I may quickly come at a knight called Sir Tristram of Lyones?"

"I am he," said Tristram. "What would ye?"

"I thank Heaven that hath led me to you, sir knight," said the other. "Here is a message from my master, King Anguish of Ireland, who is in dire peril of honour and life, and craves aid of you for the love that hath been atween you."

Sir Tristram, much marvelling, took the parchment and read: "These to you, Sir Tristram of Lyones, most noble knight, from his lover and friend King Anguish of Ireland, in sore trouble and straits at Camelot. Know ye, Sir Tristram, that I have been summoned to King Arthur's court on pain of forfeiture of his lordship's royal grace, to answer a charge whereof I knew naught till I came here. Which is that by treason and felony I caused to be slain at my court in Ireland a cousin of Sir Bleobaris de Ganis and Sir Blamor de Ganis, and of this evil deed these knights do most falsely accuse me. And there is none other remedy than for me to answer them in knightly fashion, my armed body against theirs. But inasmuch as I am old, and my wasted arm could naught avail me, and in that they are of such renown and prowess that none of my knights may hope to overcome them, I pray ye, Sir Tristram, of your ancient love for me, to come to my aid and fight for me as my champion in this most cruel charge. But if ye will not, and if ye choose to remember rather that I thrust you from my court, and would not protect you against those that meant you ill, then forgive my request, and leave me to my fate and my dishonour."

The heart of Sir Tristram lifted within him for love of the good old king, and turning, he said:

"For what day is the trial by combat which your master speaketh of?"

"For midday on the day before next Sabbath," said the knight.

"Go ye at once to your master," said Sir Tristram, "and say to him that I will not fail him, but will make all speed."

"Sir, I thank you from my heart," said the knight, and bowed. Then wheeling his horse he dashed swiftly away.

At Camelot, on the day and hour appointed, the lists were set, and knights and nobles and the common people waited to see the trial by battle which should prove the innocence or guilt of King Anguish. King Arthur was not at Camelot, nor was Sir Lancelot, for both were at Joyous Gard, the castle of Sir Lancelot, which King Arthur had given to him by the sea in the Northern Marches. In their places, King Kador of Cornwall and King Uriens of Reged were judges at the trial.

Ere noon was marked by the gnomon of the dial set up before the judges, Sir Tristram and his squire Governale rode up the lists, and were met by King Anguish and his knights. When Sir Tristram saw the King of Ireland he got swiftly from his horse and ran towards him, and would have held his stirrup; but the King leapt lightly from his horse, and with bright looks each embraced and kissed the other.

"My good lord," cried Tristram, "gramercy of your goodness which ye showed me in your marches, and of your nobleness in calling me unto your aid, for it is great honour to me that ye ask this, and I will do all for you to the utmost of my strength."

"Ah, worshipful knight," said the king, "ye are courteous and noble beyond all others to come to my aid when I am in such dire need."

"Who is he that is appointed to fight with you or your champion?" asked Sir Tristram.

"He is of Sir Lancelot's blood," replied the king, "and I wot that he will be hard to overcome, for all those of King Ban's kin are passing good fighters beyond all others. It is Sir Blamor de Ganis, a great warrior."

"Sir," said Sir Tristram, "for the great goodness that ye showed to me in Ireland and for your daughter's sake, La Belle Isoude, I will take the battle in hand for you. But ye must first swear that ye never caused or consented to the death of the knight of which you are charged, and if I avail in your battle I vail crave a boon of you which you shall grant me."

"I swear to Heaven," replied the king, "that I did neither cause nor consent to the death of the knight; and as to the boon that ye shall ask, I grant it you already."

Then King Anguish departed to the judges and cried unto them the name of his champion, and all the knights of the Round Table that were there, and the common people, were all agog to see Sir Tristram. The fame of his fight with Sir Marhaus, and his renown as a harpist and a lover of hunting, were well known unto all; but never yet had he come to the court of King Arthur.

Sir Blamor and Sir Tristram went to each end of the lists and dressed their harness and their shields. Sir Bleobaris, that was brother to Sir Blamor, went to him and said:

"Brother, now remember of what kin ye be, and what manner of man is our lord, Sir Lancelot, and see that ye suffer not shame. For never would Sir Lancelot bear it, and he would sooner suffer death."

"Have no doubt of me," said Sir Blamor, "I shall never shame Sir Lancelot nor any of our high blood; nevertheless, this Sir Tristram is a passing good fighter, and if by ill hap he strike me down, then he shall slay me and so end my shame."

"God speed you well," said Sir Bleobaris, "but he may not be so great a warrior as fame saith. For fame grows false as she goes further."

When the knights were ready, the herald of the court of Arthur stood with his trumpet and recited the cause of the quarrel and the names of the knights about to do battle. Then, lifting his tabard, he bade both knights make ready; and when his tabard fell to the ground, the knights lowered their lances in the rests, set spurs to their horses, and thundered down the lists. With a clang and a crash they met midway, and then men marvelled as they saw how suddenly Sir Blamor's horse reared in mid-career, turned right round, and upsetting its rider over its back, fell to the ground. Sir Blamor, however, was unhurt, and quickly rising to his feet he drew out his sword, crying to Sir Tristram, as that knight turned his horse and came towards him:

"Alight thee, Sir Tristram, for though this mare's son of mine hath failed me, I trust my good sword shall not fail me."

With that Sir Tristram alighted and dressed him to battle, and there they lashed at each other with mighty strokes on both sides, cutting and hacking, feinting and guarding, so that as time went on and still they fought fiercely, the kings and knights marvelled that they were so great-winded and strong.

Soon men saw that Sir Blamor was headstrong, and mad with rage, while Sir Tristram beat not so many false blows, but each was sure, though slower. Yet Sir Blamor would not rest, but like a wild man would ever dash against his enemy. Where they fought the trampled sand was stained with red from their wounds.

Suddenly men saw Sir Blamor make a heavy stroke which Sir Tristram avoided, and ere the other could recover, Sir Tristram's sword descended on his helm with so great a stroke that Sir Blamor fell upon his side. Sir Tristram leaped upon him and placed the point of his sword between the bars of Sir Blamor's vizor, bidding him yield.

When Sir Blamor got his breath he panted forth:

"Nay, nay, Sir Tristram, I will not say the word, but I require thee, Sir Tristram de Lyones, as thou art a noble knight and the mightiest that ever I found, that thou wilt slay me out of hand, for now I would not live to be made lord of these lands of Britain. Liefer I would die than live a life of shame, and therefore slay me, slay me!"

Sir Tristram started back, remembering of what noble blood was this brave knight. Knowing that he must either make Sir Blamor say the loth words "I yield," or else slay him, he went to where the judges sat, and kneeled before them and told them what Sir Blamor had said.

"Fair lords," Sir Tristram ended, "it were shame and pity that this noble knight should be slain, for ye well hear that he will not say the words of shame, and if King Anguish, whose true knight and champion I am, will suffer me, I will neither shame nor slay so stouthearted a knight."

"By Heaven," said King Anguish, "I will be ruled for your sake, Sir Tristram, as ye are the most knight of prowess that ever I saw in my long life. Therefore I pray these kings and judges that they take the matter into their own hands."

The judges called Sir Bleobaris to them and required his counsel.

"My lords," he said, "though that my brother be beaten of body by this valiant knight, he hath not beaten his heart, and so I thank God he hath not been shamed in this fight. And rather than he be shamed," said Sir Bleobaris, white and stern, "I require that you command Sir Tristram to slay him out of hand!"

"That shall not be," said the judges, "for neither King Anguish nor Sir Tristram desire to shame your valiant brother."

"We do not," said both the king and Sir Tristram.

Therewith, by the advice of the judges, Sir Tristram and Sir Bleobaris took up Sir Blamor; and the two brothers made peace with King Anguish and kissed each other and swore friendship with him forever. Then Sir Blamor and Sir Tristram kissed, and the two brothers, their hands clasping those of Sir Tristram, swore that there should forever be peace and love between them; and this did Sir Tristram swear also.

Inasmuch as, of his nobleness and generosity, Sir Tristram would not take Sir Blamor's life because he refused to yield him, Sir Lancelot and all his kinsmen loved Sir Tristram, and were ever his friends and spoke well and knightly of him.

Then King Anguish and Sir Tristram took their leave and sailed into Ireland with great joy; and when they had arrived there, the king let make a great cry throughout his dominions, of the manner in which Sir Tristram had fought for him, and how for that deed he accounted him the noblest knight among his friends, and that all should treat him with friendship and no deceit.

When, also, the queen and the kin of Sir Marhaus heard how Sir Tristram had borne himself in the trial by combat, they agreed that now they should not seek to slay him, since his great help in this matter had wiped out his evildoing in the slaying of Sir Marhaus.

So the queen and the knights of the court and the common people made much of Sir Tristram wheresoever he went; but the joy that La Belle Isoude had in her heart no tongue may tell. When Sir Tristram was led to her and they met after so long an absence from each other, men saw the lovely face light up with so sweet and high a look that they marvelled at her beauty. Yet they saw how straitly Sir Tristram held himself, and made not much of his meeting with her and did not seek her company.

Then on a day King Anguish asked Sir Tristram what was the boon he craved.

"But whatever it be," said the king, "it is yours without fail."

Sir Tristram's face went hard and white, and after a little while he said:

"It is this, my lord. I bear a request from my uncle, King Mark, and it is that you give him your daughter La Belle Isoude for his wife, and ye let me take her unto him, for so I have promised him."

"Alas," said the king, and looked full heavily into the eyes of Sir Tristram, "I had liefer than all the land that I have that ye should wed her yourself."

Sir Tristram turned away, and made this reply:

"I have given my promise, and I were ashamed forever in the world if I did aught else. I require you to hold to your promise, and to let your daughter depart with me to be wedded to my uncle, King Mark."

"As I have promised, so will I do," said the king. "But I let you know 'tis with a heavy heart."

Nor would the king say more, knowing that he might make bad worse. But the surprise and grief of La Belle Isoude, when she knew that Sir Tristram was to take her to be wife not unto himself but to a stranger, what tongue may tell and what words may say? Nightly, on the days when she was being prepared to depart, she wept full sorely in the arms of her mother or of Bragwine her faithful gentlewoman; but in hall or abroad she was ever calm and cold, though pale.

The queen, her mother, feared much of this marriage, and so sent a swift message to a great witch who dwelled in a dark wet valley in the midst of the Purple Hills, and for much gold a potent philtre was prepared. Then, on the day when, with much weeping and many sad farewells, La Belle Isoude with her gentlewomen and many noble ladies and knights were to go into the ship, the queen called Bragwine aside, and giving her a little golden flasket, said to her:

"Take this with thee, Bragwine, for I misdoubt this marriage overmuch, and I charge thee do this. On the day that King Mark shall wed my daughter, do thou mix this drink in their wine in equal parts, and then I undertake that each shall love the other alone all the days of their lives."

Anon Sir Tristram and La Belle Isoude took ship and got to sea. During the voyage Sir Tristram kept himself much with the other knights and rarely sat with Isoude; for in his heart was much grief, and he hated the fair wind that drove the ship more quickly to the time when he must give up La Belle Isoude to his uncle. He knew now that he loved none other woman in the world but her, and never would so long as he should live.

Bragwine the maid, seeing the pensive looks of her mistress, and knowing the wretchedness of her heart, determined to give her mistress what she most desired. By the aid of Governale, the squire of Sir Tristram, they poured the philtre into the wine of Isoude and Sir Tristram as they were about to sit at dinner.

They thought that the philtre being so potent, it would cause Sir Tristram to do as King Anguish wished that he would do, and take La Belle Isoude into his own home at Lyones and wed her himself.

Sir Tristram and La Belle Isoude sat at dinner and drank the wine. In a little while Sir Tristram looked at the wine that was in his silver cup and smelled at it.

"Sure this is the best wine that ever I drank," said he, and smiled at her.

"It is truly a most sweet and noble drink," said Isoude, and her heart was glad to see him smile, who hitherto had kept his face so stern.

Sir Tristram called his squire.

"Governale," said he, "what wine is this thou hast given us this day? Let us have another flask of the same."

Governale was ever ill at a deception, and began to stammer.

"My lord," he said, "I fear me there is none other."

"Ah," said his master, "and where got you that?"

"The gentlewoman of my Lady Isoude," said he, "brought it and bade me mix it in your lordship's wine."

"What?" cried Sir Tristram, rising angrily. "What means this? What trickery is this?"

"Oh, my lord, forgive me," cried Governale. "But we saw the sorrow of both your hearts, and we gave you the philtre that was meant for my lady and King Mark, and—and—my lord, you will break my lady's heart and your own if ye suffer this." But Sir Tristram would hear no further, and fiercely sent his squire from his presence.

"Ah, my lord," said La Belle Isoude, "have those two poor souls done more evil than we are doing by hiding our hearts from each other? I would have you know that no ease shall you have all the days of your life, for I know that you love me, and as to that, there is no living man in all this world that I love as I love you. If ye think it unmaidenly in me to say that—then my own wretched heart forgives me."

The gentle sorrow in her voice caused Sir Tristram's heart to swell with rage because he had promised to take her to wed King Mark.

"Lady," he said, and his face was full pitiful and pale, "Heaven knows that ye say right, and that nevermore shall I have ease after this. But no more should I have ease, but rather more shame and remorse, if I should do what my heart bids me do. I gave my promise to mine uncle, madman that I was, and I must perform it, and suffer. But I could slay myself to think that you will suffer also."

She saw the rage and sorrow in his eyes, and her heart was full of pity.

"Do thyself no harm, O noble knight and friend," said Isoude, "for thou art right, and I wrong. But I would have you promise to be my knight and champion in things both ill and good, while you shall have life."

"Lady," he replied, "I will be all the days of my life your knight, in weal and in woe, to come to your aid and battle for your dear name, when you shall send for me."

Sir Tristram gave her a ring, and she gave him another, and quickly they parted, lest they should repent them of their duty.

That evening they got to shore, and landed at the foot of Tintagel, and Sir Tristram led up La Belle Isoude and gave her into the hands of King Mark, whose looks, for all that he tried to appear satisfied, were sour as he dwelt on the noble figure of Sir Tristram. Men noticed how pale and stern the young knight seemed, and that he said few words.

In a little while, after the wedding of his uncle to La Belle Isoude, Sir Tristram said farewell to all the court, "for," said he, "he would go fight the pagans who were ravening in the north," and so departed, with Governale his squire.

Afterwards, seeing the pale queen seated in hall beside King Mark, and remembering the heaviness of Sir Tristram, some guessed how full of woe was their parting, but for love and sorrow of Sir Tristram they said naught of what they thought.

VI

The Deeds of Sir Geraint

KING ARTHUR WAS SPENDING WHITSUNTIDE AT CAERLEON-upon-Usk, and one day he hunted the stag in the forests that lay thereby. As he had given permission for his queen to go and see the hunting, she set out with one handmaiden, and rode in the misty dawning down to the river, and across the ford.

They climbed up the other bank, following the track of the men and horses which had formed the king's hunting party, until they stood on the edge of the dark forest, where the young leaves were fresh and sweetly green. The sun burst forth, and sucked up the mists along the meadow flats beside the river below them, and the water flashed and the birds sang.

"Here will we stay," said the queen, who felt happy with the sunlight upon her, and the smell of the forest blowing out from the trees, "and though we shall not see the killing, we shall hear the horns when they sound, and we shall hear the dogs when they are let loose and begin to cry so eagerly."

Suddenly they heard a rushing sound and the thud of hoofs behind them, and, turning, they saw a young man upon a hunter foal of mighty size. The rider was a fair-haired handsome youth, of princely mien, yet withal kindly of look and smile. A riding-robe and surcoat of satin were upon him, low-cut shoes of soft leather were on his feet, and in his girdle was a golden-hilted sword. A fillet of gold bound his curly hair, and a collar of gold, with a blue enamel gammadion pendant, hung about his neck.

He checked his horse as he neared the queen, and it came towards her with step stately, swift, and proud, and the rider bowed full low to Gwenevere.

"Heaven prosper thee, Sir Geraint," she said. "And its welcome be unto thee."

"Heaven accord you long life and happiness, O queen," replied Geraint.

"Why didst thou not go with my lord to hunt?" asked the queen.

"Because I knew not when he went," said Geraint. "But men told me in hall that you had gone out alone, and I came to crave permission to accompany and guard you."

"Gramercy," said the queen. "Thy protection is very agreeable to me."

As they stood talking, they heard the clatter of steel armour, and looking between the trees, they beheld a proud knight upon a war-horse of great size, wearing a heavy chain-mail jesseraunt, with coif and vizored helm, and his horse was also clothed in harness of chain mail.

Following him was a lady upon a beautiful white horse, which went with stately and proud steps along the forest way. The lady was clothed in a great robe of gold brocade, and her headcloth, of fine cambric, was turned so that her face was hidden. Behind them rode a little dark man, hairy and fierce of face, dressed as a page; and he sat on a great horse, strong and spirited, yet the dwarf held it well in hand. Hung to his saddle-bow was the knight's shield, but the device was hidden by a cloth, and two lances were fixed to the girdle of the dwarf. In his right fist the page carried a whip, long and heavy and knotted.

"Sir Geraint," said Gwenevere, "knowest thou the name of that tall knight?"

"I know him not, lady," said Geraint, "and his helm conceals his face, and his shield is also hidden. But I will go and ask the page, that you may learn his name."

And Sir Geraint rode up to the dwarfish page.

"Who is yonder knight?" said Sir Geraint.

"I will not tell thee," replied the dwarf, and scowled.

"Then I will ask him himself," said Sir Geraint.

"That thou wilt not, by my head," said the dwarf angrily, "for thou art not of honour enough to speak to my lord."

Geraint turned his horse's head to go towards the knight, whereupon the dwarf spurred forward and overtook him and lashed towards him with the long and knotted whip. The lash struck the mouth of Sir Geraint, and blood flowed, and dropped upon the silken scarf that he wore.

Instantly Sir Geraint turned, with sword half-drawn, and the dwarf cowed and pulled back. But Sir Geraint thought it would be no vengeance to carve the dwarf's head from his shoulders, and to be attacked unarmed by the mail-clad knight.

He thrust his sword back with a clang into its scabbard, and rode towards the queen.

"Thou hast acted wisely and nobly, Sir Geraint," said the queen, "and I sorrow for the insult the craven knave hath placed upon thee."

"Lady, I fear he was but copying his master," said Geraint, whose eyes flashed with anger. "But if your ladyship will permit me, I will follow this knight, and at last he will come to some town where I may get arms either as a loan or from a friend, and then will I avenge the insult which this stranger knight hath given to you, my queen and lady."

"Go," said Gwenevere, "but I beg of thee, do not encounter with the knight until thou hast good arms, for he is a man almost as big as Sir Lancelot du Lake. And I shall be anxious concerning thee until thou dost return, or send tidings."

"If I be alive," said Sir Geraint, "you shall hear tidings of me by tomorrow at evensong."

Thus he departed. All that day Sir Geraint followed the knight and the lady and the page, keeping them in sight, though at a distance. Through the forest they went first, and thereafter the road ran along a ridge of high ground, with the great downs and combes falling and heaving below their feet, the sun flashing back from lakes and streams, the bees humming at the flowers in the grass, and the larks rising with thrilling song in the warm sweet air of the spring.

Sir Geraint loved it all, but he kept his eyes ever on the knight, who flashed as he moved far before him. At length he saw the towers of a high castle, and beneath it the red roofs of a little town nestling at the foot of the grey walls. They rode into the town, and as the haughty knight passed through it the people in the booths and cabins and those beside the way saluted him. He did not acknowledge any of their greetings, but looked before him proudly, as he had done when he rode through the solitary paths of the wilderness.

Sir Geraint looked about him as he rode behind, to see if there was any armourer or knightly person whom he knew, but there was none. When he saw the knight and the lady and the dwarf enter the castle, and was sure that they would sojourn there, he rode about the little town, and found it full of knights and squires, with armourers and others cleaning arms, sharpening swords, and repairing harness. But no one did he know of whom to beg a suit of armour and a lance.

Then he took his way to a little stream beneath the wall of the town, and on the other side he saw a manorhouse, old and ruinous, standing amidst tall weeds. And thinking he might get lodging there for that night, he forded the river and went towards the manor. He saw that the hall door yawned open, and that a marble bridge led up to it, over a wide ditch full of stagnant water and thick with green weeds and rushes.

On the bridge sat an old and reverend man in clothes that once had been rich, but now were thin and tattered. And Geraint thought it was not possible that so poor a place could help him in what he desired. He looked steadfastly at the old man.

"Young sir," said the latter, "why art thou so thoughtful?"

"I was thinking, fair sir," said Geraint, "whether thou couldst give me lodging here for this night."

"Of a surety," said the old man, rising. "It is poor we are, but such as can be given shall be of our best."

He led Sir Geraint into the hall, which was bleak and desolate, and the hearthstone in the centre was thick with last year's leaves, as if it had been long since fire had flickered upon it. On the wall there hung rusty weapons and helms, and through the cracks there crept the ivy from the outer wall. The horse was tethered in the hall by the old man.

Then he led Sir Geraint to a door upon the dais, and ushered him into the bower, and there he saw an old decrepit woman, sweet of look though thin and peaked. She rose from the cushion on which she sat, greeting him kindly, and he saw that the satin garments upon her were also old and tattered. Yet Sir Geraint thought she must have been a lovely woman in her happy youth.

Beside her was a maiden, upon whom was a vest and robe poor and thin, and the veil of her headcloth was old though clean. Yet truly, thought Geraint, he had never seen a lovelier maiden, nor one with more sweetness and grace in her smile or gentleness in her voice. And the heart of him stirred with pity to see her so pale and wan, as if she fared but poorly.

"Welcome, fair sir," said the old dame. "This is my daughter Enid, who will gladly prepare food for you."

When food had been prepared they sat down, and Geraint was placed between the white-haired man and his wife, and the maiden served them.

Afterwards, as they drank weak mead from cups of earthenware, they spoke together; and Geraint asked whose was the manor in which they sat.

"Mine," said the old man, "for I built it. And the castle up there and the town were also mine."

"Alas!" said Geraint. "How is it you and yours have lost them?"

"For my sins and my greed," said the old man sadly, "and bitterly have I repented me of my wrong. I am Earl Inewl, but I have lost the lands that made my earldom. For I have a nephew, whom his father, on his deathbed, gave into my keeping, with all his lands. And I added his possessions to my own, and when the boy was a man he demanded them of me, and I would not give them up. So he made war upon me, and took everything from me except this ruined hall and one poor farm."

"Since you are sorry for the greed that hath ruined you," replied Geraint, "I will do what I may to regain your possessions, if God gives me life. But first I would ask, why went that knight and the lady and the dwarf just now into the town, and why is there so much furbishing of arms there?"

"The preparations are for the jousting that is to be held tomorrow's morn in the level meadow beside the ford," responded the old earl. "And the prize is to be a falcon of pure gold. The knight thou sawest has won the falcon two years running, and if he wins it this time he will have it for his own, and will win the title of the Knight of the Golden Falcon. And to gain it from him all those knights in the town will essay. And with each will go the lady that he loveth best, and if a man takes not his lady with him he may not enter the lists."

"Sir," said Sir Geraint, "I would willingly have to do with that knight, for he hath, by the hands of his dwarf page, most evilly insulted the queen of my dear lord, King Arthur; but I have no armour."

"As for that," said the old man, "I have arms here that will fit thee; but if thou hast no maiden with thee, thou canst not do battle."

"If, sir," replied Sir Geraint, "you and this maiden, your daughter, will permit me to challenge for her, I will engage, if I escape alive from the tournament, to be the maiden's knight while I shall live."

"What say you, daughter?" said the old earl.

"Indeed, sir," replied the maiden, gently flushing, "I am in your hands. And if this fair knight will have it so, he may challenge for me."

This said Enid to hide her true thoughts; for indeed she felt that she had never before seen as noble a youth as Geraint, or one for whom her thoughts were so kind.

"Then so shall it be," said Earl Inewl.

On the morrow, ere it was dawn, they arose and arrayed themselves; and at break of day they were in the meadow. Before the seat of the young earl, who was Inewl's nephew, there was set up a post, and on it was the figure of a gyrfalcon, of pure gold, and marvellously wrought, with wings outspread and talons astretch, as if it were about to strike its prey.

Then the knight whom Geraint had followed entered the field with his lady, and when he had made proclamation, he bade her go and fetch the falcon from its place, "for," said he, "thou art the fairest of women, and, if any deny it, by force will I defend the fame of thy beauty and thy gentleness and nobleness."

"Touch not the falcon!" cried Geraint. "For here is a maiden who is fairer, and more noble, and more gentle, and who has a better claim to it than any."

The stranger knight looked keenly at Geraint, and in a haughty voice cried:

"I know not who thou art; but if thou art worthy to bear arms against me, come forward."

Geraint mounted his horse, and when he rode to the end of the meadow laughter rippled and rang from the people watching him. For he bore an old and rusty suit of armour that was of an ancient pattern, and the joints of which gaped here and there. And none knew who he was, for his shield was bare.

But when, thundering together, the two knights had each broken several lances upon the shield of the other, the people eyed Sir Geraint with some regard. When it seemed that the proud knight was the better jouster, the earl and his people shouted, and Inewl and Enid had sad looks.

"Pity it is," said Enid, "that our young knight hath but that old gaping armour. For when they clash together, I feel the cruel point of the proud knight's spear as if it were in my heart."

"Fear not, my dear," said the old dame, her mother. "I feel that him you have learned to love so soon is worthy a good maiden's love, and I think that his good knighthood will overcome the other's pride."

Then the old knight went to Geraint.

"O young chief!" he said. "Since all other lances break in thy strong young hand, take you this. It was the lance I had on the day when I received knighthood. It was made by the wizard smith who lives in the Hill of Ithel, and it hath never failed me."

Then Sir Geraint took the lance and thanked the old earl, and looked back to where stood Enid. And his heart leaped to see how proud and calm she stood, though her lips trembled as she smiled at him.

With that the strength seemed to course Eke a mountain stream through all his body; and from the uttermost end of the meadow he pricked his horse and rushed towards the proud knight. His blow was so mighty, and the good lance so strong, that the shield of the proud knight was cleft in twain, and he was thrust far beyond his horse and fell crashing to the ground.

Then Geraint leaped from his horse and drew his sword, and the other rising to his feet, they dashed together with the fury of wild bulls; and so battled long and sore until the sweat and blood obscured their sight. Once, when the proud knight had struck Sir Geraint a mighty blow, the young knight saw, as he fought, how the maid Enid stood with clasped hands and a pale face of terror, as if she feared for his life.

With the sight of the maiden's dread and the memory of the insult done by the proud knight to Queen Gwenevere, Sir Geraint waxed both fiercer and stronger; and gathering all his might in one blow, he beat with his sword upon the crown of the knight's helm, and so fierce was it that the headpiece broke and the sword-blade cut to the bone.

Straightway the knight fell down upon his knees and craved mercy.

"Why should I give mercy to one so full of pride and arrogance?" said Sir Geraint. "Thou, through thy servant, hast shamefully insulted the queen of my lord, King Arthur."

"Fair knight," cried the other, "I confess it, and I give up my over-bearing henceforth, and I crave for mercy. And if ye give me my life, I will be your man and do your behest."

"I will give thee mercy on one condition," said Geraint, "which is that thou and thy lady and thy dwarf page go instantly and yield yourselves into the hands of the queen, and claim atonement for your insult. And whatsoever my lady the queen determines, that shall ye suffer. Tell me who art thou?"

"I am Sir Edern of the Needlands," replied the other. "And who art thou, sir knight," he asked, "for never have I met so valiant and good a knight of his hands as thou art."

"I am Geraint of Cornwall," said the young knight.

"It giveth comfort to me to know that I am overcome by so noble a knight," said the other. Then he got upon his horse, all wounded as he was, and with his lady and the page beside him took his way sadly to Arthur's court.

Then the young earl rose and came to Sir Geraint, and asked him to stay with him at his castle, for he loved all knights of great prowess and would have them to talk to him.

"Nay, I will not," said Sir Geraint coldly; "I will go where I was last night."

"Have your will, sir knight," replied the young earl courteously. "But I will ask Earl Inewl to permit me to furnish his manor as it should be furnished for your honour and ease."

Sir Geraint went back to the manor, conversing with Earl Inewl and his wife, and with the maiden Enid.

When they reached the house, they found it full of the servants of the earl, who were sweeping the hall and laying straw therein, with tables and benches as were suitable, and soon a great fire leaped and crackled on the stone in the centre. Then when Sir Geraint's wound had been washed and salved and bound, and he had placed upon himself his walking attire, the chamberlain of the young earl came to him and asked him to go into the hall to eat. Sir Geraint asked where was Earl Inewl and his wife and daughter.

"They are in the bower putting on robes which my lord the earl hath sent, more befitting their station and your honour," said the earl's chamberlain.

Sir Geraint liked it not that the maiden should be dressed in robes given by the man who had stripped her father of all his wealth, and he said coldly:

"I would that the damsel do not array herself, except in the vest and veil she hath worn till now. And those she should wear," he said, "until she come to the court of Arthur, where the queen shall clothe her in garments fitting for her."

It was so done, and the maiden sat in her poor robes while the other knights and ladies in the young earl's company glittered and shone in satin and jewels. But she cared not for this, because Sir Geraint had bidden her.

When meat was done and mead was served, they all began to talk, and the young earl invited Sir Geraint to visit him next day.

"It may not be," said Sir Geraint; "I will go to the court of my lord Arthur with this maiden, for I will not rest while Earl Inewl and his dame and daughter go in poverty and rags and trouble. And it is for this I will see my lord, so that something may be done to give them maintenance befitting their station."

Then, because the young earl admired Sir Geraint for his knightly strength, his nobility of manner and his prowess, there was sorrow in his heart for the old Earl Inewl.

"Ah, Sir Geraint," he said, "I am sorry if your heart is sore because of my kinsman's poor condition; and if you will give me your friendship, I will abide by your counsel and do what you think I should do of right."

"I thank thee, fair sir," said Geraint, "and I will ask ye to restore unto the Earl Inewl all the possessions that were rightly his, and what he should have received up to this day."

"That I will gladly do for your sake," said the young earl.

Thus it was agreed; and such of the men in the hall who held lands which rightly belonged to Earl Inewl came and knelt before him and did homage to him. And next morning the lands and homesteads and all other his possessions were returned to Earl Inewl, to the last seed-pearl.

Thereafter Sir Geraint prepared to return to the court of King Arthur, and the Earl Inewl came to him with the maiden Enid, whose gentle face went pale and red by turns. Putting her hand in the hand of Sir Geraint, the old man said:

"Fair sir, your pursuit of that knight, Sir Edern, and your revenge for his insult, I shall bless until the last day of my life. For you have done more goodness and justice than I can ever repay you. But if this my daughter, for whom ye fought yesterday, is pleasing unto you, then take her for your wife, with the blessing of myself and my countess."

Sir Geraint clasped the hand of the young maiden, and said:

"My lord, I thank thee, and if my lord King Arthur shall give this maiden unto me for wife, then will I love her and cherish her all the days of my life, if she in her heart would choose me for her husband."

"My lord," said the maiden, raising her frank eyes and flushing face to him, "I have never known a knight to whom I gave so great goodwill as I find in my heart for thee. And if thy lord Arthur shall give me unto thee, I will plight thee my love and loving service till I die."

Thereupon they proceeded on their way to the court of King Arthur, and what had seemed a long journey to Geraint when he had followed Sir Edern, now seemed too short, for he and the maid Enid passed it in much pleasant converse.

Towards evening they arrived at Caerleon-upon-Usk, and Queen Gwenevere received Sir Geraint with great welcome, calling him "her glorious knight and champion," and telling him that Sir Edern had yielded himself into her hands to do such atonement as seemed fitting, when he should have recovered from his wounds.

At the beauty of the maid Enid all the court marvelled; and the queen hastened to clothe her in robes of satin, rich and rare, with gold upon her hair and about her throat. And when she was so dressed, all were glad that one of so sweet a dignity and rare a beauty had come among them.

King Arthur gave her to Sir Geraint with many rich gifts, and Enid and Geraint were married in the abbey church, and the court gave itself up to feasting and sport, and acclaimed her one of the three most lovely ladies in all the isle of Britain.

When a year had passed in great happiness, ambassadors came from King Erbin of Cornwall, with a request to King Arthur that he should let Sir Geraint go home to his father.

"For," said the messengers, "King Erbin waxes old and feeble, and the more he ageth the more insolent and daring are the barons and lords on his marches, trying to wrest parts of his lands to add to their own. Therefore," said they, "the king begs you to let his son Sir Geraint return home, so that, knowing the fame of the strength of his arm and his prowess, the turbulent lords would desist, and if they would not, Sir Geraint would hurl them from his boundaries."

King Arthur, though very reluctant to let so great an ornament of his court depart, let him go, and Geraint and Enid went with a great party of the best knights of the Round Table, and rode to the Severn Shore, and there took ship to the shores of Cornwall.

When they reached there, all the people came from their villages welcoming Sir Geraint and his lovely bride, for the fame of his prowess, and the way in which he had won his wife, had spread over all the land. And King Erbin welcomed his son and was glad of his coming, and the next day all the chief subjects, the lords and barons holding land or offices, and the chief tenants of common degree, came into the hall, and, kneeling before Sir Geraint, did honour to him and swore fealty.

Then, with a great company of his chief warriors, Sir Geraint visited all the bounds of his territory. Experienced guides went with him, and old men learned in the marks of the boundaries, and priests, and they renewed the mere-marks that were broken down, and replaced those which had been wrongfully moved.

Thereafter men lived peacefully in the land, and on all the borders, for under the shadow of the strong young chief no border lords dared to invade the land, and no fierce baron used oppression.

Then, as had been his wont at the court of Arthur, Sir Geraint went to all tournaments that were held within easy reach of his kingdom. Thus he became acquainted with every mighty knight of his hands throughout the lands of Cornwall, Wales, and Logres; and so great in strength and prowess did he become that men hailed him as one of the Three Great Heroes of the Isle of Britain; the other two being Sir Lancelot du Lake and Sir Tristram of Lyones. And though there were other great and valiant warriors, as Sir Lamorake, Sir Bors, Sir Gawaine and his brother, Sir Gareth, and Sir Palomides, yet all these had been overcome by one or other of the three heroes. For as yet Sir Perceval was in the forest with his widowed mother, and knew no arms but a stone or a stick; and Sir Galahad was not yet born. And these two were knights stainless of pride or any evil desire, and by that force alone did strike down every arm, however mighty, that relied on knightly prowess alone.

When his fame had spread over all the kingdoms south of Trent, so that no knight that knew him or saw the device of the golden falcon on his shield would have to do with him, Sir Geraint began to seek ease and pleasure, for there was no one who would joust with him. He began to stay at home and never went beyond his wife's bower chamber, but sat and delighted in playing chess, or hearing the bards of the court sing songs of glamour and wizardry, or tell him tales of ancient warriors and lovers, long since dead.

The whole court marvelled at his slothfulness as time passed and he changed not. He gave up the friendship of his nobles, and went not hunting or hawking; and found no pleasure but in the company of his wife, whom he dearly loved.

Men began to scoff and jeer at his name over their cups in hall, or as they rode with hawk on fist to the hunting, or as they tilted in the lists. And the lawless lords upon the marches of the land began to stir and to dare, and when none came to punish them, their plunderings and oppressions grew.

Soon these things came to the ears of the old King Erbin, and great heaviness was upon him. And he called the Lady Enid to him one day, and with stern sorrow in his eyes spoke thus:

"Fair woman, is it thou that hast turned my son's spirit into water? Is it thy love that hath made his name a byword among those who should love him because he is not as he once was—a man no one could meet in arms and overcome? Is it thou that hath sunk him in slothfulness, so that the wolfish lords and tyrant barons upon his marchlands begin to creep out of their castleholds, and tear and maim his people and wrest from them and him broad lands and fertile fields?"

"Nay, lord, nay," said Enid, and he knew from the tears in her brave eyes that she spoke the truth. "It is not I, by my confession unto Heaven! I know not what hath come to my dear lord. But there is nothing more hateful to me than his unknightly sloth! And I know not what I may do. For it is not harder, lord, to know what men say of my dear husband, than to have to tell him, and see the shame in the eyes of him I love."

And Enid went away weeping sorely.

The next morning, when Enid awoke from sleep, she sat up and looked at Geraint sleeping. The sun was shining through the windows, and lay upon her husband. And she gazed upon his marvellous beauty, and the great muscles of his arms and breast, and tears filled her eyes as she leaned over him.

"Alas," she said half aloud, "am I the cause that this strength, this noble and manly beauty have all lost the fame they once enjoyed? Am I the cause that he hath sunk in sloth, and men scoff at his name and his strength?"

And the words were heard by Geraint, and he felt the scalding tears fall upon his breast, and he lay appearing to be asleep, yet he was awake. A great rage burned in him, so that for some moments he knew not what to do or say.

Then he opened his eyes as if he had heard and felt nothing, and in his eyes was a hard gleam. He rose and swiftly dressed, and called his squire.

"Go," he said to the man, "prepare my destrier, and get old armour and a shield with no device thereon, old and rusty. And say naught to none."

"And do thou," he said to his wife, "rise and apparel thyself, and cause thy horse to be prepared, and do thou wear the oldest riding-robe thou hast. And thou wilt come with me."

So Enid arose and clothed herself in her meanest garments.

Then Geraint went to his father and said, "Sir, I am going upon a quest into the land of Logres, and I do not know when I may return. Do thou therefore keep our kingdom till I return."

"I will do so, my son," said Erbin, "but thou art not strong enough to go through the land of Logres alone. Wilt thou not have a company with thee?"

"But one person shall go with me," said Geraint, "and that is a woman. Farewell."

Then he put on the old and rusty suit of armour, and took the shield with no device, and a sword and a lance, and then mounting his horse he took his way out of the town. And Enid went before him on her palfrey, marvelling what all this might mean.

Geraint called unto her and said sternly:

"Go thou and ride a long way before me. And whatever ye see or hear concerning me, say naught, and turn not back. And unless I speak to thee, speak not thou to me."

All day they rode thus, and deeper and deeper they sank into a desolate land, where huge rocks jutted from the starved soil, and there was no sound or sight of living thing, except it was the wolf looking from his lair beneath a stone, or the breaking of a branch, as the brown bear on a distant hillslope tore at a tree to get a honeycomb, and blinked down at them, marvelling, maybe, to see a knight and a lady in his desolate domain. When, late in the afternoon, their long shadows marched before them down a broad green road which they had struck upon, Enid's heart suddenly lifted to see the white walls and roofs of what looked like a rich town; for she knew not what was in her lord's mind, and feared lest his strange anger should push him to go on through the night, and so become a prey to robbers or wild animals. But she marvelled that there was no sight or sound of people; no carters or travellers going to or coming from the city, and no smoke rose above the housetops.

When they came nearer, she saw the wall of the gate was broken down, and that along the broad road beyond the wall the grass waved high across the street, and the little wooden booths and cabins beside the road were rotting and decayed. Anon they rode into a broad marketplace or forum, where white buildings rose above them, the windows gaping, grass growing on the roofs or in the crannies of the walls, and the doorways choked with bushes. And out of the broad hallway of the basilica she saw the grey form of a wolf walk and slink away in the shadows.

With a sinking heart she knew that this was one of the fair cities which the Romans had built, and when they had left Britain this town had been deserted and left desolate, to become a place where the wolf and the bear made their lairs, where the beaver built his dam in the stream beneath the wall of the palace, and where robbers and wild men lay hid, or the small people of the hills came and made their magic and weaved their spells, with the aid of the spirits haunting the desolate hearths of the Romans.

And as Enid checked her horse and waited for Geraint to come up, that she might ask him whether it was his pleasure to pass the night there, she saw, down the wide street before her, the forms of men, creeping and gathering in the gloom. Then, fearing lest they should fall upon her husband before he was aware of them, she turned her horse and rode towards him and said:

"Lord, dost thou see the wild men which gather in the shadows there in the street before us, as if they would attack thee?"

Geraint lifted up his angry eyes to hers:

"Thou went bid to keep silent," he said, "whatsoever thou hast seen or heard. Why dost thou warn one whom thou dost despise?"

Even as he spoke, from the broken houses through which they had crept to assail the single knight, dashed ten robbers, naked of feet, evil of look, clothed in skins. One leaped at the knight with a knife in his hand, to be cut down, halfway in his spring, by Sir Geraint's fierce sword-stroke. Then, while Enid stood apart, terror in her heart, prayer on her lips, she saw him as if he were in the midst of a pack of tearing wolves, and in the silent street with its twilight was the sudden clash of steel, the howls and cries of wounded men.

Then she was aware that six lay quiet on the road, and the remaining four broke suddenly away towards the shelter of the houses. But two of these Sir Geraint pursued, and cut down before they could reach cover.

He rejoined her in silence and sought for a place of lodging; and in a small villa they found a room with but one door. Here they supped from the scrip of food and the bottle of wine which Enid had brought, and there they slept that night.

On the morrow they pursued their way, and followed the green road out of the ruined city until they reached the forest. And in the heat and brightness of the high noon the green and coolness of the forestways were sweet, and the sound of tiny streams hidden beneath the leaves was refreshing.

Then they came upon a plain where was a village surrounded by a bank of earth, on which was a palisade. And there was a wailing and weeping coming from between the little mud cabins therein; and as they approached they saw, in the middle green, four knights in armour and a crowd of poor frightened folk about them.

As they passed the gate of the village a poor man ran from the group, and threw himself before Sir Geraint.

"O sir knight," he cried full piteously, "if thou art a good knight and a brave, do thou see justice done here. For these four lords would cut my father's throat if he say not where his money is hid."

"Are they his proper lords?" asked Geraint.

"Nay, sir knight," said the man. "Our land is Geraint's, and these lords say that he sleeps all day, and so they will be our masters. And they do ever oppress us with fine and tax and torture."

Therewith Sir Geraint rode through the gate of the village and approached the group. He saw where the four knights stood cruelly torturing a poor old man whom they had tied to a post, and the sweat stood upon the peasant's white face, and the fear of death was in his eyes.

"Lords! Lords!" he cried in a spent voice. "I have no money, for you did take all I had when you told us our lord Geraint was become a court fool."

"Thou miser!" jeered one of the knights. "That was two months agone, and thou hast something more by now. Will this loose thy secret, carrion?"

At the cruel torture the man shrieked aloud, and by reason of the pain his head sank and he slid down the post in a swoon. And a young woman rushed forth, threw her arm about the hanging body, and with flashing eyes turned and defied the knights.

Next moment it would have gone ill with her, but the voice of Sir Geraint rang out.

"Ho, there, sir knights," he cried, "or sir wolves—I know not which ye are—have ye naught to do but to squeeze poor peasants of mean savings?"

The knights turned in rage, and laughed and sneered when they saw but one solitary knight in old and rusty armour.

"Ah, sir scarecrow!" cried one, leaping on his horse. "I will spit thee for thy insolence."

"Knock him down and truss him up with this starveling peasant!" cried another.

All now had mounted, and the first prepared to run at Sir Geraint, who backed his horse through the gateway into the open plain. Anon the first knight came, hurling himself angrily upon him. But deftly Sir Geraint struck the other's lance aside with his sword, and as the rider rushed past him, he rose in his stirrups, his blade flashed, and then sank in the neck of the felon knight, who swayed in his saddle and then crashed to the ground.

Then the second horseman attacked him furiously, being wroth at the death of his companion. But Sir Geraint couched his lance, and caught the other on the edge of his shield, and the spear passed through his body.

And by good hap also he slew the other two, one with his lance, the other with his sword on foot.

Enid, full of fear while the fight was raging, felt gladness and sorrow when she saw how nobly her husband had smitten these torturers with justice, and she said that of a truth she had been wrong, and that there was no sloth in his heart, no weakness in the strong arm of her lord.

Then Sir Geraint took off the armour from each of the four knights and piled them on their horses, and tied them together, and bade her drive them before her.

"And do thou go forward some way," said he sternly, "and say not one word to me unless I speak first unto thee."

As he mounted his horse, the man that had been tortured came forward with his people and knelt before him, and kissed the mail-clad shoe in his stirrup, and in rude few words they thanked him tearfully, asking for his name, so that they could speak of him in their prayers.

"I am called Sir Slothful," said Sir Geraint, "and I deserve not your worship. But, hark ye, if other evil lords come upon these marches and seek to oppress thee, tell them that though Sir Geraint sleeps now, he will soon awake and they shall not stand before his vengeance."

And so he rode on, leaving the poor folks marvelling but happy.

Then in a little while they came upon a highroad, and the lady went on first, and for all his anger, Geraint was sorry to see how much trouble Enid had in driving the four horses before her, yet how patient she was.

Soon they beheld a wide valley below them, the fairest and richest in homesteads and farms that they had yet seen. A river ran through the middle of it, and the road on which they passed ran down to a bridge over the river, beyond which was a castle and a walled town.

Sir Geraint took the road towards the bridge, and soon a knight came cantering towards them.

"Fair sir," said Sir Geraint, "canst thou tell me who is the owner of this fair valley and that walled city?"

"Of a truth," said the other, "these are the lands of King Griffith, whom men call the Little King. He holds them of King Erbin, whose son, that was so famous, men say has become a worthless court dandy."

"I thank thee for thy words, fair sir," said Geraint, and would pass on.

"I would counsel thee not to attempt to cross the bridge," said the knight, "unless thou dost intend to fight the little king. For armed strangers he will not suffer to pass, and I doubt me if thy arms are of much use to thee."

And the knight smiled at the rusty arms and shield of Sir Geraint.

"Nevertheless," said Sir Geraint, "though my arms are old, I will go this way."

If thou dost so," said the knight, "thou wilt meet with shame and defeat. For the little king is a man of giant strength."

But Sir Geraint passed down towards the bridge and crossed it, and went along the road beyond towards the town. Presently Sir Geraint heard the sound of hoofs behind him, and looking round he saw a knight following him upon a great black horse, tall and stately and stepping proudly. The knight was the smallest that Sir Geraint had ever seen.

When the stranger had come up to him, he said:

"Tell me, fair sir, is it by presumption or by ignorance that thou comest armed along this road?"

"I knew not that in any of the lands of King Erbin, a peaceful man, though he be armed, could not go without hindrance," replied Sir Geraint.

"That was so," replied the knight, "when King Erbin's son Sir Geraint was a man of prowess, not a soft fool. Then his name alone kept his borders clean of robber lords and bandit knights; but now that he is less than naught, I myself must keep my land clean of thieves in rusty armour that would frighten and oppress poor folk."

"Nevertheless," said Sir Geraint, "I will travel by this road, and ye hinder me at your peril."

"Have at thee, then," said the little knight, and together they spurred towards each other.

Sir Geraint marvelled to feel how powerful were the lance-strokes of the little man, while, as for himself, so high was the little knight's horse and so small was the rider, that he was hardly able to get a good blow at him. But they jousted until at the third bout the little king's lance broke short, and then they dismounted, and lashed at each other with their swords.

At first Sir Geraint thought it was nigh unseemly that one so strong and tall as himself should have to do with so small a knight; but if he thought that he had advantage in his longer reach and greater strength he quickly saw his error.

For the little king was a man of marvellous strength and agility, and for all Sir Geraint's knowledge and strength, the other's strokes were so boldly fierce, so quick and powerful, that it was not long ere Sir Geraint found he had need of great wariness.

Soon their helmets were cracked and their shields dented and carved and their hauberks in rags, and hardly could they see between the bars of their vizors for the sweat and blood in their eyes.

Then at last Sir Geraint, enraged that one so small should give him so much trouble to conquer, gathered all his strength in one blow, so that the little king was beaten to his knees, and the sword flew from his hand ten yards away.

"I yield me!" cried King Griffith. "And never have I fought with so valiant and strong a knight. Have mercy and spare me, and I will be thy man."

"Be it so!" said Sir Geraint. "But thou hast already sworn to be my man."

And he lifted up his vizor and showed his face, whereat the little king did off his own helm quickly and came and kneeled humbly before him.

"Sir Geraint," he said, "forgive me my words concerning thee, but men told me that ye had forgotten that you had once been so glorious a man, and were softening to a fool."

"Nay," said Sir Geraint, "they were the fools that said so. And now I will depart, for I see these marches are in safe keeping in your hands, fair king."

But the little king wished Geraint to come to his castle to be rested and healed of his wounds, and Geraint and Enid went and abode there a few days. But ever Sir Geraint was cold and stern to his wife, for he was still angry at her disbelief in him.

Sir Geraint would not stay longer, though his wounds were but half-healed, and on the third day he commanded Enid to mount her horse and to go before him with the four other horses.

While the sun climbed up the sky they rode through the wilderness, by tangled woods, deep valleys and quaking marshes, until they reached a deep dark forest. Suddenly as they rode they heard a great wailing of distress, and bidding Enid stay, Geraint dashed through the trees towards the crying, and came out upon a great bare upland, and beside the wood were a knight, dead in his armour, and two horses, one with a woman's saddle upon it.

And looking further Geraint saw three small dark shaggy trolls making swift way up the hill towards a great green mound, and in the arms of one of them was a damsel, who shrieked as she was borne away.

Fiercely Sir Geraint spurred his horse up the slope, bidding the trolls to stop, but they only ran with an exceeding great swiftness. But he pursued them, and when they were within a few steps of a small door in the hillside, the one dropped the maiden, and the three of them turned at bay. And the damsel ran shrieking away down the hill.

The trolls had dark thin faces, with curly black hair and fierce black eyes, and their rage was horrible to see. They were lightly clothed in skins, and in their arms they held, one a bar of iron, another a great club, and the third a long sharp stick.

Sir Geraint commended his soul to Heaven, for he knew he was to battle with evil dwarfs who lived in the hollow hills, and whose strength was greater than any man's, and whose powers of wizardry were stronger than Merlin's.

He dashed with his lance at the one with the iron bar, but the hill-troll slipped away, and brought the great bar with a heavy blow upon his lance, so that it snapped in twain. Then one leaped like a wild cat upon the arm that held the rein, but happily Sir Geraint had drawn his sword, and with one stroke slew him. Then the two others leaped towards him, but the blows of the bar and club he caught upon his shield and slew the troll with the club.

Ere Sir Geraint could draw his sword back from this blow, he felt his horse fall under him, for the dwarf with the iron bar had with one blow broken the beast's back. Quickly avoiding the horse, Sir Geraint dashed at the dwarf, who ran towards the hole in the hill, but ere he could reach it Sir Geraint gave him a blow on the crown of his head, so fierce and hard, that the skull was split to the shoulders.

So then Sir Geraint turned and walked slowly down the hill, for he was dazed, and his old wounds had broken afresh. But he came to where Enid stood comforting the damsel mourning over the dead knight, and when he was there, straightway he fell down lifeless.

Enid shrieked with the anguish of the thought that he was dead, and came and knelt beside him and undid his helm and kissed him many times. And the sound of her wailing reached an earl named Madoc, who was passing with a company along the road from a plundering expedition, and he came and took up Geraint and the dead knight, and laid them in the hollow of their shields, and with the damsels took them to his castle a mile along the road.

Now the earl was a tyrant and a robber, and had done much evil on the borderlands of Geraint, in burning, plundering, and slaying, since he had heard that Geraint was become soft and foolish. And he had recognised Sir Geraint while he lay in the swoon, and rejoiced that now he was like to die.

As he rode along he thought that if he could prevail upon the Lady Enid to wed him, he might get much land with her, as the widow of the dead Sir Geraint, future King of Cornwall. And he determined to make her marry him.

When, therefore, he and his host had reached his castle, he ordered the dead knight to be buried, but Sir Geraint he commanded to be laid in his shield on a litter-couch in front of the high table in the hall. So that Sir Geraint should die, he commanded that no leech should be sent for.

While his knights and men-at-arms sat down to dine, Earl Madoc came to Enid and begged her to make good cheer. But, thinking to gain more from secrecy, he did not tell her that he knew who she was, nor did he show her that he knew who was her lord.

"Take off thy travelling clothes, fair lady," he said, "and weep not for this dead knight."

"I will not," she said, and hung over Geraint, chafing his hands and looking earnestly into his pallid face.

"Ah, lady," the earl said, "be not so sorrowful. For he is now dead, and therefore ye need no longer mourn. But as ye are beautiful, I would wed thee, and thou shalt have this earldom and myself and much wealth and all these men to serve thee."

"I tell you I will rather die with my dead lord, if indeed he be dead," cried Enid, "than live in wealth with you or anyone."

"Come, then," said the earl, "and at least take food with me."

"Nay, I will not," said Enid, "and never more will I eat or be joyful in life."

"But, by Heaven, thou shalt," said Madoc, furious at her resistance to his will.

And he drew her from beside the litter, and forced her to come to the table where his knights sat eating, and commanded her to eat.

"I will not eat," she cried, straining from his hold towards where Geraint lay, "unless my dear lord shall eat also."

"But he is dead already, thou mad woman," cried the earl. "Drink this goblet of wine," he commanded, "and thou wilt change thy mind."

"I will not drink again until my dear lord drink also," said Enid, and strove to free herself from the grasp of the earl.

"Now, by Heaven!" said Madoc wrathfully. "I have tried gentle means with thee. Let this teach thee that I am not to be baulked of my will."

With that he gave her a violent blow on the ear, and tried to drag her away out of the hall. And Enid shrieked and wept and cried for help, but none of the knights that sat there dared to oppose their lord.

But suddenly men started up from their seats in terror to see the corpse of Geraint rise from the hollow of the shield. Enid's cries had roused him from his swoon, and his hand as he raised himself felt the hilt of the sword beside him.

He leaped from the litter, and, drawing his sword, he ran towards the earl, who by now had almost dragged Enid to the door. Raising the sword, Geraint struck him with so fierce a blow that he cleft his head in twain.

Then, for terror at seeing what they thought was a dead man rise up to slay them, the knights ran from the hall and left Geraint and Enid alone.

Enid threw her arms about Geraint, her face bright with happiness.

"My dear lord, I thank God thou art not dead, as this man said thou wert. And I pray thy forgiveness for doubting that thou hadst forgotten thy manhood, for of a truth none is so brave, so good as thou art."

Geraint kissed his wife, smiling wanly the while.

"Sorry I am, my dear wife," he said, "that I was swooning when thou hadst need of me, and as for any doubts thou hadst of me, why, let us both forget them from this time forth. And now we must away, ere this lord's men recover their fright and pursue us."

Enid led him instantly to the stalls where she had seen the horses had been led, and Geraint took the spear and the horse of the knight whom the trolls had slain, and, when he had mounted, he took up Enid from the ground and placed her before him.

Thus they rode out of the castle, and away as rapidly as they could. And now that they were reconciled, much joyful and loving talk was between them.

But night was coming on, and Geraint was weak from his wounds and loss of blood, and Enid was full of trouble for the pain her husband suffered. She prayed fervently that soon they might reach a town where she could obtain help for him.

Suddenly she heard far away in the distance the tramp of horses, and Enid could have wept for sorrow. But she kept her face calm, though her lips trembled. Geraint also heard the beat of the hoofs, and turning in his saddle he looked up, and saw on the skyline of the narrow road the glint of spears between them and the sky.

"Dear wife," he said, with a faint brave smile, "I hear someone following us. I will put thee in hiding behind this thicket, and should they slay me, do thou make thy way homeward to my father Erbin, and bid him avenge my death."

"O my dear Geraint!" said Enid, sobbing, for all her bravery, as she thought that he would surely be slain, and that, after all their trouble, they were not to be allowed to enjoy the happiness of their reconcilia-tion. "I would liefer die with thee, my dear, dear lord. Let them kill us both, if it is to be."

"Nay, dear wife," said Geraint, "I would not have thee slain. Revenge my death if they slay me."

So, with many lingering kisses, he set her down upon the road, and saw her hide in the thickets.

By now the gloom of evening had settled upon them, and the sound of trampling horses had rapidly approached. And painfully, by reason of his stiff wounds, Geraint dressed his armour as best he could, and laid spear in rest, and drew his shield before him, and so waited in the dark road.

He heard a single knight riding before the others, and soon saw his figure issue from the gloom with couched lance. And Sir Geraint made him ready also, resolved to sell his life dearly at the last.

But as they began to spur their horses, there came the voice of Enid from the hedgerow beside them. And she cried out piteously in the dark:

"O chieftain, whoever thou art, what renown wilt thou gain by slaying a dead man?"

The stranger stopped his horse, and called out:

"O Heaven, is it my lord, Sir Geraint?"

"Yes, in truth," said Enid, "and who art thou?"

"I am the little king!" said the other, and rode swiftly towards Sir Geraint. Then he leaped from his horse and came to the stirrup of his chief.

"My lord," he said, "I learned that thou wert in trouble, and came to see if I could aid thee."

And Enid ran forward with joy at hearing this, and welcomed the little king, and told him in what a hard pass was Sir Geraint.

"My lord and my lady," said Griffith, "I thank Heaven sincerely for the favour that I come to you in your need. I learned of thy fight with the trolls and of thy slaying of Earl Madoc, and that thou wert wounded. Therefore I rode on to find thee."

"I thank thee heartily," said Sir Geraint, "and my dear wife also thanks thee. For of a truth I am spent, and must needs get me rest and a leech for my wounds."

"Then come at once with me," said the little king, and after he had helped Enid to her place before Geraint, he leaped on his own horse.

"Now thou shalt go to the hall of a son-in-law of my sister which is near here," said King Griffith, "and thou shalt have the best medical advice in the kingdom."

At the hall of the baron, whose name was Tewder, and a most knightly and gentle lord, Sir Geraint and the Lady Enid were received with great welcome and hospitality. Physicians were sent for, and they attended Geraint day by day until he was quite well again.

The fame of his adventures began to spread along the borders of his kingdom, and at length reached his own court. And the robber lords and brigands of the marches, hearing of his deeds, ceased their evildoing and made haste to hide from his wrath. Also his father Erbin and the host at his court repented of their hard thoughts and sneers concerning him, and praised the strength of his arm, the gentleness of his courtesy, and his justice and mercy.

When Sir Geraint and the Lady Enid returned home, all the people gathered to welcome them. And thenceforth he reigned prosperously, and his warlike fame and splendour lasted with renown and honour and love, both to him and to the Lady Enid, from that time forth.

VII

How Sir Perceval Was Taught Chivalry, and Ended the Evil Wrought by Sir Balin's Dolorous Stroke

IT BEFELL UPON A TIME WHEN KING ARTHUR WAS PENDRAGON, or overlord of the island of Britain, that Earl Evroc held an earldom of large dominion in the north under King Uriens. And the earl had seven sons, the last being but a child still at play about his mother's chair as she sat with her maidens in the bower.

Lord Evroc was a valiant and a mighty warrior, ever battling against the hated pagans, when their bands of blue-eyed fierce fighters landed on his coasts. And when peace was on the land, he went about on errantry, jousting in tournaments and fighting champions. His six elder sons did likewise, and all were famed for their knightly prowess.

But the mother sat at home, sad of mood. For she hated war, and would rather have had her lord and her six tall sons about her in the home. And in her heart she resolved that she would plead with Evroc to let her have her little son Perceval to be a clerk or a learned bard, so that he should stay at home with her and run no risk of death.

The sorrow she was ever dreading smote her at length. For a messenger came one day, saying that Earl Evroc her lord had been slain at Bamborough, in a mighty melee between some of the best and most valiant knights of Logres and Alban, and two tall sons with him.

As the years passed, and her little son began to run, three black days came within a little of each other, for on these days messengers came with the sad news of the death of her other boys. One of them had been done to death by an evil troll on the lonely wastes by the Roman wall, two others were slain by the shores of Humber, repelling a horde of fair-haired Saxon raiders, and the other was killed at a ford, where he had kept at bay six bandit knights that would have pursued and slain his wounded lord.

Then, in her grief, the widow dame resolved that she would fly with her little son, and make a home for him in some wilderness, where never sounds or sights of war or death would come, where knights would be unknown, and no one would speak to him of arms and battles. And thus did she do, and she left the hall where she had lived, and removed to the deserts and wastes of the wilderness, and took with her only her women, and a few boys and spiritless men, too old or feeble to fight or to think of fighting.

Thus she reared the only son left to her, teaching him all manner of nobleness in thought and action and in learning, but never suffering him to see a weapon, nor to hear a tale of war or knightly prowess.

He grew up loving all noble things, gentle of speech and bearing, but quick to anger at evil or mean actions, merciful of weak things, and full of pity and tenderness.

Yet was he also very strong of body, fleet of foot, quick of eye and hand. Daily he went to divert himself in the great dark forest that climbed the high mountains beside his home, or he roamed the wide rolling moors. And he practised much with the throwing of stones and sticks, so that with a stick he could hit a small mark at a great distance, and with a sharp stone he could cut down a sapling at one blow.

One day he saw a flock of his mother's goats in the forest, and near them stood two hinds. The boy wondered greatly to see the two deer which had no horns, while the goats had two each; and he thought they had long run wild, and had lost their horns in that way. He thought he would please his mother if he caught them, so that they should not escape again. And by his great activity and swiftness he ran the two deer down till they were spent, and then he took them and shut them up in the goat-house in the forest.

Going home, he told his mother and her servants what he had done, and they went to see, and marvelled that he could catch such fleet creatures as the wild red deer.

Once he overheard his mother say that she yearned for fresh venison, but that the hunter who was attached to her house was lying wounded by a wild boar. Always Perceval had wondered what the little dark man did whom they called the hunter, who was always so secret, so that Perceval could never see where he went or when he returned from the forest.

So he went to the hut where Tod the hunter lay sick, and charged him by the love and worship he bore to the countess, that he should tell him how he could obtain fresh venison. And the dwarf told him.

Then Perceval took a few sticks of stout wood, with points hardened by fire, and went into the forest as Tod had told him, and seeing a deer he hurled a stick at it and slew it. And then he brought it home.

The countess was greatly wroth that Tod had taught him how to slay, and she said that never more should the dwarf serve her. And Tod wept, but when he was well again the countess would not suffer him to stay, but said he should leave the hall and never come there again.

She commanded Perceval never to slay any more living things, and the lad promised. But hard was it to keep his word, when he was in the forest and saw the wild things passing through the brakes.

Once, as he strayed deep in the wood, he came upon a wide glade or laund, with two green hillocks in the middle thereof. And feeding upon the grass was a great buck, and it had a silver ring round its neck. Perceval wondered at this beast being thus adorned, and went up to it to stroke it.

But the buck was fierce, and would have gored him with its horns, but Perceval seized them, and after a great struggle he threw the animal, and held it down, and in his wrath he would have slain it with a sharp stick. With that a swarm of little angry trolls poured from the hollow hillocks with great cries, and seizing Perceval would have hurt him.

But suddenly Tod ran among them, and commanded them to release him. And in the end Tod, who came himself of the troll folk, made the little people pass the words of peace and friendship with Perceval, and ever after that the boy went with the trolls, and sported with them in wrestling, running, and other games; and he learned many things of great wisdom from them concerning the secrets of the earth and air and the wind, and the spirits that haunt waste places and standing stones, and how to put to naught the power of witches and wizards.

Tod ever bade them treat the young lord with reverence. "For this is he who shall do great deeds," he said. "He shall be a stainless knight, who shall gain from evil the greatest strength, and, if God wills, he shall beat down the evil powers in this land."

But the lad knew not what he meant, though he was very content to have the trolls for his friends.

One day Perceval was in the forest far up the mountain, and he looked over the blue distance far below across the moor, and saw a man riding on a vide road which he had never noticed before. And the man rode very fast, and as he went the sun seemed to flash from him as if he was clothed in glass. Perceval wondered what he was, and resolved to go across the moor to the road he had seen.

When he reached the road he found it was very broad, and banked on either side, and went straight as the flight of a wild duck right across the moor, and never swerved by the hills or pools, but went over everything in its way. And as he stood marvelling what mighty men had builded it, he heard a strange rattling sound behind him, and, turning, he saw three men on horseback, and the sun shone from them as he had seen it shine from the first horseman.

The foremost checked his horse beside Perceval, and said:

"Tell me, good soul, sawest thou a knight pass this way either this day or yesterday?"

"I know not what a knight is," answered Perceval.

"Such a one as I," said the horseman, smiling good-naturedly, for it was Sir Owen, one of King Arthur's knights.

"If ye will tell me what I ask, I will tell you," said Perceval.

"I will answer gladly," said Sir Owen, smiling, yet wondering at the fearless and noble air of this youth in so wild a waste.

"What is this?" asked Perceval, and pulled the skirt of the hauberk.

"It is a dress made of rings of steel," answered Sir Owen, "which I put on to turn the swords of those I fight."

"And what is it to fight?"

"What strange youth art thou?" asked Sir Owen. "To fight is to do battle with spears or swords, so that you would slay the man that would slay you."

"Ah, as I would have slain the buck that would have gored me," said Perceval, nodding his head.

Many other questions the youth asked eagerly, as to the arms they bore and the accoutrements and their uses. And at length he said:

"Sirs, I thank you for your courtesy. Go forward swiftly, for I saw such a one as ye go by here but two hours ago, and he flashed in the sun as he rode swiftly. And now I will be as one of you."

Perceval went swiftly back to his mother's house and found her among her women.

"Mother," he said, "I have seen a great and wonderful sight on the great road across the moor."

"Ah, my dear son, what was that?" she asked.

"They were three honourable knights," he said. "And, mother, I will be a knight also."

With a great shriek his mother swooned away, and the women turned him from the room and said he had slain his mother.

Much grieved was Perceval that he had hurt his mother, and so, taking his store of pointed sticks, he went off into the forest, and strayed there a long time, torn between his love for his mother, and the strange restlessness which the sight of the three warriors had caused in him.

As he wandered, troubled, his quick ear caught the clang of metal, though he knew not what it was. And swiftly he ran towards the sound a long way, until he came into a clearing, and found two knights on horseback doing mighty battle. One bore a red shield and the other a green one.

He looked eagerly at this strange sight, and the blood sang in his veins. And then he saw that the green knight was of slighter frame than the other, and was weakening before the strokes of the red knight.

Full of anger at the sight, Perceval launched one of his hard-wood javelins at the red knight. With such force did it go, and so true was the aim, that it pierced the coif of the knight, and entered between the neck and the head, and the red knight swayed and then clattered to the ground, dead.

The green knight came and thanked Perceval for thus saving his life.

"Are knights then so easy to slay?" asked the lad. "Methought that none might pierce through the hauberk of a knight, and I sorrow that I have slain him, not thinking what I did."

"He was a full evil knight," said the other, "and deserved death richly for his many villainies and oppressions of weak orphans and friendless widows."

The knight took the body of the dead knight to be buried in a chapel, and told Perceval he could have the horse. But the lad would not have it, though he longed greatly to possess it, and the green knight took it with him.

Then Perceval went home, sad, yet wild with wonder at what he had done. He found his mother well again, but very sorrowful. And for fear of giving her pain, he did not tell her of the knight he had slain.

She called him to her, and said:

"Dear son of mine, it seems I may not keep thy fate from thee. The blood of thy warlike generations before thee may not be quenched, whatever fond and foolish plans I made to keep thee from knowledge of battle and weapons. Dear son, dost thou desire to ride forth into the world?"

"Yes, mother, of a truth," said Perceval. "I shall not be happy more until I go."

"Go forward, then," she said weeping, "and God be with thee, my dear son. And as I have no man who is strong of his hands, thou must go alone, yet will I give thee gold for thy proper garnishing and lodging. Put make all the haste ye may to the court of King Arthur at Caerleon-upon-Usk, for there are the best and the boldest and the most worshipful of knights. And the king will give thee knighthood. And wherever thou seest a church, go kneel and repeat thy prayers therein; and if thou hearest an outcry, go quickly and defend the weak, the poor, and the unprotected. And be ever tender towards women, my son, and remember that thy mother loves thee and prays for thy stay in health and life. And come thou to see me within a little while."

And he thanked her, saying he would do naught that should shame her, but would remember all the nobleness of her teaching; also, that he would return to see her within a little while.

Perceval went to the stable and took a bony, piebald horse, which seemed the strongest, and he pressed a pallet of straw into the semblance of a saddle, and with pieces of leather and wood he imitated the trappings he had seen on the horses of the knights.

Then, after taking leave of his mother, he rode forth, sad at first for leaving her in sorrow and tears, but afterwards glad that now he was going into the world to become a knight. And for armour he had a rough jerkin, old and moth-eaten, and for arms he had a handful of sharp-pointed sticks of hard wood.

He journeyed southwards two days and two nights along the great straight road, which went through the deep dark forests, over desert places and over the high mountains. And all that time he ate nothing but wild berries, for he had not thought to bring food with him.

While he was yet but a little way from the court of King Arthur, a stranger knight, tall and big, in black armour, had ridden into the hall where sat Gwenevere the queen, with a few of the younger knights and her women. The page of the chamber was serving the queen with wine in a golden goblet richly wrought, which Lancelot had taken from a knight whom he had lately slain.

The stranger knight had alighted before the chair of Gwenevere, and all had seen that full of rage and pride was his look. And he caught sight of the goblet in the hand of Gwenevere, and he snatched it from her, spilling the wine over her dress and dashing it even into her face.

"Now am I well lighted here," he said, "for this is the very goblet which thy robber knight Sir Lancelot reaved from my brother, Sir Wilder. And if any of you knights here desire to wrest this goblet from me, or to avenge the insult I have done your queen, let him come to the meadow beside the ford, and I will slay him, ay, if it be that traitor Sir Lancelot himself."

All the young knights hung their heads as he mounted his horse and insolently rode out of the hall; for it seemed to them that no one would have done so daring an outrage unless, like Sir Garlon whom Balin slew, he fought with evil magic, so that the strength and prowess of the mightiest knight would be put to naught.

Then Perceval entered the hall, and at sight of him upon his rough piebald horse, with its uncouth trappings, and the old and mouldy jerkin upon the youth, the knights and others broke forth in excessive laughter, as much at the sight as to cover their discomfiture and fear of the knight who had just gone.

But Perceval took no note of their laughter, but rode up the hall to where Sir Kay the seneschal stood, wrathful at the outrage on the queen which he had not dared to avenge instantly. And Perceval looked about and saw a knight more richly dressed than the others, and, turning to Kay, he said:

"Tell me, tall man, is that King Arthur yonder?"

"What wouldst thou with Arthur, knave?" asked Kay angrily.

"My mother told me to seek King Arthur," responded Perceval, "and he will give me the honour of knighthood."

"By my faith, thou farmer's churl," said Kay, "thou art richly equipped indeed with horse and arms to have that honour."

Thereupon the others shouted with laughter, and commenced to throw sticks at Perceval, or the bones left by the dogs upon the floor.

Then a dwarf pressed forward between the laughing crowd and saluted Perceval. And the lad rejoiced to recognise him. It was Tod, who had been his friend among the trolls of the mountains, and with Tod was his wife. They had come to the court of Arthur, and had craved harbourage there, and the king of his kindness had granted it them. But by reason of the prophecy which the trolls knew of concerning the great renown which Perceval was to gain, they had been dumb of speech since they had last seen the young man.

And now at sight of him their tongues were loosed, and they ran and kissed his feet, and cried together:

"The welcome of Heaven be unto thee, goodly Perceval, son of Earl Evroc! Chief of warriors art thou, and stainless flower of knighthood!"

"Truly," said Kay wrathfully, "thou art an ill-conditioned pair, to remain a year mute at King Arthur's court, and now before the face of goodly knights to acclaim this churl with the mouldy coat, chief of warriors and flower of knighthood!"

In his rage he beat Tod the dwarf such a blow, that the poor troll fell senseless to the ground; and the troll-wife he kicked, so that she was dashed among the dogs, who bit her.

"Tall man," said Perceval, and men marvelled to see the high look on his face and the cold scorn in his eyes, "I will have vengeance on thee for the insult and ill treatment thou hast done these two poor dwarfs. But tell me now which of these knights is Arthur?"

"Away with thee," shouted Kay, enraged. "If thou wouldst see Arthur, go to the knight with the goblet who waits for thee at the ford, and take the goblet from him, and slay him. Then when thou comest back clad in his armour, we will speak further with thee."

"I will do so, angry man," said Perceval, and amid the shouts of laughter and the sneers of the crowd he turned his horse's head and rode out of the hall.

Going to the meadow beside the ford, he saw a knight riding up and down, proud of his strength and valour.

"Tell me, fellow," said the knight, who bore on his shield the device of a black tower on a red field, "didst thou see any one coming after me from the court yonder?"

"The tall man that was there," said Perceval, "bade me to come to thee, and I am to overthrow thee and to take from thee the goblet, and as for thy horse and thy arms I am to have them myself."

"Silence, prating fool!" shouted the knight, "go back to the court and tell Arthur to come himself, or to send a champion to fight me, or I will not wait, and great will be his shame."

"By my faith," said Perceval, "whether thou art willing or unwilling, it is I that will have thy horse and arms and the goblet."

And he prepared to throw his javelin sticks.

In a proud rage the knight ran at him with uplifted lance, and struck him a violent blow with the shaft between the neck and the shoulder.

"Lad," said Perceval, and laughed, "that was as shrewd a blow as any the trolls gave me when they taught me their staff play! But now I will play with thee in my own way."

Thereupon he threw one of the pointed sticks at the knight, with such force and with such sureness of aim that it went in between the bars of his vizor and pierced the eye, and entered into the brain of the knight. Whereupon he fell from his horse lifeless.

And it befell that a little while after Perceval had left the court, Sir Owen came in, and was told of the shameful wrong put upon the queen by the unknown knight, and how Sir Kay had sent a mad boy after the knight to slay him.

"Now, by my troth," said Owen to Kay, "thou wert a fool to send that foolish lad after the strong knight. For either he will be overthrown, and the knight will think he is truly the champion sent on behalf of the queen, whom the knight so evilly treated, and so an eternal disgrace will light on Arthur and all of us; or, if he is slain, the disgrace will be the same, and the mad young man's life will be thrown away."

Thereupon Sir Owen made all haste, and rode swiftly to the meadow, armed; but when he reached the place, he found a youth in a mouldy old jerkin pulling a knight in rich armour up and down the grass.

"By'r Lady's name!" cried Sir Owen. "What do you there, tall youth?"

"This iron coat," said Perceval, stopping as he spoke, "will never come off him."

Owen alighted marvelling, and went to the knight and found that he was dead, and saw the manner of his death, and marvelled the more.

He unloosed the knight's armour and gave it to Perceval.

"Here, good soul," he said, "are horse and armour for thee. And well hast thou merited them, since thou unarmed hast slain so powerful a knight as this."

He helped Perceval put on his armour, and when he was fully dressed Owen marvelled to see how nobly he bore himself.

"Now come you with me," he said, "and we will go to King Arthur, and you shall have the honour of knighthood from the good king himself."

"Nay, that will I not," said Perceval, and mounted the dead knight's horse. "But take thou this goblet to the queen, and tell the king that wherever I be, I will be his man, to slay all oppressors, to succour the weak and the wronged, and to aid him in whatever knightly enterprise he may desire my aid. But I will not enter his court until I have encountered the tall man there who sent me hither, to revenge upon him the wrong he did to my friends, Tod the dwarf and his wife."

And with this Perceval said farewell and rode off. Sir Owen went back to the court, and told Arthur and the queen all these things. Men marvelled who the strange young man could be, and many sought Tod and his wife to question them, but nowhere could they be found.

Greater still was their marvelling when, as the weeks passed, knights came and yielded themselves to King Arthur, saying that Perceval had overcome them in knightly combat, and had given them their lives on condition that they went to King Arthur's court and yielded themselves up to him and his mercy. The king and all his court reproved Kay for his churlish manner, and for his having driven so splendid a youth from the court.

And Perceval rode ever forward. He came one day towards the gloaming to a lonely wood in the fenlands, where the wind shivered like the breath of ghosts among the leaves, and there was not a track or trace of man or beast, and no birds piped. And soon, as the wind shrilled, and the rain began to beat down like thin grey spears, he saw a vast castle rise before him, and when he made his way towards the gate, he found the way so overgrown with weeds that hardly could he push his horse between them. And on the very threshold the grass grew thick and high, as if the door had not been opened for a hundred winters.

He battered on the door with the butt of his lance; and long he waited, while the cold rain drove and the wind snarled.

After a little while a voice came from above the gateway, and glancing up he saw a damsel looking through an opening in the battlements.

"Choose thou, chieftain," said she, "whether I shall open unto thee without announcing thee, or whether I shall tell her that rules here that thou wishest to enter."

"Say that I am here," said Perceval. "And if she will not house me for the night, then will I go forward."

Soon the maiden came back and opened the door for him, and his horse she led into the stable, where she fed it; and Perceval she brought into the hall. When he came into the light and looked at the girl, he thought he had never seen another of so fair an aspect.

She had an old garment of satin upon her, which had once been rich, but was now frayed and tattered; and fairer was her skin than the bloom of the rose, and her hair and eyebrows were like the sloe for blackness, and on her cheeks was the redness of poppies. Her eyes were like deep pools in a dark wood. And he thought that, though she was very beautiful, there was great arrogance in her look and cruelty in her lips.

When Perceval went towards the dais of the hall he saw a tall and stately lady in the high seat, old of years and reverend of aspect, though sorrowful. Several handmaids sat beside her, sad of face and tattered of dress. All welcomed him right kindly. Then they sat at meat, and gave the young man the best cheer that they had.

When it was time to go to rest, the lady said:

"It were well for you, chieftain, that you sleep not in this castle."

"Wherefore," said Perceval, "seeing that the storm beats wildly without and there is room here for many?"

"For this reason," said the lady, "that I would not that so handsome and kindly a youth as you seem should suffer the doom which must light upon this my castle at dawn."

"Tell me," said Perceval, "what is this castle, and what is the doom
you speak of?"

"This castle is named the Castle of Weeds," replied the lady, "and
the lands about it for many miles belonged to my husband, the Earl
Mador. And he was a bold and very valiant man; and he slew Maelond,
the eldest son of Domna, the great witch of Glaive, and ever thereafter
things were not well with him. For she and her eight evil sisters laid a
curse upon him. And that in spite of this, that he slew Maelond in fair
fight, for all that he was a false and powerful wizard. And Domna came
to my husband, when he was worn with a strange sickness, and as he
lay on his deathbed. And she said she should revenge herself upon his
daughter and mine, this maiden here, when she shall be full twice nine
years of age. And she will be of that age ere dawn tomorrow morn, and
at the hour will the fierce Domna and her fearful sisters come, and with
tortures slay all that are herein, and take my dear daughter Angharad,
and use her cruelly."

The maiden who had opened to Perceval was that daughter, and
she laughed harshly as her mother spoke.

"Fear not for me, mother," she cried. "They will deck me in rich
robes, and I shall not pine for fair raiment, as I have pined these ten
years with thee."

The lady looked sadly upon her as she heard her words.

"I fear not, my daughter, that they will take thy life," she said, "but
I dread this—that they will destroy thy soul!"

And Angharad laughed and said:

"What matter, so it be that I live richly while I live!"

"Nay, nay," said Perceval, and in his voice was a great scorn, "it is
evil to speak thus, and it belies your beauty, fair maiden. Rather a life
of poverty than one of shamefulness and dishonour. Thus is it with all
good knights and noble dames, and thus was it with our dear Lord."

Then turning to the lady, he said:

"Lady, I think these evil witches will not hurt thee. For the little
help that I may give to thee, I will stay this night with thee."

After he had prayed at the altar in the ruined chapel of the castle, they led him to a bed in the hall, where he slept.

And just before the break of day there came a dreadful outcry, with groans and shrieks and terrible screams and meanings, as if all the evil that could be done was being done upon poor wretches out in the dark.

Perceval leapt from his couch, and with naught upon him but his vest and doublet, he went with his sword in hand to the gate, and there he saw two poor serving-men struggling with a hag dressed all in armour. Behind her came eight others. And their eyes, from between the bars of their helms, shone with a horrible red fire, and from each point of their armour sparks flashed, and the swords in their grisly hands gleamed with a blue flame, so fierce and so terrible that it scorched the eyes to look upon them.

But Perceval dashed upon the foremost witch, and with his sword beat her with so great a stroke that she fell to the ground, and the helm on her head was flattened to the likeness of a dish.

When she fell, the light of her eyes and her sword went out, and the armour all seemed to wither away, and she was nothing but an old ugly woman in rags. And she cried out:

"Thy mercy, good Perceval, son of Evroc, and the mercy of Heaven!"

"How knowest thou, hag," said he, "that I am Perceval?"

"By the destiny spun by the powers of the Underworld," she said, "and the foreknowledge that I should suffer harm from thee. And I knew not that thou wert here, or I and my sisters would have avoided thee. But it is fated," she went on, "that thou come with us to learn all that may be learned of the use of arms. For there are none in Britain to compare with us for the knowledge of warfare."

Then Perceval remembered what he had heard the trolls—the people of the Underworld—say, though he had not understood their meaning. "The stainless knight," they said, "shall gain from evil greater strength, and with it he may confound all evil."

"If it be thus fated," he said, "I will go with thee. But first thou shalt swear that no evil shall happen to the lady of this castle nor to her daughter, nor to any that belong to them."

"It shall be so," said the witch, "if, when the time comes, thou art strong enough to overcome my power. But if thou failest, Angharad is mine to do with as I will."

Then Perceval took leave of the lady of the Castle of Weeds, and of Angharad. And the lady thanked him with tears for saving their lives, but the girl was cold and scornful and said no word of thanks. Then Perceval went with the witches to their Castle of Glaive.

He stayed with them for a year and a day, learning such knowledge of arms, and gaining such strength, that it was marvel to see the feats which he performed. And while he lived with them they strove to bend him to their wills, for they saw how great a knight he would become in prowess and in knightly deeds. They tempted him every hour and every day, telling him what earthly power, what riches, and what great dominions would be his, if he would but swear fealty to the chief-witch, Domna, and fight for her against King Arthur and his proud knights.

Perceval prayed daily for strength to withstand the poison of their tongues, and evermore he held himself humble and gentle, and thought much of his widowed mother in her lonely home in the northern wastes, and of the promise he had made her. Sometimes he thought of Angharad, how beautiful she was, and how sad it was that she had so cold a heart, and was so cruel in her words.

Anon the witch Domna came to him, and said that he had now learned all that she could teach him, and he must go and prove himself against greater powers than he had ever yet known. If he prevailed not in that battle, the ladies of the Castle of Weeds would become the prey of the witches, and greater power of evil would they have in the world than ever before. Then she gave him a horse and a full suit of black armour.

So Perceval took the horse, and armed himself and rode forth. And anon he came to a hermit's cell beside a ruined chapel, and he alighted and went into the chapel, and stripped himself, and laid all his armour, his lance, and his sword, before the high altar.

Prayerfully he gave his arms to the service of God, and devoted them one by one to do only knightly and pure deeds, to rescue the oppressed and the weak, to put down the proud, and to cherish the humble.

And as he ended praying, the armour stirred of itself, and though it had been black before, now did the darkness fade from it, and it all became a pure white. While he marvelled, a faint light glowed over hauberk, helm, shield, sword and lance, and there was an exceeding sweet savour wafted through the place. And ghostily, as in a silver mist, he saw above the altar the likeness of a spear, and beside it a dish or salver. And at the wondrous sight his breath stayed on his lips. Then slowly the vision faded from his sight.

He arrayed himself in his armour that was now of a dazzling white, and he rode forth and thought to go towards Camelot, where was the court of King Arthur. But he felt that some power drew him aside through the desolate ways of a hoar forest, where all the trees were ancient and big, and all bearded with long moss.

In a little while he saw a vast castle reared upon a rock in the midst of the forest. He rode up to it, and marvelled that it was all so quiet. Then he beat upon the door with the butt of his lance, and the door opened, and he entered into the wide dark hall. On the pallets under the wall he saw men lying as if dead. And in the high seat at the head of the hall sat a king, old and white, but richly clothed, and he seemed dead like all the rest. All were clad in garments of an ancient kind, as if they had lived and died a thousand years agone, yet had not rotted into dust. On the floor, about the wide heap of ashes where the fire had burned, the hounds still lay as if asleep, and on the posts the hawks sat stiff upon their perches.

Much did Perceval marvel at this strange sight, but most of all he marvelled to see where a shaft of light from a narrow window gleamed across the hall full upon a shield hung on the fire pillar beside the high seat in which the king sat like one dead.

Perceval caused his horse to pick its way through the hall, and he approached the shield. And he saw that it was of shining white, but whiter than the whiteness of his own, and in the centre thereof was a heart. As he sat looking thereat, he marvelled to see that the heart seemed to stir as if it were alive, and began to throb and move as if it beat. Then the whiteness of the shield began to dazzle like to a light that mortal eyes could not bear.

He lifted his hand and took the shield by its strap from the peg on which it hung, and as he did so, a great sigh arose from within the hall, as if at one time many sleepers awoke. And looking round, he saw how all the men that had seemed dead were now on their knees, with bent heads and folded hands as if in prayer.

The king in the high seat stirred and sat upright, and looked at Perceval with a most sweet smile.

"The blessing of God is upon thee, young White Knight," said he, "and now is my watch and ward all ended, and with these my faithful companions may I go."

"Tell me, sir," said Perceval, "what means this?"

"I am Marius," said the king, "and I was that Roman soldier who took pity of the gentle Saviour dying in His agony upon the rood. And I helped to take Him from the cross. For my pity did God, whom till then I had not known, deal with me in marvellous wise. And this shield was mine, and a holy hermit in a desert of Syria did bless it, and prophesy concerning it and me. I came to this land of Britain when it was full of evil men, warring fiercely together, and all in heathen darkness. I preached the Word of Christ, I and my fellows that came with me, until the heathens rose up and would slay me. And by that time I was wearied and very old, and wished to die. Yet I sorrowed, wondering whether God would do naught to rescue these people from this slavery to the old evil law. Then a man of God came to me at night, a man of marvel, and he caused this castle to be builded in this ancient wood, and he put my shield upon the post, and bade me and my dear friends sleep. 'For,' said he, 'thou hast earned thy sleep, and others shall carry on thy work and reveal the mercy of God and his Christ to these poor heathens, and they shall turn to God wholly. And no evil shall be able to break in upon thy repose. But when, in the distant future, men's hearts are turning to evil again, one that is of the three white knights shall come and take this shield, to ward him in the great battle against evil, and then thou and all that are with thee shall have the restfulness of death thou hast merited.' Go then, thou good knight," went on King Marius, "fight the good fight against that thing of evil whom the good man spoke of, and may my shield encompass thee and ever guard thee."

Perceval took the shield and left his own. Turning, he rode back between fines of silent forms bent in prayer. He went forth into the forest some little way, and heard from the castle the singing of a joyful hymn. And, looking back, he saw that the castle had vanished. But still above him and about him was the sound of singing, of a sweetness indescribable, as if they sang who had gained all that they desired.

Then Perceval rode forward till it was night; but never could he get sight of castle or knight's hold or hermit's cell where he could be houselled for the night. So he abode in the forest that night, and when he had prayed he slept beside his good horse until it was day.

Just before the dawn he awoke to the sound of a great rushing wind all about him. Yet marvel it was to see that the trees in that hoar wood did not wave their branches, but all were still.

Then he was aware of a sweet savour which surrounded him, and anon a gentle voice spoke out of the darkness.

"Fair White Knight," said the voice, "it is ordained of thee that thou goest to the lands of the King Pellam in the north, where an evil power seeks to turn men from the New Law which Christ brought, and to make them cleave to the Old Law with its cruelty and evil tortures. And there at the Castle of the Circlet thou shalt fight a battle for the Saviour of the world. And whether thou shalt win through all, none know as yet. But in thy purity, thy humility, is thy strength. Fare thee well!"

Much moved at these words, Perceval knelt and prayed, and then, as the dawn filtered through the trees, he mounted his horse and began his long journey to the north.

On the seventh day he crossed a plain, and saw far in the north where the smoke as of fires rose into the clouds, and here and there he saw the fierce red gleam of flames. And he passed through a ford, and then he entered a land all black and desolate, with the bodies of the dead beside the way, unburied, and the houses all broken or burned. In other places the grass and weeds grew over the hearths of desolated homes, and wild beasts made their lairs where homely folk seemed lately to have lived their simple happy lives.

No man or child could be seen anywhere to ask what all this might mean. But one day, as he walked his horse beside a brook, over the long grass, he came upon a poor half-starved peasant who had not strength to run. And the man knelt before him, and bared his breast, and said, "Strike, sir knight, and end my misery!"

But Perceval raised him in his arms and kissed him, and gave him bread and wine from his scrip, and when the poor man was revived, Perceval asked him what his words meant.

"Ah, Sir White Knight!" said the man, whose tears fell as he spoke. "Surely thou art an angel of heaven, not of the pit, such as have ravened and slaughtered throughout this fair land since good King Pellam was struck by the Dolorous Stroke that Balin made. For of that stroke came all our misery. The sacred relics of the Crucifixion fled our land, our king sickened of a malady that naught could heal, our crops rotted, and our cattle died. Yet did some among us strive to live and do as brave men should in all adversity. But into the land came an evil and a pagan knight, the Knight of the Dragon, and he willed that all should scorn and despise the good Christ, and should turn to the old gods of the standing stones and the oaken groves. And those that would not he slew, and their folic he trampled underfoot, and their herds and fields he destroyed and desolated. And I, fair lord, have lost my dear wife and my wee bairns, and I wonder why I fled and kept my life, remembering all I have lost."

"Take heart," said Perceval, "and remember that it is God His mercy that chastiseth, and that while thou hast life thou hast hope. It is a man's duty, a man's nobility, to bear sorrows bravely, and still to work, to do all, and to achieve. I think God will not long let this evil knight oppress and slay. In His good time He will cut him down."

"Fair sir," said the peasant, "I thank thee for thy cheer, and I will take heart and trust in God's good time."

And Perceval rode forward through the blackened land and found the forests burning and the fields wasted. Anon he came to the edge of a plain, and saw a great castle in the distance. And there came to him a damsel, weeping, and when he craved of her to tell him why she mourned, she stayed, and looked at him as if astounded. Then she cried with a great cry of joy.

"Oh, tell me, fair sir, who art thou? Thou hast the white armour which it was foretold the spotless knight should wear, and on thy shield is the Heart as of Him that bled to save the world."

"I know not what you say," replied Perceval, "but my name is Perceval, son of Evroc, and I seek the wicked knight that doeth all this evil."

"Then thou art the White Knight," said the damsel, "and now I pray that God aid thee, for my lady and all this poor land have need of thee. Come thou to my mistress, the lady of the Chaplet."

Therewith she led him to the castle, and the lady thereof came out to him. She was of a sad countenance, but of a great beauty, though poorly clothed.

"Fair sir," she said, "my maiden hath told me who thou art, and I sorrow that one so noble as thou seemest shall essay to overcome the fiend Knight of the Dragon. Yet if thou shouldst prevail, all men in this tortured land will bless thee, and I not the least. For daily doth the evil knight slay my poor knights, and cometh and casteth their blackened and burned bodies before my hall. And many of my poor folk hath he slain or enslaved, and others hath he caused to follow his evil worship, and many of my rich and fair lands hath he wrested from me."

"Therefore, fair lady," said Perceval, "I would seek him without delay, for to essay the force of my body upon him, by the grace of God."

"And shouldst thou conquer," said the lady, "with the fiend's death the hallowed relics which King Pellam guarded shall return to bless this land. Now, therefore, go ye towards the Burnt Land beyond the brook, for that is where is the lair of the fiend that doth oppress us."

Perceval went forward across the plain to a brook, and having forded the water he came to a wide hollow where the ground was all baked and burned, and the trees were charred and black. Here and there lay pieces of armour, red and rusted, as if they had been in a fierce fire; and in one place was the body of a knight freshly slain, and he was charred and black.

Then, as Perceval looked about him, he saw the dark hole of a cave in a bank beside the hollow, and suddenly therefrom issued a burst of horrible fire and smoke, and with a cry as of a fiend a black knight suddenly appeared before him on a great horse, whose eyes flashed as with fire and whose nostrils jetted hot vapours.

"Ha, thou Christian!" cried the knight in a horrible voice. "What dost thou here? Wouldst thou have thy pretty white armour charred and blackened and thyself killed by my dragon's power?"

Then Perceval saw how the boss of the Black Knight's shield was the head of a dragon, its forked tongue writhing, its teeth gnashing, and its eyes so red and fiendish that no mortal, unless by God's aid, could look on it and live. From its mouth came a blinding flash as of lightning and beat at Perceval, but he held up his shield of the Throbbing Heart, and with angry shrieks the Black Knight perceived that the lightning could not touch the shield.

Then from his side the evil knight tore his sword, and it flamed red as if it was heated in a fierce furnace, and thrusting forward he came and beat at Perceval. But the White Knight warded off the blows with his shield, which the flaming sword had no power to harm.

Then did the Black Knight marvel greatly, for never had a knight, however skilled, withstood him, for either the lightning of the dragon shield had burnt him, or the stroke of his flaming sword had slain him swiftly. And by this he knew that this knight was Perceval.

"Thou knowest not who it is thou lightest," said the Black Knight, with a scornful laugh. "Thou must put forth more than the skill thou didst learn of the witches of Glaive if thou wouldst overcome me. For know ye, that I am a fosterling of Domna the witch, and she taught me more than ever she taught you. Now prepare ye to die."

Then Perceval knew that this indeed was the fight which Domna had foretold, and that if he failed in this, ruin and sorrow would be the lot of many.

And Perceval began to thrust and strike full valorously and skilfully, but naught seemed to avail him. Thus for a long time they went about, thrusting and striking. Always the strength of the Black Knight seemed as unwearied as that of a demon, while Perceval felt his arm weaken, as much from the great strokes he gave, as from the burning fires that darted at him from the dragon shield.

Then Perceval cried in prayer for aid, and asked that if Christ would have this land saved for His glory, strength should be given him to slay this fiendish oppressor.

Forthwith strength seemed to nerve his arm mightily, and lifting his sword he struck at the shield of the knight, and so vehement was the blow that he cut down the shield even to the head of the dragon. Feeling the wound, the dragon gave forth a great flame, and Perceval wondered to see that now his own sword burned as if on fire.

Then, while the Black Knight marvelled at this stroke, Perceval struck at him more fiercely and beat in the other's helm, so that the fiend knight bent and swayed in his saddle. But recovering, he became so wroth that, with his fiery sword, he heaved a mighty blow at Perceval, and cut through his hauberk even to the shoulder, which was burned to the bone.

Ere the other could withdraw himself, Perceval thrust his sword to the hilt into the loathsome throat of the dragon. Thereupon the dragon gave so terrible a cry that the earth seemed to shake with the horror of it. And in its wrath and pain the dragon's head turned upon the Black Knight its master, and vomited forth fire so fiercely, that it scorched and burned him utterly, so that he fell from his horse dead.

Perceval, dizzy and weak from the battle, alighted from his horse, and went towards the knight, that he might slay the dragon. But suddenly he swooned and fell and his consciousness went from him.

When Perceval came to his senses again, he found himself upon a pallet, and the rough walls of a room were about him, while above him was the window, as it seemed, of an abbey or convent. And he was so weak he could not lift his hand.

Someone came to him, and he recognised Tod the troll.

"Ah, good Tod," said he faintly. "Where am I?"

"Now God be praised," said Tod, and smiled joyfully. "For the nuns feared ye might not win through the poison of your wound which the dragon knight did give you. 'Twas I who had followed you, lord, since that you did leave the hold of the witches, and when you swooned I brought you here, to the convent of the White Nuns. And now that I know ye live, I go to your lady mother to tell her the good news, for she is weary to know tidings of you."

"Go, good Tod," said Perceval, "and say I will come for her blessing when I may mount my horse again."

When Tod had left him, there came a nun to him, and he knew her for Angharad, who had been so proud and scornful when he left her at the Castle of Weeds. And he asked her how she had fared, and why she was a nun.

"To repent me of my evil mind," she said. "For when you left us I did not in my heart thank ye that you had saved my mother and me from death and worse. And the witches came to me and tempted me with riches and power, even as they were tempting you while you were with them. I heard how you withstood them, and I scorned you and hated you and said you would yield some day. And then you left the witches, having learned all their strong powers, yet having withstood them, and I marvelled much. I heard men say you were one of three stainless knights of the world that should achieve the Holy Grail, because of your great humility and purity, and that great honour and glory would be yours, because you put not your trust in your own strength. Then I repented, and would not listen to the evil women. But they followed me, whispering and tempting, and then for terror I sought a holy hermit, and he brought me here, and now am I at peace, and my proud heart is humble."

"By my faith, sister," said Perceval, "I am rejoiced to hear thee. For I thought when I saw thee that thou hadst a proud and a hard heart.

But as thou wert a beauteous and lovely maiden I thought much of thee; and had it not been foreordained otherwise, I would have loved thee above all women and wedded thee."

The sister's pale face flushed.

"Nay, but thou hadst a greater glory in store for thee," she said. "For thou shalt find the Holy Grail and restore it to this kingdom, and with it weak men shall forsake their leanings to the old law of hate, and cleave only to Christ and His new law of love."

"It is as God may will it," said Perceval.

In a little while he strengthened and rose from his pallet, and fared forth towards the north where his widowed mother sat in her lonely hall, waiting for him whose fame was sweet in every man's mouth.

As he passed through the land, he saw how it had already begun to smile again. Men went to their work unafraid, the corn was brightening on the hills, the cattle lowed, women sang at their work, and children played. And all blessed him as he rode.

Thus was ended at last the sorrow in the land of King Pellam which was brought in by the Dolorous Stroke which Sir Balin had given a generation before.

VIII

How Sir Owen Won the Earldom of the Fountain

NOW THE YOUNG PAGE OWEN, WHO HAD SAVED KING ARTHUR from midnight murder at the hand of the evil Sir Turquine, whom Lancelot slew, had tarried at the court of the king, and in prowess and knightly achievements was among the most famous of the knights of the Round Table. And always was he wishful to go on strange adventures, however far might be the country, or dangerous the ways thereto, or cruel and crafty the foes.

One day King Arthur was at Caerleon-upon-Usk, and sat conversing with a few of his knights in the presence chamber. With him was Sir Owen and Sir Kay, and there was also Sir Conan and Sir Bedevere. The queen sat near them, while her handmaidens stood by the window at needlework.

In a little while Arthur said he would sleep until the horn sounded for dinner. For he had come from London late the night before, and had not had his full rest.

"But," said he, "do you, my knights, continue your talk, and tell each other tales as before, and if you are hungry, Kay will give you collops of meat and horns of mead."

So the king slept on his broad seat of green rushes, over which was spread a splendid covering of flame-coloured satin and cushions of red satin were under his head.

Kay ordered a page to bring meat and bread and mead, and when the four had eaten, Sir Conan was called upon to tell how he became possessed of a dark bay palfrey, as to which all envied him for its beauty, but concerning which he always put off telling the tale of how he had obtained it.

"You must know," began Sir Conan, "that I was the only son of my parents, and the confines of my father's barony in Lothian were too small for my aspiring and my daring. I thought there was no adventure in the world too great for my doing, and when I had fought all the knights who would meet me in my own country, and had slain all the trolls that wrought evil there, I equipped myself in my best armour and set forth to seek greater adventures in deserts and wild regions. And I fared south for many weeks, over desolate mountains and wild and terrible fastnesses of rock and moor, where only the robber seemed to live, and the wild, magic people of the green mounds, and where there was no sound but the song of the lark, the plunge of the beaver and otter in the river, the growl of the brown bear from the rock, and the howl of the wolf at night.

"And I fared through all these terrors unscathed, and one day I came to a high ridge, and saw stretching below me the fairest valley I had ever seen. The grass was green and smooth, the trees were soft and of an equal growth, and a river ran gently through the dale, with a path beside it.

"I followed the path all day until the evening, but met no one, until, as the afternoon was waning, I came suddenly upon a large and massive castle, which shone in the westering sun. And I approached the green before the gateway, and saw two youths with curling auburn hair, clad richly in garments of yellow satin, with frontlets of gold upon their forehead. And they had daggers with jewelled hilts, and these they were shooting at a mark.

"And on a bench a little way from them was a handsome man in the prime of life, of a proud look, clad in a rich mantle.

"I went forward and saluted him, and he returned my greeting with great courtesy. And, rising, he led me into the hall, which, however, was but poorly furnished. And I wondered that the knight and the youths should be so richly clothed, while the hall was scanty.

"Six maidens came forward, and while three took my horse, the others unarmed me, and gave me water wherein to wash, and a dining-robe to put on. And the six maidens were fairer than any I had ever seen. Then we sat down when the meat was ready, and though the food was good, it was simple, and the vessels and flagons upon the table were of silver, but very old and dented, as if they had been long in use.

"And no word was spoken until the meal was ended, and then the knight asked me my name and whither I was going.

"I told him my name, and he told me his. And he was, he said, Sir Dewin of Castle Cower. And I told him that I was faring south seeking any great adventure, so that I might gain glory and renown. 'For,' I said, 'I wish to find a knight who is stronger and more dexterous in arms than I.'

"At that he looked upon me and smiled.

"'If I did not fear to distress you too much,' he said, 'I would show you what you seek!'

"'Tell me,' I said, 'for I am eager to obtain this adventure.'

"'Sleep here tonight,' said Sir Dewin, 'and in the morning rise early, and take the road to the wood behind the castle. Follow the path till you come to a fountain in a glade. There you will see a large cup, with a chain. Strike the cup with your lance, and you will have the adventure ye desire.'

"And Sir Dewin smiled again as if he thought the adventure was one which he deemed was beyond me, and I was angered and soon retired to my pallet. But I could not sleep, for I was eager to rise and meet this adventure, and to come back and mock Sir Dewin for his laughter.

"Before dawn I arose and equipped myself, and mounted my horse, and took my way to the wood, as Sir Dewin had told me. And the road was long and difficult; but at length I came to the glade and found the fountain. On a stone pillar beside it a chain was fastened, and at the end of the chain was a large cup.

"With my lance I struck the cup, and instantly there was a great peal of thunder, so that I trembled for fear. And instantly there came a great storm of rain and of hail. The hailstones were so large and so hard that neither man nor beast could live through that storm, for they would have slain them, so fiercely did they beat. And the way that I escaped was this. I placed the beak of my shield over the head and neck of my horse, while I held the upper part over my own head. Thus did we withstand the storm, though the flanks of my horse were sore wounded.

"Then the sky cleared, the sun came out, and a flock of birds began to sing on a tree beside the fountain. And surely no one has heard such entrancing music before or since. So charmed was I with listening, that I noticed not at first a low rumbling which seemed to come nearer and nearer.

"And suddenly I heard a voice approaching me, and I looked round just as a big knight in sky-blue armour rode swiftly up the valley.

"'O knight,' cried he, 'what ill have I done to thee, that thou usest me so evilly? Knowest thou not that the storm which thou hast sent by evil magic hath slain my best flocks on the hills, and beaten to death all my men that were without shelter?'

"He came at me furiously. I put my lance in rest and spurred towards him, and we came together with so great an onset that I was carried far beyond the crupper of my horse.

"Then the knight, taking no further notice of me, passed the shaft of his lance through the bridle of my horse, and so rode swiftly away. And it moved me to anger to think he despised me so much as not even to despoil me of my sword.

"Very depressed of spirit was I as I took my way back to the castle of Sir Dewin. And as I passed through the wood I came to a glade, in the midst of which was a green mound. And as I passed it I heard laughter, which seemed to come from the earth. And I heard a voice sneering and mocking me. And I guessed it was the voice of a troll or moundman whom I could not see, who lived in the hillock, and I wonder I did not go mad with the shame of his derision.

"And I had not the spirit to go to try to break into the mound, lest he should work magic and more disaster upon me. So I left that glade, with the sound of his hoarse laughter ringing in my ears.

"I reached the castle of Sir Dewin, and well entertained was I, and rested for the remainder of that day. And full of courtesy was Sir Dewin and his household, for none of them referred to my encounter, and to the fact that I had come back without a horse. And when I rose next day, there was a dark bay palfrey, ready saddled, waiting in the courtyard for me. That horse I still possess, though the sight of him ever brings back the memory of my defeat.

"Verily it seems strange to me that neither before nor since have I ever heard of any person besides myself who knew of this adventure, and that the subject of it should exist within the bounds of the lands of King Arthur, without any other person lighting upon it."

"It would be well, indeed," said Sir Owen, "to go to try to discover that valley and that fountain."

"Well, indeed," said Sir Kay sourly, for he had ever been jealous of Sir Owen, even when he had been but a page, "if thy mouth were not more ready to say more than thou ever carest to do."

"Thou art worthy of punishment, Sir Kay," said Gwenevere sharply, "in that thou speakest thus of a man so tried in prowess and brave deeds as Owen."

"Fair lady," said Sir Owen, laughing, "we take no heed of Kay's raw words. He ever growls like a surly dog."

At that the king awoke, and asked whether it was not time for meat. And the horn was sounded, and men came in from the tilting-ground and the playfield, and washed, and the king and all his household sat down to dinner.

On the morrow, before dawn, Sir Owen rose privily, and put on his armour and took his horse, and rode out of the town, and for many days rode over mountains, until he saw the sea like a sheet of burnished lead lying on his left hand.

Then he turned his horse's head away, and rode far through wild and distant places, into the heart of the land. And at length he arrived at the valley which Conan had described to him, whereat he rejoiced greatly.

He descended to the path beside the river, and journeyed along it till he came to the castle of Sir Dewin, as Conan had described. And the two youths were on the green before the gate wrestling together, and the tall knight of proud mien was standing by. To Owen it seemed that he was fiercer and prouder-looking than Conan had described. Nevertheless, he returned the salute of Sir Owen courteously and led him into the castle.

Sir Owen was entertained as well as Conan had been, though the hall seemed poorer, the food coarser, and the maidens seemed careworn, and not so fair as his friend had described. After the meal Sir Dewin asked Sir Owen who he was and whither he wended, and Sir Owen replied:

"I have heard of the Knight of the Fountain, and I would fight him and overcome him, if I may."

Whereat Sir Devin looked at him with keen fierce eyes, and observed narrowly the build of Sir Owen's body.

"Knowest thou aught of the prize if thou slayest the Knight of the Fountain?" asked Sir Dewin.

"Naught know I of that," answered Sir Owen; "but I would seek the adventure, and whatever it will bring."

At this the knight was silent, and seemed to brood for some moments, with dark and frowning brows. Then he laughed and said:

"Take thou the path thou seest through the wood behind the castle. Follow that till thou comest to a glade wherein is a great mound. There ye will see a stone slab. Knock on that three times, and the trollman that dwells therein will tell thee thy further way."

Sir Owen marked how evil was the smile with which Sir Dewin said these words; but Sir Owen thanked him, and then he was shown to his pallet and all retired to rest.

When he arose in the morning Sir Owen found his horse already prepared, and, having put on his armour, he rode forth along the way which the knight had indicated to him. And he came at last to the glade wherein he saw the great mound, with grass growing all over it, as if it were a little hill. In the side he saw a stone slab as if it were a door, and he struck upon it with the butt of his lance.

Three times he struck, and at the third blow he heard a voice, rough and loud, from somewhere above his head.

"Get thee gone," cried the voice, "darken not the door of my house, or 'twill be worse for thee."

Sir Owen could not see who was speaking, for no one was visible.

"I would ask thee the way to the fountain," he replied. "Tell me, and I will not trouble thee further, thou surly troll."

"The fountain?" cried the voice. "I will save thee thy journey, thou overbearing knight, as I have saved it for others as proud and as would-be valiant whom my master hath sent to me!"

With that Sir Owen received so hard and fierce a blow upon his headpiece that he was hard put to it to keep his wits and his seat; and looking round he saw the troll, a fierce dark little man, on the very top of the mound, wielding a long thick bar of iron, as thick as a weaver's beam.

Sir Owen thrust at the troll with his lance; but the moundman seized it below the point of steel, and so strong was he, that though Sir Owen drew him down from the top of the hillock, he could not loose it from the little man's hold.

Meanwhile, the troll was beating at Sir Owen with the staff of iron, which, for all its weight and size, he wielded as if it was no more than a stout cudgel. And hard bestead was Sir Owen to shield himself from the smashing blows which rained upon him. At the seventh blow his shield was cracked across and his shield arm was numbed.

Suddenly he dashed his horse forward, and the little man, still holding the lance, was thrown backward upon the grassy slope of his own mound. Swiftly Sir Owen leaped from his horse and drew his sword, and while the troll was rising he dashed at him and wounded him.

But next moment the troll was up, his dark narrow face terrible with rage, for the blood ran down the deer-skin tunic which half covered him. And then the blows of his iron rod came thicker and faster, while he moved so swiftly round about the knight that Sir Owen, though he thrust quickly and fiercely, could not strike him again.

Sir Owen was becoming dizzy and weak, and felt that not for long now could he bear up his dented and broken shield against the blows that must at length smash his arm.

Suddenly the quick movements of the little troll ceased, and he staggered. Then he dropped the iron bar and swayed like a drunken man towards the knight. He fell on his knees before Sir Owen, put his head upon the ground, and clutched the knight's steel-clad foot as if to put it upon his neck. But he could do no more, and so lay panting and spent with exhaustion.

And Sir Owen could not find it in himself to pierce him through with his sword, for the troll's subjection made pity come into his heart.

"Ah, sir troll!" said the knight, panting also, and very fain to rest. "A brave troll thou art, seeing thou hast used no magic, but hath fought me like a very man."

"Chieftain," gasped the troll, "my heart is like to break, for thou hast tried me sore. Never yet hath a knight that sought the fountain withstood my rod as valiantly as thou hast, and thou hast put my strength all to naught."

"But I know not why thou didst try to slay me," said Sir Owen, "seeing that I did but ask thee to show me my way to the fountain."

"I am the slave of him that overcometh me," answered the troll, "and I must do his bidding. Sir Dewin did conquer me by evil wizardry, and he sent thee to me with the three knocks on my door, whereby I knew he commanded me to slay thee."

"Well, and what wilt thou do now, valiant troll?"

"I must hide me from the wrath of Sir Dewin," said the troll, "until my sore wound is healed. Then will I be thy slave, sir knight, and help thee in whatever adventure thou mayst wish!"

"Get thee gone, then, good troll," said Sir Owen, with a smile. "But first tell me my way to the fountain."

Whereupon the troll showed him the way and gave him certain directions, and then said:

"Chieftain, thou wilt conquer in all thy fighting, and great honour and reward shall be thine. But beware thee of leaving the side of her that shall love thee, for more than a night and a day, or long woe shall find thee. And do thou take this, for it may find thee friends."

And the troll, whose name was Decet, held towards him a blue stone upon a silver string. The stone burned with the dazzling blue of the lightning flash, when the light caught it.

Sir Owen thanked him, put the string about his neck, and stood watching the troll as he limped, faint and wounded, into the mound that was his home.

Then, picking up his lance, Sir Owen mounted his horse, and rode forward through the wood, thinking of this strange adventure.

When he reached the fountain where a silver cup hung by a silver chain, he filled the cup with water, as the troll had bidden him, and threw it over a pillar of stone that was set beside the fountain. And instantly there came a clap of thunder as if the earth would dash asunder, and after the thunder came the shower, and so fierce and heavy were the hailstones that they would surely have slain horse and rider, but that Sir Owen, as the troll had bidden him, had put his horse's forefeet in the fountain, and kept his own hand therein, whereby the hailstones became thin rain before they touched him.

Then the sky became bright, and the flock of birds descended on the tree and began to sing. But Sir Owen heeded them not, but mounted his horse, dressed his shield and lance, and prepared for the combat.

There came a mourning cry through the wood, and a sky-blue knight on a high-stepping destrier dashed through the trees towards Sir Owen, and came against him, lance in rest. Whereupon Sir Owen put spurs to his horse, and furiously rode against the knight. At the first onset each broke his lance; whereat they drew their swords and lashed at each other most fiercely.

Sir Owen feinted, and then, quickly recovering, he smote the other so hard and stern a blow that the blade bit through headpiece, skin, and bone, until it wounded the brain itself.

Then, with a great cry, the blue knight wheeled his horse and fled, with Sir Owen in pursuit. But the other knight's horse was fleeter, and Sir Owen could not overtake him, though he kept within a few yards.

In a little while a great castle, resplendent with new stone, shone before them. The wounded knight thundered across the drawbridge, with Owen close behind him; but when the blue knight gained the street beyond, the portcullis was let fall with a rush. Sir Owen fell from his horse, and looking round he found that the horse had been cut in twain by the gate.

So that Sir Owen found himself, with the forepart of the dead horse, in a prison between the two gates, while the hinder part of the horse was outside. And Sir Owen saw that his death must be very near, for already he saw one of the soldiers who were guarding the gate run after the knight to the castle, as if for orders to slay him.

Looking through the inner gate, he saw a narrow street facing him, with booths and little houses on each side; and coming towards him he beheld a maiden, small but beautiful, with black curling hair and a circlet of gold upon her forehead; and she was of high rank, for she wore a dress of yellow satin, and on her feet were shoes of speckled leather.

She stopped when but a few steps from the gate where the soldiers stood watching Sir Owen; and he saw that her eyes were bent fixedly upon the blue stone which lay on the knight's breast. And he saw that, in the darkness of his prison, it shone with a fierce blue flame.

He looked up and saw the maiden's eyes bent on his, and he seemed to hear the voice of the maiden speaking to him, as clearly as if she stood beside him. In these words she spoke:

"Take that stone which is on thy breast, and hold it tightly in the palm of one hand. And as thou concealest it, so will it conceal thee. Thus wilt thou be able to pass unseen between the bars of the portcullis. And I will wait for thee on the horseblock yonder, and thou wilt be able to see me, though I cannot see thee. Therefore, come and place thy hand on my shoulder, and I shall know that thou art come. And then thou must accompany me to the place where I shall hide thee."

He saw the maiden turn away and go up the street, and Sir Owen did as the voice had bidden him. And looking down he saw nothing of himself, although he could see the soldiers looking in, and he saw the surprise and then the horror on their faces, as they realised that they had seen him spirited away before their eyes.

Sir Owen passed between them and rejoined the maiden, as she had bidden him. He went with her, still invisible, and she led him to a small house, and in it was a large and beautiful chamber, all painted with gorgeous colours, and well furnished. And there she gave him food, and he rested securely until late in the afternoon.

Then, as he looked out of the window upon the wall of the castle, which towered dark and high above him, he heard a clamour and sounds of a mourning coming from it. He asked the maiden the cause of it.

"They are administering extreme unction to the Lord Cadoc, who owns the castle, for he hath been wounded."

"And who art thou, that thou shouldst save me who am a stranger?" he asked of the maiden.

"My name is Elined," said the maiden, "and since thou bearest the Blue Stone of the Little Folk, I must aid thee all I can."

At that time she would tell him no more, but shortly left him to his rest, saying she would come to attend upon him again at the dawning.

In the silence and darkness of the night Sir Owen awoke by reason of a woeful outcry and lamenting; and then he knew that Earl Cadoc, the Knight of the Fountain, was dead from the wound he had given him.

Soon after dawn he arose and clothed himself; and looking out of the window he saw the streets filled with a great host of people in black, and the weeping and the mourning were pitiful to hear. Knights, with their armour craped, rode in great companies before; then came the men-at-arms with weapons reversed; then the ladies of the household, and after these the priests came, and in their midst was the bier.

And over it was a veil of white linen, and wax tapers burning beside and around it, and of the gentlemen who supported the bier on their shoulders none was lower in rank than a powerful baron, owning broad lands and great companies of retainers.

Last of all there came a lady walking behind the bier. And though her face was stained with the many tears she had shed, and was pale with sorrow, Sir Owen thought he had never seen so beautiful a lady, or one so gentle and kind of mien.

Deeply he sorrowed because he had caused the death of her lord, inasmuch as it had given her such grief.

Her hair, yellow and long and curled, hung dishevelled about her shoulders, and her dress of rich yellow satin was torn, and across it was a wide sash of black velvet. And it was a marvel that she could see how to walk, for the tears filled her eyes.

Sir Owen could not take his gaze from her, and love and pity for her filled his mind.

When the procession had passed out of the town the maiden Elined came into the room, and Sir Owen asked her eagerly who was the lady he had seen.

"Heaven is my witness," replied Elined, "but she is the fairest and the sweetest and the most noble of women. She is my beloved mistress, and her name is Carol, and she is Countess of the Fountain, the widow of him thou didst slay yesterday."

"I sorrow for that," said Owen, "for I have seen her grief. But, verily, she is the woman that I love best. And if my hand hath wounded her grievously, my arm would more willingly protect her."

"Indeed, thou art brave and bold, sir knight," said the maiden, "and much may you win, if you are as faithful in your service and devotion to her as you have been in the service of your king, the great Arthur."

And when it had passed midday, Elined said to Sir Owen:

"You must keep this chamber while I go and woo for thee. Stir not out into the city lest ill befall thee."

Elined went to the castle and found all was in confusion, with mourning and lamentation. Her mistress she found sitting listlessly looking from the window with pale sorrow on her face; and to Elined's greeting she would respond not.

"It astounds me," said Elined at length, "to find you giving yourself up to unavailing sorrow in this way."

"It astounds me also," said the countess reproachfully, "that in my time of trouble and affliction, you, whom I have enriched and favoured beyond all my handmaidens, should desert me. If I did not love thee, I should order thee to be executed."

"It was for thy advantage that I was absent," said Elined. "I reproached not thy grief when thy lord lay dying, but now you have yourself to think of. Yet you seem more willing to live with the dead than to take heed what may happen to yourself in a few hours. I would have thee remember that a live dog is better than a dead lion."

"Hence from my sight, unfeeling girl!" cried the countess in anger. "There is no one in the world to compare with my dead lord in beauty, in strength, and in prowess. Get thee gone!"

Without a word Elined turned and went from the room. But she had not gone far before she heard the countess coughing behind her, and on looking back her mistress beckoned to her.

"You are indeed hardhearted, Elined," said she, "to think to leave me in my grief, and in my need of good counsel. I will overlook thy cruelty if, as you say, you have been absent for my advantage. What mean you by that?"

"This is my meaning," said Elined. "Thou knowest that without a man of knightly prowess and bravery, thou canst not hope to guard the fountain and keep these wide dominions in the power of thyself. Thou art the prey and booty of any bold bandit lord that chooses to make war upon thee, and to capture and wed thee. And dost thou forget the wiles and treachery of thy old lover whom thou hast flouted, Sir Dewin of Castle Cower? Hath he not sworn to take thee and thy kingdom, sooner or later, by fair means or by foul? Therefore it behoves thee at once to find a noble and generous knight, courtly and worshipful, who will guard thee and love thee, and hold down the turbulent lords, thy vassals and thy neighbours."

"Hard will such a task be," sighed the countess, "for the Earl Cadoc was a man among men."

"Yet I will wager to find thee such another, even excelling him in knightly prowess, in beauty of person, and for love and devotion to thee more than his equal," replied Elined, who remembered that the dead earl had not been overly tender to his gentle countess on many occasions.

"And where couldst thou find this paragon?" said the countess, flushing a little at the reminder of her late lord's neglect.

"At the court of King Arthur," replied Elined; "for there are to be found the peerless knights of the world, men of their knightly words, and devoted to love and war."

"If it be that I must think of wedding again so soon," sighed the countess, "go then to King Arthur, and find me such a knight. But let him be gentle as well as brave, with fine and courtly manners—a man, indeed, whom I can really love."

Elined went and kissed the flushing cheek of her mistress.

"Trust me for that," she said gently. "I would do that as much for myself as for thee, my dear Carol. For did it not often go to my heart to see thee pine for gentle speech and affection, and sorrow at the harsh words thou didst suffer? I will set forth at once to Caerleon, and him that I bring shall be worthy of thee. And all others that may come and woo thee, do thou keep at arm's length until I return."

Elined departed from the castle, but she did not go beyond the town. It was in her mind to lie hidden for as long a time as it would take her to go to Caerleon and return therefrom. Meanwhile, going about disguised, she would be able to see what the many lords were doing who would essay to woo the countess, seeing that, lovely and rich as she was, she would be a splendid prize.

And things happened as she had foreseen. Every day there came into the town one cavalcade or more, with some baron or earl in flashing armour at the head of his vassals, come to try his fortune and to win the lovely Countess of the Fountain, and to possess her wide dominions.

Daily the countess was compelled to receive fresh comers in audience, and while with deft excuses she kept each at arm's length, they crowded her audience chamber, proud and insolent, humble or crafty, eyeing each other with high looks, each prepared to slay his rival if the need arose.

At last there came an earl who, as he came up the street at the head of a large company of knights, seemed to shine like the sun. For his armour was all of gold, and jewels were about his neck, and on his girdle and his wrists. Every toss of his destrier's head dazzled the eyes with the fountain of flashing lights given off by the jewels which adorned the cloth of gold about its head.

This knight called himself the Earl of Drood, but Elined was in the crowd of gaping townspeople that saw him enter, and she knew him for the old insolent lover of her mistress, whom the countess had ever despised, Sir Dewin of Castle Cower.

Sir Dewin disguised himself so that the countess did not know him. She received him in audience, and though she was startled by the magnificence of his dress, and a little moved by the gentleness of his manner, she felt that she feared and distrusted him.

The next day he craved to see her again, and then said:

"Fair and noble lady, so deeply doth thy beauty move me, that I am eager to put to the test swiftly the question whether I or some other happier knight among these noble gentlemen shall obtain thy hand. Therefore I crave permission of thee to proclaim a joust between all these knights that sue for thee, and the winner among them all shall be he that thou shalt wed."

"Sir," said the countess with great dignity, "it is not for thee to order here, but for me. I wish nothing to be done for the space of nine days, and then will I make my choice."

At which Sir Dewin, though full of rage, must needs seem content. And the countess hoped that, in the space she had named, Elined would have returned with the knight of her choice, and she herself could choose him for her lord, if she thought he was the man whom she could most trust and love.

But Sir Dewin wrought upon many of the suitors who were of his mind, and they resolved that, will she, nill she, the countess must needs abide by a contest between all her wooers to be holden on the tenth day.

And on the tenth day all the knights, barons, and earls met together in full armour in a broad green jousting-place beneath the windows of the countess, and having made the rules of contest, and committed them to the seneschal of the countess, they prepared to prove which among them all was the knight of most prowess.

Then there was fierce hurtling to and fro of knight against knight, and lances splintered, horses reared, knights fell wounded or dead and were dragged away. And for long, among the ninety-nine knights that there jousted, none of the crowds who looked on could see which were they who were gaining the day.

From her window the countess watched with a sorrowing and dreading heart; for Elined had not yet returned, and therefore the countess must be the prize of one of these suitors who had pestered her, and none of whom she cared for.

Then, when the dust of the jousting had a little cleared, and the knights had withdrawn to the sides of the lists, to breathe and rest awhile, it was seen that twelve remained of the ninety-nine.

The countess, looking from her window, knew them all from the devices on their shields, and none of them were men she favoured. Some she knew were evil men, yet, as knights, were powerful in jousting. And she dreaded which of them should be the victor, to be her lord and master.

Then the knights hurtled together again, and as one after the other was unhorsed by stronger opponents and went from the field, she went pale with fear and anxiety.

At last there were but two, and these were Sir Dewin, whom she knew as the Earl of Drood, and the other was a knight in blue armour, with a shield on which was painted a hillock or mound. And she knew him to be a man named Sir Daunt, or the Knight of the Mount, a man of fierce temper, quarrelsome and cruel.

The countess could have swooned with terror, for she knew that now she was doomed to an unhappy life, whichever of these knights prevailed. For though the Earl of Drood was soft and gentle in speech and manner, she feared that this but covered a wicked heart.

She could hardly bear to look as she heard these two, the last of all the ninety-nine, crash together in the midst of the jousting-ground. And she heard the cries of the onlookers.

"The blue knight's the better man! How he heaves with his sword! Ah, the golden knight is down!"

And looking from her window the countess saw the earl was lying wounded, and the Knight of the Mount stood over him. Then the earl surrendered and was carried off the field.

The great shouts that saluted the victor made the countess turn faint and sick with dread, so that she fell back among her handmaidens in a swoon. But, quickly recovering, she stood up, resolved to meet her fate with proud dignity.

In a few moments the door opened and the arras was pushed aside, and the groom of the chambers announced with a shout:

"The Knight of the Mound, victorious in the joust, craves leave to greet our lady the countess."

The lady bowed assent, trembling in every limb. Then the groom stepped aside, and into the chamber came a comely gentleman, clad in purple tunic, rich with chains and jewelled belt.

But it was not the knight whom the countess had expected, but a stranger, with a courtly and gentle manner and a winning smile.

Then from behind him came Elined, full of smiles, with a look of triumph in her eyes.

"My lady," she said, bowing low, "this is the knight, Sir Owen of Wales, from the court of King Arthur, whom I have brought to protect you and wed you. He hath just proved himself the doughtiest among a hundred."

The terror of the countess was changed instantly into joy, and she put forth her hand, and Sir Owen bent and kissed it, and she led him to the window seat, and commanded Elined to sit with them. And they spoke full joyously together, for the countess was much taken with the noble and gentle bearing of Sir Owen, and admired him because he had proved himself the best man of all her wooers.

In a few days she sent for the bishops and priests, and her nuptials with Sir Owen were celebrated with such feasting that all the country was full of merriment and joy. And the men of the earldom came and did homage to Owen, and he became the Earl of the Fountain.

In a little while thereafter Sir Owen told his lady that it was he who had chased the soul from the body of her former lord. But the countess was not vexed by the knowledge, for Sir Owen loved her greatly, and with all tenderness and honour, and never had the countess been so happy with Earl Cadoc as she was with Owen.

Thereafter Earl Owen defended the fountain with lance and sword against all who ventured to challenge him in his earldom. And the knights who were thus conquered he held to ransom, and the money he thus obtained he divided equally among his barons and knights. Never had they had so generous a lord, nor one of such prowess and knightly worth. And all his subjects loved Earl Owen passing well.

Thus for three years in all happiness and quiet did Owen and the countess dwell. Sir Dewin of Castle Cower had not power to hurt them, nor did any other evil light upon them.

But at the end of this space, towards the close of a summer's day, Sir Owen, by the magic whereby it was made known to him, knew that there was a knight who challenged him at the fountain. So, putting on his sky-blue armour, he went forth and found the knight.

They rushed together, and the strange knight was overthrown. But others who were with him took him away, and Sir Owen waited. But none other challenge was made, and in the twilight he retired, resolved to attend next day in case any others desired to challenge him.

In the morning the same knight came forth from the company of knights which was among the trees about the fountain. And so fiercely did Sir Owen assail him that the head of his lance broke the helmet of the stranger and pierced the flesh to the bone. Again his companions carried him off.

Then other knights came forth and had to do with Sir Owen, but all were overthrown. At length came one having over himself and his horse a rich satin robe of honour, and Sir Owen knew that he must be a man of great dignity, big of body and of knightly prowess.

They fought together that evening and half through the next day, but neither could obtain the mastery. And about noon they took still strong lances and fought most stubbornly. At length they came so furiously together that the girths of their horses were broken and both were borne to the ground.

They rose up speedily and drew their swords and resumed the combat; and all those that witnessed it felt that they had never seen such a battle of heroes before. And suddenly with a blow fiercely strong and swiftly keen, Sir Owen cut the fastenings of the strange knight's helm, so that the headpiece came off.

With a cry Sir Owen dropped his weapon, for he knew that this was Sir Gawaine, his cousin.

"My Lord Gawaine," he said, "the robe of honour that covered thee prevented my knowing it was thee with whom I fought. Take my sword and my arms, for I yield me to thee."

"Nay, Sir Owen," said Gawaine, "take thou mine, for I am at thy mercy."

Then came forward King Arthur, and Sir Owen knew him and kneeled before him and kissed his hand, and then embraced him. And there was much joy between all the knights and Owen, for all had feared that he had been slain, and the king in despair had come upon this adventure to learn tidings of him.

Then they all proceeded to the castle of the countess, and a great banquet was prepared, with joustings and hawking parties and games. They stayed three months in great happiness and diversion.

At last, when King Arthur prepared to depart, he went to the countess and besought her to permit Owen to go with him for the space of three months, that he might renew his friendships at the court at Caerleon. And though it made the countess sorrowful to lose the man she loved best in all the world, she consented, and Owen promised to return even before the time appointed.

So King Arthur returned to Caerleon with Sir Owen, and there was much feasting and diversion to welcome him. And his kindred and friends tried to make Owen forget the countess and his earldom, but they could not. For she was the lady he loved best in the world, and he would liefer be with her, to guard and cherish her, than in any other place on the surface of the earth.

One night, as the court sat after dinner over the mead cups, a juggler came into the hall and performed many tricks, and there was much laughter and gaiety at his merry quips and jests. And he craved that he might search the hands of each lord and lady present, so that he could tell them if they would be happy in love.

He began with Sir Kay, and so along the board, uttering merry thoughts on all, but speaking with serious and solemn looks, until he came to Sir Owen. And he looked long and earnestly at the marks in that knight's palm, and then said, in a croaking voice:

> "*A night and a day, a night and a day!*
> *Thou'lt grieve for thy love forever and aye.*"

None knew what this might mean, and they marvelled to see how pale went the face of Sir Owen.

For he had suddenly remembered the words of Decet the troll-man, who had said, "Beware thee of leaving the side of her that shall love thee for more than a night and a day, or long woe shall find thee."

Instantly Sir Owen rose from the board and went out. Going to his own abode he made preparations, and at dawn he arose and mounted his horse, and set forth swiftly to go to the dominions of the countess. Great was his fear that some evil had befallen her in consequence of his leaving her unprotected from the evil powers of Sir Devin.

He rode hard and fast northwards through the wild and desolate mountains, until he saw the sea like burnished lead lying on his left hand.

Then he turned his horse's head away and rode far into the deep heart of the land. But though he knew the way passing well, he could not find the road now, and wandered up and down the lonely moorlands and the dark forest rides, baffled and wearied, heartsick and full of dread.

Thus he wandered, forever seeking the way, and trying this one and that, until all his apparel was worn out, and his body was wasted away and his hair was grown long. And at length, from misery and hopelessness, he grew so weak that he thought that he must die.

Then he descended slowly from the mountains, and thought to find a hermit, to whom he might tell all his misery before he died. But he could not find any harbourage, and so he crawled to a brook in a park, and sat there wondering why this evil fate had been visited upon him, and grieving that now his beloved countess must be in wretchedness and sorrow by reason of his forgetting, and that never more could he hope to see her and tell her how grieved he had been to cause her such pain.

Then in a little while he swooned under the heat of the sun, from hunger and weakness, and lay half in and half out of the brook.

It befell that a widowed lady, to whom the brook and the land belonged, came walking in the fields with her maids. And one of them saw the figure of Sir Owen and, half-fearful, she went up to him and found him faintly breathing.

The widow lady had him taken into the farmstead of one of her tenants, and there he was tended carefully until he came again to his senses. And with the good care, meat, drink, and medicaments, he soon began to thrive again.

He asked the man of the house who it was that had brought him there.

"It was our Lady of the Moors," said the man sadly. "And though she is herself in sore straits and narrowly bestead by a cruel and oppressive earl, who would rob her of these last few acres, yet she hath ever a tender heart for those in greater distress than herself."

"It grieves me," said Sir Owen, "that the lady is oppressed by that felon earl. He should be hindered, and that sternly."

"Ay," said the man, "he would cease his wrongful dealing if she would wed him, but she cannot abide the evil face of him."

Ever and anon the Lady of the Moors sent one of her maidens to learn how the stranger was progressing, and the maiden came one day when Sir Owen was quite recovered, and she was greatly astounded to see how comely a man he was, and how straight and tall and knightly was his mien.

As they sat talking, there came the jingle and clatter of arms, and, looking forth, Sir Owen saw a large company of knights and men-at-arms pass down the road. And he inquired of the maiden who these were.

"That is the Earl Arfog and his company," she said sadly. "And he goeth, as is his wont, to visit my mistress, and to insult her, and to treat her unmannerly, and to threaten that he will drive her from the one remaining roof tree she possesses. And so will he and his knights sit eating and drinking till night, and great will be my lady's sorrow that she hath no one to protect her."

They talked of other things for a while, and then said Sir Owen:

"Hath thy mistress a suit of armour, and a destrier in her possession?"

"She hath indeed, the best in the world," said the maiden, "for they belonged to her late husband, the Lord of the Moors."

"Wilt thou go and get them for me for a loan?" he asked.

"I will," said the maiden, and wondered what he would do with them.

Before the day was passed there came a beautiful black steed, upon which was a beechen saddle, and a suit of armour, both for man and horse. And Owen armed himself, and when it was dark he went forth and stationed himself under a great oak, where none could see him.

When the earl, elated with insolence and wine, came back that way, shouting and rolling in his saddle, Owen marked him as he rode. He dashed out at him, and so fiercely swift was he, and so heavy were his blows, that he had beaten to the earth those who were beside the earl, and the earl he had dragged from the saddle and laid him across his crupper, before the earl's companions were aware of what was done.

As the countess sat in hall, sadly thinking how soon the craven earl would thrust her out of her home, there came the beat of hoofs, the great door of the manor swung open, and a tall knight in black armour strode in, thrusting another knight before him.

"I am the stranger whom ye rescued from death, my lady," said Sir Owen, bowing, "and this is thy rascally enemy, the Earl Arfog. Look you, churl in armour," said Owen, shaking the other till every piece of steel upon him rattled, "if you do not instantly crave pardon humbly of this lady, and restore unto her everything you have robbed of her, I swear to you, by the name of the great Arthur, I will shear your head from your shoulders."

In great terror the earl, who, since he oppressed women, was an abject coward, sank upon his knees and promised to restore all he had ever taken from the lady, as a ransom for his life; and for his freedom he would give her many rich farms and manors, and hostages as surety.

Two more days Sir Owen stayed at the manor to see that these things were duly performed, and then he took his departure.

"I would that you could stay with us," said the lady, who was sweet and gentle, with kindly eyes and a soft voice.

"Lady, I may not," said Sir Owen. "I seek my dear wife and her dominions, and have been seeking them these many months. But I fear me some evil necromancy hath been reared against me, so that I may not find her again, and she must be in much sorrow and misery in my absence. And if I never see my lady in life again, yet must I seek for her until I die."

"What is the name of your lady and of her dominions?" asked the lady.

"She is the Lady Carol, Countess of the Fountain," answered Owen. "Do you know aught of her, and in which direction her lands lie?"

The lady caused inquiries to be made, and her foresters said that the lady's lands of the fountain lay fifteen leagues beyond the mountains, and that his way lay through the Wisht Wood, the Dead Valley, and the Hill of the Tower of Stone, and only a knight of great valour could hope to win through these places, which were the haunt of warlocks, wizards, and trolls, and full of magic, both black and white.

Joyously Sir Owen mounted his horse, glad to learn that now he might hope to find his countess again, and the Lady of the Moors wished him Godspeed, and looked after him long and earnestly till he disappeared into a forest.

He journeyed three days through the Wisht Wood, and many were the dreadful things he saw and heard there, and great eyes, green and black and yellow, peered at him from the bushes as he sat over his fire at night. But he clasped the blue stone which the troll Decet had given him, and naught could hurt him.

On the fourth day he descended into the Dead Valley. And here he was like to die, for the air was so thick, and filled with the poison of witches who haunted there at night, that if he had not ridden fiercely and fast through its deathly vapours, he could not have reached the slopes of the Hill of the Tower of Stone, where the air was pure and blew out of the clean sky.

Long and toilsome and exceedingly steep was the way up the side of the mountain, and many times Sir Owen thought he would have to sink down for sheer weariness. And it was dark night before he reached level ground, and he could not see where he was or what place he was in.

But having said his prayers, fed his horse, and eaten from the scrip which the Lady of the Moors had made up for him, he lay down beside a thick bush and slept soundly.

Many were the terrible sounds that came from far below, where fierce witches and warlocks battled and tore each other in the Dead Valley; but Sir Owen was so overcome that he awoke not. And just as the morning broke, a great serpent issued from a rock near where he lay and crept towards him to slay him.

Sir Owen still lay asleep, and the huge creature reared his head to strike. But at that moment a great brown bear, that had sat near Sir Owen through the night, leaped forward with a fierce growl, and gripped the serpent by the head. And the serpent hissed and writhed.

With the noise of the struggle Sir Owen awoke, and marvelled to see the two animals closed in deadly combat. He drew his sword and slew the serpent, and having wiped his weapon, he went to his horse and led it forward.

But the bear followed him and played about him, as if it was a greyhound that he had reared. And Sir Owen stopped and said:

"This is a marvel, sir bear, that you would follow me gambolling, because I slew the serpent. Are ye so grateful, then, or is it that ye have been captive unto men, and are fain to see one in this desolate waste?"

The bear gambolled as if pleased to hear him speak, and went on a little way and looked back as if to see that the knight was following. And when Sir Owen would go another way, the bear stamped his foot, so that at length, with a laugh, Sir Owen said he would follow the way he wished.

Wild was that place and rocky, full of great boulders and with deep pits obscured by bushes. Full irksome was it to pass through, for besides the slipperiness of the way, the sun shone pitilessly down, and its heat was returned by the hard rocks. And there was no water.

If the bear had not led him, Sir Owen would have missed his footing many times, and been hurled down one of the many chasms that yawned everywhere.

At length Sir Owen became faint with hunger, and he dismounted and tethered his horse to a leafless thorn. Then he went and lay in the shadow of an enormous rock that reared up like a huge tower. And the bear looked at him for a little while and then disappeared.

Sir Owen wondered sadly whether he should ever win through the perils that encompassed him, and see again the lady whom he loved best in all the world. And weak with famine, he doubted whether he should not leave his bones to bleach beside the great rock.

Then he looked, and saw the bear coming towards him, and it carried a roebuck, freshly slain, which it brought and laid at Sir Owen's feet. The knight sprang up with a glad cry, and struck fire with his flint, and the bear brought dried sticks, and soon a fire was blazing, and juicy collops were spluttering on skewers before the fire.

When Sir Owen had finished eating, the bear seemed to wish him to follow him, and the bear led him to a brook in a little green patch, and there the knight quenched his thirst.

By now it was twilight again, and Sir Owen made up the fire and prepared himself to slumber; and the bear lay down beside him and blinked at the fire like a great dog.

The knight saw the sun far in the west dip beneath a cloud, and a cold wind blew across the waste. And then he heard a sigh from somewhere behind him, and then another and again a third. And the sound seemed to come from within the towering stone.

He cried out, "If thou art a mortal, speak to me! But if thou art some evil thing of this waste, avaunt thee!"

A voice, soft and sad, replied, "A mortal I am indeed, but soon shall I be dead, and as cold as the stone in which I am imprisoned, unless one man help me."

The stone was so thick that the voices of both were muffled, so that neither recognised the other.

Sir Owen asked who it was who spoke to him.

"I am Elined, handmaiden to the Lady of the Fountain," was the reply.

"Alas! Alas!" cried Sir Owen. "Then if thou art in so sore a pass, thou who wouldst guard my lady till thy death, surely my dear lady is in a worse pass? I am Owen, who won her in the jousts, and by evil fortune left her for more than a night and a day, and never have I been able to find my way back to my beloved lady. Tell me, damsel, what evil hath befallen her, and how I may avenge it instantly?"

"Glad I am, Sir Owen," cried the maiden joyfully, "to hear thou art still in life, and that thou wert not faithless, as the evil Sir Dewin said thou wert. 'Twas his evil magic that changed the landscape as thou didst ride, and so hid the way from thee. Naught evil hath my lady suffered yet, nor never will now if thou canst save me this night. But he hath changed my brother, Decet of the Mound, into some monstrous shape, and me he hath chained within this stone. Yet for seventy-seven days my magic kept him from doing further ill to my lady and me; and that space ends this midnight. Therefore am I glad that the good fate hath led thee here. Now go thee and hide, until Sir Dewin and his two evil sons come. And when they would make a fire whereon to burn me, do thou cut them down and burn them, for so shall all their evil power be stayed."

Much as Sir Owen wished to ask how his countess had fared through the time of his absence, he stole away, after he had stamped out his fire.

Towards midnight there came a great roaring wind, and a shower of hailstones, and thunder and lightning, and he saw three great black shapes descend from the sky. And he knew that these were the evil wizard knights, Sir Dewin and his two sons. They alighted upon the hill near the Tower of Stone, and took the shapes of men.

Instantly they began to gather wood and to make a huge heap. And Sir Dewin made witchfire, and began to light the pile.

Then Sir Owen crept up in the dark, and the bear went with him. And as the wizard bent to light the fire, Sir Owen raised his sword and chopped off the wizard's head, so that it hopped into the fire.

The bear had gone behind the two sons and now clawed them together, and though they struggled fiercely to get loose, the bear hugged them so tightly that they could not move. And Sir Owen slew them both with his sword.

Then together they heaped the three evil warlocks on the fire and saw them burn. And when the last of them was consumed in the fierce heat of the fire, Sir Owen felt a hand seize his, and, turning, he marvelled to see Decet the Moundman smiling into his face.

"Good luck hath been thy guide, sir knight," said the troll, "and thou hath released me from the evil dumb shape into which this wizard did change me. But all the happiness that hath been thine and shall be thine again, thou owest to thy constancy and thy devotion to the lady thou lovest best."

"Glad am I, good troll, to see thee again," said Sir Owen, "and glad shall I be to see my dear lady again. Now let us release her faithful handmaiden, thy sister."

With the master words which move the living rock, the troll caused the stone to open, and Elined stepped forth, exceeding glad to see Sir Owen and her brother again, and to feel the free air upon her cheeks.

When it was morning they went on their way with great gladness. And when they reached the City of the Fountain, the countess could not speak for joy, and all her sadness fled, and in an hour her happiness was greater than her misery had been for all the months of her sorrow.

The bells throughout the city were set ringing, and there was pub-
lic rejoicing through the length and breadth of the land, for all were
glad exceedingly that their dear lady was happy, and that their lord was
come to his own again.

Never again did Sir Owen leave his lady while she lived. Elined
was advanced to the place of Chief Lady of the Household, while Decet
was made Head Huntsman, because he loved the forest, and knew the
ways of every bird and beast that lived therein.

IX

Of Sir Lancelot and the Fair Maid of Astolat

IT BEFELL ON A TIME THAT KING ARTHUR MADE PROCLAMATION
of a great joust and tournament which should be holden at Camelot fifteen days after the Feast of the Assumption. The noise of it went forth throughout all the king's dominions, and knights and barons and earls and kings made haste to get them ready to go thither.

Sir Lancelot had but lately been sore wounded, and told the king that he could not hope to be at the joust, for fear that his wound might break forth afresh. The king was much aggrieved thereat, and would fain have made proclamation to put off the joust, but that many knights were already set forth from distant places, and great would be the disappointment.

Therefore, on the day that the king was to journey from London to Camelot, he set forth with a heavy heart. For though he knew there would be many a brave onfall and stout bickering, yet, as Sir Lancelot had become the most valiant knight in all the island of Britain, the king had greatly desired that the knight should show how he excelled all the doughty warriors that would come from all parts.

When all the knights had gone from the king's palace in London, Sir Lancelot pined in the great hall. The chatter of the ladies and the tricks of the pages became irksome to him, and he began to think how merry must be the company of the knights of the Round Table, as they rode through the leafy country ways towards Camelot, with the great Arthur at their head.

"I will see the king's leech," he said to himself, "and bid him give me some medicament that shall strengthen my wound. For I cannot abide that I stay here like some toothless old hound, while his fellows are gone to the hunting."

So Sir Lancelot betook him to the lodging of Morgan Todd, the king's physician, but found that he too had gone with the king.

When Sir Lancelot was turning away, sore aggrieved and angry, the man that had opened the door to him cried:

"Be not vexed, Sir Lancelot, for I wot well you would rather go with the king than nurse that wound of thine. Come down, then, and let me advise thee."

Sir Lancelot, thinking this would be the chief disciple or pupil of Morgan Todd, dismounted, and followed the man that had spoken, who was old and thin and gnarled, with beady black eyes. When he had examined Sir Lancelot's wound, the old man smiled strangely, and said:

"If ye take but common care of thy wound, 'twill not break out again, but your heart was ever bigger than thy wit, sir knight. Thou wilt do more than any other knight, and in thy strength ye may well maim yourself."

"Then I may go to Camelot, to the jousting?" asked Sir Lancelot.

"Ay, ye may go," said the leech. "But hearken. Stay not on thy way at Astolat. If ye do so, ye shall leave so great a wound there on one that will not harm thee, that the ill shall cause thee woe out of all measure."

"Keep thy counsel, good leech," said Sir Lancelot with a laugh. "I hurt none that desire not my hurt. And, for the rest, I will take the adventure that God will send me."

Sir Lancelot set out forthwith, thinking naught of what the leech had said. By eventide he came to Astolat, and, looking about for a lodging, he suddenly remembered the words of the leech.

"I will beg a lodging outside the town," he said, gravely smiling. "So I do not stay in the town, I may escape the ill which the old croaker spoke of."

He saw the manor house of a baron beside the way, and begged a lodging there for the night, which was freely and most courteously granted unto him. The baron was an old man, of reverend aspect, named Sir Bernard, and he welcomed Sir Lancelot warmly, though he knew him not.

At meat they were all very merry, and with Sir Bernard were his two sons, handsome youths, but lately made knights. There was also a young damsel, named Elaine the Fair, the daughter of Sir Bernard; but Sir Lancelot, though he saw how sweet and gentle she was, noted her not overmuch. Neither she nor Sir Lavaine, the younger son, could bear to take their eyes from the face of Sir Lancelot; for there was so magnificent yet gentle an air about the great knight, that they deemed he must be some very brave and noble warrior.

Sir Lancelot told them it was in his mind to go to the jousts at Camelot. Laughingly he turned to Sir Bernard, and said:

"Fair sir, I would pray you to lend me a shield that may not be greatly known, for mine has been too much seen by warriors."

"Sir," replied the old baron, "I will gladly give you your desire, for I am sure you are one of the likeliest knights of the world. This, my eldest son, Sir Tirre, whom you see hath yet the pallor of sickness, was hurt on the day on which the great Sir Tristram of Lyones gave him knighthood, and as he cannot now ride, ye shall have his shield."

"Sir, I thank you," replied Sir Lancelot, "for showing me such friendship."

"And I would crave a service of you," went on Sir Bernard. "My younger son here, Sir Lavaine, is eager to go out with some knight of proved valour and prowess; and as my heart goeth unto you, and believeth ye to be a knight of great nobility, I beseech you that you let him ride with you tomorrow."

"I shall be pleased, indeed, to have the young knight to ride with me," replied Sir Lancelot.

"Would it please you, sir," asked Sir Bernard, "to tell us your name?"

"Not at this time, sir," replied Sir Lancelot, "but if God give me

grace at the jousts, and I win honour there, I will of a surety return
and tell you."

Sir Lancelot, with his nobleness and courtesy, and his tales of fair
ladies and brave knights, so won upon them all, that it was late ere they
each departed to their beds. The maiden Elaine thought that she had
never seen or heard of a knight so full of gentleness, yet withal so mar-
tial of mien, as this stranger who would not tell his name.

In the morning Sir Lancelot made himself ready to depart, and
the maid Elaine lingered long about her brother, and would never say
that she had really buckled the last strap of his armour. Then, when
at length she could keep them no longer, she came up to Sir Lancelot,
with a face all pale and red by turns, yet striving to laugh away her fear.

"Sir," she said, "I wish you noble deeds at the jousts and much
fame. Sir, I have never had a knight wear favour of mine. Therefore,
lord, will you wear a token of mine in your helm for good fortune?"

Lancelot looked down into the lovely face and smiled:

"Fair damsel," he said gently, "if I granted you that, I should do
more for you than ever I have done for any dame or damsel living."

At that she thought he refused, and the tears sprang like jewels
into her blue eyes, and she turned away.

Sir Lancelot was grieved to think his refusal hurt one that seemed
so sweet and gentle. Then he remembered that he desired to go to the
jousts disguised, and he bethought him that if he wore a lady's token in
his helm, no one would recognise him, for all knew that never would
he consent to wear such things in joust or tournament, as was the custom of many knights.

"Stay, fair damsel," he said kindly, "I will grant you to wear a token
of yours upon my helm. Therefore, bring it me."

Instantly the face of Elaine shone with joy and pride as she looked
up quickly at the great steel-clad figure on the horse beside her. Then,
quickly running, she brought what she had in her mind he should wear.

"See," she said, giving it into his hand, "it is a sleeve of mine, of
scarlet samite, embroidered with great pearls."

"I will wear it at the jousts, fair maiden," said he, "for the sake of the kindness you and yours have shown me. And will you keep the shield which is mine own against the time when I shall return? For I will take thy brother's."

"I will keep it in my own room," said Elaine, "and will see that it doth not tarnish."

Then Sir Lancelot and young Sir Lavaine rode forth, each bearing a white shield, as if both were young knights who had not yet done some deed, in memory whereof they could blazon a device upon their shields.

So they rode to Camelot, where they found the narrow streets of the little town packed with the press of knights, dukes, earls and barons come to take part in the jousts. Sir Lancelot got them lodgings with a rich burgess, and so privily and closely did they keep the house that none knew that they were there.

On the day of the jousts the trumpets began to blow in the field where they should be held. King Arthur sat on a great scaffold which was raised at one end, to judge who did best in the jousting. So great was the press of folk, both noble and common, earls and chiefs, that many did marvel to think that the realm of Britain held so many people.

The knights held themselves in two parties and went to either end of the lists. Some called themselves the band of Arthur, and would fight all comers; and among them was Sir Palomides, Sir Conn of Ireland, Sir Sagramore, Sir Kay the seneschal, Sir Griflet, Sir Mordred, Sir Gallernon, and Sir Saffre, all knights of the Round Table. On the other side were the King of Northgales, the King of Swordlands, Sir Galahalt the Proud, and other knights of the north. These were the smaller party, yet were they very valiant knights.

Sir Lancelot made him ready with the others, and fashioned the red sleeve upon his helm. But it was in his mind to see which party fared the worse before he would choose his part; forever Sir Lancelot liked a task which was not easy.

So he rode forth with Sir Lavaine into a little wood upon a knoll, whence they could look into the lists and see the knights hurtle and crash together. Soon they saw the knights of King Arthur's band come against the northern knights, and many of the latter were smitten down. Then he saw how the King of the Northgales and the King of Swordlands with a few knights made a bold and brave stand against the many knights of King Arthur's Round Table.

"See," said Sir Lancelot to Sir Lavaine, "how that company of knights hold out against that great press! They are like brave boars in the midst of the hounds."

"Ye say truth," said Sir Lavaine; "they are indeed brave souls."

"Now," said Sir Lancelot, "if you will help me a little, you may see that great company go back more quickly than they came forward."

"Sir, spare not," said the young knight, "and I will do what I may."

Sir Lancelot spurred forward into the lists, and so fierce was his onslaught and so hard was his blow that with one spear he overthrew Sir Sagramore, Sir Kay, Sir Griflet, and Sir Saffre, and with another spear he smote down five others. Thereupon the northern knights were much comforted, and greeted the strange knight full courteously, though they wondered that he had but a white shield.

Then the band of Arthur's knights took counsel and gathered together Sir Bors, Sir Ector de Maris, Sir Lionel, Sir Blamore, and five others. These were all mighty knights and all were great fighters and close kin to Sir Lancelot. They resolved to rebuke the two stranger knights with white shields whom they knew not; and chiefly him with the lady's sleeve upon his helm did they seek to bring to the dust.

Again the knights hurtled mightily together, and Sir Bors, Sir Ector, and Sir Lionel drove at Sir Lancelot, and so great was their force that they smote Sir Lancelot's horse to the ground. By ill hap, the spear of Sir Bors pierced through his cousin's shield into his side, and the head of the lance broke off and remained in the wound.

Then Sir Lavaine, seeing his friend prone, did mightily assault Sir Mordred, who was on the other side, and hurled him to the ground; and, bringing Sir Mordred's horse to Sir Lancelot, he helped him to mount.

Sir Lancelot was exceeding wroth, and took a great strong spear, and smote Sir Bors, both horse and knight, to the ground; and likewise he served Sir Ector and Sir Lionel, and four other knights. The others retreated, for they feared his great strength.

"I marvel who is that knight that hath the red sleeve in his helm?" said King Arthur to Sir Gawaine, who sat with him.

"Sir," said the other, "he will be known ere he depart."

When the king caused the trumpet to sound the end of the day's jousting, the heralds cried that the prize was to go to the knight with the red sleeve. But when the northern knights came to Sir Lancelot and would have him go to the king and take the prize, he said:

"Fair lords, let me depart, I pray you. For I have bought my victory with my life; and now I would rather have quiet than all the wealth of the world."

Forthwith he galloped away with Sir Lavaine until they came to a great forest; and then Sir Lancelot groaned and said he could no further go, and forthwith he fell from his horse in a great swoon. Sir Lavaine went to find water in the wood, and had to go far ere he found it. But presently he saw a clearing, and there was a little hermitage and a stream running by. Sir Lavaine called the hermit, who was a man full reverend and noble of aspect, and told him how his friend lay in a deathly swoon.

In a little while they had brought Sir Lancelot to the hermitage, where the hermit took out the head of the spear and bound up the wound and gave to the knight a strong cordial. Anon he was refreshed and came to his senses again.

At the lodging of the king in Camelot, men spoke of the jousts, and wondered who might be the knight who had won the prize and who had been injured, as the northern knights had reported. Though King Arthur had it in his mind that it had been Sir Lancelot, he hoped it was not, for it grieved him much to think that Sir Lancelot was so badly wounded.

Next day the court journeyed towards London, and rested for the night at Astolat; and the town being full, it chanced that Sir Gawaine went to the manor of Sir Bernard, which lay just outside the city. When he had dined, the old knight Sir Bernard began to speak to him, and to ask who had done the best at the jousts at Camelot.

Ever since he had arrived, Sir Gawaine had seen how the fair girl, the daughter of the knight, who had attended upon him, was pale and thoughtful; and now she looked white and red by turns as he began to speak.

"There were two knights," said Sir Gawaine, "who each bore a white shield, and one had a red sleeve upon his helmet."

Sir Gawaine saw how the damsel clasped her hands together, and her face lit up with a great light and her eyes were bright and proud.

"And I swear that never saw I so valiant and stout a knight as he," said Sir Gawaine. "For I dare swear that he beat down twenty knights of the Round Table, and his fellow also did well."

"Now, blessed be God," said the fair maid of Astolat, with a great cry of joy, "that the good knight sped so well; for he is the one man in the world whom I have ever loved, and truly he shall be the last man that ever after I shall love."

"Then do ye know his name?" asked Sir Gawaine.

"Nay, I know it not," said Elaine, "nor whence he came. But I know that I love him and none other."

Then they told Sir Gawaine how they had first had knowledge of the strange knight; and the damsel said that he had left her his shield in place of the white one he had taken, so that none should know him. Sir Gawaine begged that she would fetch it from her chamber.

Elaine brought it and drew it from the case of leather in which she had wrapped it, and said, "See, there is no spot of rust upon it, for I have cleaned it with my own hands every day."

"Alas," said Sir Gawaine, when he saw the device upon the shield, "now is my heart full heavier than it hath ever been."

"Why, oh why?" cried Elaine, and stood pale and breathless.

"Is the knight that owneth that shield your love?" asked Gawaine.

"Yes, truly," said the maiden, "I love him"; and then sadly she said, "but would that he should tell me that I was also his love."

"How ever that be," said Sir Gawaine, "you should know that you love the noblest knight in all the world, the most honourable and one of the most worth."

"So thought me ever," said the maid of Astolat, proudly smiling; "for never have I seen a knight that I could love but that one."

"And never hath he borne token or sign of any lady or gentlewoman before he bore thine," said Sir Gawaine.

At these words the maid Elaine could have swooned for very joy, for she deemed that Sir Lancelot had borne her token for love of her. Therefore, she was cast more deeply in love with him than ever.

"But I dread me," went on Sir Gawaine, "for I fear we may never see him in this life again."

"Alas! Alas!" cried Elaine, throwing herself at the feet of the knight, and clutching his arm tightly, while she gazed with terror into his face. "How may this be? Oh, say not—say not that he is is "

She could not say the word, but Sir Gawaine made answer.

"I say not so, but wit ye well that he is grievously wounded."

"Alas!" cried Elaine. "What is his hurt? Where is he? Oh, I will go to him instantly."

She rose, wildly ringing her slender hands.

"Truly," said Sir Gawaine, who, though a great warrior, was a slow talker, and had no thought of the sorrow of the poor maid, "the man that hurt him was one that would least have hurt him had he known. And when he shall know it, that will be the most sorrow that he hath ever had."

"Ah, but say," cried Elaine, "where doth my lord lie wounded?"

"Truly," replied Gawaine, "no man knoweth where he may lie. For he went off at a great gallop, and though I and others of King Arthur's knights did seek him within six or seven miles of Camelot, we could not come upon him."

"Now, dear father," said the maid Elaine, and the tears welled from her eyes, "I require you give me leave to ride and seek him that I love, or else I know well that I shall go out of my mind, for I may never rest until I learn of him and find him and my brother Sir Lavaine."

So the maid Elaine made her ready, weeping sorely, and her father bade two men-at-arms go with her to guard and guide her on her quest.

When she came to Camelot, for two days was her seeking in vain, and hardly could she eat or sleep for her trouble. It happened that on the third day, as she crossed a plain, she saw a knight with two horses, riding as if he exercised them; and by his gestures she recognised him at length, and it was her brother. She spurred her horse eagerly, and rode towards Sir Lavaine, crying with a loud voice:

"Lavaine, Lavaine, tell me how is my lord, Sir Lancelot?"

Her brother came forward, rejoicing to see her, but he asked how she had learned that the stranger knight was Sir Lancelot, and she told him.

"My lord hath never told me who he was," said Lavaine, "but the holy hermit who hath harboured him knew him and told me. And for days my lord has been wandering and distraught in his fever. But now he is better."

"It pleaseth me greatly to hear that," said Elaine.

When Sir Lavaine took her into the room where lay Sir Lancelot so sick and pale in his bed, she could not speak, but suddenly fell in a swoon. And when she came to her senses again she sighed and said:

"My lord, Sir Lancelot, alas, why are ye in so sad a plight?"

Therewith she almost swooned again. But Sir Lancelot prayed Sir Lavaine to take her up and bring her to him. And she came to herself again, and Sir Lancelot kissed her, and said:

"Fair maid, why fare ye thus? It hurts me to see your sorrow, for this hurt of mine is of little account to cause you to grieve in this wise. If ye come to minister to me, why, ye are truly welcome, and ye shall quickly heal me, by the grace of God, and make me whole again."

"I would gladly serve you till you are well again," said the maid.

"I thank you, fair Elaine," replied the knight, "but I marvel how ye knew my name?"

"It was by Sir Gawaine, fair lord," said the damsel, "for he lodged at my father's house and saw your shield."

Sir Lancelot's heart was heavy at these words, for he foreboded sorrow from this adventure.

Afterwards the maid Elaine never went from Sir Lancelot, but watched him day and night, and gave such comfort to him that never woman did more kindly nurse a wounded man than she.

Sir Lancelot was full courteous and kindly in his turn, never giving more trouble than he could avoid; both were of good cheer and merry together, for Sir Lancelot deemed not as yet that the maid loved him deeply, and the maid was glad to be with him and to do him all the service that she could.

Then in a little while came Sir Bors, the knight who had wounded Sir Lancelot, who was also his cousin, and Sir Bors lamented sorely that his had been the arm that had given his kinsman so sore a wound. But Sir Lancelot prayed him not to grieve, and said:

"I have that which I deserved, for in my pride I was nigh slain, for had I given thee, my cousin, warning of my being there, I had not been hurt. Therefore, let us leave off speaking thereof, and let us find some remedy so that I may soon be whole."

"Fair cousin," said Sir Bors, as he leaned on the bed, speaking in a low voice, "there is one nigh thee, or I am much in error, that will not know whether to be glad or sorry when thou shalt be hale enough to ride away."

"What dost thou mean?" asked Sir Lancelot.

"Is this she that is so busy about thee—is she the lady that men call the Lily Maid of Astolat?"

"She it is," replied Sir Lancelot, "and kindlier nurse hath never man found."

"It is easy to see she loveth her task," said Sir Bors, and he was full of pity and kindness foi' the fair meek maid, "seeing that she loveth thee."

"Nay, man, nay, that cannot be," said Sir Lancelot, half-angry, half-denying. "She hath come to me because I was sick, and because I wore her token in my helm, that's all."

"Wise art thou in all knightly prowess, Sir Lancelot," said Sir Bors, "and full courteous and kindly art thou to all ladies and damsels. But I fear thou knowest not the heart of this fair maid. For it hath been easy for me to see by her looks this way how she is jealous of my talking to thee, and I know from her diligence about thee that she loveth thee with all her heart."

"If that be so, then, by Heaven, I sorrow it is so," said Sir Lancelot heavily. "And I must send her from me forthwith."

"Why shouldst thou do that, fair cousin?" said Sir Bors. "She is a passing fair damsel and well taught, and I would that thou couldst love her in return. But as to that, I may not nor dare not counsel thee. For I know that love blows where it listeth and will be forced by none."

"It repenteth me sorely," said Sir Lancelot, and he was heavy in spirit thereafter, and was eager to get whole again and to go away.

In four or five days he made a plot with Sir Bors, that he should rise and clothe himself in his armour and get upon his horse, and in this way show to the hermit and to the maid Elaine that indeed and in truth he was strong enough to ride forth. Therefore they made excuses and sent both the hermit and the maid away into the forest to gather herbs.

Sir Lancelot rose from his bed, and Sir Bors helped him to put on his armour and to mount his horse. And so eager was the knight to feel that he was hale again that he put his lance in rest and spurred his horse, and so furiously did he ride across the mead, as if he rode at a knight, that of a sudden his wound broke out again, and he swooned and fell from his horse to the ground.

Sir Bors and Sir Lavaine made great sorrow and dole as they raised him and carried him back to the hermitage. It befell that Elaine, who had not gone far, heard their cries and came running swiftly, and seeing Sir Lancelot borne between them pale as with death, she cried and wept and kneeled beside him, and put her arms about his neck and kissed him many times, and called to him to wake him.

"O traitors that ye are," she cried to her brother and to Sir Bors, "why have ye let him go from his bed? Oh, if ye have slain him I will denounce you for his murderers."

Therewith came the holy hermit and was right wroth, and they put Sir Lancelot to bed again, and the hermit stanched the wound and gave the knight a cordial, so that he awoke out of his swoon.

"Why have you put your life in jeopardy thus?" asked the hermit.

"For that I weary of being here," said Sir Lancelot, "and I would ride forth again."

"Ah, Sir Lancelot," said the hermit, "your heart and your courage will never be done till your last day. But now ye must do as I command, and stay till I say ye are hale again."

Soon after this Sir Bors departed, and the hermit promised that if he came back in a month, Sir Lancelot would be ready to depart with him. Thus Sir Lancelot stayed in the hermitage, and ever did the fair maid Elaine labour with diligence day and night to heal and comfort him, and to keep the time from wearying him. And never was child meeker to her parent, nor wife kinder to her husband, nor mother sweeter and more tender to her child, than Elaine was to Sir Lancelot.

The knight sorrowed that this was so; and he ever bore himself courteous, but not familiar in speech, for it grieved him that he had no love in his heart for her, however deep might be her love for him.

When the month was over, Sir Bors returned and found Sir Lancelot walking about the forest, hale and strong again and eager to be riding.

In a day they all made them ready to depart from the hermit, and to go to King Arthur's court, which was then in London. The Lily Maid went with them, sad that all her loving care was now ending, but glad to see the noble air with which Sir Lancelot bestrode his horse, and thankful that sometimes, as they rode upon their way, he turned to her smiling gravely, and spoke of the bright sunlight, the birds and trees they saw, and the company and travellers they passed.

Then they came to Astolat, and Sir Bernard gave them all great welcome, and they were well feasted and well lodged.

On the morrow, when they should depart, the maid Elaine was pale and very quiet, until Sir Lancelot came into the hall to say farewell. Then the maid, bringing her father and her two brothers with her, went up to Sir Lancelot and said:

"My lord, now I see that ye will depart. But oh, do thou have mercy upon me, for I must say that which damsels and gentlewomen are not used to say."

Sir Lancelot with grave sad face looked at her and knew what she would say, and in very heaviness of spirit replied:

"Lady, it grieves me that I have unwittingly put such grief upon you."

"O fair and gracious knight, suffer me not to die for love of you," cried Elaine, and looked most piteously and wanly upon him. "Oh, I would have none but you to be my husband."

"Fair damsel," replied Sir Lancelot, "heavy is my grief to refuse you, but I have not turned my mind to marriage."

"Alas," said Elaine, and smiled sadly, "then there is no more to be said."

"Fair maid, I would that you will seek some knight more worthy of you," said Sir Lancelot. "When I am gone, do you set your heart upon some friend or kinsman; and for all the kindness ye have shown me, I will settle upon you a thousand pounds yearly."

"Oh, of all this," said the Lily Maid, "I will have none; for if ye will not love me, wit ye well, Sir Lancelot, my happy days are done."

"Say it not, fair maid," said the knight, "for many years and much love should be yours."

But with a cry Elaine fell to the ground in a swoon, and her gentlewomen bore her into her chamber and sorrowed over her.

In great heaviness Sir Lancelot would depart, and went to his horse to mount it; and Sir Lavaine went with him.

"What would you do?" asked Sir Lancelot of him.

"What should I do," said Sir Lavaine, "but follow you, unless you drive me from you?"

"I cannot do that, so come with me," said Sir Lancelot.

Then came Sir Bernard unto the knight, lifting his grey head and wrinkled and reverend face to Sir Lancelot as he bestrode his horse, and said:

"Sir, I think my daughter Elaine will die for your sake. Forever was she quiet, but strong in mood and of a very fond heart."

"It must not be," said Sir Lancelot, "but do thou cheer her, and when I am gone she will forget me. Never did I do or say aught but

what a good knight should, and never made as if I cared for her. But
I am right sorry for her distress, for she is a full fair maid, good and
gentle, and sweet of voice and mood."

"Father," said Sir Lavaine, "my sister Elaine doeth as I do. For since
I first saw my lord Lancelot, I could never depart from him, nor never
will if I may follow him."

Night and day did the fair maid Elaine sorrow in silence, so that
she never slept, ate, or drank. At the end of ten days her ghostly father
bade her leave such grief and change her thoughts.

"Nay," she said, "I may not, and I would not if I could. And I do no
sin to love the most peerless knight in all the world, the most gentle
and courteous of men, and the greatest in all nobility. Therefore, as I
know I may not live, do thou shrive me, good father, for I must needs
pass out of this world."

Then she confessed her sins and was shriven. And anon she called
her father and her brother, Sir Tirre, and begged that they would do as
she desired as to her burial, and they promised.

In a little while she died, and a letter was put into her cold hand,
and she was placed in a fair bed, with all the richest clothes she had
about her. Then they carried her on the bed in a chariot, slowly, with
many prayers and with much weeping, to the Thames, and there they
put her and the bed in a barge.

Over all the bed and the barge, except her fair face, was placed
a cloak of black samite, and an old and faithful servant of the house
stepped into the barge to guide it.

They let it go from them with great grief, and the aged man steered
it down the river towards London, where was the court of Arthur.

It happened that, as the king and his queen were looking from a
window of the palace which looked upon the Thames, they saw the
black barge, and marvelled what it might mean.

The king made the barge to be held fast, and took the queen's
hand, and with many knights went down to the water's edge, and
there they saw a fair gentlewoman lying on a rich bed, and she lay as
if she slept.

The king took the letter gently from the fair hand which held it, and went into his court, and ordered all his knights to assemble, and then opened the letter and read what was written. The words were these:

"Most noble knight, my lord Sir Lancelot du Lake, now hath death come to me, seeing that you would not give me your love. Yet do thou do this little thing I ask, now that I am dead, for I ask thee to pray for my soul and to bury me, and think of me sometimes. Pray for my soul and think of me, as thou art a knight peerless and most gentle."

Sir Lancelot heard it word by word and went pale as ashes, so that men marvelled to see his sorrow. When it was finished, he said:

"My lord, King Arthur, wit ye well that I am right heavy for the death of this fair damsel. God knoweth that I was never causer of her death by my will, as her brother Sir Lavaine here will avouch for me. She was both fair and good, and exceeding kind to me when I was wounded; but she loved me out of all measure, and of that I was sore heavy."

"Ye might have loved her," said the queen, weeping for sorrow at the hapless fate of one so fair and fond.

"Madam," said Sir Lancelot, "I could not be constrained to love her, but I sorrow for her death exceedingly."

"Truth it is," said the king, "that love is free and never will be forced, for all the prayers that may be said to it. But thou wilt of thy worship bury this fair maid, Sir Lancelot?"

"That will I do," said the knight, "and in all richness and solemnity."

Thus was it done, and all the knights of the Round Table sorrowfully followed the body of the fair Elaine to the grave.

On her tomb in letters of gold both thick and deep were set the words:

HERE LIETH THE BODY OF ELAINE,

THE LILY MAID OF ASTOLAT,

WHO DIED OF A PASSING GREAT LOVE.

X

How the Three Good Knights Achieved the Holy Grail

NOW THE TIME DREW NIGH WHICH HAD BEEN FORETOLD BY
Merlin, before he had been snared by a greater wizardry than his, and
buried alive beneath the great stone in the forest of Broceliande.

He had prophesied that, with the coming of King Arthur, the island
of Britain should grow in strength and fame, and her knights should be
more valiant and pure in word and deed than the knights of any other
land. But that, in a little while, they would become proud, and finding
that none could withstand them, they would use their strength evilly.

To the court of King Arthur, as he sat in London, came tidings of
how his barons warred with each other in remoter parts of his dominions, seizing the strong castles of each other, putting one another to
death, and forsaking the ways of the Holy Church of Christ and turning to the idolatry of the old British pagans, some of whom still lurked
and performed their evil rites in the desolate and secret places of the
forests and the hills.

The heart of the king was heavy as he sat thinking, and he wondered why this evil was entering into the hearts of his knights and barons. He resolved to take good counsel, and therefore commanded his
clerk to come to him and bade him write down all his thoughts.

Then he gave the letter to a trusty knight, named Sir Brewis, and
bade him take it to the Archbishop of Britain, where he sat, an old and

feeble man, in his great cathedral of St. Asaph, far on the verge of the western sea. He was the king's kinsman, and already known for his great sanctity as St. David. In a month the knight brought back the answer, which was in these words:

"The time draws nigh for the trial and testing of Britain. Three good knights shall come to you, and you must pray that their spirit shall spread like fire in the hearts of all your knights. You shall have all my prayers, dear kinsman, and I bid you say to all your knights, 'Watch and Pray.'"

A few days later, when the king sat in hall before the great fire, for it was passing cold and the wintry wind snarled at the windows, the great door was flung open, and into the hall came three men bearing a wounded knight in armour upon his shield. When they had set him down, the knights that were with the king knew him for Sir Kay the seneschal, and Sir Kay looked sourly about him, and bade those that carried him take him to his pallet and fetch a leech, and not stand gaping like fools.

"How now," said Sir Gawaine, "who hath tumbled thee, Sir Kay?"

"A fool whose head I will rase from his shoulders when I am hale again," snapped Sir Kay, as he was borne away to his bed.

Then into the hall came a troll, and after the troll came a knight dressed all in white armour, who, going towards the king, knelt at his feet.

"Sir," the knight said, "I would that ye make me a knight."

"Of what lineage have ye come?" asked the king.

"I am the only son left to my mother," replied the knight, "and she is the widow of Earl Evroc of the Wolds."

"Ah," said the king, and frowned, "was he one of those turbulent lords of the north that now slay and war as if they were kin to the pagans, and threaten to bring ruin into my kingdom?"

"Nay, lord," said the young knight, "my father hath been dead these twenty years."

"Then what is your name? What have ye done to deserve knighthood?" asked the king, who was angry at the hurt his old friend and foster-brother Kay had received.

"Sir, I am Perceval who slew the Dragon Knight, and I am not yet made a knight." All those that stood there cried out in joy, and King Arthur raised the young knight from his knees and kissed him on both cheeks.

"Fair young warrior, I knew ye not," said the king, "and I repent me my churlish speech. We all have heard your great deeds, and much have I longed to see ye, and many reproaches gave I to Sir Kay, whose churlish manner thrust you from my hall."

"Sir," said Perceval, when he had clasped the hands of the knights, all of whom were eager to know him, "I vowed that I would not come to you until that I had avenged the blow which Sir Kay had given to my good friend Tod, who is my squire, and good fortune brought Sir Kay to me, or perhaps it was the will of Heaven. For as I came riding hitherwards this morning, I saw in the snow where a hawk had torn a thrush, and the blood lay on the whiteness of the ground. I stopped and gazed upon it, for I thought of the white life of Christ who gave His blood to save us all. Then I wondered whether the blood that He had shed upon the cruel Cross would ever be so pitiful a thing in men's minds that this dear Britain of ours would be rid of the evil which seems to be creeping into it, and in place thereof would turn as white as the sheets of snow that now lay over all the fields and ways. As I thought thus, I sank deeper and deeper in my thoughts. Suddenly I felt one strike me on the arm with the flat of his sword. I turned and saw a knight, who asked me why I gaped like a mooncalf at the torn bird. I told him it was my pleasure so to do. He asked if it was my pleasure to have to do with him, but I said I would liefer pursue my thoughts again. Nevertheless, he would not let me in quiet, and I drew my sword and beat him in my anger to the ground. When my squire unlaced his helm he knew him for Sir Kay, and told some passing men to bear him unto the court. So have I punished him both for the insult to my friend and squire and to myself."

Men marvelled at the quiet speech and gentle looks and manners of one whose fame for great deeds was in all men's mouths; and Sir Gawaine said:

"Of a truth, young chieftain, it had served Sir Kay rightly if ye had slain him, and he should thank thee for sparing him."

The other knights agreed that Sir Kay had done most unknightly in thus picking a quarrel with one who had not offended, and he had merited defeat.

Thereupon King Arthur knighted Perceval, and they made him great cheer and welcome; and the king knew in his heart that this was one of the three good knights whom St. David had spoken of, and he wondered who were the other two.

It chanced that seven nights before, the good Sir Bors had fared forth from the court of Arthur to seek knightly adventures. And his spirit was joyful as he rode, for he felt that some great adventure was to come to him, howbeit he knew not why he felt this was to be.

Northward he fared through the land, and the snow had not yet fallen, but so mild was the season that men's thoughts had stirred towards spring. For many days he journeyed and the ways were more lonely, the country more desolate, the rocky hills more bare. He wondered why it was that the land seemed so forsaken, as if the folk had long since left the fields to become solitary wastes.

At length it befell that one evening he could find no place wherein to shelter for the night; there was no hermit's cell nor castle nor knight's hold through all the way by which he had come that day. Towards twilight he came upon a wide moor, and the cold moon peered at him over the distant mountains. Far in the midst of the waste he saw a great pile, as of a castle, and pricked his horse towards it.

It was indeed a castle, but its walls were broken and mossy, as if long years had passed since it housed fire and gay company. He rode over the drawbridge into the great courtyard, and the echo of his horse's hoofbeats was the only sound that greeted him.

He sought the upper chambers, and found in one a rough bed of fern leaves, and, having supped from the scrip he carried with him, he composed himself to sleep, glad that at least a roof and thick walls shielded him from the freezing cold which now swept over the land.

Forthwith he slept; but at midnight he awoke and found it was deeply dark, and looking to the arrow slit in the wall he sought some friendly star. As he looked, a great red light burst through, and with that there came, thrusting fiercely, a great spear like a long flame, which darted at him, and then stayed just before him. The point of it burned blue and dazzling.

As he lay marvelling, the spear went back a space; then he grasped his sword that lay beside him, but before he could defend himself the flaming spear dashed forward again and smote him in the shoulder.

Then the spear went back and the chamber was deep dark again, and for very pain Sir Bors lay and groaned. Nor could he sleep more that night. When it was dawn he arose, thinking to ride forth, but when he went down into the courtyard to saddle his horse in the stable, he marvelled to see that where there had been an open ruined gateway the night before was now a great black oaken door, spiked and bolted.

For a long time he essayed by every means to get himself out of that castle, but he could not find a way. Yet never did he hear or see aught that showed that anyone lived there. Many times he went throughout the place, but never found aught but ruin and emptiness, and the dust and darkness of long neglect everywhere.

When three days had gone, Sir Bors was faint with the pain of his wound and the hunger with which he suffered. Then, as he sat beside his horse in its stall, he suddenly heard the clank of armour, and going forth into the courtyard saw a knight all armed, with his shield on his shoulder and his sword naked in his hand.

Without a word the stranger darted at him, and hardly did Sir Bors have time to dress his shield; and then they lashed mightily at each other, and thrust and hewed sorely. Thus for half the day they fought, and so fiercely that soon Sir Bors had many wounds, so that blood oozed from the joints of his armour. But the other knight seemed to be unharmed, and never seemed to breathe heavily. Then Sir Bors became extremely wroth, and beat so fiercely upon the other that he pressed him always backward until the stranger was nigh to the door of a chamber which opened into the courtyard; and suddenly he dashed backwards into the chamber and shut the door.

Nor would he come forth, for all that Sir Bors called him coward and recreant. Nor would he answer one word, nor had he said one word since Sir Bors had seen him.

After some time Sir Bors resolved to go back and rest himself beside his horse, for his great wounds burned him sorely; but as he turned, suddenly, without a sound, the stranger knight dashed forth, and struck a felon blow at the good knight's neck. But Sir Bors was aware of him in time and defended himself full well.

So fiercely did Sir Bors lay on, that soon the other was beaten to his knees, and then the good knight rushed at him to hurl him headlong and to slay him. Suddenly the other knight seemed to fall together as if dead; but the armour sounded hollow as it fell, and Sir Bors marvelled.

Swiftly he hacked the fastenings of the helm and tore it from the neck armour. Then a great fear seized and shook him. The armour was empty!

He knew then that he had fought with a demon. He crossed himself and prayed, and weak with deadly fear and his wounds, he went into the stall and sat beside his horse, and marvelled how he could win with life from the fell power that seemed to hold him prisoner.

Suddenly, from a dark cavernous hole in the dungeons, came a great boar, with curving tusks keen as sword-blades, and rushed at Sir Bors full fiercely. Hardily did the knight defend himself from the strength and the fierce rushes of the great beast. The boar with its long tusks tore the shield from the grasp of Sir Bors, and slashed his shield arm sorely, and then Sir Bors was wroth, and with a very fierce blow he smote off the boar's head. Immediately thereupon, with the pain of his many wounds and the weakness of his famine, Sir Bors fainted, and lay upon the frozen snow as one dead. For long he stayed thus ere he revived, and then he rose and dragged himself into the stall where lay his horse, half dead with hunger, before an empty manger.

All that night Sir Bors lay in a sad pass, for he thought that now he would never see dawn again in life. He prayed and commended his soul to God, and confessed his sins and prepared himself for death as behoved a good knight; and thereafter he slept sweetly.

At the dawn he awoke, exceeding hungry, and looking forth into the court he had it in his mind to carve meat from the dead boar. But he was astounded beyond measure to find that it was not there. In its place was a great trencher of steaming hot collops of meat, and toasted bread, with hot milk in great plenty.

Sir Bors ran towards the food, and so ravenous was his hunger that he would have devoured it instantly. But he bethought him before he had placed any of it to his lips, and dropping it he crossed himself and ran back into the stall and tried not to look forth. He knew that the food was placed there by some fell fiend or demon to tempt him, and if he ate of that unholy food, his soul would be forever lost.

Anon sweet voices sounded in the courtyard as if to attract him forth, and the smell of the hot food was wafted strongly into the stable. The fiends themselves could not enter, for there was a horse-shoe hung in the proper way upon the lintel of the door, and, moreover, Sir Bors had stuck his sword-point in the ground, and the holy sign of the cross prevented the evil things from crossing the threshold.

All that day did Sir Bors lie half dying, while the fiends tempted him, but the knight was too strong and manful of soul to yield, and would liefer die than become the slave of the powers of the Netherworld.

Then in the twilight he commended his soul to God, for he felt near to death. When he had finished his prayer, he heard great and horrible cries in the court as of rage and disappointment. Then came an old man at the door of the stable, white of hair and very reverend; and he came and put his hand upon Sir Bors' head and spoke mildly and said:

"Good and faithful knight, sorely tried have ye been, and now you shall have no more adventures here. Full worshipfully have ye done and better shall ye do hereafter. And now your wounds shall be healed and ye shall have good cheer until tomorrow."

Therewith there was all manner of sweetness and savour in the place, and Sir Bors saw as in a mist a shining vessel borne by a wondrous maiden. He knew that this was the Holy Grail; and he bowed his head, and forthwith he was whole of his wounds.

On the morrow he departed after a night's sweet sleep, and rode to Arthur's court and told of his adventures.

The king and queen and all the fellowship of the Round Table were passing glad to see Sir Bors whole and well, and they made much of him, for they felt that he would do things of great renown.

Then at the feast of Pentecost went all the court to the minster to hear their service; and when they returned to the palace the king ordered that dinner should be prepared in the hall of the Round Table, for this was one of the days when he was wont to assemble all his knights at a great feast of knighthood.

While they waited for the horn to sound, warning them that the meal was ready, one came running to the king, saying that a thing of marvel had happened. And Arthur went to the hall of the Round Table with his knights, and there in the seats about the great circular board they found letters of gold written, which said, "Here should sit Sir Bedevere," or "Here should sit Sir Gawaine," and thus was the name of a knight written in every seat.

In the Siege, or Seat, Perilous, where twice or thrice a reckless knight had dared to sit, but only to be struck dead by a sudden flashing blow of mystery, there were written the words, "In the four hundredth and fourth and fiftieth year after the passion of our Lord, shall he that shall fill this seat come among ye."

All the knights marvelled and looked each at the other.

"It seemeth me," said Lancelot, "that this is the very day on which this seat shall be filled by him for whom it is appointed, for this is the four hundred and fifty-fourth winter since Christ died on the rood."

It was seen that on each side of the Siege Perilous was written, on the right one, the name of Sir Perceval, and on the left one, the name of Sir Bors.

Then the horn was sounded to dinner, and each knight took the seat appointed for him, and young knights served them. All the sieges round the table were filled except the Siege Perilous.

Men ate and drank soberly, for they felt that an adventure strange and marvellous should happen that day, and so indeed it befell.

For when they had eaten, and the priest was saying in a great silence the grace after meat, suddenly a shrill wind sounded without, and all the doors and windows shut fast. Men looked at each other in the twilight thus caused, and many a face was white with fear.

Then the door opened and an old and reverend man entered, white of beard and head, and clothed also in white; and Sir Bors knew him for the same who had come to him at the Castle of Fiends. By the right hand the ancient man brought a young knight, clad in red armour, with a sword at his side, but with no shield.

"Peace be with you, fair lords," said the old man. Then turning to the king he said:

"Sir, I bring here a young knight, the which is of king's lineage, whereby the marvels of this court shall be accomplished, and the trial of this thy kingdom shall be brought to a happy end, if that may be. And the name of him is Galahad."

"Sir," said the king, "ye be right welcome and the young knight with you."

The old man made the young knight unarm him, and he was in a coat of red sendal, and bare a mantle that was furred with ermine. Then was the young man led by the reverend man to the Siege Perilous, and sat him thereon, and men marvelled to see that the death-stroke did not flash like lightning and slay him.

"Sir," said the old man to him, "wit ye well that that is your seat. For you are he that shall surely achieve the Holy Grail, and such of these your fellows as are pure in heart and humble shall achieve it with you."

"Sir," said the king, "if it may be that ye know, will ye tell us what my knights must do to achieve the Holy Vessel, and thus bring peace into my kingdom in place of war? For many of those that are kings and barons under me are warring with each other, and threaten to rend this island of Britain, and some are forsaking Christ and are turning to the evil faith and cruel worship of the pagan gods of Britain. And it goeth to my heart to know this, and I have much dread."

"Sir king," said the old white man, "none may tell you what shall be the end of this quest of the Holy Grail, but I can tell you and these your knights what they must do to save this land from the ruin which doth threaten it. Ye know that the Holy Vessel was that wherein Christ ate the lamb on the Thursday before he was hung upon the Cross. And Joseph of Arimathea did bring it here to Britain, and here hath it been for more than four hundred and fifty winters. And while ye and your kingdom did love Christ and did do His word, the Sangreal stayed within your borders. But now ye war with each other, and are evil livers and full of pride and mastery, and if ye do not repent and stay your dishonour, then shall the Holy Vessel pass from Britain, and ruin and death and civil war shall stalk through the land and leave it desolate."

Having spoken thus, the old man went from the hall, and none stayed him; for too many there were who knew that they had been the evil livers at whom his words had pointed.

Then up rose Sir Gawaine, who was a faithful knight and true man to his king, though a proud one and a hasty. He was filled with sorrow for the ruin that threatened his fair land.

"Now I do here avow," he said, "that tomorrow, without fail, I shall set forth, and I shall labour with all the strength of my body and my soul to go in quest of the Holy Grail, so that if I be fit to see it and to bring it hither, this dear land may be saved from woe."

So hot were his words that many of the better knights rose also, and raising their right hands did make a like avowal; and those that cared not for the quest felt that they must seem to do as the others did, and so made avowal also, though in their hearts they thought more of pride and earthly power.

"Gawaine, Gawaine," cried the king, and the great tears stood in his eyes, "I know ye do right to avow this and to cause these others to avow also; but a great dread is upon me, for I have great doubt that this my fellowship shall never meet again."

"Fear not," said Lancelot, "for bethink ye, my lord, in no better adventure can we find death than in this quest, and of death we are all sure."

On the morrow the knights armed themselves, and bade farewell to King Arthur and his queen, and there was much weeping and great sorrow. And as the knights rode through the streets of Camelot the crowds stood and wept, both rich and poor. All were full of dread to see so many brave knights depart that never more would return.

Having passed through the gates of the town, every knight took the way that he liked best.

Now Sir Galahad was without a shield, and he rode four days without adventure. At evensong on the fourth day he came to an abbey of white monks, and there was given great cheer. He found two other knights of the Round Table at that abbey, the one King Bagdemagus and the other Sir Ulfin; and the three had supper together, and made great cheer one of the other, and spoke of the adventures each would desire to have.

"There is within this abbey, as men tell me, a shield," said King Bagdemagus, "which no man may bear about his neck, but he is injured or slain within three days. Yet tomorrow I will adventure to win it."

In the morning, therefore, after they had heard mass, King Bagdemagus asked the abbot to show him where was the shield. Then was he led to the high altar in the church, and behind it was hung a shield which glowed with shining whiteness, and in the middle thereof was a red cross which seemed to quiver as if it were living.

"Sir," said the abbot, "this shield ought not to hang about any knight's neck unless he be one of the three best knights of the world, and I counsel you to beware."

"No matter," said King Bagdemagus, "I will essay it, for though I am not Sir Lancelot, yet I am a good knight enough."

This he said in his pride, and took the shield and put the strap about his neck, and bade good-bye to the other twain, and so went forth with his squire.

They had not ridden but two miles or more, when at the opening to a wood Sir Bagdemagus saw a knight in white armour on a horse, riding up and down as if to do battle with any that should venture to go into the forest drive.

When the white knight saw him he called out:

"Who art thou? Thou bearest the shield of a knight peerless, but not the armour."

"Who am I?" replied King Bagdemagus scornfully. "I am he that shall give a good account of myself with thee."

With that he levelled his lance and ran furiously upon the knight. But the other stood still, and when the spear-head was nigh his shield, he lightly turned it aside, and as Sir Bagdemagus swept by, the knight, with a quick fierce stroke of his sword, smote him so hard that the blade bit through the mail even to the shoulderbone; whereby Sir Bagdemagus fell to the ground in a swoon.

The white knight called the squire to him and said:

"Bear ye this shield to the young knight, Sir Galahad, who is at the white abbey. Greet him from me, and say that it is for him to wear this shield, and none other. And tell him that I shall meet him erelong, if God wills, and that we shall fare together to that which is appointed for us."

The squire did as he was bidden, and told Sir Galahad of the white knight's words. Sir Galahad asked him what was the device upon the shield of the white knight, and he answered, "A red heart." Then said the young knight, "It shall be even as he saith."

Sir Galahad mounted his horse and rode alone, ever northward, for he knew that the Holy Grail was hidden in a castle somewhere in the north among the warring barons. Many days he rode without adventure, until on a day he came to an old and venerable wood, dark and thick and close, where the moss hung like thick beards from the hoary branches.

There, in a laund or glade in the midmost part of the forest, he found an old and white dame, kneeling before a green cross beside the path, weeping piteously as she prayed and beat her breast.

"What ails ye, lady?" asked Sir Galahad.

"Ah, good knight," said the old dame, and as she rose it was well seen she was of gentle birth, "I weep for that I have lived to see the day when sons of mine shall slay each the other. I have three sons, and all are of the worshipful company of the Round Table. But two are wasteful livers, and have taken from me all that whereby I lived;

and ever hath my youngest boy, Sir Hewlin, withstood their evil ways. Wherefore they hated him. And yesterday did Sir Nulloth and Sir Dew, my elder sons, return, and did quarrel with my dear lad Hewlin. And now I fear they go about to slay him. Oh, if that they kill him, who is the prop and comfort of my old age, I shall surely die."

"Sad it is, lady," said Sir Galahad, and mournful was his mind, "to think that in this dear land of Britain there should be knights that are given to such thoughts of evil as to slay their own kin. Lead me to them, I pray ye."

He set the dame upon his saddle before him, and she led the way through the forest. When they had gone but a mile she started, and stopped the horse, and then they heard the sound of clashing steel. Sadly did that poor lady shriek and cry:

"Ah, they slay him now! My dear son! My dear boy!"

Swiftly Sir Galahad made his horse to leap forward, and in a little while they came upon a great meadow, where two knights on foot were together fighting another single knight with swords. Forthwith Sir Galahad cried with a loud and a stern voice, "Hold, put up your swords, ye evil brothers, that would slay each other!'

All turned at the cry. Then, seeing his mother, the young knight Sir Hewlin threw down his sword. And leaping from Sir Galahad's horse the reverend lady tottered to her youngest son and threw herself upon his breast, and he clasped his mother in his arms.

But the two evil brothers laughed scornfully at Sir Galahad.

"Who art thou, thou knight in red?" they cried. "Thinkest thou to frighten us with thy big words?"

Quickly they mounted their horses and ran upon Sir Galahad together. But the lance of one he received upon his shield, and the weapon snapped in twain; and that of the other he thrust aside and, as the knight thundered by, he brought down his sword, with so fierce and wrathful a stroke, that the head of the knight flew from his shoulders.

Seeing this, the other, who was Sir Nulloth, made haste to throw himself from his horse, and came and kneeled before Sir Galahad, praying mercy.

"I know who ye are," he said. "You are Sir Galahad, the stainless knight, who shall prevail in all thy deeds, and whom no weapon may wound until ye have fulfilled your high destiny. And I will do faithfully any behest ye may lay upon me."

"I will then," said Sir Galahad sternly, "that thou makest peace with thy mother and thy brother here instantly; that thou seekest naught of them till thy dying day, which shall not be far from thee; and that thou goest this day and place thyself in the service of Sir Bedevere, or Sir Uriens upon the coasts, and help to thrust forth the hateful pagan from the land."

The knight swore to do all this, and after he had made his peace with his kindred, he set forth to do Sir Galahad's bidding. And it was as the stainless knight had foretold, for in seven days Sir Nulloth had found death, bravely fighting the pagan pirates.

Sir Galahad went forward, sore of heart to think that such evil was in the land and in men's minds, that any could be found to wish the death of a brother and to care naught for the sorrow of an old mother.

Thus for many months Sir Galahad rode about the land, seeking out the knights who, with their bands of soldiers, fought to wrest from each other land and castles. And ever he strove to make peace between them, and to show them how, while they fought with each other, Christian against Christian, the pagan hordes were let unhindered into the land, ravening, burning, and slaying.

Some of the battling knights did forsake their evil ways, and went to Sir Bedevere and Sir Uriens, with whom they strove to push back the fierce pagans into their long black ships. But many others, so lost to honour and knightliness were they, performed not their promises, and continued to fight each with the other.

So fierce, indeed, was the fighting through all that land, that the peasants forsook the fields and hid themselves; and the pagans from the northern wilderness came over the walls and wandered, killing and burning and robbing. And thus in many parts the crops were not sown or reaped, the wheat stood unharvested and wild, and the grass and weeds grew tall on the very hearths of the poor peasants and husband-men.

The heart of Sir Galahad grew sick, seeing the evil which was come into the land, and he feared that soon the Holy Grail would be taken from the island of Britain, and that then ruin would stalk throughout the length and breadth of the realm.

Once, at the dawning, Sir Galahad looked from the door of a little hermitage where he had passed the night, and was aware of a great company of men coming over the moor. They were all horsed, and were going towards the sea, which was on the right hand, where steep and fearful cliffs fell sheer to the thundering surf beneath. And in their midst he saw they held captive a full noble knight, who seemed wounded, and whose armour was all broken and cracked, as if he had fought valiantly before he had been overcome. Him they were going to hurl headlong down the cliffs.

Sir Galahad began to arm himself full hastily to meet them. But as he dressed his armour he was aware of a knight coming swiftly from a little wood that lay towards the sea-edge. Then was the heart of Sir Galahad exceeding joyful when he saw that the knight was all in white armour, and that on his shield was the device of a heart; for he knew that this was Sir Perceval.

Sir Perceval spurred towards the band of knights, and in a loud voice called on them to release their captive.

"Who art thou?" they cried.

"I am a knight of the Pendragon of these islands, King Arthur," answered Perceval, "and thy captive is my friend, Sir Bors of Brittany."

The others laughed, and spurred furiously towards him. "Slay him!" they shouted. "We own no Arthur here. We are our own lords."

With spears in rest, seven of the knights thundered against Sir Perceval. But by this time Sir Galahad was upon his horse, and, making no outcry, he spurred upon the others.

Three knights he dashed to the ground with one lance-thrust; but then the spear broke. Therewith he drew his sword, and smote in the thick of them so furiously on the left and on the right that they could not abide him, but fled from about Sir Bors, who, wresting a sword from one of them, rode after the seven that were fighting Sir Perceval.

So valiantly and hardily did the three knights lay about them that in a little while their enemies had fled, leaving more than half their number slain.

Then did the three knights make great cheer and welcome of each other, and told each their adventures, and promised that now they were together they would never more part till death should summon them.

So, together, they fared thereafter many months, doing noble deeds, and seeking earnestly to bring men's hearts to turn to friendship and union, so that, united, the lords of the northern lands should turn upon the pagans and destroy them utterly.

It befell that, on a morn, they came to a castle on a great cliff that was in the marches of Scotland; and they heard a horn sound in that castle and much shouting. On the walls thereof were men of a savage aspect, peering and looking down at them. And those men had fair hair, with steel helms which had great horns or wings upon them. On their tall bodies were leather jerkins, with gold chains and many ornaments.

Then Sir Galahad and his friends were aware that on the topmost pinnacle of the castle was a banner, floating and flapping in the morning wind. Black was that banner, and in the midmost part thereof was a golden raven, with beaks open as if it croaked, and its wings were wide thrown, as if it flew over a field of slain men.

They knew that this was a horde of pagans who had wrested this castle from its rightful lord, and that full fierce would be the battle.

Then from a hole or cave beneath a tree near by came a maiden, richly dressed, but sad and pitiable of face and thin of form, as if from long pining.

"Fair lords," said she, "for God His love turn again if ye may, or else here ye will come unto your death."

"Nay," said Sir Galahad, "we will not turn again, for He shall help us in whose service we be entered in. Who are ye, fair damsel, in such painful guise?"

"Fair lords, I am Issyllt," said the maiden, and the tears filled her eyes. "My father is Earl Hernox, the lord of this castle. And whether he be dead by torture at the hands of his hateful enemies and these fiends, or whether he be still alive against a time when they have more leisure to torture him, I know not. But three nights ago came certain knights with a horde of these evil pagans, and stormed this castle, and for all my dear father's valiant deeds, and the prowess of my three dear brothers, they overcame our people, and my three brothers I saw slain before my eyes. When they rushed upon my father, my nurse dragged me away, and we fled hither. But I cannot go away, not knowing whether my father is dead. And if he be dead I care not whether the pagan fiends catch and slay me."

"Fair maiden," said Sir Galahad, "be of good heart, for your father may yet be delivered unto you."

"Ha, fair lord, I know not how that may be," said the maiden. Then, glancing at the castle, she saw the portcullis yawn, and some ten knights rush forth, with pagans besides on foot. Whereat she clasped her hands in terror.

"Now God be with ye, fair lords," she cried. "You have my prayers, and may Heaven grant ye victory. But dread is on me for your deaths, brave knights."

Full wrathful were the three good knights to hear the girl's sad tale, and hard was their rage to hear that Christian knights had leagued themselves with the heathen Saxons so as to get their aid in a private quarrel with the Earl Hernox. Therefore, very joyously did Galahad and Perceval leap forward, lances in rest, against the traitorous knights that rushed towards them from the castle.

Marvellous indeed was it to see the deeds of those three stainless knights that day; for when their lances were broken, they drew their swords, and their wrath, their fierceness, and their valour, none could withstand.

While Sir Bors smote with deadly blows the pagans that swarmed about him, Sir Galahad and Sir Perceval dealt death among the traitorous knights, so that not one was left alive. And seeing this, the fair-haired fierce pagans lost heart. Turning, they wished to flee into the castle and pull down the portcullis.

But swiftly on their heels dashed the three brave knights, and the pagans, never stopping, heard the hoofs of their horses thunder over the drawbridge close behind them. The horde of Saxons took flight into the hall, and there they stood and got breath. But the knights, leaping from their horses, rushed in on foot, and back to back they met the onslaught of the yelling heathens.

Very fierce was the anger in the hearts of the three knights, so that they stayed not their hands even when the pirates gave way and fled from the dreadful place of slaughter. But the knights pursued them wheresoever they tried to hide, and hither and thither about the castle they ran, and in and out the chambers, up and down the stairs, until for very weariness they had perforce to cease.

Then when they beheld the great multitude of pagans they had slain, they were sobered and sad, thinking themselves great sinners.

"Certes," said Sir Bors, "I ween that God willed that we should slay so many, for they must have done great evil."

"They are indeed foul pagans," said Sir Galahad, "and have done great wrong and cruelty in their time to women and little children through this fair land of Britain. But I doubt we have been mad this little while to slay so many mothers' sons as these."

Then from out a secret chamber came a priest, white with great age, and with a countenance that shone marvellously bright; and when he saw how many were slain in that hall, he was abashed. Sir Galahad put off his helm, and the two knights with him, and all three kneeled down and confessed the madness of their sin which had slain even those that craved for quarter.

"Ye have done more than ye wist, brave knights," said the priest, when he had absolved them; "for the evil knights that led these pagan thieves had plotted to gain this castle because of the great and holy treasures that are hidden here. And by a prophecy I know that ye are the three good knights, peerless among all, who should achieve this deed. Therefore, when ye have ordered these slain to be removed, and when the hall shall be garnished and your harness shall be cleaned of the signs of battle, ye shall see that which hath been ordained for ye."

When all had been done as they had commanded, and the place well cleansed and fresh rushes laid along the floor, the three knights sat on a bench, and the Earl Hernox and the maid Issyllt with them, and there was much cheer and rejoicing between them all.

Then the old priest called the earl and his daughter from the room, and left the three knights together. Suddenly, as they sat talking, the doors were shut and the windows were darkened, and a great wind arose with a sad sound, wailing and piping. Then the darkness suddenly went away, and they saw a great light shining in the midmost part of the hall, so bright and strong that hardly could their eyes suffer it. Soon through the light they could see a table of silver, whereon was a wide dish also of silver, marvellously and delicately wrought.

Then the doors opened and they saw angels entering; and two bare candles of wax, and the third held a towel, and in the hand of the fourth was a spear which bled marvellously from the point thereof. Going to the table the angels set the candles and the towel upon it, and the spear was placed beside the shining vessel.

Of a sudden the knights were aware that there sat one beside the table who was marvellously old and white; and he was dressed in the habit of a bishop, and his face was very winning, and a great brightness flowed from it.

On the breast of his robe were words in the Latin tongue, which said, "Lo, I am Joseph, the first bishop of Christendom, who did take our Lord's body down from the cruel rood."

The three marvelled greatly, for that bishop had been dead more than four hundred years. Seeing their looks of perplexity, the bishop smiled sweetly upon them, and said:

"Marvel not, O knights, for though I am now a spirit, I know thy weakness, and have come to aid thee."

Then the bishop took up the shining vessel from the table, and came to Galahad; and the knight kneeled down and took of the food that was within the holy dish. And after that the other two received it.

Of marvellous savour was the food, and like none that they had ever eaten or thought of at any time before.

Then the bishop said to Galahad:

"Son, knowest thou what is this vessel I hold in my hands?"

"Nay, holy man, I know not," replied Galahad.

"It is the holy vessel which men call the Sangreal, out of which our Lord ate the lamb at the feast before He was betrayed to that death upon the rood whereby He redeemed the world, if men would but choose His gentle law."

"It is what we have most desired to see, holy father," said Sir Galahad.

"And it is what, alas, no others in this realm shall ever see," said the bishop; and his countenance, which before had been sweet and gentle, now saddened and was dark. "For this night it shall depart from this land of Logris, so that it shall never more be seen here."

"Alas," cried Galahad and Perceval, "that is great sorrow to hear. O holy bishop and spirit, say not that it means that this land shall be rent in ruin and given up to heathendom again?"

"It must be so," said the bishop sadly. "Christ is not served in gentleness, nor is His law worshipped in this land, where men slay their brothers, rob their kindred, and make treaties with the pagans. And its knights are turned to evil livers, desiring mastery and proud power. Therefore hath Christ sent me to disinherit this land of this holy thing with which He hath honoured it since that time when I brought it here four hundred and fifty-five winters ago."

Hearing these words of doom, Sir Galahad and Sir Perceval wept full piteously for the fate of their country. When they had mourned greatly, they asked if there was no hope of turning the land from its evil ways.

"There is none," said the bishop sorrowfully. "Have ye three not tried manfully these last two years since ye have sought that which ye now see? And all thy labours, thy battling, thy griefs, have they availed aught? No, it is the will of God that in due time this land and this people shall be put into the melting-pot. And when the season appointed shall come, sorrow and death, rebellion and treachery shall stalk through the land, and naught shall stand of its present kingdoms; the pagans shall blot out the holy memory of God and Christ, and shall turn the fanes of prayer into the lairs of wolves, and owls shall rest where hymns of praise have been sung. And no wars of goodly knights may hinder these things of dreadful doom. But I have this message for ye two, Galahad and Perceval; that inasmuch as ye have seen this which you craved to see, and have lived purely and unspotted from pride or evil, thy souls shall go with me when I shall depart. But you, my son," he said, looking at Sir Bors, "still find in your heart the love of kin, and a longing for battle, and so you shall remain, to fight for Christ while yet you are alive."

Suddenly a fierce light came where they sat, so that Sir Bors kneeled as one blinded for a time. When it had passed, he looked and saw where Sir Galahad and Sir Perceval still kneeled, with their hands fitted as if in prayer. But there was naught to see of the holy vessel or the spear, nor was Joseph there.

Then, going to the two knights, he found that they were dead.

Sir Bors knew then that their souls had gone with Joseph and the holy vessel, and had been borne to the heaven for which their pure and humble hearts had yearned while yet they lived.

Then Sir Bors made great sorrow for his two fellows, and knew that never more would he be as joyful or as careless as he had been. With right heavy mood he craved of Earl Hernox to have a grave dug deep in the living rock whereon the castle was builded. This the earl gladly did, and very solemnly the two good knights were buried, and long did Sir Bors mourn over the grave.

In a little while thereafter Sir Bors armed himself, and departed, and after many adventures, rode southwards till he came to Camelot. And there he told the king and such knights as there were how the two stainless knights had achieved the Holy Grail, and how their souls had been taken up with the sacred vessel.

All the court mourned for the two knights, and the king commanded a history to be written of what Sir Bors had told. It was so done, and the book, richly adorned with many coloured letters, was kept in the great treasure-chest in the castle of Sarum.

Ever after Sir Bors was a silent man, for he could not forget the holy and terrible sight he had seen. Of the doom which was coming in due time upon the dear and fair land of Britain, as was prophesied by St. Joseph, he told no man, but kept the words fast locked in his heart.

XI

Of the Plots of Sir Mordred; and How Sir Lancelot Saved the Queen

AFTER THE QUEST OF THE SANGREAL WAS COMPLETED, AND ALL the knights that were left alive had returned to the court of King Arthur, there was great joy among the people, and the king and Queen Gwenevere were passing glad of the remnant that had come home again.

Especially did the queen make much of Sir Lancelot and of Sir Bors his cousin, for they were the two most noble and courteous knights of the Round Table, and none thought of them but as men peerless and beyond compare.

Sir Mordred, who was the king's nephew, was jealous of the two knights, and went about privily among such knights as were his familiars, and spoke sneering words concerning Sir Lancelot and the queen and Sir Bors. Once Sir Mordred said such words in the hearing of his brother Sir Gawaine; but that knight so heavily and wrathfully took him to task, that Sir Mordred knew that Sir Gawaine envied not the two knights, and could never be brought to think other than friendly thoughts of them.

Therefore Sir Mordred hated the two knights more than ever. Of a slight frame was Mordred, but tall, with dark hair, sallow face, and deep-set grey eyes beside a thin long nose. Few loved him, for he was never cheery nor very friendly, and ever seemed to sneer with his thin lips and his cold wolfish eyes.

In a little while strange dark rumours began to go about the court, and it was whispered that so proud had Sir Lancelot become of his fame and prowess, that he harboured evil thoughts against the king, and that he aimed to make a kingdom for himself out of the countries that lay about his own lands of Joyous Gard in the northern marches.

Then fresh rumours went about, and these were the most evil of all. It was said that he sought to slay the king, and wished to make Gwenevere his own queen, and with her he would rule over all Britain.

First, men laughed and passed the rumours with a shrug and a gesture of scorn; but when they were repeated again and again, some began half to believe them. Many said that there must be some truth therein, for Sir Lancelot was ever wending his way to the north country, and fought there many battles and overcame many knights.

But others said this was because many ladies and damsels, who had lost lands and homes and been evilly oppressed by the warring barons in those parts, had heard of his great fame for knightly deeds and noble manners, and came beseeching him to be their champion against those who had robbed them.

Others said that it was but natural that when he was at the court he should speak much to the queen, for he had from the first vowed himself to be her knight, and many deeds of daring and prowess had he done for her.

Yet others there were who believed that what rumour said might be true; and others, who were good and noble knights, sorrowed to think that such evil thoughts should be spread about by some treacherous tongues.

When men came to ask who had set these evil tongues to wag, it was always found that a certain mean knight, named Sir Pinel, had first spoken wrong of Lancelot and Sir Bors and the queen. And men noticed that it was not long before the queen began to look coldly at Sir Pinel, and then they knew that his rumours had reached her ears.

"What profit doth Sir Pinel think to gain from those false tales of her?" said Sir Brastias one day, as he and Sir Gareth came from the hawking together. "For none ever reckoned him as a knight of any merit, and all good men will now think less of him."

"I fear me," said Sir Gareth, "that there is more beneath it all than we wot of. Sir Pinel is a bosom friend of Sir Mordred's. Often have I seen their heads together in places apart. And though he is my brother, Sir Mordred is one I cannot love."

"What fear you, Gareth?" asked Sir Brastias.

"I fear naught that he may do," said Gareth, "but I think he hates Sir Lancelot and he hates Gawaine also, the chief of our party, because he hath roundly told Mordred that he is a traitor, and that he will not be drawn from his firm friendship with Sir Lancelot and his kinsmen. I think Sir Mordred would do much to cause some ill to Gawaine or Sir Lancelot, so long as his own evil body was not hurt."

"Sad it is," said Brastias full gloomily, "to think a man of such great kin should harbour hatred and murder against the chief of his kin. And that such should be, methinks, betokens that evil is about to fall upon our famous brotherhood of the Round Table, and on this dear land of Britain."

Now it befell that the poor queen had heard, through her maidens, of the rumours concerning herself and Sir Lancelot, and, taking counsel of no one, she bethought how she could prove to the remnant of the Round Table that she was free of any plots against the king or the fair kingdom of Britain.

She resolved that she would invite the knights to a privy dinner, and when they had eaten she would throw herself upon their knightly pity and honour, telling them how the evil rumours wronged and hurt her bitterly. And she doubted not that thus their manly sympathy and worship of her, their queen, would, by her words, cast out the evil effects of the slanderous tales.

Therefore, at that dinner, she had Sir Gawaine and his brethren, that is to say, Sir Gareth, Sir Agravaine, Sir Gaheris, and Sir Mordred. Also there were the kin of Sir Lancelot, to wit, Sir Bors, Sir Blamore, Sir Bleobaris, Sir Ector de Maris, and Sir Lionel. But Sir Lancelot had gone into the Scottish marches, to do battle with a notable robber and oppressor there. There were other knights, making in all the number of twenty-four. And these were all the remnant of the one hundred and fifty that had gone forth in the Quest of the Sangreal.

Among the guests were Sir Pinel and his cousin, Sir Mador.

Now Sir Gawaine had a custom of eating apples which he used daily at dinner and at supper. He loved all manner of fruit, and in especial a certain brown or russet apple, which was called Afal Coch. Every one knew of this fondness of Sir Gawaine's, and whoever dined or feasted him took care to provide such apples for his pleasure.

The queen had known this, and among the fruit for the table she had ordered such apples to be placed.

Now Sir Mordred, as Sir Gareth had suspected, hated Sir Gawaine with a deep hatred, and therefore he had, by crafty dealing, taken all the russet apples from the dish except one, and into this he had thrust a deadly poison. He guessed that, as every one knew of Sir Gawaine's fondness for that sort of fruit, no one would take it, but would leave it for Sir Gawaine, who would eat it and die thereof.

When the feast was near an end, and men laughed and jested together, the dish of fruit was handed round, and Sir Pinel, the mean knight, noticed that there was but one of the apples which Sir Gawaine loved; and to spite that knight, whom he hated, he took that apple, ere the dish went to Sir Gawaine.

Sir Mordred saw him take it, yet would not cry out to warn his fellow-traitor, for this would have revealed himself. He saw Sir Pinel's teeth sink into the brown apple, and Sir Pinel's sneering look as he glanced across at Sir Gawaine, who was searching vainly in the dish for his favourite fruit.

Then Sir Mordred saw Sir Pinel's face go red, and then deadly white. And as the poison gripped him, Sir Pinel rose shrieking from the table, crying out that some enemy had poisoned him.

Then he sank writhing to the ground, shrieking and moaning, clutching at the ground and at the legs of the chairs. Suddenly, with a great groan, he lay still and was dead.

Every knight leaped from the table, ashamed, full of rage and fear, nigh out of their wits, but dumb. They looked at each other and then at the dead Sir Pinel, and all their eyes kept from the face of the queen, where she sat on the high seat, with two of her ladies beside her.

The reason they could not speak was that they knew the queen had heard of the evil tales which Sir Pinel had spread about her, and that she must have hated him bitterly. And she had made this feast, and had invited him thereto, and now he was dead at the board, by means of deadly poison placed in the food which she had set before him.

Then for very shame some began to leave the chamber; and others could not bear to look upon the queen, who sat with a face that went now pale, now red. She had seen what happened, and who it was had been slain, and she had read the suspicion in men's gestures.

Then the voice of Sir Mador rang out, and checked men from going from the room, and drew all eyes to where he stood, a tall and burly man, red and angry of face, and fierce of eyes.

"Look!" he cried, and held between his fingers and high above his head the apple which Sir Pinel had bitten. "This is the thing whereof my kinsman, Sir Pinel, hath lost his life. The matter shall not end here, for I have lost a noble knight of my blood, and I will be revenged to the uttermost."

Then, turning, he savagely looked at the queen, and with fierce rolling eyes he roared out:

"Thou art the murderess! Thou—the queen! Hear me, knights and chieftains. I charge the queen with the murder of my kinsman, Sir Pinel, and justice upon her will I have."

Everyone in the hall stood still as if they were of stone. None could gainsay him, none could utter a word on behalf of the queen, for all had suspicion that she had slain Sir Pinel for his slanders of her.

Then suddenly the queen rose, white and trembling.

"My lords and knights, I did not cause it!" she cried in a broken voice. "I am innocent! I know not how it came!"

And therewith she fell down in a swoon.

Sir Mordred's pale face smiled with a bitter sneer. He knew not then whether what had happened would help his evil plots or no; but he resolved to say naught, and so went out with all the other silent knights, whilst the ladies of the queen took her up lamenting, and bore her to her chamber.

With the noise and the sorrow that was in the court, King Arthur came and craved to know what was the matter; but none of the silent knights would speak until he met Sir Gawaine, who replied, and said:

"Sir, the queen did invite us to a privy feast with her. And one of the knights did eat of the fruit on the table, and he is dead by poison. Therefore, I dread lest the queen will be shamed for this."

King Arthur was passing heavy at the hearing of these words, and went unto the queen to comfort her.

On the next day, when the king sat in hall with his two court judges, as was his wont daily, to hear any causes or charges which might be brought before him, all men stood with gloomy faces, and there was no laughing and jesting talk, as was usual at this time.

Sir Mador came forward and charged the queen of murder, and required that justice should be done upon her.

The king heard him with a sad face and in silence. Then he said:

"Fair lords and noble knights, heavy is my grief for this, and rather would I give my life for my queen at this moment than that my tongue should frame so evil a charge against my dear wife and your noble queen. But I am here to see that law is done, as justly to the highest as to the lowest. I doubt not that God will soon clear her of this seeming evil."

"I know not how that may be," said Sir Mador angrily, "for the evil deed is clear to any man's eyes."

"I deem this deed was never done by my queen, nor by her desire," said the king sternly, "but by some traitor that would do her evil and wishes to see her die. But as I am her judge, I may not be her champion and fight against you for her fair fame. I doubt not, however, that some good knight will take this charge upon himself, and put his body in jeopardy for my queen. For if this be not done, dost thou know what is the penalty?"

"She must be burnt," said Mador sullenly. "But she hath done the deed and will merit the doom."

"Cease, hasty man," said King Arthur sternly; "it goeth to my heart to hear ye pronounce the doom thou wouldst visit upon that fair lady. Fear not, Sir Mador, she shall find some good knight to do combat for her. Therefore do thou name thy day of battle."

"But hark ye, lord," said Sir Mador, "there is none of the four-and-twenty knights that were bidden to this dinner that hath not suspicion of the queen for this deed. Therefore, no knight can take this charge upon him in her behalf. What say ye, my lords?"

He turned to the silent, moody men about the dais.

The knights looked troubled, and were dumb for some moments; but at the last Sir Gawaine said:

"We cannot excuse the queen, for she gave the feast. And either the poison came by her will or by her servants."

But most of the knights were silent, and Sir Bors and his kindred were very sorrowful. King Arthur was heavy at the words of Sir Gawaine.

"Now, king," cried Sir Mador triumphantly, "I require ye, as ye be a righteous king, give me a day that I may have justice."

"That will I do," said the king, "as I must do, that am a just king. I give you this day fifteen days, that ye be ready armed on horseback in the meadow beside the wall at London; and if it so fall out that there be a knight to encounter with you, then God speed the right; and if there be no knight to take arms for my queen, then must she suffer by fire."

So sorrowful were the king's words that many knights had much ado to keep from weeping.

"And meanwhile," said Sir Mador, "I do require that ye keep the queen in close ward and prison, lest any try a rescue, and thus defeat the justice that is my due."

Though it went to the king's heart to have to order this, he gave the queen into the keeping of Sir Kay, who kept her in her chamber, guarded by three knights, to the great grief of her women and all the court.

Then the queen sent for Sir Bors, and when he was come she threw herself on her knees full piteously before him, and wept sorely, and begged that he would save her from this dreadful death.

"For by my confession unto Heaven," she cried, "I know naught of this wicked deed how it was brought about. And will ye not take this combat upon ye for my sake? For I am sure if your kinsman, Sir Lancelot, was here, he would not suffer this evil suspicion to lie against me. For he hath ever been my most faithful knight, but now am I without friend in this great pass."

"Madam," replied Sir Bors, "what can I do? For if I take this charge upon me for your sake, men will say I was your aider in this crime that they charge upon you. And I see not how I may fight for you except by endangering my own life without saving yours. But I tell ye, madam, what I will do. I will hasten with all speed to the north, trusting in God to get news of Sir Lancelot, so that I may tell him and bring him here within the time appointed."

"Ah, good Sir Bors," cried the queen, and clasped his hands. "Do ye do that, for I know that Sir Lancelot will never believe me guilty of so great a crime. And I will pray hourly that ye find him and bring him to me in time, so that my poor body be not unjustly given to the dreadful flames."

Forthwith Sir Bors armed himself, and with two squires set forth instantly; and sent his men in different ways, so that among the three they should not fail to hear where, in the northern marches, a knight so famous as Sir Lancelot might be found.

No rest did the good Sir Bors give to himself, but swiftly did he ride hither and thither questioning all knights whom he met, and inquiring of every hermitage and abbey and at every harbourage. Finally, when eleven days had passed of the fifteen, he found Sir Lancelot lying wounded at a broken abbey, from which, in a fierce fight, he had but two days before thrust out a band of pagans, who would have murdered the nuns and robbed the church of its holy relics.

Full wroth was Sir Lancelot when, having lovingly greeted each other, Sir Bors told him all that had passed with the queen.

"The foul traitors!" he cried, and, getting fiercely from the pallet on which he lay, he strode up and down the chamber clenching his hands and gnashing his teeth. "Do any dare to suspect her—do any think in cold blood to see that peerless lady bound to the stake, the flames devouring her noble person? That men should think such things, and move not a hand in noble wrath, shows how evil are the days in which we live!"

Then he rushed from the room, wounded as he was; and, full of a cold wrath, he ordered his arms to be brought and his horse to be saddled. And to the gentle persuasions of the nuns he said he must be gone, "for he must stay a wrong that, if suffered, would sink the kingdom in unquenchable shame and ruin."

Then with Sir Bors he rode southwards, full fiercely, and never resting to eat, but taking food as he rode. At night he would not doff his armour, but slept beside his horse; and seldom spoke, but was consumed as by a great fire of anger.

And on the fourteenth day they rode into London.

"Go beg the queen to see me," he said to Sir Bors.

Sir Bors went, and Sir Lancelot strode unto an hostelry to wash from himself the stains of travel, and to don a fitting robe in which to appear before the queen.

Now it had befallen, while Sir Bors had been absent from the court seeking for Sir Lancelot, that Sir Mordred and Sir Agravaine had made a plot with each other against him and against Sir Lancelot. And they caused it to be noised in all the court that Sir Bors had gone to seek Sir Lancelot, and that Sir Bors was privy to the plots which Sir Lancelot and the queen had made to wrest the kingdom from King Arthur and to reign together in his stead. They said that Sir Bors had gone to warn Sir Lancelot that the time was ripe to strike.

Wherefore many knights were greatly displeased to hear this news, but some would not believe it, and said that Sir Bors had gone to tell Sir Lancelot of the jeopardy in which the queen's life was placed, and to ask him to do battle for her.

"But," said some, "if he do not find Sir Lancelot, it is his intention to do combat for the queen himself, and that is great wrong in Sir Bors, for he was with us at the feast, and none but she could have caused that poison."

Daily the party which inclined to Sir Mordred and Sir Agravaine gained power, and some were for going to tell the king of the evil designs which Sir Lancelot and Sir Bors and the queen had against his person and the kingdom. But Sir Mordred said, "No, the time is not yet ripe. Wait a while."

The guard that was set about the queen's chamber was doubled, and all were knights that were well-willers to the plots of Sir Mordred and Sir Agravaine.

When, therefore, Sir Bors came and asked to see the queen, they let him go to her; but Sir Agravaine hid himself and listened to all that passed between Sir Bors and the queen. Then he went and told the others that Sir Lancelot was waiting to speak to the queen, and he counselled that they should let him come, and then when he came forth again, as he would be unarmed, they could fall upon him and capture him, and take him before the king and charge him with his treason and his plots.

And with the consent of Sir Mordred this was so agreed; and he advised that most of them should hide from before the door, so that Sir Lancelot should not think the guard was strong.

"For," said Sir Mordred, "if he sees there is no great watch kept, he may strive to free the queen, and when we take him it will be blacker against him."

When, therefore, Sir Bors came forth from his audience with the queen, he found but one knight at the door, and that was Sir Petipace of Winchelsea, a young man. Sir Bors wondered why the guard of ten or twelve that had been there before was now gone, and he was uneasy in his mind.

Going to Sir Lancelot, he told him that the queen would see him at once; "but," added Sir Bors, "ye shall not go this night by my counsel, nor should you go before there are more of our kinsmen near us to aid us in case of need."

"Why?" said Sir Lancelot.

"Sir," said Sir Bors, "I misdoubt me of Sir Agravaine and Sir Mordred. There was a great watch before the door of the queen's room when I entered; but when I came hence there was but one. And I mistrust them that stood there. For all were of Sir Mordred's evil company, and peradventure they lay some snare for you, and I dread me sore of treachery."

"Have ye no doubt," said Sir Lancelot, "for I shall go and come again and make no tarrying."

"Sir," replied his cousin, "that me sore repenteth. But if you will, I will go and seek some of our kinsmen to meet us near by. And do you not go until I have found them."

"Nay, I will not stay," said Sir Lancelot, "and I marvel me much why ye say this, for they dare do naught against me."

"God speed you well," said Sir Bors, "if that is your will, and send you safe and sound again."

Sir Lancelot departed, taking his sword underneath his arm while Sir Bors went forth to find some of their kin. He learned, however, that many of them had gone forth with the king to punish a bandit lord in the forest of the Weald, and would not return before the morrow, when the combat should be held for the queen.

Sir Lancelot came to the door of the queen's prison, and found Sir Petipace there, and demanded to be let in to see the queen.

"We thought you were in the north, Sir Lancelot," said the young knight, with a laugh, "and surely it will pleasure our lady queen to see you."

He unlocked the door of the queen's antechamber, and told her waiting-woman that Sir Lancelot would see the queen, and in a few moments Sir Lancelot was let in. The sorrowing queen told him all that had happened, and how, and he was wroth to think that any one should suspect her of so great a crime. He promised that on the day appointed he would fight for her with all his strength, as a true knight should, and God would defend the right.

Suddenly, as they spoke together, there came loud voices crying outside the chamber door:

"Traitor knight, Sir Lancelot du Lake, now art thou taken in thy treachery!"

Sir Lancelot knew that the voices were those of Sir Agravaine, who had ever been envious of him, and of Sir Mordred, whom no one loved. He went quickly to the door and barred it with the beam, and bade the terrified queen not to be alarmed. He asked her whether there was any armour in the room, which he could put on to defend himself.

"I have none," she said, weeping sorely, "wherefore I dread me sore that evil will come to you, my true and valiant knight, for I hear by their noise there be many strong knights, wherefore ye are like to be slain soon, and then shall I surely burn."

"Alas!" said Sir Lancelot. "In all my life was I never in such a pass, to be slain for lack of my armour."

"Traitor knight," cried those that were hammering at the door with the handles of their swords, "come out at once and skulk there no more, for know ye well thou art so beset that thou shalt not escape."

Sir Lancelot went to the queen and, kneeling to her, took her hand and kissed it, saying:

"Madam, I beseech you to pray for my soul if I be slain. I have been your true knight with all my power up to this time, and now I will not fail you if I may; but if I be slain, I am assured that my kinsman Sir Bors and all the others of my kin will not suffer you to go to the fire."

Then Sir Lancelot, leaving the weeping queen, wrapped his mantle round his left arm as if it were a shield, and prepared to sell his life dearly. By this time the knights outside had got a bench from the hall, and using it as a battering-ram, were dashing it against the door to beat it in.

"Leave your noise, fair lords," rang out the voice of Lancelot, "and I will open the door to ye, and then ye may do to me what ye will."

"Do it then," they cried, "and we will give you your life until we take thee to King Arthur, to be judged for your treason."

Sir Lancelot unbarred the door and held it open a little way, so that one knight only might enter at a time. One entered, a big slow man, named Sir Colgreve, and swiftly Sir Lancelot slammed the door and fastened it, to keep the others out.

Sir Colgreve turned and struck at Sir Lancelot; but the latter put the stroke lightly aside with his sword, and gave so swift and keen a blow upon the other's helm that Sir Colgreve fell down dead.

Then, while the others hammered and yelled outside the door, Sir Lancelot swiftly took off the armour of the dead knight, and with the help of the queen and her waiting-women was armed in it.

Again the knights outside had begun to dash at the door to beat it down. Sir Lancelot, when he was armed, strode to it and cried out:

"Let be your noise, and go away, for ye shall not prison me this night. And I promise ye, by my knighthood, that I will appear tomorrow before the king, and then such of ye as dare may accuse me of treason, and I will then prove that I am a true man and no traitor."

"Fie on thee, false traitor," cried Sir Agravaine and Sir Mordred, "but we will have thee this night and slay thee."

"Then, sirs," replied Sir Lancelot, "if ye will not take my counsel, look well to yourselves."

With that Sir Lancelot threw the door open suddenly, and while the others struggled and tripped over the bench between them he had run two of them through.

Then in that narrow antechamber there was as fierce a fight as ever brave knight might wish to see. Sir Mordred from behind urged on the others with evil words, telling them to slay Sir Lancelot; while he launched at that knight all manner of foul names.

Fiercely did Sir Lancelot fight, for he was full of rage; and as in the narrow place in which he stood, no more than two could come at him at once, he could not be overwhelmed by their numbers. There were ten of them, and so full of force were his blows and so skilful his thrusts, that in a little while seven lay slain, two were badly wounded, and the last, who was Sir Mordred, barely escaped with his life, and bore a deep wound with him.

Sir Lancelot, sorely wounded, returned to the queen, and said:

"Madam, I know not what is this treason with which they charge me; but I doubt not it will go ill with me, for I have killed many of the kin of the king and of Sir Gawaine this night. And I misdoubt me that the king himself will be my foe also. Nevertheless, I will save you, if it is in my power, from the danger that threatens you."

"Go ye, Sir Lancelot," the queen besought him, "ere the men-at-arms come, which are so many ye may never hope to escape them. I dread me sorely that much ill will come of this, and of the evil plots which our enemies weave about us."

Then, kneeling, Sir Lancelot kissed the queen's hand, and went from the prison; and the people who had assembled outside at the noise of the fighting wondered to see only one knight issue forth, his armour dented and broken, and dabbled here and there with the blood of his wounds.

Sir Lancelot took his way to the lodging of Sir Bors, who showed his great gladness to see him again. And when he had been unarmed and his wounds stanched and bound, Sir Lancelot told him what had befallen him.

"And now I beseech you," said Sir Lancelot, "be of good heart, in whatever great need we stand, for now I fear war must come of it all. But what is the treason they would charge me with I know not; yet I dread it meaneth much evil plotting against me and the peace of this fair kingdom."

"Sir," said Sir Bors, "your enemies and those that envy your great fame have spread many evil reports about you. They say that you plot to slay the king and to take Queen Gwenevere to wife, to reign over this kingdom with you."

With that Sir Lancelot was so astounded that for some moments he could not speak. Then he said:

"By my confession unto Heaven, this is as foul a plot against me as ever fiend could fashion. And it showeth how far they will go to pull me down and dishonour me. And doth the king know of these evil rumours?"

"I know not," replied Sir Bors, "but I doubt not that Sir Mordred will not rest his horse till he hath found the king and poisoned his mind against thee."

"Had I known of this," said Sir Lancelot, "I would have brought the queen away with me and put her in a safe place, for now I know that her enemies and mine will not rest until she and I be slain."

But Sir Bors counselled him not to attempt a rescue then, for day was breaking, the town was awake, and the court would be full of the armed retainers of the slain knights.

Then, while Sir Lancelot rested himself, Sir Bors went out to the lodgings of such of his kinsmen as might not be gone with the king, and he found that now all had returned to London with the king, that Sir Mordred had met them on their way, and had told King Arthur of the fight, and had, moreover, charged Sir Lancelot and the queen with conspiring together to gain the crown.

Sad indeed was Sir Bors to hear this; but, going about the town, he got together the kinsmen of Sir Lancelot and such of his friends as would cast in their lot with him in so weighty and terrible a thing as civil war. By seven of the clock he had got together good and valiant knights to the number of fourscore, all horsed and armed.

Then he told them to betake themselves to a privy place in a wood beyond the city walls to the north, and there in a little while came Sir Lancelot with Sir Bors, and held counsel with them. He told them all that had befallen him in the fight with the twelve knights, and they in their turn related how Sir Mordred had met them and had told his evil tales against the queen and Lancelot, and how for long the king was too wroth and too sad to listen. But afterwards, when Sir Mordred told how Sir Pinel, who had spoken of these things, had been poisoned at the feast given by the queen, King Arthur had wept, and then was very stern and quiet and said no word more.

"Now, my lords," said Sir Lancelot, when they had done speaking, "ye know well how evil are these plots, how baseless are these foul rumours against me. But now they have been launched against me, and I have slain men on account of them, I fear we shall be hard put to it to get peace again. Those men were set on to betray me; and I doubt not mine enemies will have the queen burnt, to revenge themselves upon her and upon me. Therefore, fair lords, what counsel do ye give?"

"Sir," said Sir Bors, when they had spoken together a little, "we think there is but one thing to be done first: that ye knightly rescue the queen, if your enemies force the king to put her to the stake. For if she be burnt, then it would be to your shame, seeing that you vowed yourself her true knight when she came, a young fair bride, to our king, twenty years agone. And in whatsoever way ye would rescue her, ye may count upon us to our last breath."

With a great shout all the other knights raised their right hands in the air and cried: "Yea, yea!"

Then, by the advice of Sir Lancelot, they kept hidden in the little wood, while one went into the city to learn what was being done, and in what manner the queen was to be treated.

Meanwhile, in the hall of the palace of King Arthur, men sat or stood with anxious looks, glancing in silence at the king, as he walked up and down apart, with a stern look on his face.

Then Sir Mador strode forward and said:

"Lord, I do require you to perform your promise to me, to wit, that the queen be brought to the stake, unless one be found to do combat on her behalf."

"What I have promised I will fulfil," said the king; and men sorrowed to see how heavy of anguish were his looks, and full of sorrow his words.

"Lord king," said Sir Mordred, "we have shamefully suffered much wrong at the hands of Sir Lancelot. I appeal to thee that he be seized, so that the kin of those whom he slew this last night may have vengeance upon him."

Then came Sir Gawaine forward quickly, and his face was dark with anger and his words hot.

"Lord," he cried, "listen not to such tales, for I doubt not it was only by evil plots that Sir Lancelot was forced to slay those whom he slew. For I trust not Sir Mordred."

"So God us help," said Sir Gareth and Sir Gaheris, "we too will not be known to be of the same mind as our brother Sir Mordred."

"Then will I do as I deem it best, to gain what I deem right," replied Sir Mordred.

"I believe that thou wilt do it in thine own hidden ways," said Sir Gawaine, and looked fiercely at his brother, "for in all unhappiness and evil thou art to be found, if men but seek in the darkest place and look for the most secret foe."

"I appeal to you, lord," said Sir Mordred to the king, "to proclaim Sir Lancelot a false traitor to you and to your realm."

"And I," said Sir Gawaine, "will bid ye remember, lord king, that if ye will make war between us and Sir Lancelot, there will be many kings and great lords hold with him. And I would ask you, how many times hath Sir Lancelot done noble deeds on our behalf and proved himself the best knight of us all? Did he not rescue twenty of us from the dungeons of Sir Turquine? Hath he not avenged shame upon the king and the queen, and the fame of the Round Table many a time? Methinketh, my uncle, that such kind deeds should be well remembered."

"Think ye," said the king, "that I am not loath to begin so evil and terrible a thing as civil war? Alas, it rendeth my heart to think it. And I tell thee, Sir Mordred, I will not begin it, except I have proofs of what ye charge upon Sir Lancelot. And as he is the best knight of ye all, and the most valiant, I will not judge him before I hear him. If I know him well, he will come hither and challenge the knight to combat that doth bring these charges against him, and in that will I trust, for God shall surely defend the right. Therefore, let a messenger be sent to Sir Lancelot requiring him, by his knighthood, to appear before me here, and make answer to the charges thou hast against him."

This was not as Sir Mordred desired; for he did not doubt that if Sir Lancelot came he would have little trouble to persuade the king that he was innocent. When the messenger was gone, therefore, Sir Mordred sent a servant after him, who slew him in a wood and hid his body under a bush.

Meanwhile, Sir Mordred counselled Sir Mador to repeat his demand that the king should cause the queen to be led to the stake, since no knight had come forward and offered to fight for her.

For a time the king put him off, hoping that as soon as Sir Lancelot received his commands he would come instantly. Very anxiously did the king look to the door, hoping to see the tall form of his best knight come towering through the hall.

Instead thereof came the crafty servant of Sir Mordred, throwing himself at the feet of the king.

"Gracious lord," cried he, panting as if from swift running, "I have even now come from the place where Sir Lancelot and his friends are hiding. I am one of their servants, but I hate their treason against ye, and therefore I am come to tell you of this greatest treason of all. They have slain your messenger, my lord, him that came requiring Sir Lancelot to appear before thee. Sir Lancelot ran upon him when he gave his message and slew him, saying, 'Thus do I answer the saucy words of him who shall not much longer be king.'"

The king looked at the face of the messenger long and sadly. The pain which the king suffered would have softened any ordinary heart; but the murderer was a hard and callous wretch, and his brazen eyes outlooked the king.

"Then is Sir Lancelot changed indeed," said the king, and walked away with bowed head and moist eyes.

Sir Mador pushed forward again, repeating his demand.

"Have it as ye will," said the king heavily, and went quickly into his private chamber.

"Alas!" said Sir Gawaine and Sir Gareth. "Now is the whole realm falling to ruin, and the noble fellowship of the Round Table shall be scattered in civil war."

Soon a page came to Sir Gawaine, telling him that the king would speak to him.

"Gawaine," said the king, when the knight went to him, "I have been too easy with this knight, Sir Lancelot. He hath slain eleven knights of the Round Table and my messenger. The pride and ambition of that man shall have a check. His great fame for valiant deeds hath made him mad, until it would seem that nothing but this realm will content him. Now, therefore, as justice demands, and Sir Mador requires, do ye lead the queen to the fire. She shall have the law as is right. Afterwards we will seize Sir Lancelot; and know ye, he shall have a hard and shameful death."

"Heaven forbid," said Sir Gawaine, "that ever I should see either of these things. For I will believe not these reports of Sir Lancelot."

"How now?" said the king. "Truly ye have little cause to love him. This night last past he slew Sir Agravaine, your brother, and several of your kindred with him; and also, Sir Gawaine, remember how he slew but lately two sons of yours in battle against the oppressing lords of the borders."

"My lord," said Sir Gawaine, "I know these things, and for their deaths I have grieved, but I warned them all, and as they sought their deaths wilfully I will not avenge them, nor think worse of Sir Lancelot."

"Nevertheless," said the king, "I pray you will make ready with your brothers, Sir Gaheris and Sir Gareth, to take the queen to the fire, there to have her judgment and receive her death."

"Nay, most noble lord," replied the knight sadly, "that will I never do. I will never stand by to see so noble a queen meet so shameful a death."

"Then," said the king sadly, "suffer your brothers, Sir Gareth and Sir Gaheris, to be there."

"They are younger than I," replied Sir Gawaine, "and they may not say you nay."

The king commanded the two brothers of Sir Gawaine to come to him, and told them what he desired of them.

"Sir," said Sir Gareth, "it is in your power to command us to lead the queen to her shameful end; but wit you well it is sore against our will. We will go as ye bid, but it shall be in peaceable guise, for we tell you straightway, we will not oppose a rescue, should any so desire."

"Alas," said Sir Gawaine, and wept, "that ever I should live to see this woeful day!"

Then the two knights went to the queen and sorrowfully bade her prepare for her death. Very pale was the queen, but very quiet, for now that this was come which she had dreaded night and day, she would bear herself proudly like a queen, innocent as she knew she was of any crime.

Her ladies dressed her in her meanest garments; a priest, her confessor, was brought to her, and she was shriven of her sins. Then arose a weeping and a wailing and a wringing of hands among the lords and ladies.

Between the knights and the men-at-arms she was led through the streets to the lists beyond the wall. Lamentation, cries of horror, and the shrieks and sighs of women arose from the multitude which lined each side of the narrow streets. Many were the prayers that rose from white lips, praying God to send a miracle to rescue so sweet a lady from so dreadful a doom.

The city apprentices, with stout sticks in their hands, stood in bands, and in their stout young hearts was a great rage. It was in their minds to dash upon the guard of armoured knights, to attempt a rescue, but they knew how vain their sticks would be against the keen blades of swords.

So stricken with horror were all those that looked on that they noticed not how, when the queen and her guard issued from the gates of the palace, a man in the coarse dress of a peasant, who was standing in the crowd, strode swiftly away down a narrow lane. There he vaulted, with an unpeasant-like deftness, upon a good steed that stood in the charge of a young lad; and striking spurs in the horse's flanks, he dashed away madly along the streets and through the northern gate into the fields.

Amidst the sorrowing people, with women crying and men muttering and looking darkly at the knights about her, the queen was led to the tilting-ground beyond the northern wall, and in the midst thereof was a stake. To this she was fastened with a rope, and wood was piled about her feet up to her knees. Near her stood the priest of her household, trying to cheer her with comforting words; but the queen, pale and without tears, seemed to be dazed and as if she did not hear him.

A hundred knights ranged themselves behind the queen, some on horseback, but the most on foot. Many of them had followed the example of Sir Gaheris and Sir Gareth and stood without arms; but Sir Mador was on his horse, fully armed, and prepared for combat. Others of his kindred rode beside him.

Then Sir Gaheris called upon the herald to proclaim what the king had commanded.

"In the name of the king," cried the herald, "the queen hath been found guilty of the death of a knight by treason and poison, and his kinsmen have demanded due judgment upon her. But if any knight shall take upon himself to do battle for her, let him appear instantly. If none do appear, then shall she suffer the death by burning as the law doth appoint."

The herald ceased; the people in the seats, craning this way and that, looked eagerly up and down the lists to see if any knight came.

They saw Sir Mador, in the forefront of the troop of mounted knights, glance about him; but no armed man moved forward to do battle for the innocence of the queen. Then he looked to where she stood, pale and still, and men saw him smile faintly, as if his cruel heart already rejoiced to think that she would surely burn.

A great stillness was on the multitude of people. The eyes of all the citizens of London were bent upon that long wide space of sand within the lists; many, blurred by tears, could not bear to look at the white figure in the midst of the wood and kindling.

Men and women held their breath. They saw Sir Mador look towards Sir Gaheris, as if to ask him why he delayed giving the signal for the executioner to go forward to do his duty.

Sir Gaheris stood looking down the lists towards the great entrance. His brother, Sir Gareth, was beside him, and in the hearts of both were prayers which asked that something might happen to prevent them doing this dreadful deed upon their fair queen.

"I do call upon you, Sir Gaheris, to fulfil the law!"

Sir Mador's harsh voice rang out in the silence, startling all. With the sound, Sir Gaheris threw up his hands in a gesture of despair. He turned to the executioner, who stood beside a cauldron of fire, and pointed to the queen.

Horror held the great multitude in silence, and all eyes watched the man put his torch in the fire, and then carry it blazing towards the wood.

Suddenly men heard a strange throbbing sound, as if from a distance; then quickly it changed into the fierce beat of horses' hoofs; and before many could realise what it meant, through the great gate at the end of the lists dashed knights in armour, on horses whose foam-flecked trappings showed at what a speed they had come.

At the head of then rode a great knight; and as men caught the device upon his shield a great roar of gladness burst from the throats of the people, while women sobbed for joy.

"Sir Lancelot! Sir Lancelot to the rescue!" was the cry.

As the knights entered, Sir Mador's quick commands sounded, and the knights about him ran forward and surrounded the queen. They had barely reached the place when, with a great crashing sound, the party of Sir Lancelot was upon them. Many of Sir Mador's people were at once thrown headlong to the ground by the force of the shock; but the others fought fiercely.

This way and that the battle swayed; Sir Mador trying to thrust the others from the fire, and Sir Lancelot's kinsmen striving to reach the queen. All was in confusion; the knights on foot were mingled with those on horseback, and many were cut down who did not bear arms.

Full of a mad wrath was Sir Lancelot, as he raged among the knights that stood about the fire, nor could any withstand him. So blind was he in his fury that he knew not whom he slew, except that they were men who stood between him and the queen.

So, by great mischance, at this rushing and hurtling, he slew two knights and knew not that they were unarmed, and that they were of those he loved most. One was Sir Gareth, whom he had himself knighted, and the other was Sir Gaheris. In very truth Sir Lancelot knew them not; and afterwards they were found dead where the corpses lay thickest.

Short but very fierce was that battle, for none could long withstand the fury of Sir Lancelot and his kinsmen. Many were slain on both sides; Sir Mador had his head sheared from his shoulders by a stroke of Sir Lancelot's sword, and the remnant of his party fled.

Then Sir Lancelot rode to the queen, cut her bonds, and lifted her upon his horse full tenderly. Her eyes streamed with tears as she returned thanks to God for her deliverance, and hardly could she tell her gratitude to Sir Lancelot.

Thus, with the continued praises of the people in his ears, Sir Lancelot fared forth amidst his kinsmen, and taking the road northwards he rode with the queen to his own castle of Joyous Gard.

"For," said he, "I will keep the queen in safety until I know that the king is assured of our innocence of any treason against him. But I doubt our enemies have poisoned his mind, for never else would he have suffered her to go to the stake."

But therein was Sir Lancelot in great error, as in much grief and remorse he came later to see; for if instantly he had taken the queen to the king, and had dared his enemies to prove his treason and the queen's, they would have been instantly discountenanced, and King Arthur would have known and loved him as he had ever done, for a true knight and a peerless one.

Nevertheless, Sir Lancelot would ever have had the hatred of Sir Gawaine, which was caused by his slaying, though unwittingly, the two good knights, Sir Gaheris and Sir Gareth; whereof came great bale and sorrow.

XII

Of Sir Gawaine's Hatred, and the War with Sir Lancelot

KING ARTHUR, IN THE HALL OF HIS PALACE IN LONDON, WALKED quickly up and down, thinking in great grief of the death of his queen. A group of pages stood quietly in the shadow by the door, and two or three knights gazed silently at the moody king.

Suddenly there came the sound of running footsteps; a man dashed into the hall, and threw himself at the feet of the king. It was a squire of Sir Mordred's, and he craved leave to speak. "Say on," said the king.

"My lord," said the man, "Sir Lancelot hath rescued the queen from the fire and hath slain some thirty of your knights, and he and his kin have taken the queen among them away to some hiding-place."

King Arthur stood for a little while dumb for pure sorrow; then, turning away, he wrung his hands and cried with a voice whose sadness pierced every heart:

"Alas, that ever I bare a crown, for now is the fairest fellowship of knights that ever the world held, scattered and broken."

"Further, my lord," went on the man, as others came into the hall, "Sir Lancelot hath slain the brethren of Sir Gawaine, and they are Sir Gaheris and Sir Gareth."

The king looked from the man to the knights that now surrounded him, as if that which he heard was past all belief.

"Is this truth?" he asked them, and all were moved at the sorrow on his face and in his voice.

"Yea, lord," said they.

"Then, fair fellows," he said, very heavily, "I charge you that no man tell Sir Gawaine of the death of his two brothers; for I am sure that when he heareth that his loved younger brother, Sir Gareth, is slain, he will nigh go out of his mind for sorrow and anger."

The king strode up and down the chamber, wringing his hands in the grief he could not utter.

"Why, oh why, did he slay them?" he cried out at length. "He himself knighted Sir Gareth when he went to fight the oppressor of the Lady Lyones, and Sir Gareth loved him above all others."

"That is truth," said some of the knights, and could not keep from tears to see the king's grief, "but they were slain in the hurtling together of the knights, as Sir Lancelot dashed in the thick of the press. He wist not whom he smote, so blind was his rage to get to the queen at the stake."

"Alas! Alas!" said the king. "The death of them will cause the greatest woeful war that ever was in this fair realm. I see ruin before us all—rent and ruined shall we be, and all peace forever at an end."

Though the king had forbidden any of his knights to tell Sir Gawaine of the death of his two brothers, Sir Mordred called his squire aside, and bade him go and let Sir Gawaine know all that had happened.

"Do you see to it," he told the man, "that thou dost inflame his mind against Sir Lancelot."

The knave went to Sir Gawaine, and found him walking on the terrace of the palace overlooking the broad quiet Thames, where the small trading ships sailed up and down the river on their ways to and from Gaul and the ports of the Kentish coast.

"Sir," said the squire, doffing his cap and bowing, "great and woeful deeds have been toward this day. The queen hath been rescued by Sir Lancelot and his kin, and some thirty knights were slain in the melee about the stake."

"Heaven defend my brethren," said Sir Gawaine, "for they went unarmed. But as for Sir Lancelot, I guessed he would try a rescue, and I had deemed him no man of knightly worship if he had not. But, tell me, how are my brethren. Where be they?"

"Alas, sir," said the man, "they be slain."

The grim face of Sir Gawaine went pale, and with an iron hand he seized the shoulder of the squire and shook him in his rage.

"Have a care, thou limb of Mordred's, if thou speakest lies," he said. "I would not have them dead for all this realm and its riches. Where is my young brother, Sir Gareth?"

"Sir, I tell ye truth," said the man, "for I know how heavy would be your anger if I lied in this. Sir Gareth and Sir Gaheris are slain, and all good knights are mourning them, and in especial the king our master."

Sir Gawaine took a step backwards and his face went pale and then it darkened with rage.

"Tell me who slew them?" he thundered.

"Sir," replied the man, "Sir Lancelot slew them both."

"False knave!" cried Sir Gawaine, "I knew thou didst lie."

He struck the man a great buffet on the head, so that he fell half dazed to the ground.

"Thou lying talebearer!" laughed Sir Gawaine, half relieved of his fears, yet still half doubtful. "To tell me that Sir Lancelot slew them! Why, man, knowest thou of whom thou pratest? Sir Lancelot to slay my dear young brother Gareth! Why, man, Gareth loved Sir Lancelot as he loved me—not more than he loved me, but near as much; and Sir Lancelot was ever proud of him. 'Twas he that knighted my young brother Gareth, brave and hearty, noble of mind and goodly of look! He would have stood with Lancelot against the king himself, so greatly he loved him. And thou—thou foul-mouth!—thou tellest me that Lancelot hath slain him! Begone from my sight, thou split-tongue!"

"Nevertheless, Sir Gawaine," said the man, rising, "Sir Lancelot slew them both in his rage. As he would—saving your presence—have slain you had you stood between him and the queen at the stake."

At these words, stubbornly spoken in spite of the furious looks of Sir Gawaine, the knight realised that the man was speaking the truth.

His look was fixed on the face of the knave, and rage and grief filled his eyes as he grasped the fact that his beloved brother was really slain. Then the blood surged into his face, and he dashed away.

Men started to see the wild figure of Sir Gawaine rushing through the passages, his eyes bloodshot, his face white. At length he dashed into the presence of the king. Arthur stood sorrowing amidst his knights, but Sir Gawaine rushed through them and faced the king.

"Ha! King Arthur!" he cried, half breathless, but in a great wild voice. "My good brother, Sir Gareth, is slain, and also Sir Gaheris! I cannot bear the thought of them slain. It cannot be true! I cannot believe it!"

"Nay, nor can any think upon it," said the king, "and keep from weeping."

"Ay, ay," said Sir Gawaine in a terrible voice, "there shall be weeping, I trow, and that erelong. Sir, I will go see my dead brothers. I would kiss them ere they be laid in earth."

"Nay, that may not be," said the king gently. "I knew how great would be thy sorrow, and that sight of them would drive thee mad. And I have caused them to be interred instantly."

"Tell me," said Gawaine, and men marvelled to see the wild look in his eyes and to hear the fierce voice, "is it truth that Sir Lancelot slew them both?"

"It is thus told me," said the king, "that in his fury Sir Lancelot knew not whom he smote."

"But, man," thundered Sir Gawaine, "they bare no arms against him! Their hearts were with him, and young Gareth loved him as if— as if Lancelot was his own brother."

"I know it, I know it," replied King Arthur. "But men say they were mingled in the thick press of the fight, and Lancelot knew not friend from foe, but struck down all that stood between him and the queen."

For a space Sir Gawaine was silent, and men looked upon him with awe and compassion. His mane of hair, grizzled and wild, was thrown back upon his shoulders, and his eyes flamed with a glowing light as of fire. Suddenly he stepped up to the king, and lifting his right hand said, in a voice that trembled with rage:

"My lord, my king, and mine uncle, wit you well that now I make oath by my knighthood, that from this day I will seek Sir Lancelot and never rest till he be slain or he slay me. Therefore, my lord king, and you, my fellow knights and lords, I require you all to prepare yourselves for war; for, know you, though I ravage this land and all the lands of Christendom, I will not rest me nor slake my revenge until I come up to Lancelot and drive my sword into his evil heart."

With that Sir Gawaine strode from the room, and for a space all men were silent, so fierce and full of hatred had been his words.

"I see well," said the king, "that the death of these twain knights will cause the deadliest war that hath ever raged, and never shall we have rest until Gawaine do slay Lancelot or is slain by him. O Lancelot! Lancelot! My peerless knight, that ever thou shouldst be the cause of the ruin of this my fair kingdom!"

None that heard the king could keep from tears; and many felt that in this quarrel the king's heart was not set, except for the sake of Sir Gawaine, his nephew, and all his kin.

Then there were made great preparations in London and all the lands south of Trent, with sharpening of swords and spears, making of harness and beating of smiths' hammers on anvils.

Men's minds were in sore distress, and the faces of the citizens were long and white with dismay. Daily the quarrel caused other quarrels. Many a group of knights came to high words, some taking the side of Lancelot and the queen, and others that of the king and Sir Gawaine. Often they came to blows, and one or other of their number would be left writhing and groaning on the ground.

Families broke up in bad blood by reason of it, for the sons would avow their intent to go and enlist with Lancelot, while the fathers, in high anger at such disloyalty to Arthur, would send their tall sons away, bidding them never to look upon their faces again.

Women sorrowed and wept, for whichever side they took, it meant that one or other of their dear ones was opposed to them, and would go to battle, fighting against those of their own kin and of their own hearths.

Towards midsummer the host was ready, and took the road to the north. The quarrel had been noised abroad throughout Britain, and many kings, dukes, and barons came to the help of Arthur, so that his army was a great multitude. Yet many others had gone to Lancelot, where he lay in his castle of Joyous Gard, not far from Carlisle.

Thither, in the month of July, when the husbandmen were looking to their ripening fields and thinking of harvest, King Arthur and Sir Gawaine drew with their army and laid a siege against the castle of Joyous Gard, and against the walled town which it protected. But for all their engines of war, catapults which threw great stones, and ramming irons which battered the walls, they could not make a way into the place, and so lay about it until harvest time.

One day, as Queen Gwenevere stood at a window of the castle, she looked down at the tents of the besieging host, and her gaze lingered on the purple tent of King Arthur, with the banner of the red dragon on the pole above it. As she looked, she saw her husband issue from the tent and begin to walk up and down alone in a place apart. Very moody did he seem, as he strode to and fro with bent head. Sometimes he looked towards Joyous Gard, and then his face had a sad expression upon it which went to the queen's heart.

She went to Sir Lancelot, and said:

"Sir Lancelot, I would that this dreadful war were done, and that thou went again friends and in peace with my dear lord. Something tells me that he sorrows to be at enmity with thee. Thou wert his most famous knight and brought most worship to the fellowship of the Round Table. Wilt thou not try to speak to my lord? Tell him how evil were the false reports of the conspiracy against him, and that we are innocent of any treason against him and this dear land."

"Lady," said Sir Lancelot, "on my knighthood I will try to accord with my lord. If our enemies have not quite poisoned his thoughts of us, he may listen and believe."

Thereupon Sir Lancelot caused his trumpeter to sound from the walls, and ask that King Arthur would hold a parley with him. This was done, and Sir Pentred, a knight of King Arthur's, took the message to the king.

In a little while King Arthur, with Sir Gawaine and a company of his counsellors and knights, came beneath the walls, and the trumpeters blew a truce, and the bowmen ceased from letting fly their arrows and the men-at-arms from throwing spears.

Then Sir Lancelot came down to a narrow window in the gate-tower, and cried out to the king:

"Most noble king, I think that neither of us may get honour from this war. Cannot we make an end of it?"

"Ay," cried Sir Gawaine, his face red with anger, and shaking his mailed fist at Lancelot, "come thou forth, thou traitor, and we will make an end of thee."

"Come forth," said the king, "and I will meet thee on the field. Thou hast slain thirty of my good knights, taken my queen from me, and plunged this realm in ruin."

"Nay, lord, it was not I that caused this war," said Sir Lancelot. "I had been but a base knight to have suffered the noble lady my queen to be burned at the stake. And it passes me, my lord king, how thou couldst ever think to suffer her to be burned."

"She was charged with poisoning a knight who slandered her," said the king. "I must see justice done on high and low, and though it grieved me to condemn her, I could do naught else. Moreover, if Sir Pinel spoke true, both you and she were conspiring to slay me and to rule this kingdom in my stead."

"A foul lie, a black calumny!" cried Sir Lancelot fiercely. "And I would answer for it with the strength which God might give me on any six of your knights that may say I am so black a traitor. I tell you, my lord king, and I swear it on my knighthood, and may death strike me now if I lie, that neither I nor the queen have ever had evil thoughts against your person, nor had designs upon your crown."

At so solemn an oath men stood still and waited, for few doubted in those days that if a man who took so great an oath was speaking falsely, fire from heaven would instantly descend and consume him.

The moments passed and nothing happened, and men breathed again.

Sir Lancelot looked at the face of King Arthur, and saw by the light upon it that the king believed him; and Sir Lancelot rejoiced in his heart.

He saw the king turn to Sir Gawaine with a questioning air, as if he would ask what more his nephew wanted. But next moment, with a harsh laugh, Sir Gawaine spoke.

"Hark ye, Sir Lancelot, thou mayest swear to Heaven as to some things, and there are those that may be moved by thy round oaths. But this I charge upon thee, thou false, proud knight, that thou didst slay two unarmed men—men that loved thee and worshipped thee I Forsooth, thou boastful braggart and mouthing hero, thou wilt not dare to deny it!"

Sad was the face and voice of Sir Lancelot as he made reply.

"I cannot hope to find excuse from you," he said, "for I cannot and never will forgive myself. I would as lief have slain my nephew, Sir Bors, as slay young Sir Gareth whom I loved, and Gaheris his brother. Sorrow is on me for that! I was mad in my rage and did not see them. Only I knew that many knights stood between me and the queen, and I slew all that seemed to bar my passage."

"Thou liest, false, recreant knight!" cried Sir Gawaine, whose grief by now had made him mad with the lust for revenge; "thou slewest them in thy pride, to despite me and the king, because we had permitted the queen to go to the stake. Thou coward and traitor! Therefore, wit thee well, Sir Lancelot, I will not quit this quest until I feel my sword thrusting into thy evil heart."

"Sorrow is on me," said Sir Lancelot, "to know that thou dost so hatefully pursue me. If thou didst not, I think my lord the king would give me his good grace again, and receive back his queen and believe us innocent."

"I believe it well, false, recreant knight!" cried Sir Gawaine, full of rage to know that the king verily wished to have peace; "but know ye that while I live, my good uncle will make war upon thee, and at last we will have thee in spite of thy castle walls and thy skill in battle. And then I will have thy head."

"I trust ye for that," said Sir Lancelot, "for I see that thy hatred hath crazed thee. So, if ye may get me, I shall expect no mercy."

Then, seeing how useless it was to keep up the parley any longer, Sir Lancelot withdrew. Next day spies brought in word to Sir Lancelot that, at a council of his chief men, the king had said he would take back his queen and make peace with Sir Lancelot; but that Sir Gawaine had fiercely told him that if he did not keep up the war until Sir Lancelot was taken or slain, he and all the kin of Lot would break away from the realm and their allegiance. Indeed, it was rumoured that Sir Gawaine would have made the king prisoner had he not yielded; and so powerful was Sir Gawaine and the lords that followed him, that none could have been strong enough to withstand them.

Sir Gawaine, yearning, by reason of his hatred, to get Sir Lancelot out of his castle to fight with him, now sent knights to cry out shame upon him under his walls. Thus they marched up and down, calling out insulting names and charging him with dishonourable deeds.

Until at length the very men-at-arms that kept watch upon Sir Lancelot's walls reddened for shame, and hurled down spears and stones at foul mouths. Sir Bors, Sir Ector de Maris, and Sir Lionel, they also heard the words, and going to the other knights of Sir Lancelot, took counsel with them, and decided that this could no longer be suffered.

Together they went to Sir Lancelot and said to him:

"Wit ye well, my lord, that we feel great scorn of the evil words which Sir Gawaine spoke unto you when that ye parleyed with him, and also of these shameful names which men call upon ye for all the citizens to hear. Wherefore, we charge you and beseech you, if ye will to keep our service, hold us no longer behind these walls, but let us out, in the name of Heaven and your fair name, and have at these rascals."

"Fair friends," replied Sir Lancelot, "I am full loth to fight against my dear lord, King Arthur."

"But if ye will not," said Sir Lionel, his brother, "all men will say ye fear to stir from these walls, and hearing the shameful words they cry, will say that there must be truth in them if ye seek not to silence them."

They spoke long with Sir Lancelot, and at length he was persuaded; and he sent a message to the king telling him that he would come out and do battle; but that, for the love he bore the king, he prayed he would not expose his person in the fight.

But Sir Gawaine returned answer that this was the king's quarrel, and that the king would fight against a traitor knight with all his power.

On the morrow, at nine in the morning, King Arthur drew forth his host, and Sir Lancelot brought forth his array. When they stood facing each other, Sir Lancelot addressed his men and charged all his knights to save King Arthur from death or wounds, and for the sake of their old friendship with Sir Gawaine, to avoid battle with him also.

Then, with a great hurtling and crashing, the knights ran together, and much people were there slain. The knights of Sir Lancelot did great damage among the king's people, for they were fierce knights, and burned to revenge themselves for the evil names they had heard.

Sir Gawaine raged like a lion through the field, seeking Sir Lancelot, and many knights did he slay or overthrow. Once, indeed, King Arthur, dashing through the fight, came upon Sir Lancelot.

"Now, Sir Lancelot," he cried, "defend thee, for thou art the causer of this civil war."

At these words he struck at Sir Lancelot with his sword; but Sir Lancelot took no means to defend himself, and put down his own sword and shield, as if he could not put up arms against his king. At this the king was abashed and put down his sword, and looked sorrowfully upon Sir Lancelot.

Then the surging tide of battle poured between them and separated them, until it happened that Sir Bors saw King Arthur at a little distance. With a spear the knight rushed at the king, and so fierce was his stroke and hardy his blow that the king was stricken to the ground.

Whereupon Sir Bors leapt from his horse and drew his sword and ran towards the king. But some one called upon him, and looking up he saw Sir Lancelot riding swiftly towards him.

Sir Bors held the king down upon the ground by the nose-piece of his helm, and in his other hand he held his naked sword.

Looking up to Sir Lancelot, he cried in a fierce voice:

"Cousin, shall I make an end of this war? 'Twere easy done."

He meant that, if the king were slain, Sir Gawaine would lose half his forces, and could not hope to keep up the war against Sir Lancelot singlchanded.

"Nay, nay," said Sir Lancelot, "on peril of thy head touch not the king. Let him rise, man. I will not see that most noble king, who made me knight and once loved me, either slain or shamed."

Sir Lancelot, leaping from his horse, went and raised the king, and held the stirrup of his horse while the king mounted again.

"My lord Arthur," said Lancelot, looking up at the king, "I would in the name of Heaven that ye cause this war to cease, for none of us shall get honour by it. And though I forbear to strike you and I try to avoid my former brothers and friends of the Round Table, they do continually seek to slay me and will not avoid me."

King Arthur looked upon Lancelot, and thought how nobly courteous was he more than any other knight. The tears burst from the king's eyes and he could not speak, and sorrowfully he rode away and would fight no more, but commanded the trumpets to cease battle. Whereupon Sir Lancelot also drew off his forces, and the dead were buried and the wounded were tended.

Next morning the battle was joined again. Very fiercely fought the king's party, for Sir Gawaine had commanded that no quarter should be given, and that whoever slew a knight of Sir Lancelot's should have his helm filled with gold. Sir Gawaine himself raged like a lion about the field, his spear in rest. He sought for Sir Lancelot; but that knight always avoided him, and great was Gawaine's rage and scorn.

At length Sir Bors saw Sir Gawaine from afar, and spurred across the field towards him.

"Ha! Sir Bors," cried the other mockingly, "if ye will find that cowardly cousin of thine, and bring him here to face me, I will love thee."

"'Twere well I should not take thy words seriously," mocked Sir Bors in his turn. "For if I were to bring him to thee, thou wouldst sure repent it. Never yet hath he failed to give thee thy fall, for all thy pride and fierceness."

This was truth. Often in the jousting of earlier days, when Sir Lancelot had come in disguise and had been compelled to fight Sir Gawaine, the latter had had the worst. But Sir Lancelot, loving his old brother-in-arms as he did, had in later years avoided the assault with Sir Gawaine; yet the greater prowess and skill of Sir Lancelot were doubted by none.

Sir Gawaine raged greatly at the words of Sir Bors, for he knew they were true, though he had wished they were not.

"Thy vaunting of thy recreant kinsman's might will not avail thee," he cried furiously. "Defend thyself!"

"I came to have to do with thee," replied Sir Bors fiercely. "Yesterday thou didst slay my cousin Lionel. Today, if God wills it, thou thyself shall have a fall."

Then they set spurs to their horses and met together so furiously that the lance of either bore a great hole in the other's armour, and both were borne backwards off their horses, sorely wounded. Their friends came and took them up and tended them, but for many days neither of the knights could move from their beds.

When the knights of Sir Lancelot saw that Sir Bors was grievously wounded, they were wroth with their leader. Going to him, they charged him with injuring his own cause.

"You will not exert yourself to slay these braggart foes of yours," they said to him. "What does it profit us that you avoid slaying knights because, though they are now your bitter foes, they were once brothers of the Round Table? Do they avoid ye, and seek not to slay you and us your kindred and friends? Sir Lionel is dead, and he is your brother; and Sir Galk, Sir Griffith, Sir Saffre, and Sir Conan—all good and mighty knights—are wounded sorely. Ye were ever courteous and kindly, Sir Lancelot," they ended, "but have a care lest now your courtesy ruin not your cause and us."

Seeing by these words that he was like to chill the hearts of his friends if he continued to avoid slaying his enemies, Sir Lancelot sorrowfully promised that henceforth he would not stay his hand. After that he avoided none that came against him, though for very sorrow he could have wept when some knight, with whom in happier times he had drunk wine and jested at the board in Camelot, rushed at him with shrewd strokes to slay him.

As the fight went on, the lust of battle grew in Sir Lancelot's heart, and manfully he fought, and with all his strength and skill he lay about him. By the time of evensong his party stood very well, and the king's side seemed dispirited and as if they would avoid the fierce rushes with which Sir Lancelot's knights attacked them.

Staying his horse, Sir Lancelot looked over the field, and sorrowed to see how many dead there were—dead of whom many may have been slain by their own kindred. He saw how the horses of his knights were splashed with the blood that lay in pools here and there, and grief was heavy upon him.

Sir Palom, a very valiant knight, came up to him.

"See, lord," he cried, "how our foes flinch from the fierce hurtling of our knights. They are dispirited by the wounding of Sir Gawaine. Sir Kay is also wounded, and Sir Torre is slain. Now, if ye will take my advice, this day should cease this war once for all. Do ye gather all your forces, lord, and I think with one great dash together ye should scatter their wavering knights, and this field would be won."

"Alas!" said Sir Lancelot. "I would not have it so. It cuts me to my heart to war as I do against my lord Arthur, and to trample him and his people in the mire of defeat—nay, I should suffer remorse till my last day."

"My lord," said Sir Palom, "I think ye are unwise. Ye spare them thus to come again against ye. They will give ye no thanks, and if they could get you and yours at so great a disadvantage, wit you well they would not spare you."

But Sir Lancelot would not be moved, and in pity he ordered the trumpeters to sound the retreat. King Arthur did likewise, and each party retired in the twilight from the field, where the wounded lay groaning till death or succour came; and the dead lay still and pale, until the kindly earth was thrown over them.

Some weeks passed in which the armies did not meet; for the host of King Arthur was not now so proud as they had been, seeing that they had lost many good knights; and Sir Lancelot would not of his own will sally out from his castle to fall upon the king.

But ever Sir Gawaine tried to inflame the mind of King Arthur and his kinsmen against Sir Lancelot, and he advised them to join battle with their enemy. Moreover, from the lands of his kingdom of Lothian, of which Sir Gawaine was now king in the place of his dead father, King Lot, a great body of young knights and men-at-arms came; and the king's party began to recover their courage.

Many began daily to ride to the walls of Joyous Gard, and by insult and evil names endeavoured to tempt forth the men of Sir Lancelot. Soon the young knights clamoured to King Arthur and Sir Gawaine to permit them to attack the walls, and reluctantly the king consented to call his council for next day to devise some means of breaking down the castle.

Headstrong was the counsel given by the young knights at that meeting, and greatly did King Arthur sorrow to feel that, for love of his nephew, Sir Gawaine, he would be compelled to yield to their wild demands for further battle.

Suddenly the door of the hall where sate the council was opened, and the porter of the gate appeared and approached the king.

"My lord," he said, "the holy Bishop of London and King Geraint of Devon crave audience of you."

Some of the fierce young knights scowled at the names and uttered cries of disgust.

The king's face brightened, and before any could advise him against his will, he said:

"Bid them enter instantly."

"The meddling priest and the petty king that knoweth not his mind!" sneered Sir Gawaine, looking fiercely about the room. "I pray thee, uncle," he said to the king, "listen not to their womanish persuasions, if thou lovest me."

King Arthur did not answer, but looked towards the door impatiently.

Through this there came first three priests and three armed men, and behind them stepped an old and reverend man, the hair beside his tonsure white as driven snow, and falling over his white robe edged with red, that showed his rank as bishop. Then, towering above him, a noble knightly figure, came Geraint of Devon, grown nobler still since those noble days when he had proved himself to be a strong leader indeed, while men had thought him soft and foolish.

All rose to their feet in reverence to the bishop, and fondly did King Arthur welcome Geraint, for this wise knight had from the first opposed Sir Gawaine in this war, and had refused to fight against Sir Lancelot and the queen, though he abated not his service to the king.

Dark was the look which Gawaine darted at Geraint, but quiet yet fearless was Geraint's answering gaze.

"What ye have to say," said Gawaine angrily, "say it quickly and begone. If ye are still of two minds, there seems no need to speak, and there is no need to bring a bishop to your aid."

"Gawaine," said King Geraint, and his voice was quiet, yet with a ring of menace in it, "I think grief hath made you a little mad. Let the bishop speak, I pray ye. He hath a message for the king."

"My lord," said the bishop, "I come from His Holiness the Pope."

At these words Sir Gawaine started forward, his hand upon his sword, as if he would willingly in his madness slay the holy priest.

"And," went on the bishop, his grave voice and his quiet look not bating for all the wrathful fire in Sir Gawaine's eyes, "I bear with me the bull of his Holiness—see, here it is—by which His Highness doth charge King Arthur of Britain, as he is a Christian king, to take back Queen Gwenevere unto his love and worship, and to make peace with Sir Lancelot."

The murmurs of the wild young knights rose in a sudden storm, while Sir Gawaine glared with looks of hatred at King Geraint and the bishop.

"And if ye do not this command," rang out the voice of the bishop (and there was sorrow in its tone, and silence sank on all), "if ye do not, then will His Holiness excommunicate this land. None of ye here have seen so terrible a thing as a land laid under the interdict of the Holy Church, and rarely doth she find her children so stubbornly evil as to merit it. But the Father of the Church, seeing how this land is torn and rent by this bitter war between brothers, and fearful lest, while ye tear at each others' lives, the fierce and evil pagan will gain upon ye and beat the lives from both of ye, and possess this fair island and drive Christ and His religion from it utterly—seeing all this, His Holiness would pronounce the doom if ye are too stiffnecked to obey him. Then will ye see this land lie as if a curse were upon it. Your churches will be shut, and the relics of the holy saints will be laid in ashes, the priests will not give prayers nor the Church its holy offices; and the dead shall lie uncoffined, for no prayers may be said over them. Say, then, King Arthur of Britain, what shall be the answer to the command of His Holiness which here I lay before thee."

With these words the bishop held a parchment rolled out between his hands before the eyes of the king. Men craned forward and saw the black writing on the white skin, and the great seals, or bulls, hanging from it whereon those who could read saw the device of the Pope of Rome.

"Say, is this thy doing?" cried Sir Gawaine fiercely, looking at King Geraint. "Didst thou send this meddling priest to Rome to get this?"

"That did I," replied Geraint.

"Then now I make this vow," thundered Sir Gawaine, "that though thou hast balked me of my vengeance now, I will mark thee, thou king of two minds, and be thou sure that erelong I will avenge me of this treachery, and that upon thy body and in thy blood."

"I mark thy words, Sir Gawaine," said Geraint, whose eyes flashed fiercely, though his voice was calm, "and I say again thou art mad. I will tell thee and the king, our lord and master, why I did advise the holy bishop to go to Rome and get the Pope's command. First, as ye all know, I did think this war a wicked one beyond all measure, and ever have I raised my voice against it. And what I foresaw has come to pass. As the good priest saith, while ye tore at each other's throats here in the furthest marches of the north, the sly, fierce pagan, learning how all the land was rent and weakened by this evil war, has crept up in his longships, he has landed at many solitary places on the coast, and has spread far and wide throughout the land, burning and slaughtering. The long files of his captives, our kinsmen, go day by day, even as ye fight here, brother with brother, down to the black ships, and ye do naught to save them or avenge them. Already have I, in my office as Count of the Saxon Shore, battered them back to their ships at Lemanis, Llongporth, and Rutupiae; but here in the north, for all that the old lion, Uriens of Regcd, worn with war and full of age, hath taken the field against them, here, behind your backs as ye battle, kin with kin, a great and a stubborn pagan, whom men call Hyring the Landwaster, hath entered the land and still prevails. Crafty he is and strong, for he hath made treaties with some of our weaker kin, and their women he hath taken in marriage for his leaders, and thus in our very midst there is treachery, hand-in-hand with the brutal invaders. Yet still you, Gawaine, are so mad, so lost to all care for your nation's weal, that you would see your people ruined and your land possessed by the savage boars of Saxons, while ye slake your vengeance for a private wrong. If still you so would do, I call you traitor, and, by the grace of God, I will make good my words upon your body, when we have thrust the pagan from the land and peace is within out borders once again."

While the thunder of his noble anger still rolled through the wide hall, King Arthur arose, and men marked the resolution in his eyes.

"I will that there be no more war," he said, and he looked sternly at Gawaine. "Geraint hath spoken the truth, and the truth shall prevail. I repent me that I have so long forgotten the needs of my kingdom. Do thou now, good bishop, go to Sir Lancelot, tell him that I will make peace with him and that I will receive back my queen. And do thou, good Geraint, fare south again. I thank thee from my heart for what thou hast done. Would to Heaven that all my knights were as clean-souled and as single-minded in devotion unto me as thou art. Do thou go and fulfil thy great office. Watch thou the coasts as hitherto thou hast watched them; and soon I will follow to aid thee, should the foul and savage pagans strive again to break into my realm."

But, after all, Sir Gawaine had his way in part. The bishop took the king's assurance, sealed with his great seal, whereby he promised Sir Lancelot that he should come and go safe from murder or sudden onset, and desiring him to bring the queen to the king at his hall at Carlisle. But in that parchment was no word of reconciliation with Sir Lancelot. Sir Gawaine fiercely told the king that the day on which he, the king, should clasp the hand of Lancelot in friendship, he, Sir Gawaine, with all his vassals and his men, would leave the kingdom. So deep and burning was the hatred which Gawaine bore Sir Lancelot that he even threatened that, if his will was not granted, he would join the pagans and fight against the king.

So shamed and saddened was the king at these words that, to put an end to his nephew's rage, he consented to do as he desired. Therefore, though the bishop strove to persuade the king to make his peace with Sir Lancelot, Sir Gawaine's will was done, and the bishop went sadly to Joyous Gard.

He showed his writings to Sir Lancelot and the queen, and both were sorrowful in that no word of reconciliation was said.

"I will do my lord's desire," said the knight, "but I see that Sir Gawaine's hatred of me is in no way abated. Nevertheless, do thou ride, my lord bishop, to the king. Commend me unto his good grace, and say to him that in five days I will myself bring my lady, Queen Gwenevere, unto him as he doth desire."

On the day appointed, as the king sat in hall at Carlisle, surrounded by his knights and their ladies, with Sir Gawaine standing on the high seat beside him, there came the beat of many hoofs, and into the town rode Sir Lancelot with the queen, knights and squires accompanying them. They reined up at the wide door of the hall, and Sir Lancelot alighted, and having helped the queen to dismount, he took her hand, and led her through the ranks of knights and ladies to where sat King Arthur.

Sir Lancelot kneeled upon the edge of the dais, and the queen with him; and to see so noble a knight and so beautiful a lady, sad of countenance as they were, forced many a tear to the eyes of the knights and dames who looked on. Then, rising, and taking up the queen, Sir Lancelot spoke:

"My most redoubted lord," he said, "you shall understand that by the pope's commandment and yours I have brought unto you my lady your queen, as right requireth; and if there be any knight here, of any degree, who shall say that she or I have ever thought to plot treason against your person or your crown, or the peace of this realm, then do I say here and now that I, Lancelot du Lake, will make it good upon his body, that he lies. And, my gracious lord, if this is all that there is between you, my king, and myself, there need be naught of ill thought between us, but only peace and good-will. But I wist well that one that hates me will not suffer ye to do what is in your good and kingly heart."

Sternly did Sir Lancelot look at Sir Gawaine, while the tears gushed from King Arthur's eyes, and from the eyes of many that heard Sir Lancelot's sad words.

Fierce and dark was the look which Sir Gawaine returned to Sir Lancelot.

"The king may do as he will," he said harshly and in a loud voice, "but wit thou well, Sir Lancelot, thou and I shall never be at peace till one of us be slain; for thou didst slay my twain brothers, though they bore no harness against thee nor any ill will. Yet traitorously thou didst slay them!"

"Alas, my lord," said Sir Lancelot, and the tears bedewed his face, "I cannot ask you for your forgiveness for that deed, unwitting though it was done and in my madness. Would to Heaven they had worn harness! Wit you well that ever will I bewail the death of my dear friend, Sir Gareth. 'Twas I that made him knight, and ever did I delight to see him, to hear his manly laugh ring out, and to see the light in his brave eyes that never suffered a mean or evil action. I wot he loved me above all other knights, and there was none of my kinsmen that I loved so much as I loved him. Ever will the sorrow of the death of thy brethren lie upon my soul; and to make some small amends I will, if my lord will suffer it and it will please you, Sir Gawaine, I will walk in my shirt and barefoot from Lemanis even unto this town, and at every ten miles I will found a holy house, and endow it with monks to pray for the souls of Sir Gareth and Sir Gaheris. Surely, Sir Gawaine, that will do more good unto their souls than that my most noble lord and you should war on me."

Every cheek was wet and the tears of the king fell from his eyes, yet made he no effort to restrain or hide them.

"Out upon such monkish deeds!" cried Sir Gawaine, and his scornful eyes surveyed the weeping knights and dames. "Know thee, once for all, that never shalt thou wipe away the treacherous murder of my brothers but by thy blood. Ye are safe now for a season, for the pope hath given you safety, but in this land—whatever comes of it I care not—thou shalt not abide above fifteen days, or else I shall have thy head. So make ye no more ado; but deliver the queen from thee, and get thee quickly out of this court and out of this realm."

"Well," said Sir Lancelot, and laughed grimly, "if I had known I should have so short an answer to my proffers of peace, I had thought twice ere I had come hither. But now, madam," he said, turning to the weeping queen beside him, "I must say farewell to ye, for now do I depart from this noble fellowship and this dear realm forever. Pray for me, and send me word if any lying tongues speak evil of you, and if any knight's hand may deliver you by battle, believe me mine shall so deliver you."

With these words Sir Lancelot bent and kissed the queen's hand, and so turned away and departed. There was neither king, baron, knight nor squire of all that great company who did not weep, nor think that Sir Gawaine had been of most evil mind to refuse the noble proffers of Sir Lancelot.

Heavy was King Arthur ever thereafter, and never might man see his face brighten nor hear his laugh; and the better of his knights sorrowed with him, and knew what was in his heart.

"In this realm will be no more quiet," said Sir Owen of the Fountain to his fellows as they stood upon the walls of Carlisle and saw the band of Sir Lancelot riding southwards, the sunlight flashing from their helms and armour. "The pagans have gathered strength daily while we have fought with each other, and that which would have given us the strength and the union which would hurl them from our coasts is shattered and broken. By the noble fellowship of the Round Table was King Arthur and his realm borne up, and by their nobleness the king and all his realm was in quietness and in peace. And a great part," he ended, "was because of the noble nature of Sir Lancelot, whom Sir Gawaine's mad rage hath driven from the kingdom. Nor is all the evil ended yet."

XIII

Of the Rebellion of Mordred
and the Death of King Arthur

WHEN SIR LANCELOT AND ALL HIS MEN HAD LEFT THE REALM
of Britain and had betaken themselves to Brittany, where Sir Lancelot
had a kingdom of his own, the Saxons began to increase in Britain, both
in strength and numbers. Almost daily a long black ship, crammed
with pagans, was sighted from some part of the coast; and the British,
praying that the fierce pirates would not visit their homes, would watch
the terrible warship till it passed; or else, caught unawares, would have
to flee inland in a breathless panic when the dragon-headed prow
loomed through the sea-mist, and the barbarous warriors swarmed
over the sides and ran knee-deep in the water, their eyes gleaming with
the joy of killing and their hands eager for the looting.

Then King Arthur made ready a great host, and for two years he
fought in the northern parts against the bands of the pirates. Swift were
the blows he struck, for the great wide Roman roads were still open,
not grass-grown and deserted, and with his mounted knights and men
he could ride quickly from place to place, striking fiercely and scattering the foul pagans.

Ten was the number of these battles which he fought in the north,
six against the Saxon pirates and four against the wild cats of Caledonia,
whom men call Picts and Scots, and who had ventured south in greater
numbers as soon as they heard how the king warred with his lords and

the rich land was open to plunder. Two others he fought in the south, one against an insolent band of pirates who dared even to attack his palace city of Caerleon-upon-Usk. But so heavy and deadly a blow did he strike at them then, that from that battle barely a dozen pagans were left to flee like fire to their ships.

Not without loss of many of his brave warriors did Arthur win these battles, for the pagans were good men of their hands and not easily were they beaten. Saddest of all was the loss of the noble Geraint, who, thrusting back the pirates once again from the harbour of Llongporth, got his death there with many of his valiant men.

When the fame of King Arthur's prowess and the might of his knights had gone abroad among the pagans, they were afraid and would not venture in great numbers to invade the land again, and there was peace and rest in Britain for a space.

Then Sir Gawaine, remembering his hatred of Sir Lancelot, persuaded the king to make him ready another host, with which to invade the land of Brittany where Sir Lancelot ruled his kingdom. For a long time the king would not listen to his advice, and the queen, with all her power, strove against Sir Gawaine. But that knight and his large following of knights and men-at-arms had been of great service in the recent wars against the pagans, and the king could not wholly refuse to listen to Sir Gawaine's demands.

Also Sir Mordred added his words to those of his brother, and said that men who came from Brittany said that Sir Lancelot was getting him ready a large army, and training many men, although he was at peace with his neighbours in Gaul. But the rumour went, as Sir Mordred reported, that Sir Lancelot was only waiting his time, and when King Arthur should be more than usually pressed by his pagan foes, Sir Lancelot and his great host would sail swiftly across the sea and seize the kingdom of Britain, when Arthur, exhausted by war, would be unable to withstand the fresh warriors of Sir Lancelot, and would lose both his queen and his crown.

For a time the king would not suffer these evil rumours to be mentioned in his presence, but many of his counsellors thought there was much truth in them. At length, so persistent was Sir Mordred and those whom he craftily persuaded to believe him, that for sheer weariness the king consented to take an army across to Brittany, and to demand that Sir Lancelot should own that the king was his overlord, and that he should do homage to King Arthur for his kingdom.

The host was prepared, therefore, and at a meeting of his council King Arthur made his nephew, Sir Mordred, Regent of Britain, to rule in the king's place while he should be abroad; and Queen Gwenevere he placed under the governance of Sir Mordred, as well as the officers of the court.

When they had passed the sea and landed in the coasts of Sir Lancelot's country, Sir Gawaine ordered his knights to go through the nearer parts, burning the houses and wasting the lands of the people. This he did to enrage Sir Lancelot against the king, so that he would not listen quietly to any demand which the king might make of him.

Word was brought to Sir Lancelot of the landing of King Arthur and the plundering and wasting of the land, but for some days he would do naught; for he was loath to take up arms against the king he loved, who had made him a knight.

At length Sir Bors came to him, and with that knight were others, as Sir Lunel of the Brake, Sir Magus of Pol, and Sir Alan of the Stones with his six mighty brothers.

"My lord, Sir Lancelot," said Sir Bors, "it is great shame that we suffer them to ride over our lands, burning the homes of our folk and destroying the crops in the fields."

Sir Alan also, who with his brothers were seven as noble knights as a man might seek in seven lands ere he might find a brotherhood as valiant and withal as courteous, spoke to the like purport, saying:

"Sir Lancelot, for the love of our land, let us ride out and meet these invaders in the field, for we have never been wont to cower in castles nor in towns."

Then spoke Sir Lancelot, who was lord of them all.

"My fair lords," he said, "ye wit well that I am loath to raise my hand against my own dear lord and to shed the blood of Christian men. Yet I understand how it chafes you to stand by and see your fair land ruined by those that hate me. Therefore I will send a messenger to my lord Arthur, desiring him to make treaty with me. Then when we have his reply, we will consider the matter further."

A damsel was therefore sent to the camp of King Arthur, and she bore a message from Sir Lancelot. She was brought to Sir Lucan, who was the king's butler, and she told him whence she had come and why.

"Alas!" said Sir Lucan. "I fear ye have made your journey in vain, fair damsel. My lord, King Arthur, would quickly accord with Sir Lancelot, whom he loves, but Sir Gawaine will not suffer him."

Just then Sir Gawaine happened to pass by, and saw the maiden, and knew that she was not one of their party. He turned towards her, and his fierce eyes looked at her, grimly sour.

"Whence come ye?" he said harshly.

"I come hither to speak with King Arthur," said the maiden, "for I bear a message from my lord, Sir Lancelot."

With an angry gesture Sir Gawaine seized her bridle and led her palfrey swiftly to the edge of the camp.

"Depart!" he cried harshly. "Tell your master that it is idle for him to send to mine uncle. Tell him from me, Sir Gawaine, that by the vow of my knighthood, I will never leave this land till I or he be slain. Now go!"

When this message was told to Sir Lancelot, the tears stood in his eyes and he went apart, and for that day the knights his comrades held their counsel. But they resolved that next day they would prevail upon Sir Lancelot to issue forth and give battle.

But in the morning, when they looked from the walls of the castle, they saw that Sir Gawaine had crept up in the dawn, and now was the place besieged. Thereupon there was fierce fighting, for Sir Gawaine caused ladders to be reared, and his knights strove to climb over the wall, but were mightily beaten back by Sir Lancelot's party.

Then the attackers drew off for a space, and Sir Gawaine, well armed, came before the chief gate, upon a stout steed. He shook his lance at the men over the gate, and cried:

"Where art thou, false traitor, Sir Lancelot? Why dost thou hide thyself within holes and walls like a coward? Look out now, thou timid soul, for when I may get at thee I will revenge upon thy evil body the death of my brothers twain."

These shameful words were heard by Sir Lancelot, and all his knights and kin that stood about him, and they said:

"Sir Lancelot, now ye must be done with thy courtesy and go forth and beat back those evil words upon his foul mouth."

"It is even so," said Sir Lancelot; "but sorry I am and heavy of spirit thus to fight with him, who hath been my dear brother-in-arms so long, and whose brothers I did unwittingly slay. And much evil shall come of this."

Then he commanded his strongest horse to be saddled, and bade his armour to be dressed upon him, and when he was fully armed he stood at the top of the gate and cried upon the king.

"My lord Arthur," he said, "you that made me knight, wit you well that I am right heavy that ever ye do pursue me thus; but now that Sir Gawaine hath used villainous words about me, I must needs defend myself."

Sir Gawaine, seated upon his horse below, laughed grimly, and cried upon the other.

"O Lancelot, Lancelot," he said, "what a man of words thou art! If thou darest to battle with me, cease thy babbling, man, and come off, and let us ease our hearts with strong blows."

Then Sir Lancelot issued forth with many of his knights, and a covenant was made between the hosts that there should be no fighting until Sir Gawaine and Sir Lancelot had fought together, and one was either dead or yielden.

Thereupon the two knights departed some way and then came together with all the might of their horses, and each smote the other in the midst of the shield. So strong were the knights and stout and big the spears, that their horses could not stand the shock, and so fell to the ground. Then the knights quickly avoided their horses and dressed their shields, and fought fiercely together with their swords.

So valiantly did each give and receive blows, and so heavy and grim was their fighting, that all the knights and lords that stood thereabout marvelled thereat and were fain to say, in as many good words, that never had they seen such sword-play.

In a little while, so shrewd and skilful were they both were wounded and the blood oozed from the joints of their armour, and it was great marvel to see that they could still stand, dashing their shields upon each other, and each beating upon the other with great slashes of their swords. And which was the stronger of the twain none might say.

Now Sir Gawaine had a magic power, which had been endowed upon him at his birth by a great witch who was a friend of his mother, the sorceress, Queen Morgan le Fay, wife of King Lot. No one knew of this secret power except King Arthur, and often had it availed Sir Gawaine, so that in dire perils of onfall, sudden ambush, or long battle, it had given him the victory, when all about him had been slain or wounded or taken captive.

The magic was that, from the hour of nine until high noon, the strength of his body increased until it was three times his natural strength, which itself was full great, though in that, for deep wind and breath and might of arm, Sir Lancelot was the stronger.

Now while they fought together, Sir Lancelot felt that Sir Gawaine seemed not to weaken as time went on, and he marvelled greatly. Then he felt that indeed Sir Gawaine's strength was greater than it had been at the beginning, and a fear came into his heart that Sir Gawaine was possessed of a demon.

But Sir Lancelot was stout of heart as well as old in warcraft, and knew that if he could tire Sir Gawaine he might, by one blow, get the better of him when he saw a good chance. Therefore Sir Lancelot began to husband his strength, and instead of spending it in feinting and attacking, he bore his shield ever before him, covering himself from the fierce blows of his enemy.

Thus he kept up his own strength; but hard put to it was he when, towards midday, Sir Gawaine seemed to have the might of a very giant, and the shield arm of Sir Lancelot was numbed by reason of the crashing blows which Sir Gawaine's sword rained upon it.

Great travail indeed had Sir Lancelot to stand up and not to yield; and while men marvelled how he could endure, none knew all he suffered.

Then, as the bell of the convent in the town boomed forth the hour of noon, Sir Gawaine heaved up his sword for a final blow; but his sword descended just as the last stroke of twelve had died away, and Sir Lancelot marvelled to feel that what should have been so grievous a blow that, belike, he could not have stood before it, fell upon his shield with no more than the strength of the blow given by an ordinary man.

When Sir Lancelot felt the might of Sir Gawaine so suddenly give way, he drew himself up to his full height and said:

"Sir Gawaine, I know not by what evil power ye have fought, but now I feel that ye have done. Now, my lord, Sir Gawaine, I must do my part, for none may know the great and grievous strokes I have endured this day with great pain."

With that Sir Lancelot redoubled his blows, and the sword of Sir Gawaine gave before the might of Sir Lancelot, and his shield was rent. Then Sir Lancelot gave so great a buffet on the helm of the other that Sir Gawaine staggered, and with yet another blow Sir Lancelot hurled him headlong to the ground.

Men held their breath, for now, after so fierce and stubborn a struggle, they felt sure that Sir Lancelot, hot and enraged against his enemy, would rip off the other's helm and strike his head off instantly.

But, instead, Sir Lancelot stood for a moment looking at his prostrate enemy. Then men gasped to see him thrust his sword into its scabbard with a clang, turn on his heel, and begin to walk away.

They saw the prone knight raise his head and look as if in surprise at the retreating figure of Sir Lancelot.

"Why dost thou depart?" cried Sir Gawaine, rage in his mocking voice. "Turn again, false knight, and slay me! If ye leave me thus, thou shalt gain nothing from it, for when I am whole I will slay thee when I may."

Men marvelled to hear a fallen foe use such shameful and hateful words, but they marvelled much more when Sir Lancelot, turning, cried:

"I shall endure you, sir, if God give me grace; but wit you well, Sir Gawaine, I will never smite you to death."

Many that before had hated Sir Lancelot were moved by these noble words, and by the sight of his mercy; and they deemed that there was hardly another man in all Christendom that would have shown such nobility, save Sir Galahad and Sir Perceval, and they were dead.

So Sir Lancelot went into the city, and Sir Gawaine was borne into King Arthur's tent and his wounds were cleaned and salved. Thus he lay for three weeks, hard of mood and bitter in his hatred, and longing eagerly to get well, so he might try again to slay Sir Lancelot. Meanwhile he prayed the king to attack Sir Lancelot's walls, to try to draw him forth, or to take the city by treachery.

But the king would do naught. He was sick for sorrow because of the war that was between him and Sir Lancelot, and by reason of the wounds of his nephew Sir Gawaine.

"Alas," was ever his reply, "neither you nor I, my nephew, will win worship at these walls. For we make war for no reason, with as noble a knight as ever drew breath, and one more merciful and courteous than any that ever graced the court of any Christian king."

"Nevertheless," replied Sir Gawaine, raging at the king's love for Sir Lancelot, "neither his mercy nor courtesy would avail against my good sword, once I could sink it in his treacherous heart."

As soon as Sir Gawaine might walk and ride, he armed him at all points and mounted a great courser, and with a long wide spear in his hand he went spurring to the great gate of the town.

"Where art thou, Lancelot?" he cried in a fierce voice. "Come thou forth, traitor knight and recreant! I am here to revenge me on thy evil body for thy treacherous slaughter of my twain brothers."

All this language Sir Lancelot heard, and leaning from the tower he thus spake:

"Sir Gawaine, it sorrows me that ye will not cease your foul speaking. I know your might, and all that ye may do, and well ye wot ye may do me great hurt or death."

"Come down, then," cried Sir Gawaine, "for what my heart craves is to slay thee. Thou didst get the better of me the other day, and I come this day to get my revenge. And wit thee well I will lay thee as low as thou didst lay me."

"I will not keep ye waiting long," said Sir Lancelot, "for as ye charge me of treachery ye shall have your hands full of me erelong, however the battle between us may end."

Then happened it even as before. The knights encountered first with spears, but Sir Gawaine's broke into a hundred pieces on the shield of Sir Lancelot. Then, dismounting, the knights fought on foot with swords.

Sir Gawaine put forth all his strength, hoping, with the magic power which he possessed, to dash Sir Lancelot to his knees. But Sir Lancelot was more wary than before, and under cover of his shield he husbanded his strength until the hour of noon, when, as before, he felt that Sir Gawaine's might had strangely ebbed away.

When that had come to pass, Sir Lancelot said:

"Now once more have I proved that ye fight not with a man's fair strength, Sir Gawaine, but with some evil power. And full grievously was I put to it to withstand many of thy sad blows. Now ye have done your great deeds, and I will do mine."

Then with one stroke, of so marvellous a force that men marvelled, Sir Lancelot beat down Sir Gawaine's guard, and struck him a full heavy blow on the side of the helm, beating it in so that the old wound burst again.

Sir Gawaine fell to the ground, and for some moments lay still as if he were dead or in a swoon; but he was only dazed, and soon recovering, he raved and foamed as he lay there, cursing Sir Lancelot for a traitorous coward and a base knight, and even, in his madness, thrusting towards him with his sword.

"Wit thou well, base knight," he cried, "that I am not slain yet. Come thou near and lie here with me, and we will fight this battle until we die."

"I will do no more than I have done, my lord," said Sir Lancelot, "and when thou art able to stand I will meet thee again. But to smite a wounded man that may not stand, I will not."

Then Sir Lancelot withdrew to the town, while Sir Gawaine still raved and abused him, and men marvelled both at the exceeding madness of the hatred of Sir Gawaine and the great restraint and nobleness of Lancelot. Many said that had Sir Gawaine said half as many shameful things to one of them, they would have instantly rased his evil head from his shoulders.

For a month Sir Gawaine lay sick, but was always eager to be up and able again. And at length the leech said that in three days he should ride, whereat Sir Gawaine was joyful.

"Again," said he to King Arthur, who sat beside him, "again shall I have to do with that base fellow, and ill attend me if I do not end the matter this time."

"Ye had ended it long ago, or been ended," said the king, "except for the nobleness of Sir Lancelot that forbore to slay you."

"Ay, we all know your love of the pestilent fool, uncle," said Sir Gawaine, "but we will stay here until we have made an end of him and his kingdom, if it take us all our lives."

Even as he spoke there came the clear call of a trumpet outside in the camp, and Sir Bedevere came to the door of the king's tent, his grim old face pale, his grizzled hair unkempt, and every sign of haste and travel upon his dress.

The king started up. "Sir Bedevere, ye bring evil tidings from Britain!" he cried. "Can it be that more ruin and wrong is to come than that I suffer now? What is your news?"

"O my king, it is that Mordred your nephew hath rebelled," said Sir Bedevere, "and has gathered much people about him, and hath sent many letters to all the lords and knights your vassals, promising them wealth and lands if they make him king. And Gwenevere your queen he hath imprisoned, saying that he will wed her when ye are slain."

"Mordred! Mordred!" cried the king. "Him that I thought was a quiet, strong man—turned so base a traitor!"

"Ay, he was ever the traitor, though brother of mine," cried Sir

Gawaine in a voice of rage. "A man that speaks in whispers, haunts dark corners, and ever sneers with his lips."

"Hardly with my life have I escaped to tell you this," went on Sir Bedevere, "for he placed men to watch me after I had scorned his evil offers to myself. But now, my lord, quickly ye must betake yourself and all your army from this fruitless and wrongful war against Sir Lancelot, and hasten to beat down the poisonous viper whom ye have nourished in your bosom."

Ere the day was done the army of King Arthur had raised the siege of Sir Lancelot's town and were quickly marching to the sea, there to take their boats across to Britain to punish the usurper and traitor, Sir Mordred.

A fair wind carried them across the sea, but long ere they reached the shallows of the beach at Dover they saw the sunlight flashing from thousands of headpieces of knights and men-at-arms, set to oppose the landing of their rightful lord. The king was fiercely angry, and he commanded the masters of the ships to launch their small boats, and into these the knights swarmed and were rowed towards the shore.

But the rebels of Mordred also launched boats and great pinnaces filled with knights, and when the boats of the opposite parties met, then there was fierce fighting and much slaughter of many good knights and barons and other brave men. Then King Arthur and his chief knights drew forth their horses from the holds of the ships, and leaped with them into the sea, and fiercely did they throw themselves upon Sir Mordred and his knights, and there was grievous fighting on horseback in the shallow water, which soon was dyed with the blood of the slain.

So stubborn were the king and his fighting men that the army of Mordred was forced to retreat towards the land, and then, when the king and Gawaine had trimmed their own ranks, order was given for one concerted rush against the enemy. The other side showed little fight now, and made no stand, but fled inland.

When the battle was over, King Arthur let bury his people that were dead, so far as they could be discovered in the waves; and the wounded he caused to be carried into the town of Dover to be cared for.

A squire came to the king as he stood giving orders as to these things.

"My lord king," said the squire, "Sir Gawaine lies sore wounded in a boat, and we know not whether he be alive or dead."

"Alas!" cried the king, and the knights about him were full of pity at the sudden grief that came into his voice and his looks. "Is this true? Then is all my joy of life at an end."

The squire led him to the boat in which Sir Gawaine lay, who stirred as the king approached, and feebly smiled.

"My uncle," said Sir Gawaine, "wit you well that now is my death-day come, for I know I shall not last this bout. For I am smitten upon the wound which Sir Lancelot gave me, and I feel that now I shall die."

"Alas, my sister's son," cried the king, taking Sir Gawaine in his arms and kissing him, while the tears flowed down his cheeks, "this is the woefullest day of all my life. For if ye depart, Gawaine, how solitary am I! Gawaine! Gawaine! In Sir Lancelot and in thee had I most my love and my joy, and now shall I lose ye both, and all my earthly joy is gone from me."

"Alas," said Sir Gawaine, "sorrow's on me now that I have caused you such grief, mine uncle. I see now that I have been mad with rage against that noble knight, Sir Lancelot, who slew my dear brothers unwittingly. And now I repent me sorely. I would that I could live to repair the evil that I have done to you and to Sir Lancelot. But my time is come. I shall not live till evening."

They wept together, and the knights that stood about them also wept for pure grief, to think how much sorrow and ruin was caused by the mad rage of Sir Gawaine, which had pushed the good king on to make war against his will.

"I am the causer of this rebellion by my traitor brother," said Sir Gawaine, "and my name shall be cursed for it. Had I not wilfully driven thee, thou wouldst have accorded with Sir Lancelot, and he and his brave kinsmen would have held your cankered enemies in subjection, or else cut them utterly away. Lift me up, my lord, and let me have a scribe, for I will send a letter to Sir Lancelot ere I die."

Then Sir Gawaine was set up by the king, and a priest was brought, who wrote at the dying man's dictation. And the purport of the letter was in this wise:

"Unto Sir Lancelot, flower of all noble knights that ever I heard of or saw, and once my dear friend, now do I, Sir Gawaine, King Lot's son of Orkney and the Lothians, and sister's son to King Arthur, send thee greeting and let thee know by these writings that I am this day done to death, having been wounded at the landing against rebellious traitors, and struck upon the wound which thou didst give me twice, before thy city. Whereby I have got my death. But I will have thee to wit that I sought my death of thee, and got that wound deservedly of thee, who could have slain me twice, but for thy high nobility and great courtesy. I, Gawaine, beseech of thee forgiveness for my madness, and crave that thou wilt remember the dear friendly days we have had together in times long past, and for all the love that was between us. Come thou over the sea, and with thy knights do thou press to the help of Arthur, our noble lord, who is beset by a traitorous villain, my brother Mordred, who hath dared to rebel against his rightful lord, and hath crowned himself king. Do thou hasten, good Sir Lancelot, when thou shalt receive this letter, and follow the king. But ere thou goest from this seashore do thou come to my tomb, and pray some prayer more or less for my sinful soul, that in its madness did evilly entreat thee."

Then was Sir Gawaine shriven, and in a little while he swooned, while all stood uncovered round about him. When the rays of the afternoon sun cast long shadows of the knights and fighting men who were hurrying up and down the shore making ready to depart, Sir Gawaine awoke from his swoon and looked up. For a moment he did not recognise King Arthur; then he smiled at him very sweetly and said in a low voice:

"Kiss me—and forgive me!"

The king knelt down and kissed the pallid face of Sir Gawaine, and for very sorrow he felt that the heart in his breast was nigh to bursting.

So in a little while, with the beat of the surf and the cry of the seagulls upon his ears, the light of the sun in his eyes, and the free air of heaven all about him, Sir Gawaine died. And his death was as he had ever craved it to be, under the open sky, after battle, where he had given good strokes and received them.

Now the letter which Sir Gawaine had written was given unto a young squire of Sir Gawaine's, by name Tewder, and he was commanded to depart forthwith back to Brittany, and deliver it into the hands of Sir Lancelot. But, among the knights that had stood about the dying Sir Gawaine, was a traitor, who was in the service of Sir Mordred the rebel, and he knew that if Sir Lancelot should receive that letter, and come to Britain with all his brave kin and their host, Sir Mordred would have much ado to conquer King Arthur.

Therefore the traitor knight, whose name was Sir Fergus, did accost Tewder the squire, and with fair seeming told him that he also was bidden to go back to Brittany, to bring back certain jewels which the king in his hasty departure had left in his lodging at the town of Dol.

Tewder, unsuspecting of all evil, went aboard a boat with Sir Fergus, and together they bargained with the master to take them across when the tide should rise again at dark. Together they crossed the sea that night and took the road towards Sir Lancelot's town; and in a dark wood Sir Fergus set upon the squire, who fought bravely, but was slain at last, and the letter of Sir Gawaine was taken by the traitor.

Then, returning to the seashore, the wretch went aboard another boat, and chaffered with the merchant to take him across the sea to the town of Llongporth, whence he thought to get quickly to Mordred, to receive from him the reward of his treachery and murder. But at night, as they sailed over the dark sea, a fifty-oared longship, filled with Saxon pirates, crept upon them; the pagans poured over the sides, slew men almost in their sleep, and flung their bodies overboard. And though Fergus fought well, his head was almost struck from his body by a great sheering axe-blow. When the pirates had taken all the goods they desired from the merchant vessel, they stove a hole in its side, and it sank to the bottom of the sea. So that no man ever again saw the letter which was meant for Sir Lancelot.

For some weeks Sir Lancelot lay quiet, knowing naught of the death of Sir Gawaine or of the letter desiring him to go to the help of King Arthur. Many rumours came to him, through the ship-folk, of the wicked rebellion of Sir Mordred, and though Sir Lancelot longed to go across to Britain and fight for King Arthur, his kinsmen would not consent, but said it would be unseemly, unless the king craved his aid, and sued for pardon for making war against Sir Lancelot in his own country.

Thus the precious weeks went by, and much ill fortune happened in Britain, that had ended otherwise if Sir Lancelot had been by the king.

Three days after the battle upon the shore, the king's host came up with the host of Sir Mordred on Barhamdown. Many folks had joined the rebels' side, because they hated the king for making war upon Sir Lancelot, and the king was sorely hurt in his mind to see a banner borne by one part of the usurper's army, on which was the device of Sir Lancelot's.

This the crafty Sir Mordred had commanded to be done, knowing that it would damp the spirits of King Arthur and his men.

"Verily," said King Arthur, "my evil deeds have sprung up as armed men against me. I fought unjustly with Sir Lancelot, and here are some that loved him arrayed against me for that wicked war."

"If ye would send for Sir Lancelot," said Sir Owen of the Fountain, who stood by him, "ye would learn, I verily believe, that Sir Lancelot loves and worships you as of old, and hath no mind to fight on the side of this sly fox, Mordred. Send for Sir Lancelot, lord."

"Nay, I will not—I may not," said the king. "If he cometh by the words which Sir Gawaine wrote to him, I shall know that he loves me and forgives me; but if he cometh not, I shall know he hates me, and I shall merit his ill favour. He owes naught to me since I used him so evilly, and therefore I may not ask his aid."

All day the battle raged upon the great green down, and many were the fierce fights which took place upon the top thereof, where, behind great earthworks freshly timbered, the main host of Sir Mordred stood, the banner of the great red dragon in their midst.

But at the last, so fast and fierce did the blows of King Arthur's men fall, and so stubbornly did they press on, that Sir Mordred's host gave way. Pouring forth by the upper gate, they ran pell-mell north-wards, and the knights and fighting men of Arthur kept up with them for many miles, and there was a running fight and much wounding and slaying all through the fresh green countryside, where the hedges were laden with May blossoms, and in the sky the larks were trilling.

And that day many a wounded man crawled groaning into the thickets to die, many a chalky cart-rut ran red with blood, and many a white face, with wide-open, sightless eyes, stared up at the blue sky, where the fleecy clouds sailed in the gentle wind.

For three weeks after this battle both sides rested, and like great wrestlers gathered all their strength for one great struggle. Knights and riders were sent by both sides into all parts, with letters to lords and knights, charging them to take their sides in the war. Many people from about London came to the banner of Mordred, and the parts now called Kent, Sussex and Surrey, Essex and Suffolk held wholly with him; but those in the west, as Wales, Devon, Cornwall and the middle parts, thronged to the banner of the king.

Few came from the north, for there the pagan pirates stalked with fire and sword through and through the land, and the British lords and chiefs that were alive had little power to stay them now. King Uriens was dead, slain by the dagger of a traitor, and so were two other great chieftains; so that men south of Trent sorrowfully shook their heads and said that now the north was no longer the land of the British folk, but was given over to the savage heathen hordes.

Then, to meet the many that flocked together in his favour, King Arthur drew him with his host westward beyond Sarum. There on the wide downs beside the great standing-stones of the Old Princes, which men now call Stonehenge, a great multitude of chiefs and knights and yeomen came to his banner.

But Sir Mordred avoided a battle, and, instead, kept aloof with his army, and began to burn and harry the country which was on the side of Arthur. He took Calleva and Cunetio, and put the people to the sword, and took much gear from those wealthy cities; then he stole through the great forest by night and came to Palladun, which was a rich town builded upon the top of a great hill. He thought to take this unawares, but it was well watched and well armed, and he strove to break into it and was kept about it for some days.

That delay was used well by King Arthur, for he made great haste to pass through the wild country, filled with wide marshes and thick woods as it was, which separated him from his enemy. Then Mordred, hearing through the spies of the king's approach, got his host away and thought to pass into the lands of Devon, which were those of King Dewer, son of the dead Geraint, and held firmly for Arthur.

But in the wild wasteland beside the Endless Waters, King Arthur caught up with him, and barred his further way. And the king remembered that this was that same land, full of gaunt standing-stones and haunted by trolls and witches, where Merlin had once led him, and where he had gained the sword Excalibur.

It was late in the day when the two armies faced each other, and both prepared to pass the night upon the field. Bitter was the wind that evening, and the skies were dim and leaden of hue, as if spring had been overcome by winter; and to shelter the king a tent had been put up in a little dark wood of stunted firs, called the Wood of Drood. Just in the deep dark before the dawn, when the blood in men's veins was coldest, and the life in their hearts was weakest, a dreadful cry wailed out through the dark wood, and there came the sound as of leathery wings flapping heavily to and fro above where the king lay sleeping. Men started up about their ashen fires, their faces blanching at the terror that cried in the dark, and they heard the wailing twice repeated, while none dared try to see the thing that wailed.

Then, while their blood chilled and their breath stayed, they heard the heavy flapping pass over their heads and die away towards the camp of Mordred; and there in the distance did the three cries sound again.

Men's hearts sickened as they turned and crept the nearer to each other, but few dared to utter the words upon their lips.

Two knights slept in the tent with the king, Sir Kay and Sir Owen; and they lay in the dark, trembling at the cries of terrible import. When they passed, the knights would not move, fearing to be the first to speak.

"My lords," came the quiet voice of King Arthur out of the dark, "that was the voice of the Hag of Warning. Men say it hath foretold the deaths of many of my house, but I know not. Yet will I take the issue as God shall give it me, trusting in His mercy and the blood of His Son Jesus, and Him crucified."

"Amen," said the two knights, and said no more.

When, in a little while, the sun rose, flashing his warm rays into the fearful eyes that greeted him, men's terror quickly vanished; and when fires were lit and oaten cakes were browning on the irons, or collops sputtered on their skewers, tongues were loosened and faces began to smile. But few spoke of the cries which they had heard, for all loved their king, and hoped that somehow they had dreamed an evil dream, or had but heard the cries of some foul night-bird.

Breakfast being ended, the captains and knights began to trim their men in army array, and talk was eager of the coming battle. Then were seen, coming from Sir Mordred's camp, two bishops; and these were taken at their desire to Arthur, where he stood surrounded by his knights and chieftains.

"Lord," said one of the bishops, he that was head of the great choir or monastery of Amesbury, "cannot we make accord between you and your nephew? Sad it is to see so many great and valiant warriors ranged against each other. Many are sisters' sons, and all are of one speech, one kindred. If this unnatural war doth continue, how much sorrow there will be, how many noble hearts be stilled in death or broken in grief for him that shall never return! How many puissant bodies, now quick and passionate and handsome, will be meat for snarling wolves and carrion for foul birds!"

"What says my rebellious nephew?" asked the king sternly.

"My lord," said the other bishop, a man of soft and silky speech, and he was chief of the choir of Clovesho, "he asks but little, and if ye are willing to make treaty, he also is willing. Grant him but the earldom of Kent and the Andred, with a seat at London, during your days, and do thou appoint him king after your days. For now that Sir Gawaine, Sir Gaheris, and Sir Gareth are slain, he is the only sister's son you have. If ye grant these things he will be your liege, faithful in all things, and a strong arm against your enemies."

Then some of King Arthur's knights would have him agree to these terms, but others would not, and said the king should make no treaty with a traitor, but that Mordred should come and throw himself upon the mercy of his king and uncle.

At the last, after much counsel had been taken. King Arthur agreed to meet Mordred, with fourteen of his chief men, in the space betwixt their hosts, and the king should also take fourteen knights with him. So the bishops went back with this message, and King Arthur called the chieftains of his host about him.

"I go to see this traitor, my nephew," he said to them, "whether he means falsely or truly with this talk of a treaty. But look ye, I in no wise trust him. Hold ye your men warily, and if ye see any sword drawn among us where we stand, do thou sound the horns of attack and come on fiercely, and slay that rebel and all that hold with him."

In like wise did Mordred warn his men, "for," said he, knowing how greatly he had sinned against his generous and noble uncle, "I know well that King Arthur and his knights would be avenged on me if they could."

The party from each army went forward over the stony hillside, until they met midway between the armies, and men watched them keenly. King Arthur spoke chidingly to his nephew Mordred, who, sour and dark of face, looked craftily at the faces of his uncle and his knights. And the chiefs with Mordred, men for the most part of violent and ambitious natures, looked haughtily at King Arthur's party. Nevertheless, there was no bad blood shown, and the talk was continued, and Mordred repeated the demands which the bishops had made.

"But I care not to give to thee Kent and London," said the King. "I tell thee frankly, Mordred, I would not trust thee there. I fear me thou wouldst try some crafty plot with the Saxon pagans if I gave them thee, as that rebel Caros did, who for a time made himself emperor of the Romans here in this land."

"Ha' done, then, my father," said Gorfalk, the son of Mordred, an insolent young man. "Let us cease this. I doubt not we be big enough to get all the kingdom if we fight."

The king looked sternly at the young man, and there was silence among them all as men waited for Arthur's reply.

Then it happened that a young chieftain, standing near the king, felt something bite his foot where the low leathern shoe left it naked. He looked down and saw that he was treading on a viper, which had struck him and was about to strike again. With a cry the knight stepped aside, drew his sword, and cut the reptile in two.

As the blade flashed, silvery bright in the sunlight, a great hoarse cry rose like thunder from the two masses of men watching them on either side; trumpets blared and horns squealed, and shouts of command rose sharp and keen.

Instantly the men standing with Arthur and Mordred looked about them, saw where the young chieftain stood with drawn sword, and knew that now nothing could avert the battle.

"The gods will have it so!" sneered Mordred.

Already the earth trembled and shook with the beat of ten thousand feet of the armies rushing together. A knight of Mordred's, drawing his sword, thrust it into the breast of one of Arthur's chieftains, with the cry:

"This for thy land, Sir Digon, that marches with mine!"

Instantly others fell to fighting hand-to-hand, striking on targe and helm; but Sir Owen, Sir Kay and Sir Bedevere surrounded the king, and all hurried back to the army approaching them. So likewise did Sir Mordred.

Then came the crash of battle, as line on line, with flashing swords held high, the ranks of war closed. Blades rose again, stained red, fierce strangled cries came from men in the death-grips, helms were cracked, shields riven, dirks sank home, and men who once had drunk and jested with laughing looks over the same meadboard, now met fierce eye to eye, and never parted until one or both fell in the swaths of the death-harvest.

All day the stubborn battle raged, and ever the king sought out the rebel Mordred, but never reached him. Many valiant deeds he did, wielding his sword Excalibur; and by his side were Owen and Kay, Lucan and Bedevere. So spent were they at the last that hardly could they lift their swords, and so sick of the slaying were they that gladly would they have ceased. But ever some vicious band of Mordred's knights would come upon them, and then they quitted them like men, and ceased not till their enemies had fled or were slain.

Suddenly the king came to himself, and, standing still, looked upon the field. In the morning it had been but a bare hillside of hungry, stunted grass, through which the stones showed grey and sallow, like ancient bones. Now, in the low light of the sinking orb, it was red—red, with the pallid faces of the dead stained a lighter red in the rays of the sun. Here and there bands still fought together, cries of fury rose, and the groans of the dying mingled with them.

"Alas!" cried the king, and looked behind him. "Where are all my noble knights?"

There were but two with him now, Lucan and his brother Bedevere.

"Where is Owen, and Kay?" he asked.

"Alas, lord," said Bedevere, "Sir Owen got his death-wound by the thorn where we fought those five knights but now, and Sir Kay suddenly fell as he walked. And when I knelt to speak to him, I found him dead."

"Alas," said the king, "that ever I should see this doleful day, for now is my end come. But would to Heaven that I wist where is that traitor Mordred, that hath caused all this sorrow and ruin."

Then, as he spoke, he looked towards the east, and saw where, by a tall standing-stone, a man leaned as if spent with a wound. And he was aware that this was Mordred.

"Now give me my spear," said the king to Sir Lucan, "for yonder is the traitor, and he shall not escape me."

"Lord," said Sir Lucan in a weak voice, "let him bide, for he hath none with him, while we three are still alive."

"Now, betide me death, betide me life," said the king, "now that I see him yonder I will slay the serpent, lest he live to work more havoc on this my poor kingdom."

"God speed you well," said Sir Bedevere, and gave the king his spear.

Then the king ran towards Sir Mordred, crying:

"Traitor, prepare, now is thy death-day come!"

When Sir Mordred heard King Arthur he raised his head, then came towards the king with his sword in his hand.

And there, in the shadow of the great stone, King Arthur smote Sir Mordred under the shield, with so keen a stroke of his spear that it went through the body and out beyond. Sir Mordred, feeling that death was upon him, thrust himself along the spear almost to the butt thereof, nigh where King Arthur held it, and grasping his sword in both his hands, he struck his uncle on the side of the head, with so keen and fierce a blow that the sword pierced the helm and the skull.

With that stroke Sir Mordred fell stark dead to the earth, and the king sank in a swoon upon his body.

Then Sir Bedevere and Sir Lucan, who were both sore wounded and weakly, came up, and between them, with many rests upon the way, took the king to a little combe beside the waters, and there they took off his helm and bathed his wound and bound it. After which the king felt easier.

"We may do naught else with thee here, lord," said Sir Lucan, "and it were best that we got thee to some town."

"It would be better so," said the king, "but I fear me I have my death-wound."

When they had rested Sir Lucan tried to rise, so as to take up the king.

"I may not rise," he cried, his hands upon his head, "my brain works so."

Nevertheless, the knight staggered to his feet and lifted up the feet of the king. But the effort was too much for him, and with a deathly groan he fell to the ground, and when he had twitched and struggled a little he lay dead.

"Alas," said the king, "this is to me a full heavy sight, to see this noble knight so die for my sake. He would not complain, so set was he to help me, and now his heart has broken."

Then Sir Bedevere went to his brother and kissed him, and closed his eyes.

"Now," said the king, "come hither to me, Bedevere, for my time goeth fast and I remember me of a promise. Therefore," he bade Sir Bedevere, "do thou take Excalibur, my good sword, and go with it beyond the combe side there where a low thorn grows, and when thou comest there, I charge thee, throw my sword in that water, and come again and tell me what thou seest."

So Sir Bedevere departed with the sword, and on the way he looked at the sword, and saw how noble was the blade and how shining, and how the pommel and haft were full of precious stones.

"If I throw this sword into the water," said Sir Bedevere to himself, "how great a sin 'twould be to waste so noble a weapon."

Therefore he hid it in the branches of the thorn and returned to the king.

"What sawest thou?" asked the king when Bedevere returned.

"Sir," he said, "I saw the wind beat on the waves."

"Ye have not done as I bid thee," said the king. "Now, therefore, do thou go again and do as I bid thee; and as thou art dear to me, spare it not, but throw it in."

Then Sir Bedevere went back and took the sword in his hand; but again he could not bring himself to throw away that noble sword, so again he hid the sword and went back to the king.

"What sawest thou this time?" said the king.

"Lord," said Bedevere, "I saw the waters ebb and flow and the sedges trembling."

"Ah, traitor untrue!" said the king, deep sorrow in his voice, "who would have weened that thou who hast been so true and dear to me, and who hast been named a noble knight, would betray me for the jewels on a sword? Now go ye again, I charge thee, and as thou shalt answer for thy sins at the last day, throw ye the sword far into the waters."

Then in heavy mood Sir Bedevere went the third time, and took the sword from its hiding-place, and looking away from the weapon lest its beauty should soften him, he bound the girdle about the hilt, and then he threw the sword with all his might far out over the water.

As he looked, inwardly lamenting, he saw the jewels flash in the low light as the sword passed through the air. Then suddenly, when it neared the water, he marvelled to see a great arm and hand come up through the waves. The hand caught the weapon by the haft, shook it and brandished it thrice, and then vanished with the sword under the waves.

With some fear in his heart Sir Bedevere went back to the king and told him all that he had seen.

"It is well," said the king. "Now have I performed my promise. Help me hence to some village, for I am cold and would die beneath a roof, if I may."

Then Sir Bedevere took the king upon his back, thinking that he would find some road in a little while which should lead them to a hamlet. And as he went along, he passed by the waterside, near the low thorn whence he had thrown the sword into the water.

There, in the sedges, he marvelled to see a barge draped all in black cloth, and in it sat many fair ladies, all with black hoods on. When they saw Sir Bedevere with the king upon his back, they shrieked and wept.

And one that looked a queen, so fair and stately, yet so sad was she, held out her arms towards the king, and cried unto him in a voice wondrous sweet, "Come to me, brother!"

"Put me into the barge," said the king to Bedevere, "for there I shall have rest."

Softly did Sir Bedevere lay him in the barge, and the fair ladies wept over the king with much mourning, and one laid his head in her lap and caressed it with soft hands.

Then, without sails or oars, the barge went from the shore, and fear and sorrow shook the soul of Sir Bedevere to see them go from him.

"Alas, my lord Arthur," he cried, "what shall become of me if ye are leaving me lonely?"

"Comfort thyself," said the king in a faint voice, "and do as well as thou mayest, for in me ye may no longer trust. For I will go into the vale of Avalon to heal me of my grievous wound, and if thou hear never more of me, pray for my soul."

Sir Bedevere stood watching till the barge went from his sight in the mists of evening, and then he wept a little, and so fared forward through the night, weeping as he thought how all the glory that was Arthur's was now past, and how he himself was very old and very lonely.

When morning broke he was aware of a little chapel and a hermitage between two hoar woods upon a knoll beside the marshes, and entering therein he got cheer of the holy hermit and rested.

NOW, WHEN KING ARTHUR HAD GONE WESTWARDS TO COLLECT his host, Sir Owen, marvelling that Sir Lancelot had sent no word in reply to the letter of Sir Gawaine, had charged a trusty squire of his to go across to Brittany, to tell Sir Lancelot of all that had passed and how King Arthur longed for his aid and his love. Nigh mad with grief was Sir Lancelot when he had learned all, and so deep was his sorrow and so wild was his regret, that hardly could he wait till the ships were ready to take him and his knights and army across to Britain.

When they arrived at Dover, Sir Lancelot sought out the tomb of Sir Gawaine, and there with much weeping he prayed long and earnestly for the repose of the soul of that dead warrior, his once dear friend. All the other knights prayed likewise for the soul of Gawaine, and Sir Lancelot gave one hundred pounds for masses to be said, and the others gave according to their means.

Then word was brought him of the daylong dreadful battle in the west, and how King Arthur was gone, mortally wounded, none knew whither, and how all the knights of the Round Table were dead.

Silent was Sir Lancelot at this news, but men saw how his stern face paled; and for a time he walked apart and would suffer none to speak to him. Then he came to his knights, and all could see how his looks had changed. Grief was deeply lined upon his face, and he had the air of an aged and weary man.

"My fair lords," he said, "I thank you all for your coming with me, but we came too late. But now I go alone to find the body of my dear lord, and if I may, I will see my lady, Queen Gwenevere. And do ye all go back into your country, for now we have no place in this."

Thus Sir Lancelot fared forth, and would suffer none to go with him. First he went to Amesbury, and in the convent there he saw Queen Gwenevere. Few but very sad were the words they spake. Sir Lancelot offered to give her a home in Brittany, away from the trouble and the ruin of the land, but she would not.

"My lord is dead," she said, weeping, "and this dear kingdom may not long stand, but while I live I will stay on its dear soil."

Then Sir Lancelot fared far west through the wastelands, and came to the battlefield; and there he wept sorely to see the long lines of dead. Many were the dead knights of the Round Table whom he found unburied, and these with his own hands he laid in the grave, and he procured a priest to say prayers over them.

Further he went beside the shores of the Endless Waters, until one day he found a black barge, and stepping therein he was taken without sail or oars far over the wide sea, until the twilight. Then, raising his sorrowing eyes, he was aware of a fair green island with a valley between two sweet hills, and there was a chapel, and all about it were trees all laden with blossoms.

A little bell began to ring just as the barge lightly touched the shore, and stepping therefrom, Sir Lancelot went into the chapel, and heard mass. Afterwards a bishop came unto him where he kneeled, and a hermit, and the latter seized his hand; and when he looked up Sir Lancelot knew it for Sir Bedevere. Neither could speak for the great tears that rolled down their grim faces, but Sir Bedevere drew him forth and led him to where a great white marble slab was lying, freshly cut, in the midmost part of the chapel.

Thereon Sir Lancelot saw the words, cut deep and wide, in black letters:

HIC JACET

ARTHURUS REX

QUONDAM REX QUE FUTURUS

Then did Sir Lancelot's heart almost burst with sorrow; and when he had finished praying and weeping, he kneeled unto the bishop and prayed him to shrive him and assoil him. Afterwards he besought him that he might live with him, and the holy man granted his request, and there ever after did Sir Lancelot, putting off all the fame and glory which he had gotten in the world, pass all his days and nights, serving God with prayers and fastings and much abstinence.

When, within a year, Queen Gwenevere died in her cell at Amesbury, Sir Lancelot, having been advised in a dream of her death, braved the bands of lawless men that now ravaged the fair land of Britain, and brought her body to the isle of Glastonbury. He laid it solemnly beside the body of her dear lord Arthur, and thereafter he endured greater penance.

"For," said he, "by my stiffnecked pride did all this evil come. If I had gone straightway to my dear lord, and cast myself upon his love and justice, my lady the queen would not have been led to the stake, and I should not unwittingly have slain young Gareth. I am the causer of all the ruin and the sorrow that hath come upon this land, and never while I live may I forgive me."

Thus evermore he prayed and mourned, day and night, but sometimes he slumbered a broken sleep. He ate but little, and neither the bishop nor Sir Bedevere could make him take comfort. And if you would know the time and place where Lancelot was happiest, it was when he was lying on the tomb of King Arthur and Queen Gwenevere.

At last, on a sweet morn in June, they found him lying there, stark dead, but with a gentle smile upon his wasted face. And when they had made the mass of requiem, they laid him in the tomb at the feet of the king and the queen, and on the slab that covered him they caused these words to be graven:

HERE LIETH

SIR LANCELOT DU LAKE

WHO WAS CHIEF OF ALL CHRISTIAN KNIGHTS;

THE MOST COURTEOUS MAN AND THE TRUEST FRIEND,

THE MEEKEST DOER OF GREAT DEEDS, AND

THE GENTLEST TO ALL LADIES AND WEAK CREATURES.

R. I. P.

CLUNY MEDIA

Designed by Fiona Cecile Clarke, the CLUNY MEDIA *logo*
depicts a monk at work in the scriptorium,
with a cat sitting at his feet.

The monk represents our mission to emulate
the invaluable contributions of the monks
of Cluny in preserving the libraries of the West,
our strivings to know and love the truth.

The cat at the monk's feet is Pangur Bán, from the
eponymous Irish poem of the 9th century.
The anonymous poet compares his scholarly
pursuit of truth with the cat's happy hunting of mice.
The depiction of Pangur Bán is an homage to the work
of the monks of Irish monasteries and a sign
of the joy we at Cluny take in our trade.

"Messe ocus Pangur Bán,
cechtar nathar fria saindan:
bíth a menmasam fri seilgg,
mu memna céin im saincheirdd."